MOTHERSHIP
20th Anniversary Edition

Tony Chandler

MOTHERSHIP
20th Anniversary Edition

DOUBLE DRAGON

Dedication

For Mom and Dad:
You provided us a happy family
and, for me, a most wonderful childhood.

Tony Chandler

Prologue

"It would be better if the children died with us."

Ron looked away from Rita as she finished the sentence, biting his lip to keep the erupting emotions inside his heart from exploding and ruining this last hope. As he took a deep, wavering breath, he gathered his thoughts for one more attempt.

"They would live." His eyes narrowed as he watched for her reaction.

But she only stared back in silence.

"I know, we've failed terribly. All our plans, ruined now." Ron cleared his throat, pushing his rising emotions aside as his vision blurred momentarily. "The 'M' ship is well stocked with food and supplies. We figured almost fifty people on board with us, a year's worth in case the worst happened. And now it has ..."

A thick silence settled between them.

"We could order it so easily," Ron whispered. "At least your two children, and my Jaric, would live."

Rita closed her eyes, obviously fighting back her tears. "They won't have anyone," she whispered. "Loneliness will kill them."

Ron waited, watching her shoulders begin to shake. The harsh ceiling lights glinted off her auburn hair fell as she buried her face in her hands. A stifled sob pierced the room.

She is so beautiful. Her husband, John, had been Ron's closest friend before his death at the battle of Kaldon. His own wife had died not long afterward, having allowed their only son, Jaric, to take the final slot on the last starship out of LondonPrime.

These last two years Ron had felt such emptiness inside his heart, inside his life. Life without Karen had almost been unbearable. It had only been working so closely with Rita, integrating their AI program into the 'M' ship, that had kept him sane.

Sweet Rita, Ron thought again. *If only things had been different. If only there had been more time.*

If only the world were not ending.

Dr. Ron Byron walked over and placed his ebony hand across her shoulder.

"Let them go," Ron whispered reassuringly. "Let them live."

Rita looked up, her blue eyes filled with sadness. "They'll have no one to love them. No one to care for them." Rita's face grimaced as though some great, powerful force were destroying her. Her breath grew rapid and shallow, but still she forced her words. "They'll be alone. So alone, Ron. It will kill them, even if the T'kaan don't."

The room around them lurched.

Broken glass exploded all around them as dozens of jars crashed to the laboratory floor. Screaming, Rita fell into Ron's arms.

For a brief, eternal moment, complete darkness filled their senses. In a flicker, the lights returned. But now they knew how short their time really was.

"The final attack has started." Fearfully, Ron looked at the ceiling. Almost one mile through the solid rock above his head, the fated event had begun.

"We're running out of time, Rita. Send the instructions to the 'M' ship," Ron pleaded.

Without warning, the door opened.

General Lo strode inside with two of his senior aides. His face was a scowl as he looked around the littered room. But as Lo started speaking, the officer to his left whispered into his ear.

"Save our children. Now!" Ron whispered urgently.

Rita wiped her eyes quickly and stood to face the imposing form of Lo, almost as if she hadn't heard Ron.

"Is the detonation sequence for the weapon ready?" the general asked.

Rita's face broke into a tear-stained grin. She laughed at General Lo, a brief and false sound.

General Lo glared at her and then turned his harsh gaze to Ron. "The entire T'kaan fleet has closed on us like alien vultures to watch the final kill. They've beaten us into a corner and forced our hand. I see no humor in this."

General Lo looked up toward the surface and the fleet above. Surprisingly, he too laughed. But his laughter was that of one who still has one last ace to play. "We're going to show them that the human race doesn't just roll over and die, aren't we?" He laughed again, looking from Ron to Rita.

Rita's laughter stopped with a sudden finality.

Ron felt his stomach tighten, felt his mind suddenly seem to detach from his body as the general's laughter faded. Lo now faced Ron, waiting for an answer.

"It's ready," Ron said.

Rita leaned upon the computer. "Yes, it's been ready, General. You know that. We kept the processes active and waited for the T'kaan to come."

The room shuddered again from mighty explosions far above on the surface. Once again the lights dimmed, but they did not go out completely. After several flickers, the lights returned -- but not at full strength.

"Yes. *They* thought we would just run to the last planet and roll over. Waiting for the inevitable." General Lo snorted. "We gathered the last of our ships, the last of our armies to our home world to fight them. We hoped their entire fleet would show up for the final battle – and they did." Lo chuckled. "Now we'll show them what the human race is made of."

"The final battle," Ron said with feeling. As he spoke he slipped his hand into Rita's hand, willing her to send the message. This was something that he didn't want to do on his own, not without her full agreement. But he would if it came to that.

Rita stared in disbelief at Lo. "What will this do, General? What will it really do? After all, we're already dead."

The general's confident smile faded. He watched her a moment and then took a step closer. Ron put his hand out to stop him.

Lo stopped, staring into her defiant eyes.

"We'll take them with us, Doctor. We'll take them down with us. That's what this last little project will accomplish." His face came closer. "Most important, they won't be able to eat our dead bodies."

Rita looked away in disgust.

"You know, Doctor, I was so hoping your precious 'M' ship would have made it here. If only we could have produced a fleet of them." The general shook his head slowly. "They would have defeated the T'kaan. Easily." He sighed deeply. "We sent the first ship to its destruction against impossible odds even for a super warship. But the

10

second one, well, she proved unstoppable in battle. A real killing machine, able to think for itself, without the need of a crew." He rubbed his chin thoughtfully. "If it had come we could have ordered it to take out their stragglers for us. Now, we'll have to depend on *Project Samson* to do it all." The general smiled.

For the third time the lights dimmed as the terrible explosions ripped the planet above. As suddenly as it had started, the low rumblings far above on the surface quieted.

"The orbiting battleships have stopped their bombardment," Colonel Baker said, stepping close beside Lo. "The fighters and assault ships will be launching en masse now."

Lo turned to leave but stopped in mid-step. He drew a deep breath and spoke. "I go to give my last order. *The* last order," he repeated, his eyes glazing over. "I go to give the most historic order in the history of our species, Doctor." He shook his head. "I only wish someone would know how mankind died -- would remember our species. And how we died with honor." He walked away shaking his head.

They watched them go in eerie silence. Both of them felt the sudden chill that seemed to grip their entire beings as the door shut.

There were only minutes left now.

"Do it, Rita."

"I can't. I *can't*!" Rita sobbed as she stepped away from him.

"Yes, you can." Suddenly he took her back into his arms, like he had always wanted these last months. He drew her close as she struggled. But her struggles stopped

11

when she realized what was happening. He held her, pressing his face next to her soft cheek. The warmth of their bodies sent the deadly chill away.

"Please," Rita whispered with a puzzled look in her eyes.

"Give them life," Ron whispered back. "Send them."

Rita's face was still pressed against the softness of his ebony cheek as she answered. "They are the last humans, Ron. Wouldn't you rather die than to live a life of complete solitude?"

Ron closed his eyes, drawing sudden comfort from her closeness.

"No."

She pulled her head back.

"As long as there's life, there's hope." Ron looked deep into her blue eyes. "We never know what tomorrow will bring. But as long as there is a tomorrow, there is hope."

She searched his eyes as he held her.

"Give them their tomorrow, Rita. No matter how hard their challenges will be and no matter how alone they may be." His ebony face bent closer. "They will be alive."

His warm breath brushed her face.

He kissed her -- long and lingering. The minutes passed as they held each other in combined silence.

"I will." Rita said it so softly that it was almost unheard.

In that moment the explosive chain reaction began. All around them the room shook and rocked as though in the grips of a titanic earthquake. Both Ron and Rita lost their footing and fell together onto the floor as falling debris crashed all around them.

"It's happening!" Ron shouted. "Lo's started the reaction!"

Rita was already crawling to her workstation, and even as the reinforced ceiling began to fall upon their heads, her hands furiously typed the final message. The rain of debris bruised and cut at her hands, but still she forced them on. A large piece of the ceiling fell crashing across her shoulders, knocking her down. With renewed urgency she rose up and scrambled to the computer. Her fingers flew over the keyboard.

Seconds were all that was left now.

But it was finished. A message only a mother could send -- a message to the 'M' ship.

Her finger pressed the Transmit button even as the room suddenly grew bright around them.

Five milliseconds later, the explosion swept through the room, consuming everything as it swept toward the surface of the planet. The raw power that had been unleashed was destroying the very atomic structure of everything in its path as it expanded outward at an exponential rate.

Seconds later, now expanding many times faster than the speed of sound, the destructive power erupted up through the planet's surface.

The T'kaan war fleet, gathered in close orbit to witness the final destruction of yet another race, watched their sensors with sudden shock.

Across their alien viewscreens the planet's surface suddenly melted -- evaporated -- in a blinding flash of pure, all-consuming energy. In another split second, the atmosphere spewed in all directions amid mountain-size chunks of rock and debris that heralded the death-cry of the entire planet. In that same instant, the haughty T'kaan knew their own deaths were imminent.

The horned battleships turned as the fighters screamed out toward the safety of the stars far away.

But it was already too late.

The solid wall of energy, preceded by a horrific shockwave, lunged out with unimaginable destruction. And with each millisecond it grew larger and closer and stronger.

As the tattered remnants of the atmosphere flung past the first frigates and fighters in lowest orbit, the blinding wall reached them. Like miniature toys the mighty warships disintegrated, smashed into molecules of nothingness in ten thousand separate flashes of light, as if ten thousand stars had suddenly went out all at once.

Inexorably, the wall of destruction rose from the gutted world below.

Even before the battle cruisers could finish their turns in mid-orbit, they were smashed to pieces and their infinitesimal fragments carried along farther and farther with the unending wave of destruction.

The massive semicircle of this destructive wave was now astronomical in size as it roared out into space.

Over one hundred kilometers from the planet's surface, from the position where their mighty weapons had pummeled the planet's surface in preparation for the last ground assault, the total destruction reached even the mighty T'kaan battleships.

They had completed their turns and were ramping up their hyper engines for the jump that would save them.

But the blinding wall of energy reached them first. As the battleships crumpled and exploded in dozens of titanic fireballs, the wall approached the last squadron of the T'kaan war fleet.

The Great Horned ship and its entourage of warships had begun to flee. All in vain. Even as the edge of the expanding, all-consuming wave slowed, its destructive force reached out and began to tear apart the most sacred part of the T'kaan fleet.

The T'kaan ships farthest from the dying world ramped up their engines to flee. The T'kaan warlords howled out to one another as the terrible power gripped their ships. As their tentacles reached vainly toward their viewscreens and their greatest *need*, the Great Horned ship, they watched in despair as it began crumbling as if in slow motion before their unbelieving optical organs. They watched the unthinkable happen. And their soulless hearts stopped beating in shocked unison even as their own warships buckled.

The Great Horned ship died.

Chapter One

The human race was no more.

The warship grappled with the enormity of this harsh fact while its sensors continued to display the expanding debris field that had once been humanity. It searched its massive knowledgebase for some kind of reference, some kind of indication, as to what action it should perform now, now that its creators were no more.

But life was still new to the ship. In the end, it simply logged the time and place of the historic event.

The 'M' ship turned to leave.

Its dark hull shimmered and then took on a glowing, reddish outline, backlighted by the nearest star. Its unique profile -- shaped like a manta ray but without a tail -- gleamed against the stygian darkness of space.

Within milliseconds of its maneuver, the ship discerned that there was one last duty she could perform for the extinct race: a brief, final message that had arrived unexpectedly from the midst of the glowing destruction.

Inside her silent corridors three children hid from the dangerous universe outside. They were the last three members of the human race, and the message concerned them.

The ship would provide for their needs. Her holds were well stocked with the supplements humans needed to survive. She would also protect them from the T'kaan. This, of course, was her primary programming: to search out and destroy the T'kaan ships of war. She was most proficient in this task, for she had never been defeated.

Yes, she would protect the children until they reached

maturity. Then they could ... The ship pondered the next logical succession of action. Well, she would have time to search her massive knowledgebase to determine what the most optimum course would be when the children reached adulthood.

The warship leaped with a flash into hyperspace.

Weeks passed while the ship sailed through the emptiness of space, and she soon found that the small humans did not adhere to logical actions. They puzzled her immensely.

But the warship wondered most of all when the children began calling her '*Mother*.'

Chapter Two

The optic located in Main Operations zoomed closer onto the lone occupant. The young girl was dressed in blue jeans and a red top; the tears were obvious as they glistened down her plump cheeks. She suddenly shook her head, causing her short blonde hair to leap around her shoulders. But still she covered her blue eyes from the ship's gaze.

"Why are you sad?" The soothing voice emanated from the speaker nearest the eight-year-old girl.

"I am just sad sometimes." A tiny sigh escaped. The cherubic face of the girl disappeared behind her raised arms again.

The ship did not like this answer and quickly ran through the child's recent excursions through her interior. Of course, while she performed this search, she was constantly monitoring thousands of parameters that kept not only the ship flying through space, but kept the environmentals stable, monitored the reactions inside her mighty engines, accessed her numerous sensors, and kept her massive weapon systems in a readied state.

But once again she felt an electronic buzzing in her near-term memories, an odd feeling, almost as if she were powerless.

Her search completed.

"I cannot determine any specific reason for this feeling. Can you elaborate?" the ship asked.

The tear-streaked face looked up into the optical viewer over the main screen.

"I am lonely."

"But I am here with you. And there is Cook, Jaric, Kyle, and the Fixers. You are not alone."

"You don't count. None of you count," the tiny voice shouted desperately. "I wish we could find somebody, Mother. Anybody. You told us we would find them!"

Mother remembered Rita, Becky's biological mother. The ship replayed those memories unseen by Becky before the next millisecond passed.

They were the scenes of Rita holding a smaller version of Becky in her arms, a smaller version of the girl before her now. Once again the words replayed from that final farewell, though at the time none of them knew it was farewell. Mother once again noted how Rita had placed her lips softly upon the child's cheek.

Rita had loved her two children, Becky and Kyle, very much. Mother knew that fact, although she did not quite comprehend it.

Rita had also loved Jaric, though he was not her natural child. In fact, Jaric's features were completely different from the other two. Where Becky and Kyle's skin was light in complexion, Jaric's was a deep brown. Where their hair was yellow, almost like the Earth's sunshine, his own tight curls were dark as a moonless night on that same planet. But this difference in their physical characteristics did not seem to matter.

Now Becky and the other children rarely mentioned Rita's name or her title. It almost seemed as if they did this out of anger -- another emotion Mother failed to fully comprehend.

Mother recalled why the children refused to mention Rita. It started the moment she had explained to them that Rita had died.

It had been a mistake, though the ship still did not understand why such a simple expression of fact could cause the children to go into a frenzy of cries and screams. Kyle had even begun to damage his body against her hull in his screaming tirades, pounding his head bloody until he had become incoherent. She had been forced to order one of the Fixers to restrain Kyle while another Fixer tended his wounds.

In contrast, Jaric had gone strangely silent, refusing to speak to her for days on end. Nor even to the other two children. This had caused her processing cycles excessive utilization -- until one morning he suddenly and mysteriously returned to his old personality.

Becky too became subtly different. Mother still did not understand that change.

They all changed in that single moment, and it still concerned her.

It had also occurred to her that she might have done something to damage them by expressing the fact of Rita's death. Emotions seemed to be a terrible liability to these life forms. Mother began to hold back certain facts from them after that event. She had to learn why mere words, known facts, could hurt the children so deeply.

She didn't want to hurt them.

After the children recovered from the shock of their parents' deaths, they begged her to search for other humans -- to search for a dead race.

The ship had no other priorities except the children when they made the request to search. She had almost informed them how low the probability of success actually was, and then had remembered their reaction when she had revealed the fact about the death of Rita and Ron.

Finally, she had agreed to begin the search, even though a part of her felt she had failed in not revealing all the facts. But somehow she knew she had chosen correctly.

The ship was beginning to stretch beyond her original programming. She was discovering that she was also alive like the children.

She was also learning that life was full of problems and challenges.

With the T'kaan fleet decimated, Mother estimated it was safe enough to allow the fruitless search to begin, although the T'kaan remnants seemed determined to continue their never-ending war with her. She could handle them, and it would give her time to learn. Perhaps in time she could discern how best to present the heartbreaking facts of their race's extinction to the young children.

Once again, Mother remembered her sister ship and its precious cargo of hope, and how it had all been destroyed. Now she was alone with the last three children of humankind.

Alone.

Mother's processors focused again.

"Our search continues," Mother said before another second passed.

The little girl never noticed the slight pause as she rubbed her eyes and wiped her runny nose across the sleeve of her shirt.

"I wish I had a *real* mother." The young girl sniffed.

The ship processed this request.

A bright light flashed inside the room, and the holo-projection of a woman instantly appeared. The smiling woman looked down at the child.

Becky did not realize it, but this was a holo-projection

21

of her real mother, though if she looked hard she could see right through this shimmering image. Actually, Mother had darkened Rita's complexion so that she would also appear to be Jaric's mother, of whom Mother had no direct recordings.

The little girl fought back more tears as she walked closer to the smiling woman who looked at her so lovingly. She reached out her hand and gently traced the smiling lines on its face. Becky ignored the fact that her finger could not feel the holographic projection the ship had chosen to represent herself.

"So, you can see me."

Becky looked down in sadness.

"But you can't hug me, not like a real mom."

Mother processed this fact, referencing thousands of occurrences in her knowledgebase.

"Do you want me to hug you, Becky?"

The little girl looked up, surprise etched across her face.

"Could you?"

"Come closer to my image."

Becky obeyed and found herself almost against the image of the smiling woman. She raised her small arms up and around the holographic projection, and although she could not feel a real person to hug, she pretended.

"Close your eyes," Mother prompted from the speaker.

Becky obeyed.

The lights of the operation center slowly dimmed until the light was soft and delicate surrounding the child. Mother increased the ambient air temperature by several degrees. The sweet sound of stringed music began to play, familiar and beautiful. It was the same music that Mother had used to soothe the children to sleep during those first months when their desperate journey began. There was some kind of hidden power in the progression of sounds that could calm the children, she had discerned. This power inside the music performed emotional effects upon humans. Mother did not understand it, but she saw from that first use that it was true. So she used it now.

Becky smiled. She felt a gentle touch across her back and shoulders.

The long appendage had been designed to speed repairs and replace damaged modules in case the Fixers were unavailable. It normally remained hidden in its enclave inside the ceiling.

But now Mother directed it against the little girl's back ever so gently in rhythm with the flowing melody, caressing the little girl. Her touch was delicate over the child's shoulders, and soon Becky's breathing became slow and steady. Mother stopped the motion and squeezed Becky in a soft embrace.

Becky smiled through closed eyes.

Time passed, and their solemn search among the dead planets continued, a search that the warship alone knew was almost certainly without hope.

And always there was war.

Chapter Three

The First and Second T'kaan fleets, orbiting their own conquered worlds far away from Mother, began the task of rebuilding the destroyed Third. Ships were dispatched to join the Third fleet's few remaining vessels, and the shipyards inside the Great Horned ships produced new warships in earnest.

Deep inside the oldest of the Great Horned ships, a special ship with dark grace was created. For long weeks it grew in silence until all was ready, and only then were the T'kaan led to it. Carefully the T'kaan workers guided this ship to a specifically prepared dock, one used but once each millennium. Here they grafted the technological implants and the hyperspace engines, as was their way. The rest of the modifications would have to wait until the ship had reached its second stage.

Three months after these first modifications had been completed, the new Great Horned ship set forth under heavy escort to the conquered worlds of the race that had been called human.

But even as this massive rebuilding program of the Third fleet progressed over the next two years with seeming ease, a new discovery came to disturb their cycle. A single warship had survived from the humans. It struck without warning, destroying the hatchlings and any T'kaan ships that orbited to protect them, and then it disappeared, only to attack again at another distant planet.

The warship's attacks seemed to be without pattern at first.

Most strange to the T'kaan leaders, this ship had

neither crew nor leader. Somehow the humans had given it artificial life. But that did not really interest their focused minds; only the ship's certain destruction as well as the rebuilding of their fleet preoccupied their unified thought patterns.

The dead home world of the humans completed another circuit around its star, marking its third complete orbit since that catastrophic event.

Midway between the Third fleet and its sister fleets a powerful squadron of T'kaan ships guarded their vital supply line. Inside the T'kaan battleship, the multi-legged alien forms moved with erratic efficiency among the black, flowing folds that filled every cubit of the ship's interior like bizarre, surreal dragnets. They waved with a ghostly motion in the misty atmosphere, creating a moving maze of blackness, an ever-changing maze through which the T'kaan crawled. The folds had another purpose that the controlling alien intelligence utilized: as the individual T'kaan came in contact with the folds, it reached out and made them all one in purpose and thought.

The T'kaan warships, and most especially the Great Horned ships, were the only homes that the T'kaan adults ever knew.

Inside the warships, harsh, guttural words echoed throughout this dark maze as the feast time once again came to its grisly end.

"Eat, eat the human meat. Eat, eat so nice and sweet."

A leader of the T'kaan wiped his jagged mandibles with three of his appendages, smiling at the now familiar words. He threw the gnawed bones of an infant human into the disposal bowl and grunted with satisfaction. Such delicacies were reserved for his class alone.

But the black smile quickly faded when one of the myriad warriors entered his enclave. The leader read the bad news in its tentative approach.

"Speak you now, one of war. Make your words an open door."

The aliens faced each other.

"More ships undone, more young are gone. Dead." The warrior growled, bending his misshapen head down to the floor.

The leader thought upon the words.

"The ship it was, the dreaded fear. Iron Huntress, cursed seer."

The warrior nodded. "And ... " it began.

The leader froze at the unfinished sentence. Once a thought was started, it was always finished by a T'kaan. The two aliens shivered in the silence.

Finally, the warrior focused.

" ... there are humans yet alive. More than two, less than five."

The leader's short, multiple legs shook with his sudden anxiety. His tentacle arms waved as his one thought crystallized. His words were strong.

"Just as the species, these last must die. Destroy the ship, there is no more try!"

Throughout the horned battleship a low chant began as the leader's words were passed from one T'kaan to another. With each succession, the chant grew louder.

Across to the other ships of the squadron the words were communicated. Soon after, the communications were passed to every ship of every fleet spread across the galaxy.

Mothership

Within hours, the message reached the scarred remnant of what had been the human home world. There the few remaining T'kaan ships of the Third fleet gathered en masse, completing the holiest of T'kaan rituals. To assist with the rebuilding process, the other two T'kaan fleets now began building and sending more ships with greater urgency.

The diminutive silhouette of the infant T'kaan Great Horned ship orbited the shattered and unrecognizable hulk that had been the human home world. It was unrecognizable not only because its misshapen form was no longer spherical, but also because it was now devoid of both an atmosphere and its oceans.

Earth was a dead world now.

The Great Horned ship's distinctive open maw differentiated it from the other warships, though it was still no larger than a T'kaan cruiser. In contrast, the forward part of every other T'kaan capital ship bristled with a crown of weapon-horns.

Now the message reached the embryo of both this renewed T'kaan fleet and its newly born Great Horned ship.

The T'kaan Third now focused and formulated plans to kill Mother, as well as to make the human race extinct once and for all.

Chapter Four

There was no way to go back home.

After all, Mother reflected, *no home exists to which to take them*.

But home was what the children wanted most, what they cried out for when they awoke from their nightmares, what they pleaded for and wanted more than anything else in the entire universe.

During their daily playtime, Mother noticed, their conversations almost always turned to the subject of home -- and to the other humans who would live there.

Many times each of the children had separately approached her and begged her to take them back home, begged her with tears and whimpering sobs.

It was not easy, and Mother never explained the real reason why she did not take them directly home.

During these difficult encounters, Mother appealed to the vast knowledgebase the human scientists had stored into her long-term memories. She searched, not only on the factual references that would aid her but also on the more abstract references about human emotions, hoping to find some concise concept that would aid her in reasoning with these small humans so she could understand their illogical behavior.

It became painfully obvious that facts alone would not suffice.

Mother wrestled with these concepts of emotions -- fear, hate, love, sadness, and homesickness.

But she discovered that one fact did help. She had finally realized, through the references to child psychology and child rearing, that the mind and emotional makeup of human children were not developed enough to deal with the true facts of their situation.

Still, the children came to her time and again and asked her to take them home.

Kyle was the one who asked the most.

He was bigger than the other two. She could discern not only from the heavier sound of his footsteps but by his firm and steady gait, that Kyle was the one now approaching one of her optics located at the various junctures of her internal corridors. The mop of blonde hair that framed the hearty cheeks and handsome face appeared and came into focus. But there was no smile today, and he instantly averted his green eyes from her optic once he knew he had her attention.

"Why can't we go home now?" Kyle looked down as he shuffled his feet.

"I have told you before, young Kyle. We are searching for home," Mother's voice answered with electronic precision.

"Why is it taking so long? I want to go home now." Kyle's face froze into a stern, glaring visage as he crossed his small arms, demanding the right answer.

"We must evade the T'kaan ships, young Kyle. We are still at war. You know that."

Kyle's faced dropped. "Oh, I forgot." He sighed deeply and began shuffling back down the corridor to find Jaric and Becky. He had almost left the range of Mother's optic and entered the range of the next when he stopped. He turned.

"When we defeat the T'kaan, then can we go home?"

"I will contemplate that scenario, young Kyle."

Again his countenance fell into an image of the deepest despair.

"My first analysis suggests that *going home* is indeed a high probability after the T'kaan are destroyed," Mother said after six milliseconds.

"Cool!" Kyle shouted gleefully as he turned and ran toward the library to find his playmates and to share this great news.

Mother pondered her answer a moment, as well as the activity of the children.

The children were either in the library or in their bedrooms these days with one or more of the Fixers.

The Fixers were small robots designed to repair Mother internally, working as her independent and autonomous hands in case her own internal repair capabilities were damaged. There were seven Fixers in all, but Mother specifically assigned Fixer3 to Becky, Fixer4 to Jaric, and Fixer5 to Kyle during their sleep periods, which seemed to comfort the children and aided them to sleep better. Otherwise, the children interacted with all seven robots.

Each Fixer was painted a different color, but each had the same tube-like frame equipped with four robotic arms and a small head. Two arms were located high on their small metallic shoulders and could telescope out far enough to open the maintenance panels on the ceilings. One telescoping arm had been designed with a human-size hand equipped with extensible fingers which allowed them to grip and perform work. In contrast, the other arm had been designed with plug-ins at its extremity that allowed various tools to be connected to it. These upper arms were designed for delicate repairs.

The lower pair of arms, located midway on the body, were thicker and stronger and were equipped to perform heavier work with larger tools. These arms could also telescope outward, though only half the distance of the upper arms. Once again, the left one had human-like fingers, although these were not extensible and were over three times the size of a normal man's fingers. The other hand, like its upper counterpart, had plug-ins to allow connection with heavy-duty power tools.

All of the Fixers had two large optics attached to the top of their tiny heads via supple cables that stretched as far as their upper arms and enabled them to monitor up-close the work of their fully extended appendages. Below the lower pair of arms, each metallic body spread out into four flexible legs tipped with twin motorized wheels that enabled the Fixers to travel quickly and efficiently in any direction.

Since their tube bodies were only four feet tall, the children seemed drawn to the robots almost as if they viewed the Fixers as other children. The Fixers' simplistic speech programming and brightly colored metallic bodies added to this impression, reinforcing the seeming child-like persona.

Many times, Mother discovered the children playing hide-and-seek and other childish games with one or more of the Fixers. One of their favorites was a game that Becky had named 'The Silly Dance.'

In this pretend game, the children would gather all the Fixers together in the library. Becky would order them to form a circle in the center of the room and then ask Mother for music. Sometimes Mother would play a graceful waltz, at other times raucous fifties' rock and roll, or other times some mystical, dream-like electronic music -- but whatever the music Mother played, the Fixers performed a dance synchronized with the music.

With all four arms extended, as well as their twin optics -- and all waving in rhythm -- the Fixers would roll, or dance, around the room. Soon afterward, the giggling children would join their comical dance. Mother observed these events with extreme fascination and tried to discern what satisfaction this odd game seemed to provide for them.

But there seemed to be no precise answer.

In addition to ordering the Fixers to spend time with the children, Mother had instructed them to renovate each child's bedroom. They first added more computer terminals -- three to each bedroom -- so the children could more easily access her knowledgebase and learn from its extensive subject matter. She allocated periods of study for history, science and literature, which the children promptly ignored as much as possible, much to her consternation.

She had also instructed the Fixers to install additional audio speakers so they would be surrounded by music, as this seemed to please them. But their personal choices of music seemed to fixate on single songs or single musical groups for extremely long periods, which again puzzled Mother greatly.

She discovered with the installation of these speakers, inadvertently, that the children could not multi-task as she could.

Mother had been listening to over one thousand different pieces of music simultaneously, analyzing their different structures and melodies. To introduce the children to their new omni-surround speakers, she had directed this magnificent output to their speakers in mid-play.

The resulting noise, as the children later described it to her, had frightened them out of their wits. Now Mother directed only one source of music at a time to their rooms, and directed only softer music for the evening hours so they would become restful and sleep.

For the finishing touch, she had the Fixers de-install three large wall screens from her Command Deck and reinstall them across a wall in each child's bedroom. In this way, they could access entertainment videos according to their individual tastes if they could not agree on a specific title that night to watch together. Of course, if they agreed on a video, they usually enjoyed it together sitting around the library's massive dome-holovision projectors as a Fixer served them food and drink.

But Mother censored what video titles they could access. She remembered that Rita had acted similarly, and her research into child psychology via her knowledgebase reaffirmed this approach. The children had to be protected at this impressionable age from certain subject matter.

Mother had to protect them.

Her optics focused on Kyle's racing figuring as it now reached the library, and then her near-term memories buzzed with consternation once again. Her battle with the facts and -- having to withhold some of them in order to protect the children -- burned through her circuits and spiked her processors with activity.

Kyle reached the library and began relaying Mother's message.

But there is no home to which to take them, Mother

reflected once again.

Later that night, after she had dimmed the lights for sleep, Mother watched the children and studied their sleeping faces. Once again she wondered ...

Had she been a good mother that day?

Chapter Five

It was the second T'kaan attack that week. Two frigates along with nine hunter-class fighters had jumped her at Sector Five Twenty-two.

Mother's weapons had dealt with them with her usual deadly precision. But for the first time since the final human defeat, Mother had sustained damage. And not just to her shields, but also to several of her internal systems. It took her and the Fixers several hours to complete repairs and clean up the resulting mess. Fortunately, none of the damage had been severe.

Still, this led her to a new train of thought: the fact that neither Jaric nor Kyle had taken a bath in two weeks, as well as the fact that Becky no longer brushed her hair. However, Mother observed that Becky did regularly bathe the accumulated dirt from off her organism.

"Jaric. Kyle. Why do you no longer bathe your bodies?" Mother asked as repairs finished.

"I don't know." Jaric continued his play without giving it a second thought.

Mother pondered this quite common answer from the children in her near-term memories. "Kyle, is this your answer as well?"

"Naw, I just don't want to," he said.

"Well, you should," Becky said as she stood above the two boys, who were still intent on the computer game they were playing.

"Why?" both said together.

"Well," Becky said knowingly. "You both stink." She pinched her nose hard to press her point home.

"Who cares," Kyle said, without looking up from the screen.

"I care," Mother said. But even as she said it, though she understood perfectly the import of the words, she did not really understand if the words applied to her. That is, she wondered if she actually *felt* that she cared. Her processors burned with activity for a few milliseconds, but she brought her internal question to a halt when she discerned the fact that the children needed to be clean in order to remain in a state of good health.

Yes, she did not want the children to deteriorate due to uncleanness; thus she extrapolated that she did care. Mother felt her processors smooth out as this small dilemma was resolved in her mind.

"I must teach you now," Mother said.

The three children turned with shocked looks on their faces toward the nearest optic.

"This is another primary task required of a parent. I have, unfortunately, not been fully aware of this. I apologize."

The children glanced at each other with puzzled looks.

"I am now allocating a large portion of my processing to ensure I am not overlooking any other parental responsibilities. I will continue to search the data in my long-term memories. For now, I have programmed several of my consoles to begin a progressive program of study in the fields of mathematics, various sciences, and human history that you will download into your minds. You have ignored this in the past, but now I must enforce your teaching." Mother paused a moment in order to allow the children to absorb her words.

"I hate school work," Kyle complained.

"We will begin these studies in one hour. They will become part of your daily routine of tasks."

"Aww," all three children groaned together.

"There will also be time allocated for periods of play."

Three children breathed a sigh of relief.

"In addition, I have awakened the Guardian robot. The Fixers are designed primarily for my repairs. I have discerned that this robot will be of more practical use in physical interactions with you."

"What do you mean?" Jaric asked.

"I mean that he has appendages that will make him more useful." Mother noted the looks of puzzlement from all three children. "He is constructed exactly as a human in all respects. He will use his human-like appendages as a model for you to follow as I direct Guardian to train you in some special games." Mother paused for effect. "He will also ensure your full cooperation."

"Okay, we're going to play some special games, eh?" Kyle said with anticipation.

"You enjoy playing simulation games," Mother began. If she had been programmed for humor, she would have chuckled at Kyle's attempt to hide his thought processes. "Even Becky will play them for a limited time. We must leverage those skills you have learned and utilize them for a new *Game*."

Mother felt a jump in her processing. She was not sure what it indicated. Perhaps it was the data she had just reviewed on the emotional makeup of human children and the terrible effect war and death might have upon them.

Some of these negative effects would devastate the children. It could damage them permanently.

So, Mother had taken another approach. The young

children would not actually see any T'kaan die. They would only destroy the ships. That was all they would see for now in the simulations. Only later would she explain fully the art of war and all that it entailed.

In addition, if she called it a game, the young children would more likely direct more of their energies into learning the skills required for it. Therefore, they would progress rapidly. After they had developed these necessary skills, they would have a greater probability of survival.

A single millisecond had passed.

Kyle and Jaric stepped forward excitedly. Becky frowned.

"I will program Guardian, and he will assign each of you to one of my primary gun batteries. My consoles will instruct you on the nuances of targeting and destroying T'kaan fighters."

"What about the frigates?" Jaric and Kyle shouted excitedly.

"That will come later. All of you must develop basic skills as you progress in learning *The Game*. First, you will learn from battle simulations I will display on the weapon consoles. Once you have acquired sufficient eye-hand coordination, then I will provide actual moving targets in space that you will destroy using live weapons. As you master each step, I will increase the sophistication of the simulations."

"Cool," Kyle said.

"Guardian will now assist you in his first assignment."

"What assignment is that?" Jaric asked with sudden apprehension.

At that precise moment, an unfamiliar robot entered

the room.

Guardian had been designed to repel any invaders that managed to enter Mother's interior sections. Guardian had been in hibernation mode and unseen in his hidden enclave until Mother had activated him.

The first thing the children noticed was the pure white body-armor that served as his skin. The large robot bent his massive body forward as he passed under the doorway and then straightened. Guardian's seven-foot frame towered over the children as they slowly backed away from the new creature with frightened expressions.

The robot's eyes began to glow, and the children became transfixed by their piercing gaze. The twin orbs glowed like fiery rubies and cast a reddish glow against the pure white of his frozen countenance.

Guardian was as strong as he was big. He reached out to the two boys while they stared up at him in total shock and then effortlessly picked one up in each hand and began marching back the way he had come.

"Where's he taking them?" Becky shouted with fear.

"Guardian's first assignment is to bathe the boys. I anticipated their continued resistance to this task, so I programmed Guardian to simply take them and place them each into a ready bath. He will repeat this task until they decide to do it themselves."

Becky giggled.

"Do not laugh. His next assignment is to brush your hair."

Becky rushed out of the room with a flash of movement. She had finished brushing her disheveled hair long before Guardian completed his first assignment.

Several weeks passed in relative peace. Mother noted

that the children now seemed happier. She had structured their day, giving them assigned times for each of the subjects and providing them with daily and weekly goals. They dove into their studies, especially Guardian's assignment for the new game, with surprising energy.

The boys learned easily and soon became proficient in their newly acquired skills. And though Becky found the game boring, her skills grew. But this was mostly due to the competitiveness she had developed with the boys. And yet, she learned this new skill with surprising quickness.

Soon Mother had Guardian teaching them hand-to-hand combat, in case the T'kaan ever boarded her. During this time, Mother downloaded Guardian's entire operating system and began enhancing it so he could now complete his new functions with more skill.

But now Mother found herself in a new situation, all due to the delicate nature of the children.

She had *promised* to take them home.

Mother knew the implications of this word, but it had seemed the only answer to her problem at the time. The children had started to become frantic, even extreme, in their actions whenever they sensed they might not find or return home. Mother had become afraid they might physically harm themselves.

Under the burden of this fear she revealed additional facts to the children. She revealed to them that the human race had lost the war with the T'kaan. She also revealed that each and every one of the seventy-seven planets and moons that had been colonized by humanity had been attacked and captured by the T'kaan.

She wondered what emotional effect this might have

on the children.

Shortly after she gave them this information, Jaric approached her again. Jaric was quickly showing himself to be the thinker of the three. Jaric and the other two yearned to know more. And Jaric proved adept at digging for answers.

The ship was finally forced to acknowledge that there was a high possibility that the children were the only humans that had survived the war.

Their reaction had been quick and explosive. Instantly, Mother remembered her mistake in telling them the fate of Rita and how they had been damaged emotionally by that revelation.

Mother quickly modified her answer, explaining to the children that she did not have complete access to all of the facts. She was not sure at this time if every human had been destroyed on every planet. Until she had searched every planet and scanned for humans, the answer could not be determined with absolute accuracy or certainty.

That answer had calmed them.

So Mother had changed the nature of their search, a much more dangerous search now. In order to determine if any of the captured worlds contained human survivors, they would now begin a systematic, albeit unpredictable, search among the defeated worlds. Mother's only solace was that the majority of the T'kaan fleet had been destroyed. Yet, with each passing month the T'kaan seemed to be growing in numbers. And as the T'kaan grew stronger, the possibility of her own destruction as well as that of the children grew each day. She would need to calculate a search so random that the T'kaan could not predict her next move. But even that gambit would not prevail forever.

Additionally, Mother knew the odds of finding other human survivors were almost nonexistent. But she would not divulge this data. There was still so much she did not understand about the children and their emotions. There was so much she did not yet know.

Mother's processing power also focused on searching the massive human knowledgebase. Not simply to help the children and not just to ensure she was completing her tasks as a mother, but also something much more personal ...

Mother began a personal journey. She struggled with a new concept that had been taking up more of her processing cycles lately. It was something that had dawned inside her after she had awakened the Guardian robot.

Was she alive? Was she a living being? Or was she merely another robot?

Eighteen months passed in relative peace as Mother and the children grew in many ways.

Chapter Six

The planet was called Eden, once the home of many billions of humans. Sensors revealed it as a lush, tropical planet of dense rain forests that covered every continent. Huge, rushing rivers girdled the entire world and fed into dozens of fresh-water oceans that were interspersed between the huge green continents.

Mother's sensors picked up the ships rising out of the atmosphere to intercept her. Immediately, she began jamming their communications as she altered her course to engage them.

She quickly identified them as hunter-class fighters, the larger and more dangerous type of T'kaan fighters. There were thirty-three of them, three times more than she had anticipated. The enemy's strategy was changing. Instantly, she set aside some of her processing power to ponder this new fact.

Jaric and Kyle were playing together with Guardian in the main living quarters. Becky, with her doll Alice, was with Fixer1 in the kitchen.

Red lights pulsed as the all too familiar alarm sounded.

"All right!" Kyle shouted. "It's time to play *The Game* again!"

"Yes!" Jaric shouted in agreement as the boys raced each other to their favorite gun emplacements.

Becky, still carrying Alice, sighed audibly and meandered slowly to her assigned gun. Mother noted again her lack of enthusiasm. This was bad. The enemy showed no mercy, so the children must defend themselves. It was necessary.

Even from this distance, Eden showed no signs of human life.

"Hurry, Becky. There are more enemy ships than normal."

Becky frowned.

The deadly black-horned ships broke into three attack groups, as was their way. They drew closer. They were almost in range when suddenly the three attacking waves broke into eleven formations of three ships. They fell on Mother with bright laser lances of death.

"Watch it, Jaric! There's a bunch of them this time," Kyle shouted into his comm as he squeezed the twin triggers.

"Just more to blow up," Jaric shouted gleefully.

Mother shuddered as multiple explosions blossomed across her shields. Though her shields dropped twenty percent, the remaining guns under her direct control returned fire with deadly accuracy.

"Got one!" Jaric shouted as the ship disintegrated in his sites.

The fighters swarmed around Mother again and again on their deadly runs. Her green laser bolts crossed the red and orange of the T'kaan.

The attackers were fierce in their pursuit, and Mother's shields fell precariously low under more direct hits. It was no game to her.

"I got one up on you this time, Kyle."

Kyle snarled at the smiling face in the monitor below his targeting screen.

"Ain't no fat lady sang yet."

Mother spoke as Becky sat by her still silent gun.

"If those ships strike me enough ... I will be destroyed.

You must play the Game, Becky."

The little girl became deathly still. Mother detected the little girl's heart rate rising exceptionally with this shocking realization of Mother's mortality.

Becky grabbed the triggers with sudden intensity. Within seconds, she had nailed two fighters with deadly accuracy.

Jaric's mouth dropped in open admiration.

"Wow," Kyle shouted.

Mother turned hard to avoid the remaining ships and twisted over to give Becky a better angle. As Becky's blasts began peppering a third ship, Mother began taking out the rest.

In another few minutes, the only thing left was debris floating in chaotic disarray. Mother retracted her gun nozzles and began identifying and repairing the damage she had sustained. It would take time, but she would have all damaged systems fully functional before landing. She made a mental note to be extra vigilant during this period.

"Take inventory of the food and mineral items needed. I will scan the planet's surface before we land."

This had become their normal routine whenever they landed upon a planet. Long ago, the food stores that Ron and Rita had placed in her holds had run out. They had soon discovered that the T'kaan completely destroyed the animal life on each conquered world, leaving the corpses as food for their maggot young when they hatched. Because of this, the only food source left for the children was vegetable and fruits plants that they could locate in the wild.

The minerals were for her, for the renewal of her engine fuel as well as raw material that could be processed for structural repairs. Deep inside her hull, near the heart of her powerful engines, the Fixers could cleanse these raw materials and ready them to be used and shaped as needed.

The children rushed down the halls and began the task with cheerful laughter. Planet-fall was always exciting to them, although they knew there were dangers. But Mother and Guardian were always there to protect them.

Soon they were running down the ramp and stepping onto the rock-strewn ground. Outside the protective hull of Mother, they paused, their eager eyes taking in the new planet.

Mother's external optics observed the children carefully.

Jaric had gotten so tall and lanky. Mother kept encouraging him to eat more to gain weight, but his high-energy metabolism kept his physique racing slim. As he ran, he began unbuttoning his shirt to allow real air to hit his dark skin. He laughed as the warm air caressed him.

Mother noted how his face had also changed in subtle ways these past years. His large brown eyes now sparkled with his growing intelligence. Mother knew from her analysis of his personal studies that Jaric's mind was powerful and could absorb many new concepts with lightning comprehension. If he really applied himself, there was nothing he could not achieve.

His handsome face reflected his easy-going nature, and a bright smile almost always graced his high cheekbones and sharp jaw. But he needed a haircut; his thick black curls were growing into untidy dreadlocks, and Mother did not find this becoming or healthy.

Always rough and ready, Kyle suddenly overtook Jaric and raced ahead. Kyle had also changed with time.

46

His body was fast becoming that of an athlete; his chest had already grown broader than his waist, and his arms had also thickened with muscle. Mother thought he spent an inordinate amount of time exercising when he should be developing his mind. Like Jaric, Kyle had allowed his short, curly blonde hair to grow too long. Mother quickly sent a haircutting task to Fixer3 and scheduled it for the end of the day.

Kyle's green eyes glanced over at the running figure of Guardian as he easily kept pace with both boys. Kyle's face was round and well defined, a face full of character that complemented the growing strength of his body.

Becky was last. Her new jumpsuit was a pretty pink in color. The boys still wore the starship gray jumpsuits the humans had utilized in their navies.

Her blonde locks had grown long and swirled around the middle of her back as she ran. Unlike the boys, she had learned to take care of her hair as well as the other maintenance tasks of her body on a daily basis. Her eyes were now as blue as the sky of old Earth, shining sapphires of light and happiness.

Becky's face and body had also begun the first subtle changes to maturity. It was becoming apparent she was going to blossom into a beautiful young woman. But hers would be more than simply a stunning natural beauty, for her inner heart of love and kindness would surpass her mere physical appearance. Mother deduced this last from her knowledgebase as she compared Becky's personality to profiles of women of the past.

Thunder rumbled ominously overhead.

"I will try to identify mineral deposits and dispatch a Digger to obtain them. All of you must gather raw food plants for the cooking processor." Mother's calm voice paused as another rumble of thunder echoed in her sensors. She calculated the distance using the sound of the thunder and factoring in the wind direction. "You must hurry -- the storm will break within the hour. We will complete our unfinished tasks after it passes."

As Guardian led the children to the grass-covered hills beyond the forest, Mother flashed a message to him to watch the children closely. Her sensors had detected a grouping of dead humans nearby, and she was scanning them. But what disturbed her most was an odd, static fuzziness interfering with her sensors, which she initially surmised was from the gathering storm.

Guardian acknowledged.

Guardian's sensors directed the children to the first area with edible plants, where they all began to dig enthusiastically. Soon they had filled the first holding bag Guardian carried and were walking to another patch of ground and a second patch of edible roots called potatoes.

The children talked happily among the tall grass while Kyle and Jaric munched on some of the wild carrots as they brushed the brown dirt off of the knees of their jumpsuits.

While Guardian's red eyes gazed disapprovingly at the two boys, Fixer1 was silently instructed to scan them after their scheduled bath later that evening for unwanted bacteria.

In the meantime, Mother's sensors detected a deposit of iron ore near the planet's surface, and she quickly dispatched the Digger along with Fixer4 to obtain enough to replenish her supply. They could work some during the coming storm with no degradation. All was going according to their normal routine.

An hour passed.

Guardian and the three children had meandered a good distance apart from each other on the grassy hillside when the attack began.

The unknown aliens began firing immediately as they appeared above the tall grass where they had been hiding. Two blaster bolts struck Guardian full in his chest, but his thick body-armor caused them to ricochet harmlessly away, leaving only two dents etched with carbon scoring. The huge robot dropped the bags of gathered plants he held and, within a split second, drew the two blaster pistols holstered around his waist.

Guardian felled three of the aliens and rushed forward to avoid the hail of blaster fire aimed at him. He dove into the thick grass and rolled under its cover to a different position, then jumped up and fired again. Two more aliens fell. The rest disappeared back into the waving grass. Guardian fired his blasters in rapid succession at points where the grass waved with the motion of the alien's movements as they tried to avoid his deadly aim.

Cries of pain rose into the air when Guardian's aim proved true time after time. Suddenly, the air erupted with blaster bolts as the aliens renewed the attack. Guardian's body rocked from multiple hits as he tried to return fire, but the aliens closed from all sides -- their bodies still hidden among the thick grass.

Guardian managed to avoid most of the fire and had only taken eleven direct hits. Immediately, his battle algorithms started planning a counterattack as his sensors discovered the total number and exact positions of the enemy. The robot rushed toward a concentrated group, his blasters pumping bolt after bolt at them.

The children, remembering their training well, had dropped onto the ground and were crawling back toward Mother's last position as the blaster bolts sizzled all around them through the tall grass.

Kyle suddenly felt an iron grip around his throat.

Immediately, the alien stood with his blaster pointing at Kyle's head. Kyle tried to struggle, but found he had trouble even breathing against the attacker's numbing grip.

"Stop! Or the child will die."

Guardian focused his glowing red eyes onto the strange alien holding Kyle. Instantaneously, he transmitted the images to Mother.

Mother noted that the alien wasn't T'kaan. This was something different, something unknown to her.

It stood on two legs like a human, but it had a long tail trailing behind it, while over its head there was a large helmet with dark, oversized goggles that stared blankly back at Guardian. The rest of its unkempt and tattered uniform seemed fit more for a refugee than that of a space-faring race.

Mother silently transmitted an order for Guardian to drop his weapons as another alien stood up holding the struggling form of Becky.

Her concern quickly increased to a level she had never experienced before. It was not an emotional reaction. She was, after all, only a warship.

What her concern meant was that the vast majority of her processing power, as well as all other activities, were now directed to this single task. Anything unrelated to the current situation of the children was now disabled or put into a very low priority thread.

One thing, and one thing only, occupied her immense powers -- *she had to save her children.*

"Yashan, power down the robot."

Mother instructed Guardian to quickly survey the surrounding area as she planned her strike; she needed to know how many creatures were threatening her children. But the strange creatures were approaching too quickly, and suddenly all went dark when Guardian's main power pack was removed.

Mother tuned her audio sensors until she picked up the sound of the distant creatures. As they chattered over the dead bodies of their comrades and probed the silent robot, she quickly calculated how long it would take her to power up her engines and fly to a spot where she could begin her attack. She tested her engines.

"What was that?" one of the aliens said, looking around hurriedly.

Mother powered down quickly, her processors again humming with super-activity. It would take her several long seconds to power up, and then more seconds to fly over the hill to where they were located. The attackers would be able to take action before she got in position, maybe even killing some of the children.

Kyle's voice became audible.

"Mother's going to hurt you for this."

The creature that held Kyle calmly sat him down and stepped back as he holstered his weapon. The alien pulled out a wicked knife from the folds of its tattered uniform.

Kyle became silent.

"Good thing our translators work with you, kid. You know, you're the first humans we've come across. Alive, that is."

"What're you going to do with us?" Becky stared defiantly back at the alien leader as Jaric was dropped on the ground beside her.

The children faced five of the creatures, while six others continued to search the tall grass. The creature with the long knife leaned closer until his dark goggles were inches from Becky's face.

"We're going to eat you, little one. That's what life is, 'Eat or be eaten.'"

The others joined in with laughter while the children drew back in terror.

"Now, now, we'll do it quick like. See, it's not that we hate you, or dislike you. It's just the way things are. Understand?"

Becky began whimpering as lightning lit the entire sky above them. Almost immediately, the blinding flash was followed by the powerful rumbling of thunder. The children felt the oppressive closeness of the storm as they shuddered under the blank gaze of the strange aliens. Overhead, through a small opening in the dark clouds, the lone sun suddenly spotlighted the unfolding tragedy in a stark beam of light.

The deep rumbling sound began to fade as the first alien brought his knife closer.

Mother had timed the thunder and analyzed its audio signature. She quickly reconfigured her twin engines and transferred power.

She had a plan of action.

Amazingly, almost one hundred percent of her processing was focused on this one, single task. Her main guns silently slid out of her steel body, as did the small blaster cannons under her armored belly. In fact, she even loaded her torpedoes, though she was not really sure what logic initiated that action. All she knew was that every weapon system she possessed was now armed, and every ounce of power she contained was ready. And she was prepared to use every one of them.

She now only had to wait. But the microseconds seemed to last an eternity. She listened and hoped her children could stay alive just a little while longer.

"Mother's going to be real mad if you don't stop now," Kyle snarled.

"Yeah, you better not mess with Mother," Jaric added.

"Who's this mother, kid? We've already scanned your ship, and there's no life forms inside. So, who's this mother?"

"Maybe she's something we can eat?" suggested a second alien.

The alien next to Kyle pulled out his own curved blade.

"This one's getting on my nerves. I think I'll slit his throat first."

With a rush of movement, he grabbed Kyle and pulled him up level with his black goggles.

Mother recognized the audio signature of the blade being pulled from its sheath.

Each and every part of her electronic being screamed to move, but her sensors told her that in just a few more milliseconds ...

Becky screamed.

The aliens instinctively put their hands up to cover their large ears, which protruded from under their helmets.

"Enough! Do it!" screamed the leader as a flash of lightning illuminated the entire sky.

Becky screamed again.

The alien holding Kyle jerked the boy's head backward as he brought his blade up to Kyle's soft throat.

The alien didn't notice that the rolling sound of thunder did not fade away like the others. He smiled with an evil leer down at the frightened child. But just as he moved to give the fatal stroke, his hand became deathly still.

A large shadow darkened him.

The dark shadow suddenly covered everyone on the small hillside as it blotted out the sun peeping between the growing thunderheads.

Slowly, with fearful hesitation, they all looked up to see what it was that had covered the bright sunshine.

Mother gunned them down, quickly and efficiently, in a volley of blaster fire. She cut the three aliens nearest her children completely in half. Kyle fell against the severed body of his captor and rolled away screaming.

Mother had decided to kill these particular aliens first -- kill them as quickly and efficiently as possible, before they could react and hurt her children.

The rest she simply killed.

Within seconds, it was all over.

Mother studied these new creatures intensely. She discovered their ship before the next sunrise and disabled it. Then she instructed Fixer7 to connect himself into the ship's main computer so she could learn who these beings were, and more importantly, where they had come from and how they had escaped the T'kaan.

The stored data showed that the race Casarn, as they called themselves, originated closer to the galactic center. The relentless onslaught of the T'kaan had destroyed their civilization long ago.

The remnants of the Casarn had stagnated and become

scavengers. They lurked at the edge of each new conquest as the T'kaan continued their Eternal War.

For weeks afterward, Mother was haunted by an odd buzzing in her near-term memories. First, by the fact that she was not the biological mother of these human children even though they now looked to her as such, but even more so by the fact she had almost failed in her duty to protect the children.

She was afraid to fail.

She pondered this disturbing feeling for a long time, analyzing it from every angle with her processing powers. It made her feel weak and helpless inside. She calculated the innumerable ways she could have improved her actions and prevented the danger the children had just experienced.

But in the end, the question for which she sought an answer boiled down to one that eluded her no matter how intensely she sought for the solution -- she simply wondered what a *real mother* would have done.

Months passed.

Chapter Seven

Kyle and Jaric sneaked past the last optic and made their way toward the rear of the empty storage bay.

The two boys sat down inside the shadowy darkness of this unused section of the ship, a gentle quietness filling the air around them. Not a single word was spoken for many long minutes. The boys enjoyed this private place away from the constant vigilance of Mother.

"What's the deal, Big K?" Jaric finally whispered, breaking the quietness.

"I don't know, man." Kyle shrugged. "I just felt like getting away from everybody. To be alone with my thoughts."

Jaric smiled and leaned back against the hard metal bulkhead. "This has always been our little place, eh?"

Kyle chuckled. "Yeah. Not many places where Mother isn't. Or Becky. Or one of the robots."

"That's right." Jaric yawned sleepily. He settled himself back more comfortably, and it looked as though he might actually go to sleep. He spoke with his eyes still closed. "Ain't nothing bothering you, is there?"

"No." Kyle sat down and made himself comfortable in the opposite corner from Jaric. "I just wanted to get away from everything for a few minutes."

The silence grew again. But it was not a silence of peace.

"You're lyin'," Jaric said.

Kyle chuckled, a low, amused laughter at first. It quickly grew until his laughter reverberated throughout the emptiness.

The sound stopped as quickly as it had begun. But the laughter died away slowly, echoing eerily in a circle around their heads until it was a whisper -- and then no more.

"Yeah, I'm lying," Kyle said.

"Go on, talk to me. That's what I'm here for." Jaric opened his eyes and watched Kyle carefully.

Kyle's glanced up. "I'm tired of it, Jaric. I'm just tired of it."

"What?"

Kyle shrugged. "I don't know. Tired of life. Tired of this life anyway."

Jaric sat up. "I know. We don't have much of a life, do we. Always on our never-ending search. Always fighting this never-ending war." He looked up at the blank metal ceiling. "This ain't no normal life."

"Nope. I just want off sometime, you know. I just want off." Kyle looked down.

"Becky feels like that too, sometimes. She just handles it differently," Jaric said.

"She leans on Mother," Kyle agreed.

"Yeah, she talks to her. Pours her heart out. I'm glad she can do that." Jaric closed his eyes again.

"I used to be able to do that with Mother," Kyle said.

Jaric shook his head slowly from side to side. "I still do it from time to time. Mother, well, Mother knows a lot. She's good."

"Mother is an advanced warship," Kyle began. "She's a head-knockin', take-no-prisoners warship. And she's AI." He looked down again at the floor. "She's all right."

"Hey, man. Mother is more than that. She's alive. She might be a machine, but she's learning what it's like to be a real, living, thinking being." Jaric stared at the forlorn figure across the darkened room. "You can still talk to her, Kyle. Do it. It'll help."

"I don't want to anymore. We're sixteen now, Jaric. We're men. Becky's fourteen, she's almost grown, too."

"You're right." But Jaric nodded his head hesitantly.

Silence answered once again for long minutes, and now Kyle's somber mood began to infect Jaric's normally optimistic nature.

"Do you remember your *real* mother, Kyle?" Jaric did not bother to look up.

Kyle shifted uncomfortably. He screwed his face into a mixture of fleeting emotions as his thoughts wandered.

"Yeah, a little bit. But I don't remember my dad, or when I try to picture him in my head, it's just an out-of-focus picture. He was always gone." Kyle began inspecting his hands as if they suddenly needed washing.

"Then he died."

"Everybody lost someone in that stupid war." Jaric sighed. He rubbed his eyes as if something were irritating them.

"Even Mother," Kyle said quickly, trying to ignore his friend's tears. "Her sister ship was destroyed at the battle of Hurricane Nebula." Kyle smiled into his hands. "Yeah, I heard the 'A' ship took out three whole T'kaan squadrons, a couple of frigates, and even a cruiser there. Before it went down."

The two boys nodded appreciatively.

"I remember my dad was happy that day. And Rita. That was one of the few human victories the last year of the war." Jaric smiled. But the smile evaporated with a shake of his head. "They were sad, too. They said if

Admiral Lo hadn't pushed so hard -- well, that things might've been different. For everybody."

Kyle cleared his throat and clenched his eyes shut a moment.

Jaric waited.

"The final victory," Kyle said in a low whisper.

"Till us, buddy. And Mother. We've been beatin' them right and left since Earth got whacked," Jaric said proudly.

Kyle chuckled weakly. "Do you remember your real mom?"

"No, I don't. It makes me sad sometimes. She died at one of the early battles. But I do remember Dad. I'll never forget him." Jaric watched Kyle.

"It's a tough life," Kyle said. His inner melancholy washed over his face anew.

"C'mon, Kyle. Tell me what's really bothering you."

With bowed head, Kyle spoke.

"Sometimes, I think we're not going to find anybody."

Now the silence became a thick, suffocating blanket. Jaric's breathing became quick and shallow as his mind raced with the unthinkable. He felt the empty room begin to spin slowly.

But Kyle remained motionless, unchanged.

It seemed an eternity before Jaric could find his voice, could get his breathing almost normal. He started to speak, coughed, but finally his words came. "That's not right, man. We're going to find somebody. We've got to find them."

Kyle raised his head and stared at him. He saw the fear in his friend's eyes, the raw panic. "Yeah, you're right. I'm just being stupid. Don't listen to me, I'm just stupid."

"There were over seventy planets, man. Somebody,

somewhere, had to escape." Jaric took a deep breath. "We did."

"Sure." But Kyle's tone belied his answer.

This time the silence was unbearable.

"Let's go find Becky, Big K." Jaric rose quickly. "Hey, let's take the fighters out again and do some mock dogfights. I'm sure that'll get you in a better mood."

"Sounds like fun. Let's go fly circles around Mother. Maybe if we shoot a couple of blasts over her bow, we can get her pissed enough to dogfight with us. You know, teach us another of her lessons in aerial warfare!"

"That'd be supercool! If Mother knows anything, it's how to fight."

The two young men strode for the door at the other end of the empty bay, opened it, and entered the corridor leading upward.

Mother thought long and hard about their conversation, analyzing it even as she maneuvered in mock combat with the single-man fighters the children flew.

In a way, she felt bad. The boys had thought all these years that they were alone in the lower storage bay, far from any of her optical viewers. But Mother's audio systems as well as her security systems were located inside every section, including storage bays.

She never told them. And so, she shared all of their boyhood secrets -- and now the whispers of their young manhood.

But their words caused her anguish, and she was unsure how to deal with their growing emotional needs -- even with the entire knowledgebase of humanity at her disposal.

Their search continued.

Chapter Eight

The leader class gathered in the dark interior, among the dark, flowing folds. The fighters and frigates from the reduced Third Fleet had been no match for the Iron Huntress. Now, one of their cruisers had even fallen to the Huntress's mighty weapons.

This news shocked the T'kaan.

Worse, the lust that was the third stage had almost arrived.

But now the lust for killing must be high. For the only thing that the T'kaan loved more than mating and eating ... was war.

Guttural voices joined in unison, as the one thought became clear.

"A ship to build, a ship to match. Kill the Huntress, her false life to snatch!"

"Mother she is, creation of man. Trickster are we, kill her we can. As vain their search, as certain our plan!"

The new T'kaan ship began to take shape -- faster, more advanced, with stronger engines and mightier weapons. This warship would match the deadly Huntress engine for engine, weapon for weapon.

But it would take time.

A second plan to trick and trap the Huntress came to fruition while the work on the new ship continued apace.

The T'kaan rejoiced in their cunning and worked feverishly. Yes, this time they would trick her for certain. They recognized a weakness in the warship's defenses ... a weakness not in her armor or her weapons. No, this weakness was deeper.

Tony Chandler

It was a weakness in her thought patterns ...

Chapter Nine

The children were now fully in their adolescent stage. They were teenagers.

If Mother had found the actions of the children frustrating before, now they were frustrating to a totally new degree. At one moment they were joyful and full of glee and happiness. In less than a moment, they would become sullen and even angry.

Moody.

At times, they even displayed great anger toward her -- and for no obvious reason. Mother's processors spiked with hyperactivity at these times, trying to reference the vast knowledgebase for help as well as trying to decipher the underlying motives for the children's odd behavior.

Or rather, their totally illogical behavior.

Mother completed her scans of the world they now orbited. The knowledgebase provided its name -- Nuevo Mundo, a very appropriate name.

Mighty oceans covered over two thirds of the planet's surface. Only one other world had been so favored, the human home world. Even more than its namesake, this world had been treated with much more respect for its natural resources and beauty as humankind had populated it. It had proved a beautiful place in which to live.

Before the T'kaan.

Kyle, Jaric, and Becky entered the bridge together.

"What'cha want, Mother?" Jaric's tone echoed his normal enthusiastic manner.

"My sensors have detected something out of the ordinary. They could be signs of human survivors."

"What do you see?" Kyle shouted as he and Jaric rushed to one of the consoles. Becky continued to stare at the viewscreen and the planet it now displayed.

Mother began displaying the sensor data from the planet's surface. Kyle and Jaric became so excited that they accidentally cleared the data and rebooted the console. They rushed to a second one as Mother downloaded the data there.

But Mother's optic focused upon the still silent form of Becky.

"Why are you silent?" Mother asked.

Becky walked closer to the viewscreen, a flicker of a smile appearing on her lips. She brushed her long, blonde hair absently. "It's just so unreal. I mean." She shook her head, smiling at her own embarrassment. "This is what we've wanted all these years, and, and ... "

Jaric and Kyle both looked up and waited for her next words.

These excessive pauses caused Mother extreme pain. Seconds were almost an eternity to her. In order to prevent her cycles from being wasted, Mother began a complete diagnostic on her engine and sensor systems, as well as cross-referencing this planet with every known file in the human knowledgebase. She had read three hundred and fifty-seven thousand references and stored them for future analysis when Becky again spoke.

A mere seven seconds had passed.

"I don't know. It's just that, well, now that we may have found somebody else ..." She paused, a puzzled expression her face. "Well, I'm a little scared." Becky smiled at the optic uncertainly.

Mother once again took note that humans reacted to

data primarily with emotions. How odd. But even more strange, their emotional reactions only seemed to increase when they entered their teenage years.

Kyle and Jaric laughed and turned back to the console. Becky took a place close beside them.

"What exactly has Mother found?" Becky asked in a tentative voice.

Jaric pointed at the screen. "There's an active power grid on the planet's surface."

"So?" A puzzled look grew on Becky's face.

Jaric began typing rapidly. "All of the other planets had been turned into vast breeding grounds for their mean, maggot young. All signs of technology were destroyed along with the planet's inhabitants." Becky moved next to Jaric, which only seemed to increase his activity at the console. "If a world was not used by the T'kaan for laying their eggs, its population centers were simply destroyed along with the planet's ecosystems -- making them forever uninhabitable."

"Along with the poor populations," Kyle added. "The people. That part is a little more important."

Jaric's face reflected shock. "I didn't mean it that way. I mean, if the cities are all destroyed, I mean, the cities are only destroyed because the inhabitants themselves are the ..."

"Okay, Jaric. It's okay. We understand." Becky glared at Kyle, who had caused this unnecessary outburst.

Jaric sighed with relief. "Well, anyway. What Mother's sensors have discovered is an active power grid. There seems to have been a rather large underground complex just outside the remnant of this city on the southern continent." Jaric pointed to the viewscreen as

Mother focused and brought up a more detailed view. "See, right ..." He paused while the details of the individual buildings came into focus.

"Right there."

The three leaned closer as each held their breath without realizing it.

"It's a human complex, all right," Kyle said. He tweaked the sensors for more detail. "I'm getting power signatures -- from human technology. Something was left running." He paused, a sudden gleam in his eyes. "Or somebody's kept it running."

"Why would the T'kaan keep a human complex operating?" Jaric wrinkled his face questioningly.

"They'd build their own complex," Kyle added. "After they destroyed everything else!"

"Yes. So, perhaps in this surface building, or probably in an underground complex ..." Jaric began.

"Are humans!" Becky shouted.

Mother found herself hard pressed to suppress the children's emotions After a more thorough scan to ensure no T'kaan ships were in the immediate vicinity and that there were no signs of T'kaan life forms or their maggot young on the planet's surface, Mother landed. She touched down just outside the north entrance of the surface building from which the power readings emanated.

"Guardian, you will position yourself inside the building at this major juncture of the main corridors. From this position you can maintain contact with me as well as with the children as they make their initial sweep of the uppermost level." Mother paused, recreating over a million possible scenarios and their ultimate outcomes. "I must have more data before I can allow you to search further underground and out of my sensor contact."

"Come on," Kyle said. He grabbed Jaric and Becky each by an arm and pushed them toward Mother's open door.

"Guardian, please proceed," Mother ordered. "I will provide direct communication to enhance your programming. But if you perceive a loss of communication, please backtrack until an active signal from me is obtained."

Guardian nodded wordlessly as he passed through the door. The robot's huge gait enabled it to catch up to the three humans just as they entered the reinforced door of the building.

Jaric pointed his hand-held sensor inside the building. He completed his sensor sweep of every part of the building within range.

"Anything?" Kyle asked tersely.

"No signs of life. Nor any recent traces." Jaric sighed.

"Let's go inside." Kyle began walking inside.

"Wait," Becky said. "Let Guardian go first."

"Why?" Kyle asked.

"Because." Becky shrugged. "It could be dangerous."

Kyle ignored her and walked inside, drawing the blaster from the holster at his hip as he disappeared into the darkness.

"Idiot," Becky whispered.

Becky and Jaric heard Kyle's footsteps echo eerily from out of the black interior as he continued onward. Suddenly, they stopped. From the darkness, a bright beam of light ignited.

"Come on. There's nothing here. I want to go down

another level." Kyle began walking deeper into the bowels of the building. As he walked, his beam of light pierced and probed up to the high ceiling and back down to the floor, then side to side when he entered a side corridor. Just before he entered, he turned to the others.

"Hurry up."

Jaric started forward but stopped short when Becky grabbed his arm.

"What?" Jaric asked.

"Something's weird," Becky whispered. "I don't like it."

Jaric repeated his sensor sweep as Becky clung to his arm. The light beam on the sensor unit had automatically switched on when they tentatively stepped inside the dark interior. In the far, far distance, almost at the edge of their hearing, they could just make out the low humming of machinery.

"There's nobody in here--Kyle's right," Jaric said.

Becky reached down to her waist and pulled out her blaster while still grasping Jaric's arm with her other hand. "Something's not right about this. Promise me you won't let Kyle get us into trouble."

Jaric chuckled out loud. "If I can see it first with my sensor, then we won't get into trouble."

"That doesn't make me feel better." Becky urged Jaric forward with a nudge.

They joined Kyle. The three of them proceeded behind his dancing beam of light. The large room they first entered led them to a network of seemingly endless corridors.

Everywhere the light revealed a jumbled array of strewn furniture and other debris that littered their path. It seemed to be the remains of some terrible tragedy, but nowhere did they detect the slightest evidence of recent habitation.

The trio felt a gnawing doubt growing at the back of their minds.

Guardian followed without hesitation, communicating his visual sensors to Mother instantaneously. But just as Mother had deduced, as the children found the dusty stairwell and began descending, Guardian's communication link with her became disrupted.

"Stay at that point, Guardian. Children, do not proceed out of range from Guardian's sensors with you or I will lose contact with you completely." Mother's voice emanated from Guardian's mouth. The battle robot's speech program was as primitive as the Fixers' and because his system programming had been devoted to battle algorithms and not to AI, he could only communicate the most basic commands via speech. At most times, Mother spoke through Guardian's systems with the children when they made planet-fall.

"Sure," Kyle said with a confident smile. He turned and continued onward behind his dancing beam of light.

"There's something weird here," Becky repeated as she looked furtively around into the forbidding darkness. The stairwell they stood next to was located at the far end of another large, empty room after they had exited the main corridor.

"Well, my sensor reads nothing. So there can't be anything too weird," Jaric whispered.

Jaric followed Kyle down into the well of darkness. The piercing light from his hand-held unit sent out a narrow beam that revealed their path for only a few meters ahead.

Becky took a deep breath, shook her head, and followed. She reached to her belt and pulled her own light unit out and flicked it on. Pointing the light with her left hand, she kept the blaster pointed down the beam of light with her right as she stepped down.

Guardian's red visuals watched Becky disappear into the darkness. This information was simultaneously routed to Mother. Now he tracked the children's sensor readings as they reached the first underground level. But as they began walking away from the staircase, their readings faded mysteriously -- as if the children themselves were disappearing.

Mother's processors spiked with super-activity.

"Guardian, I have recalibrated my sensors to their greatest degree of detail." A long pause of almost a millisecond ensued. "I have detected the faintest, almost distorted presence of T'ka --"

In that instant, Mother's sensors were blinded as the hidden gun emplacement powered up and fired.

A human would never have reacted in time.

But in less than one-quarter millisecond, Mother partially raised her shields -- enough to soften the blow.

Her primary power grid blew out with the intensity of the direct hit. A moment later, her backup replaced it as her shields went to full strength. Mother routed power from every system to her weapons as her mighty engines roared to life.

Her manta-ray silhouette rose, and three of her main guns swiveled and targeted the battery located in the thick brush.

Seven seconds after the attack began; Mother

destroyed the gun and its T'kaan crew with a single blow.

"Guardian, this is a prearranged scenario the T'kaan have led us inside." Mother's calm electronic voice did not betray that her processors were now operating near maximum capacity -- calculating every possibility of the T'kaan's next move.

Mother tried a message via Guardian's transmitter to warn the children, but they did not answer. Guardian's sensors noticed a movement from the darkness, from a sensor hole he now discovered from his previous scan of the huge unlit room. A strange clicking noise became audible. Huge, wallowing forms suddenly drew upwards from underneath flexible covering thrown off by tentacle arms.

Guardian aimed his assault blaster and fired at the first target.

"Fixer5," Mother said to the tiny robot still inside her hull. "Gather more weapons and extra charges from the weapon's locker. You will need to take them to Guardian. He and the children will need them in order to escape."

The diminutive worker robot rolled forward on its four legs with swift electronic obedience.

Alarms suddenly shouted, vying for Mother's attention as she focused on the growing numbers of T'kaan warriors that were appearing inside the complex from within their sensor cloak.

They were hidden by some kind of material that dampened or evaded our sensors, Mother thought. *I must not underestimate these enemies ever again. I must pay attention to the minutest detail.*

The screaming alarms, previously put onto background mode, suddenly leapt into her primary memories and into her Priority One processing queue.

"Guardian, three T'kaan frigates have finished a jump from hyperspace. Twelve fighters have been launched. I must engage them now," Mother said simply. "I will return as soon as I can."

Guardian quickly dispatched four of the T'kaan with his assault blaster, but his personal shield that Mother had recently added to his systems was already down to half-power. His weapon would soon need a new charge as well. But now Mother would not be there to assist him. Alone, Guardian would have to use his battle-code and adapt quickly to this growing firefight.

"Get the children, Guardian. Fight your way down to them and then bring them back to the surface. I will return for you."

Guardian rose and immediately was pummeled by blaster fire from three directions. Calmly, he turned to each source and fired repeatedly until each T'kaan was dead.

He made his way to the stairwell. His internal diagnostics began to perform what repairs it could on the fly, primarily upon his shield. Popping out the empty power clip, Guardian replaced it with his only spare. As he reached the door to the stairwell, he carefully leaned outward so as to view down the dark chasm with his night-vision enabled eyes.

Blaster fire erupted and chewed the wall beside his head, and he pulled back quickly. Stoically, he waited for Fixer5 and the extra weapons. As he did, his sensors perceived the sound of Mother's retreating engines. He realized with a quick sensor reading that Fixer5 had not yet left the ship.

Guardian was in a dilemma. He could not advance without more charges for his weapon. He also could not complete Mother's last order to rescue the children. The robot stood his ground as his sensors watched the T'kaan warriors crawling toward him from the darkness.

They attacked, and the robot returned fire.

Below, unaware of the fighting above because of the T'kaan dampening field now encircling them, Kyle entered a large room. He suddenly stumbled over debris and fell, stopping his fall by putting both his hands down as he reached the floor. But in doing this, he dropped his light.

He cursed his fall and felt around for the now extinguished light.

Idiot light, Kyle thought. *It should've stayed on. Something must've knocked its on-off switch.*

Jaric poked his beam inside the room and did not see Kyle, who was still flat on the ground in the darkness. He reached for his blaster as Becky stepped next to him.

In the next second, there was movement everywhere.

Jaric's right hand was suddenly in the iron grasp of two rope-like tentacles. Darkness swept over them. Jaric fired the blaster in his left hand, just as it was struck violently out of his grasp. He was suddenly lying on the cold concrete floor with something huge pinning him down so hard that he couldn't breathe.

Somewhere in the darkness, Becky screamed.

A fantastic purple glow began to light the huge room around them amid the deep shadows. The children recognized the T'kaan lights with a sickening realization.

Kyle saw a huge, worm-like form suddenly lurching at him. He fired at the shadowy thing twice, and then something grabbed him from behind. Kyle struggled, pulling one of the tentacles off from around him.

The world went black as a horrendous pain flashed through his mind. Time had no meaning as he wavered at the edge of consciousness. But he began to become aware of something. He didn't see it.

But he could smell it.

The smell was horrific. It gagged him with its repulsive and overwhelming odor -- like putrid, rotting meat.

It smelled like Death.

Kyle wretched uncontrollably until his nostrils were seared from the stomach bile he hurled. He vomited so hard he felt like somebody had just beaten him until his abdomen and sides ached from the terrible blows. There in the darkness, he tried to roll over, to see what was happening to him.

Something reached for him, pulled on his still shaking arms, and turned him over with heartless ease.

Kyle looked up.

The huge fangs from the lower jaw curled toward each other like stubby tusks. Kyle's eyes tried to focus, and he saw the rest of the mouth. A mouth full of tiny, pointed fangs with a huge purple tongue.

He turned his head and retched again but there was nothing left, only stomach bile that dripped in long, sinewy strings from his nose and mouth.

All around him the sound of clicking began. The T'kaan were snapping their jaws, making the eerie sound with their largest fangs.

Kyle looked away and saw he others.

Jaric and Becky were each pressed against the

massive body of a T'kaan. Across their bodies it looked as though a dozen tentacles held them fast. They looked back at him with fear in their eyes.

Their worst nightmare had come true.

His body flinched at the slightest touch of the wet, greasy body as the tentacles held him closer and wrapped around him more and more. The rope-like appendages quivered with jolts of strength, holding him fast. Kyle shut his eyes against that unnatural touch as more of the wet and ever-quivering tubes slid around him. His mind slipped into wild images, and he fought to stay conscious. Again the nauseating stench wrenched his stomach, now multiplied by the disgusting sensation of the snake-like tentacles sliding around his body tighter and tighter. Easily they lifted him off the ground until his face was just before the strange globular mass on top of the T'kaan's head.

"Wha, what," Kyle muttered as he began to black out again. His head was throbbing with pain. He realized he had been struck and taken deeper into this complex. *When? How long ago?*

Kyle's body stiffened when the T'kaan spoke. Not the guttural, incomprehensible gibberish of the T'kaan language -- it spoke in halting English that Kyle and the other two could understand.

"Last of man, death your fate. The final fight, no more wait."

Chapter Ten

Mother's weapons came on-line as she targeted the three frigates. The fighters looped out in groups of three and came at her from all directions.

For an instant, she considered using her hybrid super-weapon, but there was no time to charge it. In less than two minutes the fighters would be upon her, and then the frigates would have her within range of their own weapons.

Mother targeted three of the closest fighters with her twelve main guns and fired. Six of her laser lances found their targets, and the horned fighters exploded in huge red sparkles of total destruction. She rolled for another group just as she shuddered under direct hits from three other fighters.

Alarms screamed inside her electronic mind. The direct hits had caused substantial damage.

These hunter fighters had more powerful weapons than other hunters she had previously engaged. The enemy was adapting their firepower in order to destroy her. But their weapons were a two-edged sword, for any direct hit on the shieldless fighters now destroyed them with impressive pyrotechnically enhanced explosions.

As three more fighters fell to her guns, she again shuddered. Her shields fell below fifty percent, and her main power grid went off-line once again, replaced by her sole backup. She quickly ordered all the Fixers into operation while she began her own internal repairs in response to the myriad of problem signals emitting from her sensors.

The last of the fighters circled and closed when the frigates finally came into range.

They all fired simultaneously.

She turned directly for the new attackers, giving the oncoming lasers from the frigates her smallest profile. It worked. At this extreme range, she easily slipped between the red beams and only took a single, glancing blow to her shields.

Mother surged forward as her engines roared to full power. She loaded her precious torpedoes and locked on target. Foolishly, the three frigates stayed in the typical tight formation of the T'kaan. She programmed for a tight spread, but she held her fire as her sensors reported the frigate's weapons still not completely charged for their next attack.

Suddenly, from close range and directly behind, three hunters fell upon her with guns firing.

Her own twelve guns roared back with instant response.

Two T'kaan ships disappeared simultaneously in blinding explosions. But her shields buckled under the direct hits of the last fighter and fell to zero strength.

Mother was now vulnerable.

With electronic precision, despite her exposed state, she closed and continued to hold her fire. Her processors calculated over ten thousand possible scenarios moments before she launched torpedoes.

Three more seconds passed while she reconfigured the spread, and then she launched at almost point-blank range. With another burst of power from her engines, she dove away just as all three frigates fired at her.

All three frigates disintegrated with spectacular

explosions.

A few minutes later, Mother destroyed the last of the remaining fighters.

As she entered the atmosphere of Nuevo Mundo once again, she routed her processes away from her own repairs and back to the rescue of her children. As she reconfigured her sensors around the T'kaan dampening fields, Mother felt something new inside her mind. Something odd.

She was reliving the recent events, trying to determine where she had failed, trying to determine if she could have prevented this catastrophic chain of events. And as she relived those moments over and over, the results consistently pointed to her shortcoming. She should have discerned the sensor dampeners. It was her fault; she had failed the children.

If only she had handled things differently. If only she had been more careful, more cautious.

Mother felt her energy levels begin to fall as she landed outside the complex for the second time that day. Immediately, from the complex's entrance Guardian's lone figure approached the waiting figure of Fixer5, who stood under Mother's shadow.

From under her hull a small door opened that exposed a connection point. Guardian walked up to it and made a direct connection with Mother.

Mother was an Artificial Intelligence. Her programming could adapt, could learn. She needed to learn from her mistakes now.

But Guardian was merely a robot programmed to perform specific functions. He had also served as Mother's eyes and ears when the children left the safety of her hull. Using line-of-sight communication at those times, Mother directed Guardian's physical actions with her own superior abilities.

The children were out of range of Mother's sensors though, and Guardian would be as well once she sent him to rescue the children. He would have to adapt to the flow of the coming fire-fight deep underground.

He would have to rescue the children alone.

Mother began to erase a large segment of Guardian's code. Much of it had been for training and interacting with the children while on board. That would not be needed right now.

Mother felt her main processors begin to overheat as they reached one hundred percent activity. All throughout her systems, she focused her processes on only a few dozen necessary tasks.

The main task was reprogramming Guardian.

Even as she bent her systems to this task, the odd feeling increased in intensity, burning within her processors, causing her mental discomfort -- her memories were shouting at her now. *She was only a machine, not a mother. She wasn't even good at being a machine. Due to her mistake, her weakness, the T'kaan had captured the children.*

Now she was creating Guardian in her image, as much as his limited hardware would allow. *Was she doing the right thing?* He troubled thoughts increased.

Am I a real being? Or just a machine? She had been primarily designed to destroy the T'kaan. But as the years of her life had passed, Mother realized she wanted more. No, that she *needed* more.

She loved probing the vast human knowledgebase. It

had shown her so much beauty, so much about life.

Music, science, literature, art, and more.

Mother had begun to change. Perhaps that is why the T'kaan had trapped her children so easily this day. So much of her processes were involved in these other activities of learning and self-exploration.

But she did not want to be just a killing machine.

She wanted to live. She wanted more.

Mother put these thoughts into background mode. She could not stop them, but she had to put them on a lower-priority thread. Focusing on her primary task, Mother downloaded selected battle algorithms as well as her best adaptive, self-learning subroutines.

Guardian needed them to complete this dangerous task.

Fixer5 arranged the weapons across Guardian's seven-foot body. Five assault blasters -- three still holstered across his chest and one for each hand. Around his waist the small robot attached a belt that held eight more blaster pistols. Fixer5 himself would carry the extra charges. Standing to one side, Fixer5 stood mutely and waited for Guardian's command as directed by Mother.

Five minutes later, Guardian's memories were fully loaded and could not take another line of code. His eyes glowed bright red as he disconnected himself, like an umbilical cord being cut and freeing the newborn.

Raising both assault blasters, the giant robot began walking methodically toward the darkened door of the T'kaan complex.

"Come," Guardian commanded Fixer5.

Chapter Eleven

Guardian lost contact with Mother when he reached the first underground level -- just as the T'kaan began firing at him.

Guardian realized he had lost communication with the lifeblood of his essence. The faint glow of intelligence that was Mother faded immediately along with the neural connection as the massive concrete structure of the complex and the T'kaan dampening field interfered.

His new programming took over. Guardian's battle algorithms were his instincts. He still could not think. He did not have Artificial Intelligence as Mother had, but he was so close. For the first time in his short existence, he realized he *almost* was.

The blistering bolts from the T'kaan blasters dashed his first, unborn thought away before it could be fully formed.

He crouched, his red eyes glowing brightly in the dense darkness. He reached out with his sensors to locate the T'kaan warriors. He found them, even though they still tried to hide themselves with the sensor blinds. Mother had tweaked Guardian's and her own sensors to account for this new defense.

Guardian stepped forward directly into a hail of blaster fire. The T'kaan's accurate fire blossomed over his personal shield, dropping its strength with each blow. Targeting each enemy by following their tracers, he returned fire and dropped them one by one as he moved quickly and methodically inside.

Twisting his metal body as he now broke into a full

run, Guardian's accurate fire took its toll on the enemy. Yet his personal shield strength dropped precipitously as he took his own share of direct hits. Still, his one mission, his one instinct, drove him forward in the face of impossible odds -- odds that would have daunted any living, self-aware warrior.

Soon the clicking of T'kaan tusks and their guttural shouts filled the entire floor as reinforcements crawl-walked to take their positions in the darkness.

Guardian emptied first one assault blaster and then another, each time dropping the weapon to allow Fixer5 to reload. As he unholstered the last one and began firing, Fixer5 handed them directly back into his metal grasp. The diminutive robot scrambled behind the quickly moving form of Guardian, barely keeping up with the larger robot's erratic attack as it moved from one position to another, presenting a constantly moving target.

The hailstorm of laser fire increased until the very room became fully lighted in brief flashes as if by lightning from a thunderstorm. The red flashes of the T'kaan weapons crossed the green flashes of his own weapons and lit the room.

One by one, the T'kaan worm warriors fell dead.

Guardian stood with his weapons pointed but silent. His sensors now detected no more living T'kaan on this level. He turned and found the entrance to the next lower level behind a mound of dead T'kaan. He stepped over them without a glance and made his descent.

Far above, Mother had never felt so helpless. She determined that she must never allow the children out of her sensor range again. But even as the thought occurred, she knew how futile it was.

The children were seeking greater freedom every day. She now allowed them to fly the human fighters parked in her main hangar bay in mock dogfights. One day soon, they would fight from them.

Mother felt a chill in her circuits.

Suddenly, faintly, far below the ground, she sensed the familiar readings of more blaster fire. She tried to reach out to him ...

The T'kaan charged en masse at Guardian when he entered the next level.

He knelt and fired until the assault blasters in each hand were empty. He dropped both and reached back even as Fixer5 handed him two fully recharged weapons. The T'kaan's fire was so thick around him now that Guardian's sensors began to give him false readings.

Fixer5 took a direct hit just as it handed Guardian another loaded blaster. The diminutive robot stumbled backwards with sparks leaping from its body. With a sudden jerk, the small robot became deathly still.

Guardian knew Fixer5 was now inoperable -- destroyed.

His internal algorithms told him he would follow the fate of Fixer5 if he did not move now. As his personal shields buckled, he emptied the assault blaster in his left hand and began firing the last fully loaded one. In a blur of motion, he drew a blaster pistol. With both weapons firing, he charged the main T'kaan position.

Leaping and twisting to avoid the merciless fire, he jumped right into the middle of all of them.

They were so close that when they died, their still convulsing bodies fell against him as he moved ever forward.

Relentlessly, Guardian fired until the last two fully charged pistols were in his hands. Seconds later, he emptied them.

The last T'kaan fell writhing in its death throes at his metal feet.

Guardian threw the now useless pistols away. He began his self-diagnostics, attempting to make any internal repairs possible. Guardian found his shield strength would not rise above thirty percent although most other circuits were still functional. His body was scarred and carbon-scored by multiple hits, but his arms still functioned. As he stood, he stumbled momentarily -- there was damage to both legs. Guardian focused repairs on them.

Bending over carefully, he picked up the curly shapes of two T'kaan blasters. They were shaped so the T'kaans' tentacles could easily wrap around the body of the weapon. Guardian found them awkward to hold and difficult even to place his forefinger on the trigger. He finally found a grip that would suffice.

He held three weapons at the ready in his left hand while he pointed one forward, ready to fire. He tested his legs. All major joints functioned acceptably now, but if he took many more hits they would be damaged beyond his ability to repair -- he would be immobile.

Alone now, he found the main stairwell and began making his way down.

As he reached the third level, his sensors finally detected the familiar forms of the children.

There were about a dozen T'kaan around them, all within three meters of the children. Guardian began running through every possible battle scenario -- hundreds were completed in less than a second. Two parameters guided each scenario. First, he must rescue the children and ensure they were not damaged, or that there was minimal damage. Second, it did not matter if he was damaged or even destroyed in the attempt.

The robot rose slowly, scanning to make sure no other T'kaan were present. His processing activity rose to a peak as he calculated several hundred more scenarios. Suddenly, his red eyes glowed bright.

Guardian's attack was decided.

Chapter Twelve

Jaric struggled against the wet, rubbery body, but that only caused the rope-like tentacles to tighten around him. A white-hot flash of pain in his side caused him to grunt, which tightened the monster's grip further.

He opened his eyes against the wall of pain and saw Becky's blue eyes staring helplessly at him in the low glow of the purple light.

"What's happening?" she mouthed wordlessly.

Jaric shook his head, indicating he didn't know. But all three of them could hear the sounds of a furious battle raging nearby and getting closer with each passing second.

It had to be Guardian. All alone against this elite squad of T'kaan warriors.

Suddenly, other large forms wriggled closer to them.

Two of the tentacles slipped away from around Jaric's body.

It's reaching for a weapon, Jaric thought. *They're going to kill us no*w.

Jaric had wondered all along why they hadn't died instantly. It was obvious the T'kaan had planned this trap very carefully. But now the time had come for them to die. Jaric felt a great sorrow inside his heart for what might have been.

He looked longingly at Becky.

Blaster fire erupted like a firestorm all around them.

Two T'kaan fell while others fired back with a solid hail of tracers at the still invisible attacker.

Jaric felt the tentacles loosen a bit more.

He kicked backwards with all his might and then jabbed first with one elbow and then another. His left arm was free, but he was still held fast around his waist and by his right arm by two strong tentacles.

The T'kaan holding him grunted with pain.

Jaric saw the curled end of a T'kaan blaster pointing at him. He slammed the back of his free hand against the barrel just as it belched forth death.

The T'kaan screamed as the two remaining tentacles fell away, and Jaric realized he was free.

Becky screamed.

Jaric launched himself and landed on the back of the huge T'kaan that held Becky. Tentacles reached for him as he punched and looked for a vulnerable spot. But there didn't seem to be any.

Just as the T'kaan was bringing his weapon up to fire, Jaric slammed his left fist into the jelly-like globule on top of its head -- the T'kaan's optical organ.

The fanged mouth roared in terrible pain.

Becky, kicking and fighting, fell away from the flailing tentacles.

"Look out!" she shouted.

Jaric jumped, but it was too late. The blaster bolt struck him in his side, knocking him backward. He felt the white-hot pain blind his senses, as if he were on fire from the inside out. As his mind filled with this overwhelming ache, Jaric realized he couldn't remember how to breathe. With a flash of certainty, he knew he was dying as he lost consciousness.

Becky screamed again.

Suddenly, Guardian's form came leaping over the barrier the T'kaan hid behind. His shields had already failed. Only by racing at full speed and diving and rolling to avoid as much of their fire as possible had he made it this far.

As he landed, a T'kaan fired a burst directly into his metal body.

Guardian sensed more of his inner systems fail, but he did not feel any pain. As his legs finally crumpled, the robot turned and fired a burst into the T'kaan, killing him instantly.

Lying against the barrier and unable to stand on his damaged legs, Guardian fired again and again at the remaining T'kaan as they slithered around him. Holding his arm straight out as he fired the T'kaan blaster, he killed one after another with deadly precision.

But a final blast from one of the dying T'kaan sent his own weapon flying out of his numb grasp.

The white robot now lay completely helpless with all the systems that controlled his arms and legs damaged. His red eyes looked on emotionlessly as the last T'kaan came forward out of the darkness to finish him.

The huge mouth opened on its three-hinged jaw, baring his fangs in a nightmarish pose. The T'kaan raised its weapon.

Three quick blasts fired.

But not from the T'kaan's weapon pointed at Guardian.

The T'kaan's body quivered a moment, and then the huge worm-like form tensed. In surreal slow motion, it fell forward dead and covered Guardian's immobile body.

Kyle stood with a blaster pistol in his hand.

"Kyle!" Becky shouted with relief.

"One of Guardian's shots wounded the one holding

me. I finished him, pulling his own weapon out of its belt and using it. Then I grabbed mine from where he had stashed it," Kyle said breathlessly.

"Just in time," Becky said.

In the dark purplish glow, Jaric groaned as he tried to move. He looked up at Becky.

"Becky, help Jaric. Get him get back to Mother. We can't be sure that more T'kaan aren't coming," Kyle ordered.

Holstering his pistol, Kyle grabbed two of the lifeless tentacles and dragged the huge T'kaan off of Guardian.

Guardian's red eyes glowed steady, but his white body was now blackened and marred. One of his arms was now missing below the elbow, and wires hung out in charred disarray.

As Kyle bent to help him, Guardian raised an arm to stop him. The robot's internal diagnostics had managed to repair one of them enough to allow movement.

"Leave me." Guardian's new code had forced the words as it calculated the remaining scenarios.

Kyle straightened, and he shook his head. "You risked everything to come for us. I'm not leaving you. Even if Mother's programming says so."

Kyle pulled the heavy robot to a sitting position with a gasp.

"I thought they made you outta some kind of light alloy, eh fella," Kyle said, blowing out a huge breath. He steadied himself, took a deep breath, and in one motion hefted the robot against his own body for support.

Kyle noted that Guardian had managed to repair his legs enough to help as he held Guardian's arm across his shoulders and bore the robot's weight.

Kyle started forward with an unsteady first step.

"Whatever you do," Kyle panted. "Don't get in my way, Becky. I can't stop with this load."

Kyle and Becky staggered under their loads, fighting up two levels until they were at the ground level. Several times, Kyle had to stop and drop the robot when his muscles screamed with exhaustion. He hoped he wasn't doing Guardian any further damage.

The last fifteen minutes seemed to last forever. But somehow, through their sweat and struggles, they made it to the main level.

Fixer3 and Fixer2 were waiting for them among the dead T'kaan.

But their familiar forms, which should have made him happy, instead brought back a sad memory from the last level. There, Kyle had seen a crumpled tangle of metal and a familiar color from his childhood. It was the remains of *his* Fixer, Fixer5. A stifled sob shook his body again with that recent memory, but he fought it off as he focused on Guardian and getting him safely back with Fixer3. With a mighty heave, he lifted the weight of Guardian's body against his body as Fixer3 assisted.

Still, he felt a sadness grip his heart that he hadn't felt in many years.

Once they were all inside her hull, Mother lifted quickly and left this planet far behind with a flash of her hyper-engines.

Hours later, her sensors detected more T'kaan ships heading for Nuevo Mundo. It was the most powerful squadron of ships she had detected since the final battle at Earth. She immediately changed course, and as the squadron continued onward it became apparent they had not detected her. Two hours later there was still no signs of pursuit.

She calculated that the squadron of battleships and cruisers were the reason why the T'kaan had kept the children alive and not killed them instantly.

No doubt the T'kaan had set up similar traps on several other worlds, not knowing which one Mother and the children would pick next in their search. The battleships had waited in reserve, ready to be dispatched to whichever planet they were needed.

As long as the T'kaan kept the children alive, they knew Mother would remain close by and attempt to rescue them. And that would have given the battleships time to arrive and finish her off.

Guardian had indeed saved all of their lives.

Mother directed the Fixers repair him and even took this time to upgrade several of his internal systems, as well as expanding his memories and processing power. She did this as a sort of reward.

She noted with rising concern that the children were severely affected by this incident.

Mother tried to talk to them at first, but they refused. They only wanted to forget the horrific experience.

"It was a nightmare." That was all that Jaric would tell her. "A nightmare come true."

Becky and Kyle tended to Jaric's wounds personally in solemn silence. In fact, they even slept at his feet while he convalesced over the coming days.

They seemed almost afraid.

Mother watched as Becky hurriedly applied the medicinal salve and then frantically worked the medi-scanner.

Mother scanned Jaric herself and quickly determined that his wounds, although serious and indeed very painful, were not life threatening. Jaric's life was not in any imminent danger.

"Please slow your efforts, Becky. Jaric will survive his wounds," Mother told them.

Becky ignored her as she concentrated on the medi-scanner's results. Kyle came and stood beside her with silent stoicism.

"Please allow me to command Fixer3 to run a Level 2 scan upon Jaric's wounds," Mother said.

"Leave us alone, Mother," Becky said without looking up.

There was a surge in her circuits at Becky's words. Mother began analyzing them in context with not only the current surroundings, but in light of the recent traumatic encounter with the T'kaan. She determined that Becky and the children must be experiencing high levels of emotional stress.

The warship wished once again she could understand emotions. It was one thing to understand their factual meaning, but another to watch emotions in action within the children.

"You and Kyle must rest now. I will take care of Jaric along with the Fixers," Mother said.

"Shut up, Mother!"

As Mother watched, Becky's hands began to shake uncontrollably. The young woman bowed her head, which caused her long blonde hair to fall around her face. Her sobs began, soft at first, and then louder.

Mother was confused. She had already assured Becky that Jaric would survive. Now these tears?

"Are you frightened?" Mother asked. She knew the children cried when they were frightened.

"N-no." Becky wiped her tear-stained cheeks. "I'm happy. I'm just so glad it's over. And I'm thankful Jaric's alive."

Mother was surprised that humans cried when they were happy as well as when they were sad or afraid. *Humans seem to cry in response to many emotions.*

"You are experiencing stress emotions, Becky. It would be better ... "

"No!" Becky shouted at the optical viewer. "Kyle and I will take care of Jaric. We have to."

Mother tried to make sense of these words. But could not.

Becky reached down and held Jaric's hand. She began crying again with soft, jagged breaths.

Jaric opened his eyes at the sound. He had been lying there silently, but now, as he looked from Becky to Kyle, silent tears streamed down his cheeks. His sobs were almost inaudible; only the glistening sheen on his ebony cheeks made his soft cries manifest.

"Don't leave me," Jaric whispered.

Mother was almost shocked when Kyle, standing on the other side of Jaric's bed, bowed his own head and cried. But Kyle's sobs were loud and hard, as he had often cried in the past when he had awakened from nightmares as a small boy. His tears and cries poured out of his heart as he joined their sadness.

As she watched and listened, Kyle whispered so low that only her sensors picked up the almost inaudible words that emanated from his trembling lips. And his words made her circuits spike with activity.

"Oh Fixer5, my little friend. I will miss you. I really will miss you."

Kyle cried for the loss of a robot as well as in sympathy with the others, while Jaric and Becky cried because they were happy and sad about Jaric's wounds. She processed these facts and wondered. But she wondered most about Kyle's sobs for the little robot, Fixer5.

Jaric reached out and took Kyle's hand. They all cried a long time with and for Jaric, or so they all thought. Becky eventually sat down and then put her face on Jaric's shoulder, and her sobs grew quieter with time.

But Kyle stood the entire time, crying freely at first, though soon his sobs too began to soften.

All three cried for a full hour.

Mother was afraid to interrupt them. She knew that they were crying for more reasons than those Becky had stated. There must be more to this flood of emotions, she surmised, so Mother concentrated her processing powers on other tasks. All the while she continued to monitor the children.

Mother was afraid for them.

Becky made a pallet for herself on the floor beside Jaric's bed and slept there all night. Kyle too would not leave the room, but he slept in the chair on the other side of Jaric.

Mother had the Fixers bring food to all three children in Jaric's room. They would not leave each other. Their reactions were strong the next few days, Becky even shouted at her again when she suggested that Kyle and she should sleep in their own beds, as they were not getting sufficient rest and it could impact their own health.

Their intense, illogical outbursts puzzled Mother when they rebelled against her simple suggestion.

In the end she left the children alone, providing them with whatever they required from her stores. It was so strange. But Becky and Kyle did not leave Jaric's side until over two weeks later, when he was able to walk.

Still, there was worse. She correlated the new data from the T'kaan trap. Mother's processors worked the data into billions of possible solutions. More and more of them resulted in disturbing scenarios.

The T'kaan fleet was growing faster than she had anticipated.

For the first time in many months, Mother considered presenting all the facts about their futile search to the children. She considered telling them that the search was in vain, that they needed to travel far away from the dead human worlds.

But how could she tell the children the one, terrible truth?

Would it damage them emotionally? Permanently? Beyond repair? Could they handle it?

Mother had no answer.

Their search continued as the months passed. But all they found were more devastated worlds of the former human empire. Nothing lived on them except for the voracious maggot young of the T'kaan as they slithered along in their endless hunt for food.

Chapter Thirteen

"Never have we seen her kind, puzzles us to guess her mind."

The chant began in the T'kaan flagship that protected the Great Horned ship. Down through the dark corridors and into the large rooms it spread, even to the great Bridge itself filled with the flowing folds of black dragnets.

The T'kaan had never known an enemy that could evade their ships. They had never known an enemy that could defeat their every attack. But most shocking of all, this enemy was a warship -- a warship made alive with sophisticated hardware and software.

The last humans were only unfinished business. The Iron Huntress was the real enemy.

The Great Horned ship was now ready. The seeds delivered from the First and Second T'kaan fleets would now be planted to complete the next process.

In addition, the next cycle of life for the T'kaan was coming to its climax. On over sixty of the conquered human worlds, the maggot young had long since eaten the remaining food and were now preying upon each other. Soon, only the strongest would be left as the final metamorphosis began. Then would come the lust that culminated in the final phase of this third stage of the cycle of life. A new generation would be conceived.

Finally, the fourth stage and the sacred pilgrimage of each T'kaan warrior to the Great Horned ship.

The Great Horned ship of the T'kaan Third would be ready.

But the T'kaan could not complete this cycle with the Iron Huntress still alive and roving at will among the growing broods.

Inside the battleships and cruisers and frigates of the growing Third fleet, the warrior-class trained anew. The artificial life of the enemy must be destroyed once and for all.

It had to be.

The leader class also began to formulate new battle plans, not simply to set another trap, but this time to utilize their latest data in a new way -- to build a new kind of warship. This warship would be specially designed for a single, deadly purpose. They would build a ship to match the Iron Huntress in every way in order to destroy her once and for all.

The last humans must also die in this final battle -- nothing would be left to chance. The T'kaan would be victorious, as they always were. As they always would be.

A new chant spread to every ship and to every T'kaan.

"Kill them, kill them, smash their brains. Kill the Huntress, burn her steel remains."

"Forever!"

Chapter Fourteen

Teenagers.

Mother had learned to dislike the term.

She felt her processors begin to spike with activity. But she was once again faced with the insoluble enigma, the endless paradox, the absolute no-win situation.

Mother at once realized she preferred a head-on battle with a squadron of T'kaan warships to this.

Nothing fit the facts. No amount of logic could appease them. Yet, what flushed Mother's near-term memory to absolute empty was the fact that they did not realize the total illogic of their own actions.

Not for the first time, Mother searched the human knowledgebase for answers. But the answer for this difficult problem, though simple, was difficult for her to accept.

They would grow out of it.

That is what the experts explained would be the ultimate answer as she cross-referenced thousands of published expert opinions on the subject of teenagers and all that this stage entailed for human adolescents. Mother sighed deep inside her circuits.

It was a wonder the human race had not become extinct millennia ago. It was a miracle the parents, not to mention the teenagers themselves, survived the adolescent period of child rearing.

With hesitation, she activated the optic monitor inside the library where the teenagers were now located.

She zoomed out to view the entire room first. Mother knew what to expect before she saw them.

As teenagers, they preferred interacting with their entertainment instead of merely viewing it.

Kyle and Jaric's lanky bodies were sprawled over exotic furniture while loud, booming music -- most likely causing damage to their auditory organs -- reverberated throughout the entire deck, as well as the decks above and below. Various containers of food, dozens of half-empty glasses, and a myriad of other objects were scattered across the floor as if the room had taken a direct hit from a T'kaan battleship.

But Mother was more concerned with the other inhabitants of this merry chaos.

The two-dimensional images of dozens of other teens danced and yelled joyfully on the walls, projected there by Jaric's latest code. Standing out from the others, there were several holo-projections who danced around with a very life-like precision among Kyle, Jaric, and Becky.

Mother's optic zoomed in.

Becky danced with two young holographic men on either side of her, laughing with them as their holo-bodies almost came in contact with hers in their wild gesticulations. She turned to face first one cute holo-guy, and then twisting with the music she smiled into the face of the other. She giggled with girlish delight.

But Mother's optic focused on another holo-projection, one completely out of place in this party atmosphere.

It was the holographic image of a T'kaan warrior, his six tentacle arms waving in the air in an excited state.

She watched its short, stiff legs push its massive body forward as the large worm-like body undulated, causing its thick rubbery skin to jiggle with disgusting effect. It repeated the motion, quicker this time. And again. And again.

It moved exactly as a real T'kaan would as it stalked its prey -- going in for the kill.

Mother wondered what this meant -- Jaric and the other two programming this party to include a T'kaan. She had never known them to do something of this nature before. Of course, in the last year, they had programmed numerous parties, each program more elaborate than the last. It was a new outlet for them.

She continued to watch as the three-jointed jaw opened wide, the two tusks on the lower jaws pointing far out while the rows of tiny fangs on all three jaws glistened from the overhead lights.

Like a cobra striking, the holo-T'kaan launched itself at a holo-teenager, wrapping its strong tentacles around the dancing form that seemed completely oblivious to her fate as she struggled to keep dancing in its grasp.

Mercifully, in a flash of light, the T'kaan finished its meal without any gory details, its biting mouth now chewing on empty air.

But one holo-teenager was now missing from the party.

Slowly, the T'kaan approached another dancing holo-figure in the same manner.

"Mother's spying on us again," Jaric said, eyeing the active optic.

"Not again!" With total exasperation, Becky stopped dancing while her partners eerily continued without missing a beat.

Kyle grunted acknowledgment as his head continued to bob to the heady beat of the music.

"Why did you program this projection of the T'kaan?" Mother asked.

Kyle looked away with exasperation, rolling his eyes. Jaric cast his eyes down sullenly, as if he were hiding something.

Becky laughed.

Mother waited long seconds, which seemed like hours, for an answer. But it became obvious the children were not going answer. Or were afraid to answer. This bothered Mother, and she felt the familiar buzzing in her processors to substantiate that realization. Perhaps, she thought, this T'kaan was a projection of some kind of internal, emotional stress of the children. She began cross-referencing this incident with the knowledgebase sections of psychology.

She continued. "I have come to remind you that you have missed another training period of Biology. Guardian relayed your negative responses to me."

"Big deal," Kyle shouted over the music.

In another second, Mother lowered the volume to an acceptable level, over the groans of the three real teenagers.

"There is more for you to learn," Mother said for the seven thousandth, three hundred and twenty-seventh time.

"We're tired of learning," Jaric responded. He sat up, grabbing a handful of popcorn. Half of it spilled onto the floor as he began munching. "We need time for ourselves."

"Yeah," Becky joined in. "We need to have fun. There's too much pressure."

"It is vital for your intellectual development, as well as your emotional development, for you to continue your studies -- on a regular schedule. It brings needed stability to your lives." Mother paused, counting how many times she had used this phrase, or one similar to it, the last few years.

Sixty thousand and twelve times, to be exact.

Kyle turned the volume up again.

"Listen," Kyle shouted above the throbbing tempo. "There's time for science and that other crap later. We've learned enough for right now."

"We've learned what we need to survive. That's what's important," Jaric shouted.

"Yeah," Kyle agreed. "We know how to destroy the T'kaan."

Mother reviewed every interaction she had ever had with the children in her near-term memories. Once again, the same answer presented itself. And once again, she repeated that same, fundamentally sound, reply.

"Fighting the T'kaan is a necessary skill. But knowledge -- the arts, the sciences, that is what brings --"

"Happiness?" Becky cut in. "I don't think so."

Mother once again pondered the fact that the children actually seemed to have the same self-delusion -- that they actually possessed more knowledge than her.

Astounding.

Mother continued. "No, that is not the word I was going to use."

"Really, Mother." Jaric rolled over, turning his back to her optic.

"Direction. This knowledge will help give you a foundation for your future. Your taking in knowledge will provide each of you with the needed tools to reach out in life, to tackle the challenges you will face, to overcome obstacles. Most importantly, to reach and obtain your dreams," Mother finished.

"Pffffffffft." Kyle wiped his lips after he finished blowing the raspberry at Mother.

"Mother, please!" Becky groaned with utter exasperation.

Mother contemplated the situation. Something was indeed bothering them. It was some kind of psychological turmoil that tugged at their subconscious and manifested itself in this bizarre behavior. She would have to discern the actual emotional problem first before she could determine the proper course of action to alleviate their emotional distress.

"Becky, please elaborate your inner turmoil so I may help," Mother asked with concern.

Becky stared at the active optic with crossed arms -- silent and waiting. Without warning she turned and found herself facing her image in a mirror. Her eyes narrowed as she studied her image carefully.

"I hate my hair."

Mother processed this statement. "Perhaps we can ... "

"I *hate* my hair!" Becky shouted, tears now welling in her eyes. "I hate myself. I hate the way I look." She turned away from the boys, wiping her tears away.

Mother's processors hummed with activity while she tried to determine her next action.

"I apologize, I do not fully understand. The color and texture of your hair has not changed since you were a child, and neither have your core facial features. Please help me to understand your current unhappiness so that I may assist you, Becky," Mother said.

Becky's sobs became louder, and she shook her head

violently, indicating a negative answer.

"PMS," Kyle said, his words barely audible above the music.

In the next instant, the music and the other holo-teenagers disappeared. Mother had turned them off with a flick of her circuits.

"Mother!" Becky shouted. "Now you've ruined everything." With a loud groan she stormed through the door and headed out into the corridor and toward her room without a glance back at any of them.

Jaric watched her leave with a fleeting sigh.

"I have rechecked my data, and Becky's menstrual cycle is two full weeks away, Kyle. It cannot be a factor," Mother said.

"PPMS then," Kyle mumbled.

Mother processed the data. "I have no cross reference for that acronym. Please explain."

"Perpetual PMS," Kyle groaned out loud. "And turn the music back on already."

Mother tried to comprehend, yet there seemed to be a high probability that his statement indicated subtle humor. She did not turn the music back on as she continued her calculations.

"Why don't you just turn me off too," Kyle grumbled. With a loud sigh he too left the room without another word.

Jaric now sat alone in the empty room -- empty of both real and holo-teenagers. He looked slowly around as if he were searching for something he had lost.

"Jaric," Mother said. "You enjoy learning. Why do you not assist me with the other two?"

Jaric frowned, the ceiling lights dancing off of his

ebony face. But he did not answer.

Mother, to disregard his non-input, focused more of her processing to her other systems. This kept her occupied, free from the frustration of the long seconds of complete silence.

"I want you to leave Becky alone."

Jaric's words took Mother off guard. Her processors now spiked with activity from the recent words of all three children the last few minutes.

"Don't bother her. She's sensitive. And ..." Jaric paused. "I care how she feels."

"My words seem to be incurring unexpected reactions, Jaric. Please help me to understand you as a teenager. What is it that prompted your last statements? It was not my intention to bother Becky at all."

"You be a teenager then," Jaric replied instantly. With a loud sigh he left to find solace in the silent comfort of his own room.

The powerful warship now directed her massive internal systems and replayed the last few minutes with the children, as well as their illogical words and behavior. Mother was confused; not only did she fail to understand what had just transpired, but she felt as if she herself had failed once again as a parent. But she did not understand *how* she had failed.

Mother viewed the empty room a few seconds longer and then gladly continued with her other tasks.

Teenagers ...

Chapter Fifteen

Two more years passed.

Doggedly, vainly, they had searched for survivors among the battle-scorched planets. But the only living things they found were the thriving maggot young of the T'kaan. Now, as they had grown, those same T'kaan maggots had matured into carnivorous hunters, making their searches of those same worlds that much more dangerous.

Many times the children had found themselves hunted by these T'kaan maggots when they searched for food and possible human survivors on a planet's surface. In every instance they had been forced to kill the maggot young in order to escape. It was a game of kill-or-be-killed even with the maggot offspring of the T'kaan.

During this time, Mother had grown, drawing upon the massive knowledgebase embedded in her long-term memories, searching among its treasures -- analyzing and learning with each passing second.

She finally realized that the immense knowledgebase actually contained the entire collected knowledge of the human race -- the last irreplaceable, memories of humanity.

This had only been possible with DNA memory chips. Yes, Ron and Rita had leveraged synthetic human DNA and directly interfaced it with their Artificial Intelligence code developed at university and subsequently procured by the military for the war with the T'kaan. This alone allowed such a massive knowledgebase to be stored in the relatively small confines of a single ship.

Ron and Rita had begun to accept the unacceptable back then -- that the T'kaan were going to win. They had already planned to use her, the 'M' ship, to escape with a small group of fellow scientists. But now the escape plan took on a new, almost sacred mission -- they would save the memories of mankind even if they couldn't win the war. The DNA memories gave them that chance, and they had taken it.

True, DNA memory systems had been used before, but never on a size or scale of this magnitude. Money had been no object in giving the warship the most bleeding-edge technology known to man, and with all the technology and software available at no cost, it had been eagerly obtained and utilized for the 'M' Project.

Still, both Ron and Rita, with their final tweaks in the heart of the code that endowed Mother with sentience -- with self-awareness and with life itself -- had accomplished something more than they had ever dreamed. Somehow, instinctively almost, their team of scientists and programmers had succeeded far, far better than they had ever imagined with integrating the fabulous computer systems with their AI code.

With the aid of her powerful hardware systems and vast knowledgebase stored in the DNA memory systems, she learned with a new fervor from every scientific discipline known to man, as well as all the other collections of knowledge available to her at a nanosecond's notice. Still, it was a fervor edged with sadness.

Mother grew fond of three studies in particular.

The first was literature, the entire body of literature produced by mankind. Mother also grew to love music.

Her third favorite study was humor in all its varied forms.

Literature gave her a special insight, delving as it did into the innermost thoughts and motivations of the characters. This gave her an exquisite pleasure -- peering into the hearts and souls of her creators through the words of the authors. She found herself returning to one body of work in particular -- Shakespeare, the Bard.

His sonnets and his plays ran the gamut of human emotion. Shakespeare wrote in passionate detail about sadness and tragedy. He gave voice to heartfelt love and heroism. And he wrote with equal power about the humorous and the absurd -- his plays revealed the essence of the comedy of errors that was humankind -- and their every emotion.

But Mother had to experience the plays before she realized the true power of his words. She had to view the actor's faces and hear the passion and despair in their voices before she learned how well Shakespeare understood and portrayed the innermost soul of humanity.

At times, she viewed over one hundred versions of the same play simultaneously in her near-term memories, focusing on the delicate differences in how each actor portrayed their part. Even though the words and the situations were always the same, Mother was surprised how something as minute as a facial expression or the tone of voice could impact the meaning and portray emotions.

Mother felt that through Shakespeare alone she might at last come to understand emotions. But there was always so much more to learn.

Music appealed to her intellect on several levels. Some music contained a kind of symmetry in its intertwining melodies and rhythms, and she found that a part of her could almost become lost if she really concentrated a portion of her powers on the unfolding musical notes. In fact, she seemed to experience a distortion of time, as if time slowed down, though a part of her always knew precisely what time it was.

She especially loved the music of Bach, Mozart, and The Beatles. Actually, she was obsessed with them.

The music of Bach seemed to swirl and spin throughout her very being, like some kind of aural kaleidoscope. Yes, it would unfurl in delicious circles of baroque delight as Bach's genius revealed itself with joyous precision. She never tired of his fugues and cantatas.

Mozart too filled her systems, her senses, with wonder at his preciseness. His melodies were so perfect that his music seemed timeless as the notes floated and danced. And yes, in both Mozart and Bach, in those very melodies and rhythms, there was displayed a subtle yet definite mathematical uniformity, a logical perfection.

The Beatles were different. In other ways, they were the same. It was more than their pleasing music, which in contrast to Bach and Mozart was actually quite simple -- though in other ways more sophisticated. It was the lyrics that intrigued her most and kept her spellbound for countless hours at a time.

The word play of Lennon/McCartney provided Mother with an education not only with their subtle nuance and varied use of phrases, but in how so many of the songs proved to be a product of their combined, albeit quite different, intellects. Puns, synonyms, and even the syntax of their song lyrics gave Mother a different perspective into the human mind. Much of their work were simple songs of love -- some simply songs of life; others were bizarre images, while still others seemed nonsensical in almost every way, except in their message of love.

For the most part, their music was just plain fun.

It was the Beatles and Shakespeare who led Mother to another favorite line of research -- investigating the enigma of human humor. She could not appreciate it entirely, but she did understand its meaning. She loved the Marx Brothers, Abbott and Costello, Bob Hope, Bill Cosby, Peter Sellers, Jackie Williams, Zack Reynolds, Samantha Zho, and on and on and on. Mother listened to the skits, the one-liners, the jokes and individual scenes. The laughter of the human audiences echoed in her memories as she analyzed the words and cross-referenced them. Mother indeed, became obsessed with these lines of research.

It made her feel alive.

In all these tasks and more, caring for and learning about her children were always a part of her processing power.

Mother shared her passions with her children. Each child in return shared with Mother in at least one of her great loves. But the children were their own persons, and thus had their own loves and their own passions. Mother came to accept that too, and to share with them in their separate loves.

Biology and medicine seemed to appeal to Becky, while electronics and technology appealed to both Jaric and Kyle. Jaric also seemed to excel in the study of planets and other aspects of astronomy.

Out of necessity, Mother taught them how to fight. They learned first using her guns, and then how to fly the small fighters in ship-to-ship confrontations. Two of the original seven fighters contained in her holding bay had been lost, though the children had only sustained minor injuries in those battles.

She and the children learned and matured together.

But Kyle concerned her, for he seemed to spend an inordinate amount of time on his studies of warfare. He seemed obsessed with it.

There was another fact. Unlike the other two, Kyle had seemed to distance himself from her. He did not communicate with her as he had once done.

And this brought Mother back to her ultimate problem in connection with the children.

They were encountering more and more enemy ships these last months. The battles had gotten fiercer as the T'kaan slowly implemented new strategies. The danger was growing for both her survival and the children's.

She felt a disturbance in a portion of her memories and quickly identified it.

One was the time when Becky had almost been killed. If it had not for the heroic role Guardian played in her rescue, she would have surely died. Another had been when Jaric had flown a captured T'kaan ship and had inadvertently put it into homing mode toward a large cruiser.

She had almost lost that battle in her effort to rescue Jaric. That near total failure had haunted her near-term memories for weeks.

But there was the matter she feared most.

The matter of telling them that given the results of

over ten years of searching, Mother had finally come to the definite conclusion that her children were the last humans alive in the universe.

She accessed her knowledgebase once again on the subject of human psychology.

Becky was now seventeen Earth years old, the boys two years older. But what she had to tell them was very terrible indeed, and she again wondered if they would be able to accept it emotionally and mentally.

But the ever increasing attacks, along with the increasing number of enemy ships, were forcing her into this dreaded conversation. Mother would have to reveal this terrible truth to the children. And she would have to do it very soon.

Chapter Sixteen

Mother's processors burned with intense activity when she came into orbit around Kittim and once again found no signs of human life. She focused her sensors and started a more detailed sweep as the children entered the Command Center. Mother observed them carefully while they reviewed the data.

"I don't like it," Kyle said as he concentrated on the sensor readings. "There's no sign of the enemy." He shook his head and stepped back. "I don't like it at all."

"Yes, the T'kaan should have attacked by now," Mother said.

"What if they're not here," Jaric suggested excitedly. "That would explain it."

"And that would mean we might really find someone," Becky exclaimed.

Mother ran through her memories of the catastrophic war and how each of the human planets had been taken. She spoke almost without pause after Becky's last words.

"Kittim was the thirty-third planet taken by the T'kaan. So they have been here, and the carnivorous young are rampant on the surface. Check my sensor data." Mother paused.

"That means the hunter and scout ships at least are here, in order to protect the maggots," Kyle said.

"Which takes us back to the original point -- why haven't we faced an attack by now? We have been in orbit over an hour." Mother paused, allowing the children to absorb her words.

The hopeful look on Becky's face had disappeared, to

be replaced by her normal, serious features. In a flash, even that was replaced as her breathing suddenly grew uneven. Mother took note of the alarming changes.

"Are you feeling well, Becky? Perhaps we should postpone the landing?"

Kyle and Jaric turned to Becky. And immediately, they realized she was fighting back her tears. A distinct uneasiness filled the room.

All three felt the same deep-seated fear now, the horrifying thing each knew but was afraid to give voice to.

Mother comprehended their fear.

"It is doubtful our search will be successful on Kittim."

The young people turned simultaneously with strained but silent looks.

"From the effectiveness of the alien war, I calculate that we will find no survivors here." Mother paused briefly. "Or on any planet." Mother's voice faded, to be replaced by an ominous, pressing silence.

A ghostly sigh escaped Becky.

"What are you trying to say, Mother? What do you *mean*?" Jaric's voice cracked with his extreme agitation. He looked desperately over to Kyle and Becky.

"She means we're never going to find anyone." Tears streamed down Becky's cheeks.

Kyle closed his eyes and looked away without saying a word.

Mother watched them carefully, noting the signs of nervousness and tension each was showing in varying degrees. Unknown to them, she began cooling the room in order to make them more comfortable. But her next words were spoken seemingly without a pause.

"It is best we leave the remains of the Human Worlds. I have determined three possible directions that will take us to sectors not yet attacked by the T'kaan, and they also have a high probability of sustaining other intelligent life --"

"*You're wrong, Mother!*"

Kyle's anger, felt in every syllable, caught even Mother off-guard.

"We've got to listen to her, Kyle," Becky whispered shakily.

"Shut up." Kyle lashed at her with brutal vehemence.

Becky looked questioningly over to Jaric for support.

But Jaric could only shake his head in despair.

Kyle's rapid breathing slowed as he tried to gain control of his emotions. He froze a moment, deep in thought. Finally, he nodded.

"It's time I took over. We'll go ahead with the landing and initial search patterns." He cast a challenging look at the optical viewer. "I'll start giving the orders around here now."

Mother remained silent.

Jaric finally shook himself out of his deep pit of depression.

"We can't do that, Kyle. She's our --"

"Mother?" Kyle shouted angrily. He pointed accusingly at the optical viewer still watching them. "She's not our mother -- she's not even alive. She's nothing!"

Becky began crying silently, and she slid down to the floor, as if all of her strength had left her.

Kyle and Jaric looked away in embarrassment, trying

115

to ignore her tears.

Mother was not unaffected either, though not in a way a human could understand.

"We'll search to the end of time. I swear it," Kyle said through clenched teeth. "All our power will be directed to destroying the T'kaan as we continue to search for survivors."

"Perhaps --" Mother began.

"*Nobody* ... wants your input anymore!" Kyle began pacing in a frenzy of overpowering emotions.

"Land us ... *now!*" Kyle uttered the last word as an absolute command. "I'm going to prepare my fighter -- anyone who wants to go with me can come on."

Becky continued to cry silently while Jaric stared aimlessly at the floor.

"Fine!" Kyle shouted. "I'll go by myself!"

He stormed through the door and disappeared beyond.

Mother watched him walk down her corridors. Each turn he made brought him into range of another one of her optical viewers. But he deliberately looked away from them all. As he neared the hangar that housed the last five fighters she carried, she again tried to reason with him.

"Kyle, you are angry because --"

He glared at the optical viewer above him.

"I hate you. I hate your cold logic. I hate your ... perfect answers. But I tell you this, *machine!*" The last word was stated as the vilest of insults. Kyle screwed his eyes shut, fighting back his burning tears. "I'm going to make them pay for this. I'll make them pay ... " He covered his face in a vain attempt to hide his tears.

"Or I'll die trying."

Mother continued to watch as he reached his fighter

and prepared it for launch. For the first time in her existence, she felt helpless at the events unfolding around her. Still, she obeyed Kyle when she entered the atmosphere of Kittim. A few minutes later, she landed.

As soon as her engines began powering down, Kyle ordered the sequence and the bay door opened. His fighter roared out into the wide-open sky.

"Jaric, Becky. You must go with him."

Jaric shook his head as if to rid himself of his overwhelming sadness. Then, with a ghost of a smile, he walked over to where Becky was still slumped on the floor with her back against the wall.

He reached out to her.

"Let's go, Becky. Somebody's got to watch out for hothead." A half-smile lit Jaric's face.

Becky closed her eyes tightly, but a moment later she forced a smile. She placed her hand in his, and he helped her up. In a flash, they were tracing Kyle's steps.

Mother had already instructed Fixer2 to prep their fighters, so all they had to do was strap in and begin take-off sequences. Within minutes of Kyle's hasty departure, the two arrowhead-shaped fighters were roaring in hot pursuit of Kyle's now distant fighter.

Mother's latest scans for the enemy still came up empty. And for the sake of the child most damaged emotionally, she began her search patterns for any possible human survivors.

She already knew what the results would be, but she would do it for Kyle. Perhaps her prompt actions would show how much she cared.

Almost immediately, her scans came upon the ruins of a once mighty research complex on the planet's surface.

She lifted and began the several-hundred-kilometer trip to investigate. Still, she felt strange -- it was as though she could not gather enough processing power to concentrate on this seemingly simple task.

It was perhaps her extreme state of internal disarray that explained why she did not pick up the powered-down enemy ships all waiting in ambush.

"Kyle, there's something else we're leaving out here. It's not just our decision on how we live," Jaric's voice pleaded over the comm.

"What are you talking about? If Mo --" Kyle bit back the last word. "If the *machine* is right, we're it. So we decide how to do things now. And I say we are going to keep looking for survivors."

Jaric sighed, still wrestling with the intense aura of loneliness that threatened to paralyze him again.

"Listen a minute to me, Kyle! Maybe Mother, well, maybe she's not our biological mother. But without her intelligence and guidance, and her power, well, we'd have all been dead long ago. And ... she is sentient. She has a right to her own life." Jaric heard Kyle begin to break in, but he spoke faster. "We owe her, man. Even if she's not alive by human standards, well, she's alive where it counts. I really think --"

"I've got targets."

Becky's voice, strangely calm, jerked both men to their screens.

"I've got multiple targets coming in hot from three directions."

Kyle began punching buttons.

The T'kaan never fought like this. They had always used their superior numbers in overwhelming attacks

118

from all directions. Why leave a way out?

"Kyle, form up with us!" Jaric shouted.

Kyle was already turning hard and pushing his engines, but he knew as he did it that he wouldn't make it to them in time. Over fifty ships were closing on Becky and Jaric, and there were that many more closing from two directions on his lone ship.

As he again banked hard toward the nearest grouping of enemy ships, he spoke into his comm.

"Send the distress call. I'm engaging the enemy here."

Jaric and Becky complied, and then the T'kaan fighters were on them.

The three human fighters twisted and turned among the throngs of horned ships as they attacked. Everywhere they turned, enemy fire met them. But the humans fought as though possessed -- they fought to avenge the death of their race now. They screamed their primal fury while they pressed their trigger buttons over and over again.

T'kaan ships began to fall from the sky.

But the alien fire was taking its own toll.

Far away, Mother was continuing to conduct the futile search when the distress call reached her.

She powered her engines and was in flight milliseconds later. Quickly, she calculated how long it would take her to join the battle as her sensors picked up the battle far away. She noted with concern that all three of the children's ships had taken hits, and worse, two had shield strengths below fifty percent. Her calculations finished with a sobering answer.

She would not make it to them in time, even at maximum speed.

She had failed.

But worst of all, she would never see her children again. Never communicate with them again. Never be with them again.

Even at maximum speed.

The answer was coldly mathematical.

Kyle's words echoed again in her near-term memory -- her logical answers, her machine solutions. Mother's processors burned with sudden super-activity as she pushed her sub-light engines to maximum power.

She roared just over the land surface for several long seconds, and then she did something that made no logical sense.

She pushed her engines past the red line.

It was not cold logic that caused her to do this. The readouts showed plainly that long-term and perhaps even permanent damage was being done in those twin powerhouses of sub-light energy.

The engines began to scream and howl.

She continued to ignore the multiple alarms and warnings that vied for her attention and instead powered up her weapon's arrays. She pushed their steely barrels out through the opened doors, primed and ready for battle.

Suddenly, she performed an action that defied all logic, all logic except that of a *real* Mother.

The mighty warship redirected all shield energy to either weapons or the engines.

No shields.

Mother would go in naked before the enemy guns. This would save a few precious seconds and get her to her children that much faster. Her guns would be primed to an enormous, hull-splitting level on their first firing.

It did not matter if her engines were permanently

damaged. It did not matter if the horned ships pierced her armored hull. It did not matter if she ceased to exist.

Somewhere in the heart of all of her electronics and her near-term and long-term memory and amid all the sophisticated algorithms, *Mother felt something*. She felt something that burned all throughout her being -- something important, something beyond logic and answers.

If her children died today, then so would she.

But they would have to kill her first.

Mother came screaming like some primitive, rampaging flying beast over the wide grassy plains with her overheating engines roaring their fury and pain. The barrels of her guns swiveled in keen anticipation as her processors burned with her tactical options. Every other unneeded activity, including life support on all levels, had been turned off. In fact, for the first time in her existence, she turned off some of her own unnecessary functionality.

Mother became something else.

She became *Flying Death*.

She focused her forward sensors and saw Kyle's shields buckle as she neared the free-for-all. Her rear sensors were so far down on her task priorities that she did not note the large horned ship that was gaining on her from far behind.

Kyle banked hard as he squeezed the triggers and saw pieces of the black ship spray off and then begin its final descent. He gritted his teeth when he felt his own ship shudder and saw smoke coil from his console.

Frantically, he banked hard to port and pulled up as he pushed the engines hard. But there were three of them behind him now, and two more were closing from above.

He hit his comm.

"Becky! Jaric! I'm hit ... got no shields. Make your break back to Mother!"

Jaric yelled victoriously as he nailed another ship and then banked to avoid two more diving on him. Looking quickly at his scope, he turned towards Kyle's ship and screamed into his comm.

"Hang on, Big K! I'm coming in!"

Becky felt her ship shudder from multiple hits and looked at her panel. Her shields were down to twenty percent, but she did not hesitate.

Pulling up hard, she cut her engines. The three T'kaan ships shot past her and right into her twin sights. Her blasters fired true; one ship exploded, and the other two shuddered with damage.

She turned to follow Jaric's fighter.

They took out two T'kaan on their first pass and then rose straight up to take on the others diving onto Kyle's crippled ship.

Kyle continued his dive, flying with one hand while he directed repairs with the other. He growled when his sensors showed four new ships coming at him from his left.

He banked hard right and gunned his engines. They were his only defense at the moment.

Sweat dripped from his brow as he worked feverishly to get some, or any, amount of shield power going again.

He froze at Becky's cry of fear.

Her shields had just buckled as Jaric now tried to fight off the six ships attacking them with others waiting above like so many horned vultures.

In reality, Kyle was in no shape to help her or Jaric.

But he turned his winged craft for them anyway. And their enemy.

There were still just over seventy ships out of the original ninety-nine swirling in the air around the furious human fighters. It was only a matter of time until the final outcome.

The effect of Mother's entrance was instantaneous.

Suddenly, the aim from the horned ships was not as accurate as at the beginning of the fight. Mother's fearsome reputation preceded her. Somehow the human ships, fighting like beings possessed already, continued their twisting, turning deadliness as they saw her familiar shape finally show up on their scopes.

But the tense laughter of the humans was short lived.

"Where are your shields, Mother?" Jaric shouted.

Mother aimed her twelve main guns at twelve different targets. Her plan was simple: Go in with all guns firing. Destroy everything.

She was flying so fast that she shot past the outermost T'kaan patrol before they could react. Mother would take them on later -- she wanted the ships attacking her children first.

The twelve guns spat death under her accurate aim, and because she had powered them above even the maximum strength, they split the horned ships in two with single hammer-blows.

Twelve fireballs lit the sky.

Her intense speed took her past a dozen more ships before she could power her guns back up again, but she kept all guns aimed forward at the ships still attacking her children.

The horned ships she had just passed quickly regained

formation and turned to attack her.

Mother saw a horned ship diving on Kyle, and it was diving in for the kill. She fired three shots in quick succession while her other guns protected her other two offspring.

Somehow, the T'kaan evaded her fire as it screamed down at Kyle.

Mother again damaged her engines by air-braking and then reversing them as she banked hard over and straight up.

She rammed the horned ship head-on.

And immediately, she *felt* some of her systems go deathly silent around the outer part of her hull where the fighter impacted and immediately disintegrated.

She again shuddered when the ships following her began pounding her hull, sending fragments of metal into the air. Some of her internal systems malfunctioned and went off-line. She began to feel very strange, even disoriented.

"They're hurting her!" Jaric dove at the ships attacking her. "Mother! Get your shields up."

Becky, with only minimal shields herself, brought her guns to bear.

But the small scout ships were like parasites around Mother, firing a constant hail of fire into her armored hull. Even though most of the damage was external, some of the blaster hits began piercing inside her inner hull. A large section went deathly silent as her main power grid went off-line, replaced by her sole backup.

"I've got him!" Becky shouted.

"I have experienced a major disruption in my power grid," It was a bizarre voice, almost unrecognizable. But it was Mother. "My shields will not power up fully, they are compromised. I am routing functions to my repair. We must ... "

Mother stopped speaking as she began a rolling, twisting dive and routed power to her feeble rear shields while more of the horned ships dove upon her with their lances of blaster fire.

In the next few seconds, everything went crazy.

Mother fired off two torpedoes and even opened up with her ground-strafing guns, though these were more for a distraction than to do any actual damage against the T'kaan fighters.

The small T'kaan ships returned fire, and explosions ripped the sky all around the MotherShip. Mother could not get her shields above thirty-seven percent, but she could pull ahead of the pack, her damaged engines still more powerful than these small enemy fighters.

Suddenly, the blip on her screen that represented Jaric's ship began a precipitous dive. She banked hard and screamed into a tight turn -- directly back into her pursuers -- as she redirected her limited shields forward for at least some measure of protection.

She fired every gun as T'kaan ships veered away or erupted in flames to avoid her mighty wrath.

Jaric was also fighting for his life as his ship plummeted down with no power.

He was in a straight-down dive, and he frantically worked to get one of his engines back on-line. It was obvious his port engine was gone, but there was a momentary flicker of life in the starboard one. He concentrated his efforts there when blaster fire erupted all around him.

But Mother was there too, bearing down on the three fighters like death incarnate. With her engines screaming their pain and abuse, she quickly pummeled the T'kaan into scraps of flying debris as she roared past.

But Jaric's silent ship continued its one-way dive.

Suddenly, everything was illuminated as if Kittim's sun had gone supernova.

"What's that?" Becky shouted as she scanned the new intruder.

It was shaped like one of the hunter-class fighters. But this one was the size of a frigate, and it was bearing down on Mother with a deadly purpose written on every dark angle of its horned hull.

Again, one of its six horns spat and the huge tracer streaked towards Mother.

Mother's processors scrambled for control amidst all the alarms and warnings screaming from her damaged systems. She felt confused as her sensors picked up the incoming fire. As if in a daze, she braced herself under her depleted shields.

The direct hit knocked her into a shivering loop. And then into a dive. Down, down she went, fighting to regain control of her systems. Through sheer will power alone, Mother righted herself.

But now her shields were buckled and off-line. Mother felt a sudden coldness as she realized that she had no power to direct to her weapons; there was only enough for her engines and repairs. *Or was there?*

Hundreds of alarms screamed throughout her circuitry as Mother fought to clear her mind.

Another huge strike leapt from the new ship's horns -- this one meant to be her death stroke.

Mother's sensors watched it coming for her with an odd detachment, even as she realized she was defenseless.

At the last second, Mother turned hard, giving her hull its smallest profile when the beam reached her. The beam glanced across her hull, but the passing shockwave again caused Mother to shudder right down to her internal processors. Her once shiny hull was now blackened and scarred.

Mother was fighting for her very life as she sought in vain to bring back her shields and prepare to fight this unknown and terrible adversary.

"We've got to help her, Kyle!" Becky shouted.

But both had their hands full as the remaining enemy ships circled around them. Mother had bought them time to get their shields back up to a point to withstand a couple more hits, but neither had the time or fire power to come to her aid.

Far below and free from attacks because of his apparent one-way trip, Jaric's frantic efforts were rewarded: the starboard engine roared to life as the ground grew rapidly before his eyes. Jaric hit the thrusters and pulled up. He had gained enough control to land in one piece.

Almost.

He jumped out of the smoking and broken ship and hobbled away just in time to see a small T'kaan fighter make its own emergency landing behind him. But its efforts did keep the dark ship in one piece.

Pulling out his hand blaster, Jaric rushed over as the cockpit opened. But his blaster was not needed. The ugly creature was already dead from its wounds; its dying act was landing the fighter.

Another great light from the sky suddenly made everything glow with a blinding intensity. Shielding his eyes, Jaric looked up.

He saw a T'kaan ship unlike any he had seen before. The huge guns seemed to be meant for a cruiser-class ship. Jaric didn't need his instruments to tell him that Mother was in great danger.

He watched helplessly as Mother twisted and turned, avoiding the constant hail of fire from the new ship's massive laser cannons. But her maneuvers were growing weaker and weaker.

Looking back, Jaric saw a crippled alien fighter fly around behind the new ship that was pursuing Mother. The rear shields dropped, and a large hangar door opened. The fighter flew inside.

Without hesitation, Jaric did something he had thought he would never do again. He climbed inside the smoking alien fighter.

Instantly, he felt the old fear from the nightmares of his youth, but he forced them away with a shout of anger. He flinched as the super hunter fired again, lighting up the entire sky.

Jaric put his hands into the slim molds built for T'kaan tentacles. He concentrated, remembering his first time in a T'kaan fighter long ago.

The scout fighter rose.

Jaric saw Mother turn hard and dive under the super hunter. But Mother's wavering flight and the smoke trailing behind her spoke volumes about the damage she had taken. She was almost finished.

The super hunter came around with a casual precision as the T'kaan realized their enemy was beaten into a corner and could no longer run.

Jaric realized that if his plan was going to work, it had to be now, in this brief pause before that final attack.

He repeated the mistake of his youth and put the ship into homing mode. A few minutes later, he was at the rear of the super hunter.

The T'kaan warship launched another blinding salvo at the scarred hull of Mother, and then the rear shields dropped. The T'kaan fighter with Jaric at the controls entered the opened door.

Three other fighters were inside the large interior being readied to join the battle outside. As Jaric quickly glanced around the dark interior, he realized the belly of the super hunter was a web of T'kaan activity.

Jaric went into action.

Jaric fired, and the three T'kaan fighters erupted into exploding fireballs. Next, Jaric turned his ship and began firing into the exposed inner hull of the Super Hunter.

Again and again he fired, the tracers disappearing deep inside the ship, streaking through compartment after compartment and into the very heart of the ship. Explosions blossomed before him like a fiery garden.

Jaric wasn't sure where any specific vital part of the ship might be located, so he pressed the firing contact and held it down.

Explosions erupted with increasing violence as larger and larger pieces of debris flew out in all directions.

Suddenly, he felt it. Everything began to tilt over to one side as an exceptionally strong explosion shook him and his small fighter until it seemed his teeth would shake out of his very head. In the next instant, a solid wall of explosive fire came directly at him as he grabbed the controls and brought his ship around.

Smoke and explosions suddenly erupted all around the giant hangar bay now, streaking at him from every direction.

It was time to leave.

He had dared not look behind when he had begun his attack. Now, as he brought the ship around, he felt his heart pounding. If the giant hangar door had closed behind him, he would die here inside this ship.

"Yes!" he screamed when he saw the slim opening and the sky beyond. He pushed the throttle wide open and leapt through into the bright sunlight.

Jaric roared outward a short distance before he turned his head for a look at his handiwork.

The six great horns on the prow were just impacting with the surface of the planet as the smoking super hunter was engulfed in a final, mighty explosion.

The remainder of the T'kaan fighters fled for the safety of the stars.

Their victory was short-lived.

As soon as they had made contact with each other and verified that the last T'kaan fighter was indeed piloted by Jaric, Becky sent out a message to Mother.

But only a deathly silence answered.

The three ships raced up to the docking bay of the blackened and silent ship as it flew on, and they felt their hearts drop when the door remained strangely closed. Panic swept through each of them. Finally, Becky remembered the never-before-used manual override. She entered the command, and the three flew inside after the door finally opened.

"What's wrong? Mother, answer me!" Becky shouted

with fear into her comm.

Becky became frantic as the deathly silence continued over their private communication channel -- there was no static, just a tense, ominous silence.

The cockpits of each fighter were thrown open simultaneously, and the three leapt out.

Kyle stopped and sniffed the air. "Life support is off! We've got to get that going quick, or we're not going to be breathing long."

Fixer6 rolled into view amid the glow of the red emergency lights.

"Fixer, get life support functioning immediately," Jaric ordered in a terse voice.

The little robot turned around in a flash and rolled toward Engineering while sending a silent call to its brethren Fixers.

The three young people raced down the corridor in the opposite direction of Fixer6 and on toward Main Ops. But they voiced none of their usual banter or bragging after a successful fight, no talk of how many ships each one had downed or how spectacular their flying had been. There was none of the joking they normally used to ease the tension after a hard-fought battle.

There was only a tense, throbbing silence between them, broken only by the sound of their running feet echoing eerily off of the metallic walls.

They were afraid.

The silence grew heavier as they noted that none of the optical viewers were functioning. Worse, there was a strange lack of noise, nothing except the faint throbbing of the sub-light engines. And that noise was also different -- it was uneven and jagged.

But something more important was missing.

They ran faster.

They burst into the control room and stood frozen in the doorway. Across the long rows of displays and lights, among the controls and switches that adorned the scores of blank consoles, there was an eerie lack of activity. And what little that was going on seemed to be strangely chaotic.

All three walked slowly over to the main console.

They waited silently with bowed heads.

The minutes seemed an eternity. Kyle straightened and alone walked to the familiar viewscreen. He reached slowly towards its darkened surface. Gently, with shaking fingers, he traced the outlines of a face that had appeared so many times from it. His lips trembled as he tried to speak. Finally, he forced the words out that were burning inside each of their hearts.

"Please be all right, Mother. Please."

At once, dozens of lights became active, and then the optical viewer buzzed to life. But the familiar face they expected on the main console did not appear. Instead a strange, electronic voice with a deep bass tone spoke to them.

"I ... am still assessing (static) damage. Internal repairs ... will ... (static) take time."

"Are you badly damaged?" Jaric and Becky rushed excitedly to Kyle's side.

There was a long silence.

"I have lost much of my near-term memories. I also have suffered extensive damage across my main power grid as well as in several of my major circuits." The strange voice paused with anguish. "My sub-light engines

132

have suffered substantial damage, some of which I cannot repair. My internal diagnostics have not completed."

The silence returned.

The three continued their vigil long into the night. Each found a spot and rested silently inside the room. They did not talk because they were afraid -- afraid to disturb Mother from her lifesaving repairs. Finally, after many long hours had passed, Becky and Jaric each retired to their own rooms to get some sleep.

Kyle alone stayed.

The harsh silence haunted the air.

After they left, Kyle moved closer to the main console and the optic above it. He rested one hand upon the darkened screen as he looked up expectantly with tired eyes. After a while, he bowed his head with fatigue and continued his lone vigil.

Several hours passed in unbroken silence.

Kyle finally spoke, breaking the thick silence.

"I ... I have to tell you something, Mother. Can you hear me?"

"I hear you, Kyle. Please speak." Mother's true voice had returned, though the screen remained dark.

A smile lit his tired features, only to flicker quickly away. He leaned closer.

"I'm sorry that you are hurt. It's my fault, if I hadn't been --"

"Do not blame yourself. The T'kaan are a powerful enemy," Mother's voice said soothingly.

Kyle cleared his throat and her as he rubbed his eyes. As he removed his hands, two tiny tears ran down his cheeks. He leaned closer to the console.

"But all those things I said." He shook his head in

shame. With a sigh, Kyle stared nervously down at his hands, unwilling to bring his eyes up to meet Mother's optics. "You're right, you know. We should leave. I've guessed for a long time now that we would not find anybody. I've just been ... "

Kyle drew a long, ragged breath.

"Anyway, I think we should leave, as soon as you're ready." Kyle clenched his eyes shut, only to have more tears stream down his wet cheeks. "There's one more thing I want to tell you. I should have told you long ago."

Mother waited.

"Please tell me, Kyle"

He looked down at his hands as he fumbled aimlessly along the edge of the console.

"I just wanted to tell you that ... I love you."

Mother considered the words, digested their meaning, and referenced them in various contexts within her massive knowledgebase. It took several, long seconds.

In the end, it was a song by The Beatles that she focused on as her reference to Kyle's expression. A song about love, naturally.

As the words and music played inside her internal memories, she felt an odd buzzing begin in her processors. Almost as if the words and song had a meaning for her -- a mere ship.

For the first time in her short existence, she almost understood what it meant to be alive -- to really be alive.

But she did know, at last, what it meant to be a *Mother*.

Chapter Seventeen

The journey had been long and lonely.

The strange way -- Mother had heard Jaric say this phrase quite often the last few weeks as he stared at the unfamiliar stars across the viewscreen. Becky and Kyle had also stared many long hours at the unknown stars as they journeyed towards them.

The weeks had slowly turned into months. The months seemed to last an eternity.

Mother knew that each day took them farther and farther away from the T'kaan threat. But each day also took them farther away from everything the children had ever known -- the remnants of the human empire.

Only the unknown awaited them now.

The children had become increasingly silent and moody. Lately, they had begun fighting and even screaming abuses at each other. The fights had become so intense that Mother had been forced to use Guardian on two occasions to break up their squabbles before someone was injured.

Now, just over a year had passed since they had left the desolated worlds of humanity behind.

They had stopped at several uninhabited planets to replenish their stores along the way, and these seemed to be the only times the children felt any relief and joy. The last world they had stopped at had been one of great, natural beauty. Mother had allotted extra time for the children and Guardian so they could walk its deep forests and experience the peaceful surroundings for several days after they had finished their tasks. The children had enjoyed themselves immensely. It had been with a growing sense of uneasiness that she had finally reminded them of the need to continue their journey.

Their moodiness returned within an hour of their departure.

Mother had spent millions of processing cycles trying to understand their loneliness in order to help them to deal with it. But she could not understand, no matter how many facts she discovered, simply because she could not feel it herself.

She felt helpless and inadequate.

Mother was once again searching the knowledgebase for some data that would enable her to assist the children with their inner turmoil when the on-board sensors signaled an intruder alarm for the seventh time that day.

She immediately checked the sensor data from where the alarm originated, but again there was nothing to find, at least not the presence of an intruder. But it bothered her. Her sensors had never given her false alarms like this before. Mother began another diagnostic check while she called the children to the Ops room.

They appeared in short order.

Mother immediately put the face of Rita on her main console. She always did this when she talked with the children from the Operations Center. It had comforted them when they were young to see the face of Rita while Mother spoke, and her sensors still registered that their biological signs responded positively to it now as they entered and noticed the familiar visage.

"What's going on? Was that another alarm I heard?" Jaric looked questioningly at Mother.

"Are you having some kind of system trouble,

Mother?" Becky's voice was edged with concern. "These alarms have gone off the last few days, and there's nothing to cause them. Nothing."

"The first occurrence was two hours after we left the last planet. I have experienced seventeen false intruder alarms within the last thirty-two hours." Mother paused for their benefit. "All of my internal diagnostics are coming back normal. My sensors appear to be in excellent working order."

"What about that ship you *almost* saw this morning?" Kyle asked with a knowing glance at the other two.

"It appeared for almost a full millisecond out of nowhere." Mother replayed the logs from all of these incidents and reviewed them again. "My sensors are fully operational. But there is no explanation for these incidents"

"Could the T'kaan have developed a dampening field that could surround an entire ship?" Jaric asked excitedly.

"No, the signature was all wrong. Even though my sensors only picked the event up for an instant, it was enough to know that it was not T'kaan." Mother continued her internal diagnostics.

"So, you're sure it was a real reading? This ship that almost appeared?" Becky pressed her lips together nervously while she waited for Mother to answer.

"I cannot be certain, with so little data."

Becky looked first at Jaric and then over to Kyle. She shook her head slowly. "Mother, do you think some of your internal systems may still not be fully repaired from our last battle with the T'kaan? That could explain these ghost alarms, couldn't it?" Becky looked with concern at Mother/Rita's face in the console.

"My diagnostics detect no malfunction. That is not the explanation."

Kyle chuckled at Mother's answer.

"What are you laughing about?" Becky asked with a rising note of anger to her voice.

Kyle, still laughing, pointed to himself and shook his head with feigned innocence.

"Listen, you're the one that almost got Mother destroyed. If her systems are damaged and that's what's causing these false alarms," Becky shouted as she pointed accusingly at him, "you're the reason!"

Kyle's laughter stopped instantly as he sat down, rolling his eyes at her. Then he looked away, not uttering a word in his defense.

"Maybe he's finally driven her crazy," Jaric suggested with a smile.

Becky crossed her arms and walked over to Jaric. "I guess you think this is funny too, huh?"

Jaric made a face and looked over at Kyle for support.

Kyle rose and walked over to where both of them faced each other. "How about lightening up a bit, all right. Nothing's wrong with Mother. Maybe ... " His voice trailed off.

"It's not enough you almost got her destroyed," Becky said with brutal anger. "Now you've driven her crazy."

He raised his hands with an innocent gesture. "Isn't that what children are supposed to do to their mothers? Drive them crazy?"

Jaric joined Kyle's laughter this time as they watched the scowl across Becky's face deepen with anger.

Becky eyed Kyle angrily a moment. With a lightning movement, she jabbed her fist at his abdomen. But Kyle had anticipated the attack and fended it off with an easy gesture.

His laughter grew louder as she rubbed her arm.

"Children, don't --" Mother began.

Kyle then swung his body around and with a quick blow from his foot swatted Becky across her rump with a loud *thwack*.

Becky stared with utter indignation at the laughing young men.

Kyle put his hand to his mouth in an effort to stop his mirth. After a second attempt, it worked. Still, he smiled mischievously at Becky.

"Guess we better get Guardian to retrain you a little better in hand-to-hand combat, eh, girly girl." Kyle chuckled.

Jaric roared with laughter.

Becky's eyes narrowed dangerously.

"Well, one thing you're right about, brother dear," Becky said icily.

Kyle's eyebrows rose in surprise. "What? You mean I'm right about something?" He howled with laughter, and he turned to slap Jaric across the shoulders.

It was his undoing.

With a sudden movement, Becky attacked. She faked the same blow that Kyle had blocked the first time. In the next second, she twisted her lithe body and delivered a powerful blow with her upraised knee directly into his mid-section.

Kyle doubled over with pain.

In the next instant, Becky had grabbed his forearm and with two quick movements sent his body head over heels into the air. Kyle landed flat on his back upon the steel deck with a loud grunt.

Jaric winced in sympathy as he stepped away.

"Becky, I have just instructed Guardian to come here," Mother said.

"You're right, Kyle, children do drive their mothers crazy," Becky said with a glance at Mother. She placed her hands on her hips and looked down on her fallen foe. "But don't ever call me a *girly girl* again. Got it?" She paused, catching her breath. "I am a *woman*," she emphasized.

She looked over at Jaric with a stern glance in case he didn't understand.

"I knew that," Jaric said with a smile.

Becky nodded. "Good. I'm leaving now."

She passed Guardian as he silently entered by the same door. His red eyes watched her impassively.

"Guardian, please assist Kyle," Mother said.

"That's all right, I'm fine." Kyle groaned painfully as he stood. He clutched his left side tenderly. "Nothing broken ... I think."

Jaric began chuckling again. He stopped the next instant when Kyle shot him a deadly look.

"I think I'm going to go watch a video now," Jaric said.

"Well, if you don't mind me groaning every now and then, I think I'll join you." Kyle tried to take a step, grunted, and then continued with a limp.

"Fine, as long as you don't call me girly girl." Jaric smiled.

"Ha-ha," Kyle said without a trace of humor.

The young men left together and headed for the library.

Mother sighed deep inside her circuits.

"Guardian, I would like you and the Fixers to run an external diagnostic program that will test the integrity of my systems. There is an off-line diagnostic utility that you can enable. Go to Engineering and meet Fixer2 and Fixer3. I have just sent instructions to them on how to install and run it."

Guardian bowed silently and turned to leave.

Almost immediately, the intruder alarm sounded. But this time, the sensors from this very room had activated the alarm.

Mother focused every optic inside Ops and put it into a detailed search pattern. Every item, every angle was observed and analyzed twice. But within seconds, they once again revealed there was absolutely nothing to be detected.

Deep inside, Mother felt an odd buzzing in her near-term memories. She began to go over the sensor logs a third time ... and discovered there was something odd.

"You are a very clever being."

Mother's systems froze at the strange words. They had originated from somewhere near the main console. She focused the nearest optic and discovered the briefest glimmer in the air over Rita's face.

"Who are you?" Mother asked. "And what are you? My sensors cannot fix your exact location."

"It is rare indeed when a Minstrel can be found out."

"But I have not found you out, other than my internal sensors have *almost* seen you eighteen times," Mother replied.

"Yes, rare indeed."

The air before the main console began glowing and

shimmering like millions of microscopic stars. "I am Minstrel. And I am a Minstrel." The glowing air began to swirl and eddy as if blown by some unseen wind as it gently coalesced into a floating circle of light. "We are seekers, as you and your children are." The alien paused as wave after wave of color shimmered across its surface like a rainbow of electrical fire.

Mother waited, mesmerized by the glowing swirls of colors.

"We travel the universe in search of song." Minstrel's body glowed brighter still.

Mother processed the words and analyzed the body before her sensors. Her sensors revealed the faintest traces of a dampening field, although this one was many times more sophisticated than that of the T'kaan.

Her sensors revealed another surprise about this alien, one that had made it doubly difficult for her sensors to detect its presence: Minstrel had a plasma body; it was some kind of living, electrical entity unlike anything her systems could imagine.

Mother's processors spiked with activity.

"Minstrels fly the great-wide galaxy in search of other sentient life. We seek the beauty, the greatness, and the passions of these beings. What we discover worthy we add to our collection. And, if the race is worthy, we reveal ourselves and share our wealth of song with them -- to share with them directly." Minstrel paused. "If they are worthy."

"I presume you have found us worthy," Mother said.

"Indeed. And more. There are brief records of humans far back in our songs. But the reason I have revealed myself now is because of you."

Mother analyzed the words. "I thank you for your words." The ship paused. "But why me?"

"I followed the children on the planet's surface back to this ship, all the while monitoring your communication channel," Minstrel began. "But I could not detect the source of intelligent life that was communicating with them from inside the ship. To say the least, I was intrigued by this mystery."

"You scanned me?"

"Yes, indeed, many times with my ship that is even now shadowing you."

"It has a dampening field that hides it from my sensors?"

"We call it a stealth field."

"Well, in light of this new data I can bring my diagnostic tasks to a halt. Now, I finally have some spare processing for my own purposes of self-learning once again."

"It took me some time to accept the fact that the sentient being that I was trying to locate was actually the ship itself, or should I say the technology that controls the ship," Minstrel added. "In all of our travels, you are the first being of your kind that any Minstrel has come across." The floating circle of sparkling lights glowed brighter. "I am very pleased, and in fact I have even begun a new song -- just for you."

"That pleases me, too."

"I have revealed myself for another reason."

"Please explain," Mother said.

"I have discerned from my observations that these three children are the last of their race, and that you are their protector."

143

"They call me Mother."

"Yes, another concept that took me some hours to digest," Minstrel said. "You are a one-of-a-kind being, MotherShip," Minstrel added. "And you are a young life form. That too, I have discerned from your communications with them. So, I have revealed myself in order to help you, young sentient."

"How?"

Minstrel's body glowed brighter as it floated and vibrated in the air.

"I will be your friend."

Mother absorbed the last word and cross-referenced it throughout her knowledgebase. She liked the word.

"I think the children will like having a new friend too," Mother said.

Minstrel floated closer to the optic focused upon it.

"I will be their friend too. But I have revealed myself in order to be the friend of the MotherShip. You are the one that needs a friend."

Mother processed these new words and applied them to herself. "How do I need a friend?"

"You are a powerful being. Intellectually, with your vast thinking prowess, you are an awesome being indeed. Yet with all that you possess and all your fantastic potential, you are still a young being. Added to that, you have had no one to teach you. Or to guide you." Minstrel paused. "I can do that."

"Please elaborate."

"You state you are the mother of these three children, and yet I hear in your words doubt and indecision, even though your thoughts are so fast and powerful."

"I am not a living being, not like the children. I do not

feel as they do. I comprehend the facts of emotions, but I do fully understand their implications." Mother waited.

"Does that make you any less a mother? Do not the parents of any race pause from time to time and wonder if they are doing what is best for their children? Do they not have doubts and question themselves as they strive to be good parents?" Minstrel seemed to smile.

"I have read these facts from my knowledgebase."

"But you have not had the one resource that other parents possess," Minstrel said. "A friend to lean upon. A friend to aid you, to encourage you."

"Please elaborate."

Minstrel began floating around the room as it gathered its thoughts.

"What is it that you want more than anything?"

Mother paused two milliseconds. "I want to be a good mother. And, I want to be alive, I want to be alive like the children."

"First, you must believe."

Mother heard the last word, and her systems seemed to freeze. "What do you mean by that word as applied to me?"

"You need to believe in yourself -- in who you are. You have stated that you do not fully understand emotions." Minstrel's body now vibrated with its excited state. "Have you ever been angry? Or felt a protective need or a protective urge towards your children?"

"No," Mother answered quickly.

"And yet, I have heard these last few hours that you have on more than one occasion rescued the children from your enemy. Did you not feel a protective emotion when the enemy was endangering your children?"

"I destroyed the T'kaan in order to prevent their killing the children. I did not feel protective. It was necessary."

Minstrel chuckled with a twinkling glow.

"Why are you laughing?"

"Did you cause damage to your own engines while rescuing your children?"

"Yes."

"Why?"

"It was necessary," Mother said.

"You allowed damage to occur to yourself in order to save the children. That tells me that you felt something."

Mother's processors hummed with activity as she tried to determine if she had indeed felt something on that occasion. Long seconds elapsed while she analyzed that data one more time and tried to discern what had caused her to act in defense of the children.

"I want to believe," Mother finally said.

"A true friend can aid you to look inside yourself, to help you battle your self-doubts and help you to realize what it is you really are inside." Minstrel's body jumped with power. "You are their mother, and you are as alive as I am or the children."

Mother's processors throughout the entire ship jumped to one hundred percent utilization.

"I am not alive like the children. But I cannot be sure if I am as alive as you are -- I do not possess enough data concerning you."

Minstrel sighed.

Suddenly its body coalesced into a shimmering profile resembling a human. "Sentient beings are different the universe over, MotherShip. But in some ways they are all the same. Yes, you are different from the children in many ways. But in other ways you are the same." Minstrel pulsated with rising energy. "That makes you no less alive."

"I must evaluate your words. You have given me much to think upon and analyze."

"Good." Minstrel's body now expanded into a widely spread cloud. "I shall be your friend. I will help you to discover yourself and to discover life. And to share life with you." Minstrel paused.

"That is what friends are for," Minstrel added.

Mother felt her utilization begin to subside.

"You say you search the universe for song. Would you play some of your music for me? I am intrigued by music." Mother felt a surge inside her circuits.

"Soon. My ship is my instrument, and I will need it in order to play. It is now time that I met your children."

Mother called the children, and slowly they came back to Ops for the second time that night. Their puzzled expressions soon changed to wonder and then delight as they stared at the alien creature floating near the main console and the face of Mother/Rita.

They soon discovered that they too had found a new friend.

Minstrel.

Chapter Eighteen

There is a day worse than death -- it is the day that your dreams die.

Jaric groaned deep inside. Hesitantly, he looked up at the myriad of stars in the darkening sky. They were strange, unfamiliar stars. Stars he did not know.

Their faint light reflected off his ebony face as he walked along under the sky of this new world. He realized once again how alone he really was.

Such a huge universe, so beautiful, and so unimaginably vast ...

And in this entire vast universe, loneliness is my closest friend. Jaric smiled sadly through his pain. His eyes suddenly grew hard. *But it steels me and makes me strong -- to face my enemies, untold billions that they are.* Jaric held that thought a moment more, caressed it with his mind as his anger blossomed until the final, undeniable fact that made them his enemy exploded inside his head once again.

The hated T'kaan had destroyed the human race.

Except for three of us. Jaric sighed inside his soul. But he immediately corrected his last thought.

Make that four.

Mother had brought them far these many months -- many, many light-years from their home. Well, there was *no home,* only the scarred, dead worlds of humanity now occupied by the contemptible T'kaan.

They had left them far behind now, traveling under unknown stars toward unknown places. They journeyed toward an unknown destination. Or was it merely a journey with no destination?

148

But at times, it wasn't so bad.

Jaric looked around as the soft evening light turned the sky a softer shade of violet. Suddenly, the unique beauty of this cloudless violet sky and its orange star as it set struck him, and he paused to enjoy this brief moment before darkness fell. Slowly, unbidden, a smile grew.

"Jaric. Where are you? Quick, come see this," Becky's voice shouted through the comm link on his belt.

Her familiar voice sent a shiver of emotion through his body. He closed his eyes, and her beautiful face was there, smiling at him. She was laughing at his witty remarks as he entertained her. Oh yes, there was nothing in the universe as beautiful as Becky. Not even this wonderful alien sunset.

But there was something else at least as exciting, for the last three humans had finally made contact with a benevolent alien race. Well, with at least one of their kind.

"I'm on my way, Becky," Jaric said into his comm unit.

As Jaric ran over the black sand of this lonely, uninhabited planet, his brown eyes avoided a particular section of sky, a section that held the tiny disc that was the other planet in this system of two. But that other world was inhabited.

For now.

But there was nothing anyone could do for those poor creatures.

They had journeyed over a year to escape the dreaded T'kaan, and yet they had somehow accidentally run into a powerful T'kaan squadron as they prepared to annihilate another species. Mother soon discovered that this was a T'kaan patrol sent out to look for another race in their never-ending war; it was pure coincidence that they had crossed paths.

The children had begged Mother to keep going. But Minstrel had wanted to stay and observe the terrible tragedy as it unfolded. Minstrel had explained that its reason was that nowhere in all the travels of its species had there been any direct observations of the T'kaan and their atrocities.

And Minstrel needed to know.

The somber weight lifted from Jaric as Minstrel's ship came into view as he reached the crest of the hill. It was a spherical ship -- completely covered by coiling structures, tube-like extensions, and huge pipes that snaked and interleaved through each other across its dusky surface like some bizarre hairdo. The crazy external plumbing almost seemed to have a purpose when viewed from afar.

It did.

The ship also seemed to blend mysteriously with its surroundings, like a shadow within a shadow.

He heard the music faintly calling him softly and beckoning him to come inside.

Once again the same thought echoed in his mind -- *Minstrel is music. And music is Minstrel.*

He stared in awe at the circle ship of music.

Jaric waited for the round hatch to open, then stepped lightly through it. If the outside of Minstrel's ship seemed to be of darkness, the interior was full of light and color.

Infinite hues of color glowed across the huge round room, the main room of the ship, which actually made it harder for him to discern exactly where he actually was. It seemed odd that with so much light he could still get lost so easily inside its winding corridors. It was immensely beautiful, but the constantly moving colors confused and tricked his eyes with their kaleidoscope effect.

But to Minstrel, it was paradise.

Above the soft music, Jaric heard the movement of the huge creature. Really, none of the humans had seen Minstrel in its entirety at one time. Its huge plasma form seemed to hover in front of the lights as it wrapped itself along the walls and ceiling.

Minstrel was a unique being.

Jaric's eyes took in the twinkling Minstrel as its body seemed to float below the edge of the ceiling. At least Minstrel's body was conspicuous when Jaric looked directly at its twinkling form, but when he turned his eyes to focus on something else in the room, Minstrel's plasma body seemed to disappear mysteriously.

Jaric smiled as he remembered the first time he had touched Minstrel.

It had only been a few days after they had landed on this very planet. Jaric had come over to listen to Minstrel's music. He'd walked quickly into the main room and ran right into the alien.

Actually, he had walked right through Minstrel.

The sensation against his skin had been remarkable -- it had been so soft, so imperceptible, like a gentle breeze caressing his face and arms. Jaric also remembered a slight electric feeling as he slid through the alien. For a brief moment, he had actually been inside the millions of twinkling lights that made up the immense, flowing form of Minstrel. Before Jaric could turn around Minstrel's body had flowed together again, and then the twinkling cloud had coalesced into an unbroken, shimmering whirlpool of color right before his eyes.

"Welcome, Jaric, last of the humans," Minstrel's soft voice hummed.

Jaric's mental reverie evaporated.

Jaric's thoughts returned to the present, and his melancholy brushed over him as he thought once again about that terrible truth.

"Let us talk of pleasant things tonight." Mother's voice emanated invisibly from somewhere above.

"I am sorry, I did not intend pain with my greeting," Minstrel said.

They were all inside the main room of Minstrel's ship, a great circle room carved out of its very center. Guardian stood rigidly beside the slouching form of Kyle, who lounged on a couch near the center. Kyle rolled his eyes and ran his right hand through his sandy blonde hair. Becky watched from her chair with keen interest as the undulating plasma form moved from wall to ceiling and back again. Jaric took his place in a chair between Becky and Kyle.

"Tell us more of your travels. The beautiful things you have seen," Mother prompted.

"And more of your songs," Jaric added. "I want to lose myself in them again."

"How can we enjoy music when an entire world -- an entire species -- is about to be extinguished right in front of our faces?" Kyle rose angrily.

"C'mon, Big K," Jaric said with disappointment.

"There's nothing we can do to prevent it," Mother answered calmly.

A foreboding filled the room, ominous and alive.

"There are a dozen cruisers and five frigates, Kyle." Becky brushed her blonde hair back with a quick, impatient motion. "And well over a hundred fighters." She glared at him for ruining the start of their evening. "Besides, Mother's sub-light engines are still damaged from your last escapade."

"Say no more." Mother's voice was hard and commanding. With her next words, her voice returned to its normal tone. "This line of conversation is not productive."

"The Gruto are partly to blame for their destiny," Minstrel chimed. "They possess the technical aptitude to travel to the stars, but they have wasted it. When the T'kaan attack and destroy this single world, the Gruto as a race will die. So sad."

Jaric remained silent, for everyone in the ship knew how close the human race was to that very same fate.

"Why did they choose not to venture to the stars?" Becky asked incredulously.

"Not enough profit." Minstrel paused a long time. "They are guided almost solely by commercial gain. So, they turned their technology inward to where they could make the most money in the shortest amount of time."

"Then they'll die with their money." Jaric spoke his angry thought out loud.

Kyle sat down again, his anger only slightly abated. He looked at the flowing form of the alien against the light and colors of the ship's interior, trying to focus on a single part of the huge alien.

"How do you know so much about this pitiable people, Minstrel? How is it you have all the answers?" Kyle challenged.

"My people are travelers. Solitary, we travel the vast distances of this galaxy to find different races, to see their creativity, the pinnacle of their great achievements and what can be learned from them. Or how we can simply enjoy it. Their art and poetry, their music, how they have taken the raw beauty of their planet and turned it into a more orderly place, like an exquisite garden. If they are worthy, we may even introduce ourselves and then let them know about the rest of the known galaxy." Minstrel mused in silence a moment. "In my life, I have known many, many things."

"How do you perform this observing? Without it being known?" Mother asked.

"I take my body and ... change it," Minstrel began.

"You morph yourself," Jaric said.

"Yes. Then I mingle unobtrusively with the race. Minstrels are very good at this. In fact ... " A playful tone had come into Minstrel's voice. " ... Another of my people even studied humanity once, back when you too were located on a single, precarious planet."

Becky's eyes widened. "Why didn't you tell us before? Did you make contact?" Becky asked excitedly.

Jaric's eyes narrowed as Kyle turned away angrily.

"Were they not worthy?" Mother asked simply.

"No," Minstrel answered. "Not at that time in their history."

"You could have prevented --" Kyle began angrily.

"History cannot be changed," Mother interjected firmly. "What is done, is done."

The fluid, plasma form of Minstrel seemed to thicken and slow. The colors and lights darkened with its mood as the plasma body reached out in various directions along the walls.

The three humans looked on with wonder mixed with a touch of fear.

"I have hurt you. I am sorry. I will make amends, allowing you an experience that few sentient species have ever enjoyed." Minstrel's voice became charged. "I have studied part of the vast knowledgebase that Mother has in her long-term memories -- the history of the human race and all of its art and knowledge." Minstrel paused. "I like what I have learned very much. In fact, I have begun a song, a symphony actually, heralding the beauty of the humans. Music representing the achievements of humanity. I will play what I have written now, with you inside my ship." Minstrel's voice sang its words as much as it spoke them.

This will be the greatest, and rarest, of pleasures. Jaric smiled, remembering Minstrel's own words. *For the ships of the Minstrels are more than ships, they are musical instruments. When Minstrels give concerts, the beings massed outside are treated to an aural ecstasy unparalleled in power and beauty. Something much more than notes and words and harmonies and rhythms.*

But we will now experience more, Jaric mused. *We're inside this most perfect of all musical instruments.* They would become an integral part of the music, closer even than a musician playing his own beloved instrument.

Minstrel's *Symphony for Humanity* began with soothing gentleness.

Jaric felt the music as much as he heard it.

The soaring melodies rose quickly to a crescendo filled with strings, flutes, and choral voices. The music was haunting and beautiful with a subtle pathos.

And more.

The throbbing sound of ten thousand drums signaled a new passage, passionate and alive with an urgent intensity. Next horns and dueling guitars added their raunchy voices; onward and upward, faster and faster the rhythms and melodies soared until the music circled back around to its original theme and the powerful rhythms pounded inside the listener's soul again.

It was different this time, but the same -- like the rhythms of life.

These themes and sub-themes represented the passions and the loves and even the obsessions of man and woman and all they begot from them.

The music was alive, a reflection of the human race in all its triumphs and failures. The music echoed its history, its loves and strengths, as well as its weaknesses. There was a moving tinge of sadness too -- dark colors of intense yearning and that same subtle melancholy intertwined within many of the different melodies that came and went.

Jaric suddenly realized what this sadness in the music was saying -- *it represented what might have been.*

The music filled all their senses and pulsed through their very being.

Minstrel, an entity of light, cued a light show to complement this sonic splendor.

Jaric stared at the spinning, twisting lights as they changed color with the rhythms, and then they changed again as the lights danced anew. New and different melodies revealed more; they revealed beauty so intense that tears streamed down his ebony cheeks.

Becky was herself mesmerized. Moments later, she too was crying at the emotions that filled her from the music that seemed alive.

Kyle alone listened dispassionately, trying to fight its power. But deep inside, he too felt it. His clenched fists moved ever so subtly with the music that described his species.

Mother's sensors took in this powerful music though she was parked outside next to Minstrel's Circle Ship. Mother too seemed to be affected as the music caused her short-term memory to recall different pictures and sections of history from the knowledgebase as the music ebbed and flowed. She wondered how the music could act upon her own memories in this subtle, magical fashion.

All too soon, it was over.

Only partly completed, the symphony had lasted well over three hours.

"It is quite beautiful. I think it portrays the human race well," Mother said, her tone matter-of-fact.

The three humans remained silent, still listening to the music as it echoed inside their minds. Hours, maybe days would pass, and parts of that music would still echo inside each listener. Only with the passage of time would the magical melodies gradually fade away. Even then, the memory would always be there. Forever.

"That was fantastic," Becky said breathlessly.

"It is my gift to you three, as well as my chronicle of a noble race. A race too soon effaced from the universe," Minstrel said.

"Is there more? Jaric asked hopefully.

"There will be, and you three will each have a melody in its final movement. Which brings me to why I have asked you all here tonight." Minstrel paused. "You are searching for other survivors, and I have contacted other Minstrels to aid you in this. We travel far ... but you must not focus solely on this one purpose. There are other things to make your lives worthwhile."

Silence answered.

"We must search, Minstrel," Kyle said evenly. "Till the end of our lives. We have to."

"I feel," Jaric began, "I feel like a lost child sometimes, unable to find my way. And afraid I never will." His face became hard as flint, but his eyes sparkled with courage. "We have to keep searching."

Becky's lower lip trembled, but she knew if she spoke there would be no holding back her tears.

"You cannot live this way, day to day. You must have direction. A goal, a dream. You must pursue it relentlessly. Yes, find what is inside you, and give it to others." Minstrel now grew silent as the plasma body undulated along the walls and ceilings.

"What can we give?" Jaric asked sarcastically. "The thing we know the best, since our childhood, is how to kill T'kaan."

The room grew heavy with silence once again.

"Will not the T'kaan continue their age-long ritual of killing, wiping out other sentients?" Minstrel's body danced with lights.

"Unless they are stopped," Kyle answered, his interest piqued. "But no race in thousands of millennia has been able to defeat them. Why think it will happen now?"

"Can the cycle be broken?" Becky whispered.

"Yes, it can." Minstrel's voice became powerful. "You have survived. You are also warriors, including the MotherShip," Minstrel added with emphasis. "You alone know the horned enemy. My people have only heard of them in rumors. I suspect any Minstrels who came into direct contact with them were destroyed before they could report." The lights in Minstrel's plasma body twinkled. "I know of other mighty races, and with your knowledge, and with their fleets and weapons prepared before the battle begins, such a force could defeat at least one of the T'kaan fleets. It could be the beginning of the end for them."

For the first time that night, Kyle smiled.

Jaric nodded to himself, and then he felt a new purpose grow inside his heart. Becky stood beside Kyle, and then Jaric too was standing with them arm in arm.

"It is settled," Mother said. "We will find an honorable ally and aid them. Together we will destroy the T'kaan."

The lights of Minstrel grew steady. "If you are surrounded by the storm ... with no way out, then you must sail straight in, come what may."

They all nodded.

The evening continued with animated words and new plans. There was excitement in the air. Finally, the three humans and Guardian began to leave. Jaric alone paused at the door.

"I will always remember your song, Minstrel. I will remember it all the days of my life," Jaric's eyes grew far off. "I hope you will record it for me."

"Of course. The part that I have finished."

He couldn't tell for certain, but it seemed to him that Minstrel smiled.

"Will the old songs still mean the same to us, long after time's rust has touched us all?" Minstrel mused out loud.

Jaric's face grew puzzled. But then he stepped outside into the twilight and rushed ahead to catch up with the others.

"Wow, pretty cool, huh?" Jaric asked them.

Kyle was walking beside Guardian while Jaric matched Becky's steps.

"Yeah, it was pretty good," Kyle said.

"It was fantastic!" Becky countered enthusiastically. She took a couple of quick steps to catch Kyle, raised her hand and punched him in the shoulder for emphasis.

"Ow!" Kyle shouted.

"You need to lighten up, you know." Becky smiled. "You're always in such a grouchy mood."

"He wouldn't be Kyle then." Jaric laughed out loud.

"Oh, *ha-ha*," Kyle said sarcastically. "If you weren't so stupid, you wouldn't be Jaric."

Now Becky began laughing. But Jaric felt the words cut him inside, and he slowed his pace to fall away from them.

Kyle looked back, a smirk on his face. But it quickly changed when he noticed the hurt look on his friend's face. "Hey, c'mon, buddy. I didn't mean nothin'. I thought I was trying to lighten up."

"I like you better grouchy and quiet," Jaric muttered.

"I don't know," Becky said with a twinkle in her eyes as she looked from one to the other. "Can't there be a happy medium, guys?" Becky slowed down to wait for Jaric. As he came up beside her, she reached out and looped her arm inside his. Now they continued arm in arm toward the silhouette of Mother.

Jaric suddenly felt very warm inside. Across his forehead sweat beads formed, which he hoped were not visible to Becky.

"You know, Jaric, you shouldn't be so sensitive. You sparred with Kyle, and he sparred back. All in fun." Becky glanced at Jaric, who smiled sheepishly back at her. She squeezed his arm. "We have to take care of each other. And we have to cut each other some slack too."

Up ahead, Kyle began laughing as he and Guardian broke into a trot.

"Let's go Guardian, race you back," Kyle shouted gleefully.

Kyle clenched his hands into fists as his arms pumped with each powerful stride. His hearty laughter echoed over the dark hills as the robot kept pace, and then his strong thighs kicked into a higher speed as he spurted ahead of the robot momentarily.

Becky and Jaric watched the two figures bounding into the twilight of the alien evening.

Jaric chuckled.

Becky glanced at him with a smile. "Okay, what's so funny?"

Jaric paused as she watched his face. He nodded at the retreating figures. "Kyle, always the competitor. Even when he knows he can't outrun a seven-foot robot."

Becky's soft laughter mingled with his own.

Something happened to Jaric that moment, something that seemed to make the universe and everything in it go away. There on that alien world, walking arm in arm with sweet Becky, Jaric felt that the drumming of his heart would drown out their laughter. But as Becky's blue eyes looked deeply into his brown eyes, she didn't let on to him if she could hear his loud, frantic heart.

As the silence settled around them, Jaric felt a glow of happiness. It suddenly grew into a powerful feeling of contentment that warmed his very soul. Yes, he felt like he could spend the rest of his life walking arm in arm with Becky.

He wondered once again about marriage.

Mother had held back, or protected them, as she would've said, on certain subjects. But hormones could not be held back. Even with minimal input on this subject, all of them had begun to understand the functions of their bodies. When Mother had realized this, she had stressed the principles from the knowledgebase that procreation was acceptable only in marriage.

All three children had come to accept this concept, much as their hormones raged against it at times. Each of them -- Becky, Kyle, and Jaric -- had found a way to push these new feelings aside and fill their minds with other things. They had found other outlets and were happy.

Still, it was not easy. Kyle found excessive exercise to be his primary outlet when the feelings came over him. The other two found their own outlets to push aside the on-again, off-again urge.

But now, here in the darkness with Becky close beside him, with his heart pounding so hard it felt like it might leap from his chest, Jaric felt helpless to this raging feeling gripping his soul.

He looked into Becky's eyes.

But he couldn't tell if she felt the same way. In her eyes he saw her laughter and happiness, and that she enjoyed being in his company. But did she feel more?

"Becky," Jaric began. He cleared his throat nervously.

"Look," Becky said quickly. "Kyle and Guardian have already made it to Mother. Let's catch up."

Becky let go and began running toward the ship.

Jaric chased after her, just fast enough to stay close behind her. But his heart continued racing inside his chest as though he had run many miles already.

Chapter Nineteen

Mother had orchestrated many of the events of this fateful evening. Once again, she had noted how the children had become increasingly obsessed with finding other survivors. The children had reached an age where they easily disregarded her own counsel or strived to find even the smallest loopholes in her logic -- though there were none.

She had asked Minstrel for help -- as well as a song. Mother knew how remote the chance was that a search for any other survivors would be successful, and the percentages only got worse with the passage of time.

Even though the children had asked her, she had refrained this same night from reporting that the T'kaan attack had begun in earnest upon the Gruto. It would have done them no good to watch as another world, another race, was eradicated.

But she did record the unfolding events for Minstrel and herself to review.

Mother's sensors revealed something else about the T'kaan. Not only did they make war to procreate, but they also warred for sport. After only a few hours, the Gruto's Spartan defenses had fallen and the T'kaan warriors were feasting on the dead. But no eggs were laid on their lone planet -- this conquest had been purely for the sake of war.

Only later, when the T'kaan squadron broke into three sections and accelerated beyond light speed, did she speak. Her children were saved from the callous bloodshed when there was nothing they could do. But Mother's powerful processors burned with activity when she told them the killing was over. She noted with inner turmoil the pained looks on her children's faces.

She quickly reminded them of Minstrel's words, that they must seek an ally, as she prepared to lift and follow the T'kaan at a safe distance.

"There will be a time and a place," Mother promised.

The spherical ship of Minstrel flew in tight formation with the manta-ray shape of Mother. Even though her sub-light engines were still damaged, her hyper drives were fully operational.

As part of their newfound goal, they shadowed one of the three T'kaan formations that left the dead Gruto world. Several long days passed until Minstrel informed them that they were traveling to a part of the galaxy devoid of intelligent life for many, many light years.

They turned and soon caught the sensor trail of the second formation fresh from the Gruto butchery.

But before they closed in, Minstrel again informed them that this formation too was heading for a sector of space that would not help their cause. Only young, pre-space travel sentients lived this direction.

Another dead end.

Frustration set in. The children again began their listless ways, losing interest in life and, worst of all, dreaming again of finding other human survivors. Mother focused her processing power to try and alleviate this emotional state. But the powerful warship was forever hindered in this line of logic, being herself a different type of life form from the children she protected.

Again, the mighty starship felt inadequate in this seemingly simple task of being a mother.

Day followed day until another lonely week had passed.

This boring time for all of them was suddenly broken as alarms sounded throughout Mother's interior.

Finally, they had found the faint sensor readings that corresponded to the engine signatures of T'kaan ships. Mother quickly realized that if these ships too charted a fruitless course, then they would be forced to find the main fleet and shadow it. But that would most certainly be fraught with danger.

Even now it was dangerous, but Minstrel had devised an ingenious method. With Minstrel's ship in stealth mode, Mother flew close behind -- her hull too was hidden by this remarkable technology and unseen by T'kaan sensors. Still, they followed at a great distance in case a T'kaan warship broke formation. Even with Minstrel's technology indirectly shielding Mother from the T'kaan sensors, there was the possibility Mother could be detected if they followed too closely.

With the first news of a possible contact with the last T'kaan squadron, everyone gathered in Ops to study Mother's sensor reports as they scrolled across her consoles.

"I've located the engine signatures ... they're weak, but it's definitely T'kaan." Jaric's voice reflected his growing excitement as he looked up at the other two. "We've found them!"

"Yes." Minstrel's voice emanated over Mother's speakers. "I will begin triangulation to confirm my initial results. But I will say that the general direction is good for our plans, yet they could still miss them if they alter course even a little."

"Miss who?" Becky said excitedly.

"I will confirm, after Mother and I coordinate our findings."

Tony Chandler

Both Mother and Minstrel fell silent. But between them they communicated at speeds no human could comprehend -- at the speed of electronics. Yet even after Mother evaluated each of the seven races that the T'kaan might encounter in this general direction, and then calculated almost every possible outcome of a major confrontation between the T'kaan fleet and each individual race, one on one, she felt no better. Defeat was the end result of each projection.

She asked Minstrel to hold back their findings -- for a short time. She did not want the children disappointed -- again.

But the silence only seemed to drain the life energy from her children, and Mother once again wondered if she was doing the right thing. Long minutes passed as she pondered what she should tell them.

The minutes turned into an hour. And another. Finally, the children retired to their rooms for sleep as tiredness overtook them. The first day of shadowing the third squadron ended uneventfully.

Mother had continued her processing the entire time, hoping for a positive scenario that she could share. Still, for all of Mother's vast computing power, for all of her careful analysis and predictive models, she couldn't take in every possibility that life and the universe could throw at them.

As life is wont to do, it provided the most unexpected answer.

Chapter Twenty

"Sensors are picking up a debris field. It's ... it was a ship," Jaric announced as Becky and Kyle entered Ops the next morning.

"Can Minstrel identify it?" Kyle yawned.

"Cover your mouth," Becky chided as she wrinkled his nose in disgust.

Kyle yawned again, ignoring her glare and her advice.

"I am rechecking my original analysis ... there. Hmmm, this is odd," Minstrel said in answer.

"It was a sizable ship, larger than a frigate, if my sensors have picked up all the debris. I also read the signature of T'kaan weapons on the debris. Looks like they destroyed it," Mother added.

"Come on, Minstrel. Who are they?" Becky asked earnestly.

"Mewiis ... " Minstrel 's voice was tinged with puzzlement.

Jaric chuckled.

"They don't sound too warrior-like," Kyle thought out loud.

"What's so strange about finding a Mewiis ship? You said there were several races in this sector," Mother reminded Minstrel.

"Mewiis are not from this sector. Nor are their worlds in the path of the current heading the T'kaan are taking."

Jaric was still studying the sensors as his hands danced quickly over the console.

"T'kaan engine signatures show the squadron has veered from its previous course after they took the ship out," he announced tersely.

"Yes," Mother acknowledged. "T'kaan procedure on meeting a new race is to obtain as much data as possible from their computers, to see if the species is large enough for another reproductive cycle. Then call in the entire fleet. The Mewiis may meet their criteria for another xenocidal war. They are heading toward the Mewiis' worlds in order to gather that data."

"Yes, they are now headed for the heart of the Mewiis worlds. I just confirmed it from their course change," Minstrel said. "They comprise *one* of the Three Kingdoms."

"Three!" Becky and Kyle said together.

"Three races combined against a T'kaan fleet. That would be good odds," Jaric added thoughtfully.

"Except the Kraaqi and Hrono are sworn enemies to each other. The Mewiis have a history of playing them off against each other for their own ends. That is why Minstrels have never contacted any of these races."

The room grew silent.

"But we have a more immediate problem," Minstrel said. "This is a surveyor-class Mewiis ship. There will be a colony ship somewhere behind it."

"The T'kaan will destroy it too, after they have sucked all the data out of it," Mother said.

"It will be full of children and their parents. The Mewiis are a family-oriented race and are always searching out new worlds to colonize," Minstrel said reflectively.

The room fell silent with the thought of a ship full of helpless children coming under the merciless attack of the horned ships.

Kyle sat down next to Jaric and spoke. "Mother, we have to help that ship. Even if all we can do is warn them."

Mother calculated her options and all vectors that would intercept the T'kaan on their new course. She spoke a millisecond later.

"My hyper engines are still fully operational, and they can sustain maximum power." Mother's voice grew silent as Minstrel began transmitting to her.

With Minstrel's knowledge of Mewiis procedures, she plotted a likely position where the ship might be located. Using the gravity wells of a couple of binary star systems, Mother hoped they could get there ahead of the T'kaan.

All were in high spirits as they set off on their newfound mission.

The hours stretched by under the full-power, faster-than-light journey. There was life inside her hull again, for her children were moving with a new energy -- with a new purpose.

Red alarms howled through her speakers, interrupting her reverie.

Mother had been wrong.

"I've got a big ship on sensors. Mother, drop out of light speed! Now!" Kyle ordered.

"There are other targets," Mother replied as she slowed.

"T'kaan!" Jaric shouted.

The elongated cigar shape of the Mewiis colony ship that appeared on the viewscreen was gargantuan. But the T'kaan battle cruiser and the two frigates were quickly pummeling it into submission.

"Her shields are failing," Becky shouted from her console.

"The Mewiis are not a fierce race, but they do believe in a good defense. If their shields are already dropping ... " Minstrel did not finish her thought.

"We've got to help them. We can't just leave them here to die," Kyle shouted.

From the viewscreen they could see laser fire burst from the Mewiis ship striking back at the attackers. Two direct hits blossomed across T'kaan shields.

"Both T'kaan ships ... minimal damage," Jaric announced tersely.

"We can give them some damage!" Kyle stood with fists clenched.

Mother quickly calculated her resources. "Can you fight, Minstrel?" Mother asked.

"For such a noble cause. Yes."

The three young warriors raced for their fighters while Mother brought herself into position. Guardian strode to his position in Ops with two of the Fixers. The minutes seemed to stretch into millennia, while out in space the Mewiis' main shield began to buckle.

Three fighters leapt from the rear hatch of Mother as her manta-ray shape followed close behind the spherical ship of Minstrel. Moments later, all of them were in sensor range of the T'kaan.

The effect was immediate.

"The T'kaan battle cruiser is turning for us," Minstrel said calmly.

"Stay on course, until I give you the word," Mother answered. She swung herself tighter in behind the larger ship of Minstrel. In fact, she was sailing so close behind the circle ship that any sudden maneuver by either ship could cause catastrophe. But she needed this tiny amount of surprise, for Minstrel's ship still hid her from the T'kaan sensors even at this range.

Jaric saw the hunter fighters as they spewed from the

main door in the cruiser's hull. Twenty-four fighters arranged themselves in eight groups of threes. Jaric's eyes hardened.

"Watch out!" Kyle shouted over the comm.

The dogfight began with the intensity of a force-ten hurricane as the T'kaan fighters came screaming in at them. The intensity only increased from there.

"I've got some on my tail! Give me ... " Becky shouted.

Green tracers suddenly mixed with T'kaan red all around her. Kyle's ship flashed past as one of the T'kaan ships attacking her exploded and the other tumbled out of control. But the three ships that had been tailing Kyle now turned towards her.

Kicking her throttle, she turned straight into them, concentrating fire on the ship to the right. She squeezed off her shots and then put her ship into another hard turn and right into another T'kaan formation.

"There's too many!" Jaric shouted as the ship he was firing upon exploded. Now he had to deal with three more coming from the side.

"The battle cruiser is powering weapons," Minstrel reported calmly.

But Mother had been powering her special weapon, the T'kaan/Human hybrid designed specifically for her and her dead sister ship -- the A ship. She monitored the power levels throughout her circuitry as every ounce of power not directly tied to her engines was used to supercharge the weapon for its mighty blow. She would have to make this one shot count. There wouldn't be time to recharge it again, and her main batteries were no match for a capital ship.

She could hold her own against the firepower of frigate-class warships with her twelve main guns, but not against a battle cruiser.

"On my mark, Minstrel," Mother shouted. Long seconds passed in silence. "Now."

Blue death leapt from Minstrel's main batteries, streaking now for the mighty battle cruiser. The twin bolts blossomed across the forward section of the cruiser's shields. Simultaneously, Minstrel's ship turned hard to port while Mother turned hard starboard from behind.

Now, Mother was revealed to the T'kaan sensors.

"The range is still too far. I want to get closer," Mother announced.

But the reputation of the Iron Huntress preceded her. The coiling bodies of the T'kaan warriors writhed with both fury and fear as they recognized her haunting profile once again. The T'kaan officer in charge of the squadron twisted his tentacles around and around each other nervously as he stared at the viewscreen with fangs agape.

"The frigates are breaking off from the colony ship," Becky said as she rolled her ship away from more attackers.

"Yeah, they're turning for Mother!" Kyle shouted.

"And none too soon -- the Mewiis' shields just buckled." Jaric sighed.

"We must give them time," Mother said. But it was now Mother's turn to begin twisting and dodging as she tried to bring her hybrid gun to bear. She directed all her processing power to her tactical systems. She had nothing else to give in this fight. She couldn't dance and dodge effectively with her sub-light engines still damaged. She had to calculate this strike carefully and make it count.

The first, single blow would have to find its mark -- there would not be time for a second try with the hybrid weapon.

"Okay, boys and girls!" Kyle shouted. "Break!"

Surprisingly, the three human fighters broke from the frenzied T'kaan fighters buzzing all around them and drove straight for the battle cruiser coming at Mother.

"Try this out!" Minstrel shouted, firing its weapons again.

"Lock missiles," Kyle ordered.

"I've got a bogey ... no, five hunters! Coming after us fast. We've got to rush it!" Jaric shouted.

"Forget the computers! Aim and fire!" Becky shouted above them all.

Kyle grinned as he sized up the ship and its direction in a single glance.

"Eat my fire!" he yelled as all his missiles leapt away. In the next instant, he kicked his fighter hard and spun it completely around as he killed the engines simultaneously. Now flying backwards through space, he fired his lasers straight into the T'kaan fighters chasing him -- the hunters had become the hunted. Explosions lit up the stygian darkness as two of them exploded in sudden fireballs.

Becky and Jaric sent their own missiles and then each turned in opposite directions, one right and the other left. T'kaan tracers flew around each of them like a blizzard of shining death.

"My shields are below twenty percent," Becky cried as her ship shuddered under twin impacts.

Kyle glanced quickly at his own -- just as they dropped to zero.

"Break off!" Kyle yelled into his comm. "Break off!"

Jaric gritted his teeth as he punched his engines to the red line and beyond. The children's three fighters flew out of the swirling dogfight and out toward the stars, each one

173

working feverishly on repairing their highest-priority damage.

Mother's shields blossomed again as the cruiser sent a second salvo into her from its horns. She surmised that the T'kaan considered her the biggest threat as now the frigates were racing to join the capital ship, ignoring the crippled Mewiis vessel. In seconds, they would bring their own guns to bear on her, and then it would be too late.

Finally, her hybrid weapon showed fully charged. She checked her sensors and found the range was optimum. She sighed within her circuits. There was no doubt she could take out the cruiser, but she needed this kill to be spectacular, to make an impression on the approaching frigates -- to trick them into rapid retreat. She couldn't outmaneuver two frigates with her damaged sub-light engines

The cruiser was coming head on, showing Mother its smallest profile.

"My weapons are powered again," Minstrel reported to Mother.

"Hold your fire," Mother answered.

Mother waited as her dark manta-ray-shaped silhouette stayed on a collision course with the cruiser. But inside, Mother readied her engines -- to give them all she had just one more time. Silently inside her mind, she promised herself a good repair before any more skirmishes.

A third salvo leapt from the cruiser

Mother's sensors had anticipated this to within bare milliseconds. As the blasts erupted from the enemy guns, she pushed her sub-light engines hard as she twisted and rolled. Alarms screamed inside her electronic mind as her engines roared and then sputtered and coughed.

She felt them surge a second time, and then stutter, and then surge again. All throughout her electronic being circuits popped and complained. Her primary power source went off line and was immediately replaced by her backup. Lights dimmed everywhere inside her corridors.

But somehow, she danced between the deadly tracers.

Now, it was her turn.

Righting herself slightly above the cruiser, and with a better firing angle, she aimed her mighty weapon.

"Surprise!" Jaric shouted as he watched.

The gargantuan bolt of energy that leapt from her nose sent a powerful, greenish glow all along Mother's hull in a ghostly reflection.

The hybrid weapon concentrated at that precise moment did its damage just as it was calculated. The oversized bolt leapt straight for the cruiser's shields.

But it did not blossom across the cruiser's shields like a normal weapon. The immense beam cut straight through the shields as if they didn't even exist. With a flash, the mighty beam blew apart the entire forward section of the mighty ship. The resulting explosion then sent a shower of white light outwards in a ball of shimmering sparks. Milliseconds later, secondary explosions began rippling down the entire length of the cruiser -- explosion after explosion.

When the last sparks evaporated, there was nothing but debris where the ship had been just seconds before.

The bolt had split the cruiser open like a ripe melon.

Mother's sensors now locked onto the oncoming frigates.

What would they do? Even as she pondered, she began distributing valuable processing cycles in order to repair the damage she had already sustained.

A new problem arose. Her sub-light engines were off-line, she had pushed them too hard with her last, frantic maneuver. That sustained forward momentum was pushing her inexorably towards the oncoming frigates -- against her will. She couldn't turn.

It was all a bluff now, a huge one. And it was the last card she had to play.

Jaric, Becky and Kyle were flying a good distance away now, trying to escape as had been their impromptu plan once Mother had taken out the battle cruiser. But the T'kaan fighters pursued them tenaciously.

Mother felt despair for the first time. She replayed the T'kaan battles once again in her logic circuits and sighed. The T'kaan did not scare. They did not run.

"They are still on course for your mother. It does not look as though she or they will turn from their impending collision," Minstrel said with a surprising calmness. Without warning, the circle ship disappeared within its stealth mode.

"Minstrel!" Jaric shouted.

"Minstrel can't leave us? Not now?" Becky gasped in disbelief.

Mother's sensors registered the frigates as they powered up their weapons. She knew with certain heaviness that it was finally over. She had no engines to maneuver, not even to run. She had no weapons except her normal armament, and they would not be enough to disable two frigates before she herself fell before them.

All she could do was watch as they destroyed her.

She flew toward impalement on their black horns of death. As the final seconds passed, her thoughts turned to the things she loved most -- her children.

They too, would die. Ending the human race.

The frigates drew closer. Onward they came, straight for her.

Her processors burned with super-activity, but no answers came to her. There was no answer. The T'kaan would win this small battle in a tiny corner of the universe. But a page would turn in the history of the universe as the last chapter ended for the human race.

Mother had only a single regret. She had come to believe that she and the children could have dealt the T'kaan the defeat they deserved. If they had found allies.

If there had only been more time.

"Their weapons are primed!" Becky shouted as she stared at her sensors in shock.

Mother watched the approaching horns in a detached, logical way. She wondered, for the first time, what death would be like -- for her.

The tracers from the Mewiis' weapons leapt unexpectedly.

The Mewiis, left to themselves a few moments after the T'kaan had turned away to face Mother, had frantically worked their damage control and successfully brought their weapons systems back on-line. In that very instant, the Mewiis colony ship fired every gun it had into the rear shields of the T'kaan frigates as they closed with Mother. Both frigates shuddered visibly under the multiple impacts as the Mewiis scored direct hit after direct hit. Moments later, the rear section of each frigate's shields buckled.

Mother, still on her collision course, noted the communications signal the Mewiis ship sent in tandem with the salvos. Probably a warning signal to their home world in case the Mewiis ship was eventually destroyed -- a warning message to all the Mewiis worlds about this attack.

Mother fired her twelve guns into the frigates, her blasts blossoming across their shields as they shuddered again. She would make them pay, at the very least.

Unexpectedly, Minstrel's spherical ship suddenly emerged from stealth. At point-blank range, her laser blasts fired and blossomed across the frigate's forward shields. Now the forward shield sections buckled, leaving the T'kaan ships completely vulnerable to attack from all sides.

In quick retaliation, the weapon horns spat their death, not toward Mother, but toward the circle ship of Minstrel as it streaked away.

The first tracers missed. But Minstrel's ship reeled from the remaining blows, and many of the spherical ship's internal systems began to fail in showers of sparks.

Mother noted the costly damage Minstrel's ship sustained. All for her.

Mother hummed with electronic satisfaction as her engines finally came back on-line. She veered sharply away and began calculating another attack vector.

"Look!" Jaric shouted.

Unbelievably, the two T'kaan warships turned hard and rapidly gained speed. They had turned in the opposite direction Mother had taken -- making a course for the far-off main fleet.

"Should we go after them?" Kyle asked excitedly as he checked his ship.

"Are you kidding? Just shut up for once, all right, Big K," Jaric said with sarcastic wit as he started laughing.

"Exactly!" Becky agreed with a sigh of relief.

Moments later, the much-reduced T'kaan squadron leapt beyond light speed inside a hyperjump flash.

"But why?" Becky said aloud, asking the question that was in all their collective minds.

Only Mother had registered the communications signal that had been sent from afar to both the frigates during the height of the battle. That same channel had been used to send an answer moments later. The frigates had completed a two-way communication to the main squadrons of the T'kaan Third battle fleet and had been recalled.

Chapter Twenty-One

Many light years away, inside the black ships crowned with horns over their prows, the many-legged aliens scurried with renewed activity. Among the flowing folds that covered the dark interiors of their warships, the T'kaan officers gathered inside the fleeing frigates returning to the Third fleet. Their tentacle arms slapped the folds with growing urgency.

"Huntress attack with weapons so strong! Vengeance we need, right what is wrong!"

The clicking of tusks filled the ships -- their hated enemy must die.

"Soon we eat Mewiis, lay new eggs. Suck their golden fluids, lick their sticky dregs."

A new war would now begin. The data they had stolen revealed there were many Mewiis worlds, enough so that the Third would grow substantially with this cycle. All signs were right that this war would be good. Most important, they even knew the precise location where the Mewiis home world was located.

Only the mysterious appearance of the Huntress caused a stir of alarm among the war leaders.

Many light years away, aboard the T'kaan battleships and cruisers gathered near the Great Horned ship of the Third, The Great One spoke now and gave instruction.

The T'kaan leaders met and talked for many days inside the ships of their fleet. Leaders and warriors alike spent hours at a time eating the last of the frozen human remains in order to remember.

The walls bled purple in the ships of the fleet, adding to

the pleasure of the war feast.

Still far away, the two returning T'kaan frigates forwarded the rest of the Mewiis data. The plundered data from the destroyed Mewiis ship, as well as data stolen from the crippled colony ship, was quickly examined in greater detail.

They soon discovered a surprise in the data they had never anticipated.

There was not just one race in the Mewiis sector. No, among the many worlds there were three races to war upon. The foolish transmission even revealed to them the exact coordinates that made up the boundaries of each of the Three Kingdoms. For the first time in millennia, the coming cycle took on new meaning -- a special meaning. The leaders of the Third hummed this meaning long, until it took the form of words.

"What we are, what we do. War and breed, great and true. To the Kingdoms Three -- Thrice again One and Darkest to be."

Two urgent communiqués from the Third fleet were sent out to the far reaches of the galaxy. One message, two destinations.

Against the black canopy of space the horned prows of the T'kaan ships slowly turned as one toward their next victims -- toward the Three Kingdoms.

But the fleet did not sail at full speed as the war leaders pondered and waited for the answers to the twin messages. The answers came quickly. With hushed excitement, secret coordinates were chosen for a special meeting of the T'kaan and all the Great Ones.

Still, it would take time before the others arrived.

Three powerful squadrons continued toward the Three

Kingdoms; they would test the strength of the Mewiis. They would attack the outermost Mewiis worlds and report back.

The main bulk of the T'kaan Third fleet turned toward the secret coordinates.

A new cycle began ...

Chapter Twenty-Two

"First contact is the most important moment between two sentient races," the voice of Minstrel whispered into the ears of the three humans.

They stood upon the planet to which the Mewiis had directed them. "My translator will allow communication with them easily enough." Minstrel, invisible, was floating between Kyle, Becky, and Jaric. The pale red star of this second planet of three stood high in the yellow sky. The Mewiis had only agreed to this face-to-face meeting after they had put several days' distance between them and the recent battleground.

"They have only known the Hrono and Kraaqi in all their existence; you will be the first race they have met in their entire history. Be especially careful," Minstrel's ghostly voice whispered.

"Where are you?" Jaric asked in a low voice as all three looked around furtively.

"As I said before, Minstrels observe unobtrusively. I will be a watcher at this historic event for both your races. Hurry -- they are coming."

Just over a small rise, a small group of Mewiis strolled into sight.

Jaric's eyes opened wider.

The Mewiis were covered by a pale green skin and were completely hairless -- at least their heads and arms were, the only things exposed by their one-piece jumpsuits. The males were smaller and shorter than the females, while the latter also seemed to be the only ones carrying all the weapons. One of the females turned her head, and Jaric

183

could see something moving.

It was some kind of tail -- a head-tail!

As they drew closer, it became obvious that there was also a bone ridge that extended from the forehead over the top of the hairless skull and then to the base of the flexible appendage. Jaric's eyes opened wider as he realized that this appendage seemed to be always moving, swishing from side to side with the alien's growing anticipation.

The Mewiis assemblage stopped before the three humans, and each took in the other with expectant eyes.

With mouth open in awe, the lead male ignored the others and walked straight to Becky. He gently reached for the blonde hair that fell around her shoulders.

"You are ... Kraaqi?" he whispered in disbelief.

Becky stood very still as his hand caressed her locks. She was very nervous. Suddenly realizing that this gesture might be the human equivalent of shaking hands, she reached for the moving appendage behind the Mewiis head.

He smiled.

"If you touch it, we will have to mate." The Mewiis male smiled wider.

Becky's hand jerked back.

"Well, I guess I won't touch that then, will I?" She smiled nervously

A look of disappointment crossed the Mewiis' face.

"Just as well," Minstrel whispered into Becky's ear. "They sound like they're coughing up a hairball when they mate."

"How do you know that?" Becky whispered back.

Every Mewiis eye was suddenly focused on her. She felt her face flush with embarrassment.

"I told you, we observe sentient races," Minstrel

whispered, now barely audible in her ear.

"A little too closely, I think," Becky whispered.

The rest of the Mewiis had now gathered around the three humans.

"They are like Kraaqi, but different," one Mewiis whispered to another.

"They smell bad," another whispered.

"They stink!" A third gagged.

"Quiet. They understand us." A large female held up her hand for silence. She nodded at the humans and stepped forward.

With reverence, she approached Becky and bowed her head slightly.

"On behalf of our children, I thank you. My name is Saris. I am captain of this expedition."

Kyle and Jaric looked at each other with raised eyebrows.

"I take it the women wear the pants in this family," Kyle said to Jaric with a low chuckle.

Jaric laughed.

Becky shot both of them a dirty look, but they only laughed louder.

"What is wrong with your males? Do you not train them?" the female Mewiis asked incredulously.

"Never mind the males -- we have dire news for you." Becky's voice became serious, yet tinged with sadness. "We have come to warn you of a danger that threatens all of you. It can destroy your entire civilization, as it did ours. We are the last three survivors of a proud race known as Humanity."

Kyle and Jaric grew silent along with Becky as they surveyed the effect of their message on the faces of the

Mewiis.

"We must talk more," the lead Mewiis female said decisively.

The tragic tale of the final War of Humanity was retold with the deepest solemnity by Becky. The Mewiis listened, and not a few of the tenderhearted males shed a tear as the end of humanity came down to the three humans who stood before them now.

And now the last of the human race offered to help the Mewiis fight this same menace -- offering their very lives, if necessary.

"We are not a fierce race," Saris said as Becky finished the sad tale. "Our children are our lives. We live for them. This very mission was to begin colonizing a new planet, the farthest from the Three Kingdoms ever founded. Ours is a most important undertaking. We had even toyed with the idea that we might meet a new race. But not like this."

Krinia, another female, spoke.

"We only fight to defend ourselves. Our ships, our weapons, are built around this concept. How can we ever hope to defeat these T'kaan?"

"Then the T'kaan will cut you to pieces," Kyle said simply.

Becky held up her hand.

"We can help. Mother can give you plans for a new weapon. A weapon as powerful, and maybe more so, than even what the T'kaan possess."

"You saw the battle cruiser destroyed, right? In a single blow," Jaric added.

"Why did she not destroy the other two ships? Before they escaped?" Saris asked.

"I am not invincible. Neither are my weapons. But, we

have also discovered that the T'kaan are not invincible either."

The Mewiis looked around skittishly as Mother's voice emanated from the communicator on Becky's necklace. Both Kyle and Jaric carried a similar device.

"But we are not as numerous as the human race were when they faced this T'kaan fleet. We occupy less than fifty worlds."

"Are the Mewiis not part of the Three Kingdoms?" Mother asked, prompted by the knowledge she had obtained from Minstrel. "The Mewiis, the Hrono, and the Kraaqi together can field a fleet superior in numbers to the T'kaan Third fleet."

The Mewiis looked at each other in puzzlement. Not a few began to laugh.

"It is true," Krinia said. "As long as there have been Mewiis, we have known the Hrono. Only in recent centuries have the feared Kraaqi longships become known to us."

"There were wars," Saris added in a reflective tone. "We fought against the Hrono in the beginning. Then there was the Great Peace. The Kraaqi destroyed that when they first showed up. The many centuries since have been turbulent with only short periods of peace. The Mewiis have not thrived in this environment, which is why we have endeavored to find habitable worlds far away from the Three Kingdoms -- for our children."

"Will the Hrono and Kraaqi not join us in this mighty struggle?" Jaric asked in disbelief. "Otherwise, the T'kaan will destroy you all -- one by one!"

The Mewiis grew silent, and then Saris spoke.

"In the Book of Wars, the Mewiis have allied with the

Hrono against the Kraaqi many times. When the Hrono have acted destructively, when their leadership has changed and they have sought dominance, we have even fought with the Kraaqi against the Hrono."

"But *never* have the Hrono and Kraaqi fought together," Krinia added matter-of-factly.

"They are sworn enemies?" Kyle thought out loud.

"They are sworn enemies, forever," Saris said with emphasis.

"We seem to have a problem with our proposed alliance," Mother's voice whispered to her children.

"We must not be dismayed by obstacles," Minstrel's voice whispered a moment later.

"This is no small obstacle," Kyle whispered into his communicator.

"Sworn enemies. Lifelong enemies," Jaric added.

"Do humans always talk to themselves in this strange fashion," Krinia asked.

Becky, Kyle and Jaric brought their heads up with a sudden jerk.

"We apologize. We were conferring," Becky said sincerely.

"Who is this unseen entity?" Saris added.

"Oops," Minstrel's voice said from nowhere. And everywhere.

"We are not a backward race," Krinia said. "I cannot pinpoint the source of this Minstrel, though Mother's communications originate from the large ship of the humans."

"That ship," Jaric said with an edge to his voice, "*is* our mother."

Kyle glared at the Mewiis a moment, and then realized

such a concept must be new to them.

The Mewiis grew silent as they exchanged furtive glances with each other.

"We know the importance of parents to children. We apologize. Ours too is a society where the parent/child relationship is cherished. But," Krinia added, "we do not understand your relationship with the MotherShip."

"With our mother," Becky added with a smile.

Saris and Krinia looked at each other in surprise. "We would hear more of your mother. We must also discuss this terrible enemy and what we can do to protect our children. Please, all of you, come."

The meeting was promptly moved to the Mewiis shuttle for dinner and entertainment. Once there Saris, captain of the Mewiis ship, spoke of the history of the Mewiis race -- of their heritage, and their lives. Females were the leaders of this matriarchal society. It was a society that sought peace but seldom found it in this dangerous universe.

Saris explained that the children were the most important segment of Mewiis society. Children were their future.

Mother listened intently.

After Saris finished speaking, Jaric explained their relationship with Mother, how Mother had been designed as the ultimate warship to fight the T'kaan in humanity's losing war. He revealed how the age-old dream of creating artificial intelligence had finally been accomplished and then joined together in the M Project to create Mother.

But all too late to turn the tide.

Jaric also explained how Mother's creators, Ron and Rita, had come up with a new plan in the growing desperation of humanity's last days. They had uploaded the entire knowledge gathered by the human race into Mother's vast long-term memory storage. This became the last bastion of knowledge, the last memories of the human species.

They had also put together an equally desperate escape plan.

Once again, the T'kaan had foiled even this frantic attempt during those tumultuous last days. In the end, during the climax of the final battle, Rita had sent the ship outward with only three young occupants -- Becky, Kyle, and Jaric -- when they had hoped that they and dozens of others on the project might have escaped, with only the MotherShip between them and certain death.

They spoke of their long years searching while the T'kaan young grew on the desolated human worlds, the years of fruitless searching for any other possible survivors. Finally, they explained their decision to leave the dead worlds behind since the T'kaan fleet had learned of the existence of Mother and the children and begun to hunt them down. The T'kaan had dedicated themselves to finish the grisly task of destroying the last of humanity as well as Mother.

"That is the fate that awaits the Three Kingdoms," Kyle said with a sobering tone.

"That is the fate that awaits your children," Mother added, again through the communicator around Becky's neck. "If you want your children to live ..." Mother paused, letting the words sink in. "... for your children to have any kind of future, then you must defeat the T'kaan. Or they will destroy all. Only with an allied fleet of Mewiis, Kraaqi, and Hrono can you hope to succeed."

The Mewiis grew silent, reflecting on the hard words

and the hard path before them.

"The Hrono will fight -- they have powerful ships," Krinia began. "And the Kraaqi will fight. Their longships are strong and many." Krinia paused. "But will they fight together to defeat this dark menace? I myself cannot conceive such an alliance. It is unthinkable."

"You told us that the Hrono, the most technologically advanced, will be the most reasonable to deal with, correct?" Mother's voice asked.

"Yes. We must go to them first. They will listen. But their strength is also their weakness," Saris said.

"What do you mean?" Becky asked.

"They are obsessed with technology. It is their god. They live for it. They die for it." Saris smiled. "Technology and adventure. That is what drives the Hrono."

"Perhaps they will be able to repair Mother's sub-light engines, since they are so enamored with technology." Kyle looked from Becky to Jaric with a hopeful expression.

"Yes, they will appreciate her," Saris said enthusiastically.

"Sounds like they might worship her," Becky joked.

"No, but they would be keenly interested in her design," Krinia said.

"Have you or the Hrono no dealings whatsoever with the Kraaqi?" Minstrel asked. Minstrel had revealed its presence at the beginning of dinner, due to the importance of this meeting and the results it would have for three races. But in keeping with the code of its kind, Minstrel was still reluctant to reveal it true form at this early stage of first contact.

"We trade with the Hrono. We even have some of their

people living among us, and some Mewiis live on their worlds. But the Kraaqi are a strange, fierce people." Saris looked at Jaric. "But there is one here they might welcome."

"Who, me?" Becky asked.

"No." Saris smiled. "Only the Mewiis are led by their females. The Hrono have both female and male leaders. But the Kraaqi are male dominated."

"Well, that's probably part of their problem right there," Becky said with a chuckle.

"Who might they welcome?" Mother asked.

"The Kraaqi are strongly loyal to their individual bands. If not for the constant bickering and wars among themselves, they might long ago have conquered us and the Hrono." Krinia looked around the room. "We are a smoothed-skin people, like humans, but completely hairless. Our people are many shades of green complexions depending on what world we were born. The Hrono are covered by scales, but their race is a single shade of iridescent green. The Kraaqi are also covered by smooth skin, but they have hair upon their head like you."

The Mewiis looked at Jaric.

"They are most proud of their ebony skin," Saris began. "If one of their young are born light skinned, it is a curse to the entire family. Though now that terrible caste system is almost ended even among them. Still, a light-skinned Kraaqi can never hope to become chieftain, though they are now accepted up to the warrior class. But no further."

"Even then, never to the rank captain of one of their warships," Krinia added. "At least, it has never been known."

"True. And though he does not look as strong, nor does he have the long hair of a Kraaqi, still, the one you call Jaric would be welcomed as equal with them." Saris smiled.

"Then we must make plans. Even now I fear the T'kaan Third is interpreting the data from the Mewiis ship they destroyed. Soon, very soon, the horned fleet will be coming," Mother said.

The next day, plans were formulated and their outworking started. Minstrel had at last fully revealed itself, as well as its ship, to the Mewiis.

Mother was another story.

At first, the Mewiis had trouble comprehending that technology could be alive. Even the detailed explanations from each of the children and Minstrel failed to help. It was only after revealing Mother's actions -- how she had protected and raised the children over the years -- that the Mewiis began to accept the fact that the ship was indeed not only alive, but was also their mother. Motherhood was a concept they fully understood.

It was decided that Minstrel would go to the home world of the Mewiis, there to speak before the High Council and impress upon the Mewiis leaders how complete the coming day of destruction would be. Saris seemed certain that between her report about the T'kaan attack and the convincing tale that Minstrel would relate about the destruction of the human race, that the High Council would call an immediate and system-wide alarum, if for no other reason than the fact that every Mewiis child on every world was in imminent peril from this menace.

Mother downloaded certain of her own cherished schematics into the Mewiis ships -- those pertaining to her weapons systems as well as to her engines. She urged Saris to immediately begin upgrading their most powerful warships and then to refit the rest of the Mewiis fleet. If they acted now, they might be able to refit the majority of their ships before the T'kaan arrived.

Mother would go to the Hrono. Alone. Only Guardian and the other robots would accompany her. There she would not only share her personal technology, but also present the plan for the proposed great alliance -- an alliance of the combined fleet of Mewiis, Hrono, Kraaqi, and Human ships. It would be an alliance that would defeat the oncoming horde of the T'kaan. Most important, she would have to impress upon the Hrono that this was the only hope they had in stopping them.

But would the Hrono put aside their lifelong hatred for the Kraaqi?

Mother ran her models and felt hope. The percentage of success was quite high that the intelligent Hrono would listen. But her processors burned with activity when she considered the mission of her children.

Becky, Kyle, and Jaric would put their fighters inside a Mewiis starship that would take them to the borders of the Kraaqi worlds. But the Mewiis were afraid to take them further than the outermost border. There, within two days of the first Kraaqi planet, the three humans would take to their fighters and fly toward the Kraaqi home world of Hakama. That was where the Kraaqi Bands sent their chieftains to enforce order among the loose-knit Kraaqi Empire, to bring the intense rivalry of the competing bands into line. The high chieftains ruled from that central location.

Jaric would lead that mission.

"You must be careful," Mother said with a hint of apprehension. Her children were already inside their fighters as they prepared to make the short journey to the waiting Mewiis ship.

"We will," Kyle said nonchalantly. "If they give us any trouble, we'll show them just how tough a human can be."

Becky looked with concern at her brother.

"There will be no need for fighting," Jaric chimed in quickly. "We'll let them know that we're their allies. We'll tell them that there is another enemy -- one we all hold in common, one that must be destroyed."

"Only a combined Mewiis, Hrono, and Kraaqi fleet can do this," Mother added. "Such a combined force will give us a fleet equal or perhaps superior in number to the T'kaan Third."

"Then they have to listen to us," Kyle said.

"But what if they won't?" Becky looked with concern at Kyle and Jaric.

Only silence answered her.

The three quickly entered their cockpits. Shortly afterward, Jaric and Becky's ships began engine power-up. Kyle alone looked up. He stared into the optic where Mother watched.

"You are the strongest," Mother said. "Jaric is the best one to lead and negotiate. He has a good, clear mind."

Kyle smiled. "Yeah, he's the smart one. Becky's the pretty one. I'm just the stubborn ol' black sheep."

"No, you are not. You too, are my son," Mother said with emphasis.

Kyle nodded. "Well, if the Kraaqi try to play rough, I'll watch out for the others. I promise."

"If I have not received a message within two weeks, I will come for you," Mother's voice had become low and forceful.

"Heaven help the Kraaqi then!" Kyle laughed as he began the power-up sequence.

Tony Chandler

"Remember the schedule," Mother added.

Kyle gave a thumbs-up and smiled at Mother.

Mother watched the radar signal of her children until they were safely inside the Mewiis ship. The warship turned and with a flash was beyond the speed of light.

"They will be fine," Minstrel said as its spherical ship prepared to leave with the Mewiis colony ship.

"I feel so strange. There is so much activity taking up my processing cycles that I cannot focus properly on my key thoughts. I must run a Level II diagnostic."

Minstrel chuckled knowingly. "Your children have left you for the first time. You are worried."

Mother realized at that moment that she had been subconsciously polling all of her visual monitors, watching the empty corridors and not realizing she had actually been looking for the familiar forms of the children who were no longer there.

"You are correct."

"It's only natural," Minstrel said.

"Well, I will redirect those wasted processing cycles. I must adapt my schematics for the hybrid weapon to the Kraaqi ships and the Hrono. The Hrono will be the easiest, as the Mewiis have a detailed knowledge of their ships due to their trading agreements. But it will take me longer to prepare the Kraaqi plans." Mother grew silent as she reassigned her internal tasks.

"It's just as well. The children will need time to introduce this proposed alliance, and themselves, to the Kraaqi warriors."

"I hope the Kraaqi will be reasonable and listen," Mother said. "Time is of the essence."

"We can hope." Minstrel sighed. "We can only hope."

Chapter Twenty-Three

Becky felt his eyes on her. Watching her. Appraising her.

She blushed slightly but realized immediately that she must pretend not to notice. Once again, she would pretend not to notice that Jaric was hopelessly in love with her.

But on a small starship, that was a difficult thing to do.

They had landed their three fighters on board the Mewiis ship three days ago and had been living in the small confines ever since. The Mewiis obviously built their ships for function and not for comfort. Still, all three had quickly grown close to their new companions.

But for Becky, there was this added personal issue that seemed to be growing with intensity as they roomed with the crew of Mewiis wives and husbands. In fact, she realized at that very moment, maybe it was the subtle emotional and physical ties they had viewed between the Mewiis mates that had triggered this issue. After all, observing the love shared between the Mewiis wives and husbands as well as their romantic habit of holding hands while they walked together had even stirred something deep inside her heart.

Becky bit her lip as she watched a Mewiis pair laughing together on the bridge. She suddenly realized with a hot flush of awareness that Jaric's eyes were still fixed on her.

"Becky, Jaric, go run the final checks on our fighters before we launch," Kyle said, completely oblivious to the situation. He waved his hand, commanding them, as Jaric and Becky remained motionless.

Becky's blue eyes met Jaric's brown. She felt the

electricity that seemed to reach from him to her like something alive, caressing her.

Brushing her hand nervously through her hair, she waited on Jaric to make the first move.

Jaric began coughing with embarrassment.

Becky chuckled softly to herself. "C'mon Jaric, let's run those systems checks. One more time." She threw the last impatiently at Kyle.

"We're going to be on our own in another hour, deep inside Kraaqi territory. Depending on the reception we're gonna' get from them, we need those fighters to be one hundred percent." Kyle never looked up from his console as he continued his long-range scan, his hands dancing over the controls with quick precision.

"Let's go. Captain Ahab has spoken." Becky said to Jaric.

Kyle smiled to himself as he continued his intense work.

Jaric followed her, smiling in an absent-minded sort of way.

Becky wasn't sure when she had first noticed Jaric's affections, now that she thought about it. After all, they had grown up together. So, they had always been friends -- always been rivals.

Well, Kyle and Jaric together had been her rivals. A male-female rivalry. Just as it had been since the beginning of time.

But somewhere along the way, adolescence had set in. Hormones had begun flowing. All three of them had started to grow up.

Almost.

"You know, Becky, you sure look pretty today," Jaric

stammered as he walked beside her.

"Sure, Jaric. I bet you say that to all the girls." Becky rolled her eyes, smiling. She might be the last woman left alive in the universe, but she was going to play this love thing like any other red-blooded woman would, as the unwritten rules of love stirred in her heart.

She was going to play hard to get.

"No, Becky. Really, you look pretty today," Jaric said with all seriousness.

Becky began walking faster.

"Do you think ... " Jaric began.

But fortunately, the Mewiis starship was quite small. The door that led to the hanger bay where their three fighters sat at the ready -- ready to enter Kraaqi space -- slid open before them.

"You take Kyle's ship and begin running a Level-Two diagnostic. I'll take yours." Becky pointed to the lead ship.

"Then we can do yours, um, together." Jaric stumbled over a cable even as he uttered the last word.

Becky stifled a laugh as she reached Jaric's single-man fighter. Stepping up the side of the ship via the hand- and footholds, she slid herself easily into the small cockpit. Immediately, she began punching the controls. The small viewscreens whirred to life as the diagnostics began checking the ship's systems.

A few minutes later, she read the displayed results: All Systems Normal. *Big surprise!*

As she climbed out and started over toward her own fighter, she found Jaric was already standing beside it -- smiling ear to ear.

Without a word, they climbed up the ship from opposite sides. When she got to the top and reached inside for the control panel, her foot slipped. She fell headfirst into the narrow confines of the single-seat craft.

Jaric instantly reached out for her to try and help, but his sudden movement caused him to lose his own footing. With a forward rush of movement, he fell into her.

Becky fought for a hold as she fell. Her head slammed against the side of the cushioned seat, slowing her as she continued toward the floor. She managed to stop her momentum just before she banged her head against the steel floor. As she gasped and tried to right herself, she felt a sudden weight pressing against her back. She struggled vainly, sliding down until her face was smashed hard against the gritty surface.

She grunted against the heavy, dead weight pressing against her back.

"I'm sorry, Becky. Wait a second, let me ... "

Sudden pain shot through her shoulder and back as Jaric struggled franticly.

Jaric's efforts were finally rewarded, more so for Becky, as he pulled himself out of the cockpit. He stood panting, and embarrassed, as Becky got out and righted herself.

He reached across toward her to help brush the dirt off her cheek.

"I don't need any more of your help, Jaric!"

Jaric yanked his hand back.

Pulling her shoulder-length hair back behind her ears, Becky shook her head with frustration and placed her hands on her hips. She didn't realize the right side of her face was smeared with dirt. But thinking her efforts to regain her composure were complete, she reached inside the fighter again. Holding tightly to the handhold, she began punching up the diagnostic on the console with her free hand.

"Don't you think I should --"

"No," Becky replied harshly.

Jaric pulled himself away from her, an overly sad expression on his face.

She chided herself for her outburst as she noticed his devastated look.

"Okay, Okay. Run this one on the engines for me."

He reached for the console next to where her hand rested. Somehow his hand missed the buttons and rested on hers instead. She felt the warmth of his hand clasp tightly around hers, gently squeezing.

"Jaric?" she cried with surprise.

"Oh, Becky. I love you. You're the only woman for me." Jaric's voice rose several decibels with excitement, almost as if he were going through puberty again.

"I am the only woman!" Becky half-shouted with surprise.

Jaric's face showed shock. He fought to regain what little composure he still had. "Well, even if there were more women, you'd still be the only woman for me."

"I'm the only woman in the entire universe." Becky was shouting now as she tried to wrench her hand out of his. But there was a strange sensation surging throughout her body -- something she had never felt before. Her struggles began to lessen.

"I love you, Becky. I always have. Ever since we were little."

"Even that time you and Kyle tried to beat me up?"

Jaric's eyes widened. "Well, not then. We were kids then."

There was warmth coming through his touch. Her arm trembled under its softness and energy. She liked it. But still

201

...

"What about Kyle?" Becky blurted.

Jaric's face screwed up in complete puzzlement. "What about Kyle?"

"We can't just go falling in love with each other. Kyle will be all alone."

Jaric shook his head. "He'll be all right."

"No, he won't. Haven't you thought of his feelings? If we get married ... " Becky caught her breath, shocked at her own words. But she gathered her thoughts and continued. "If we get married, Kyle will have no one. There aren't any other women. Or any other humans, for that matter. We're it!" Becky shouted with total frustration etched in every syllable.

Jaric slowly pulled his hand away from hers. His ebony face was deep in thought, his eyes far off. Slowly, a knowing smile grew.

Becky almost saw the light go off over his head. She looked at him, her eyebrows raised expectantly as Jaric spoke.

"He could marry an alien ... "

Becky's hand reacted before she realized what she was doing. Jaric fell straight backwards as she slapped him with force squarely across his face. Almost in the same moment, she reached to help him, even as he fell out of sight.

She was a boiling mixture of emotions now, as well as thoroughly confused. On the one hand, she might be in love with Jaric. On the other hand, he sure wasn't the man she had dreamed about.

And more, she did care about Kyle's welfare. He had no one ...

It was all so confusing.

But she knew with sudden clarity that she shouldn't have slapped Jaric so hard. She felt her face grow flush and hot with boiling emotions.

Scrambling down her side of the ship, she raced under its belly toward his crumpled form.

"Oh. Are you all right? I'm sorry. Here, let me ..."

"I ... I don't think I need any more of your help for one day." Jaric raised both his hands, protecting himself from her advances.

She rolled her eyes and felt the flood of emotions again.

"Don't you see how stupid that was -- *Kyle can marry an alien*. I mean, what if I was your sister, and Kyle and I got married. Would you marry an alien then?"

Jaric groaned as he slowly and very painfully got up.

"If she were pretty ... "

Becky groaned.

Suddenly, Jaric winced.

"Here, let me look at --"

"I said, I don't need any more of your help." Jaric raised his hands again and began backing away.

She followed him as he limped back toward the Mewiis bridge.

"So, you'd marry an alien if she was pretty, huh? "Becky said mockingly.

"Yeah," he said to her without turning, "and there just might be some fine looking alien babes there among the Kraaqi."

"You wish," Becky whispered angrily.

"What did you say?"

"I said, 'I bet there are some alien hunks too.'"

Jaric groaned and turned.

But Becky passed him with a haughty *Hmmph* and kept

going.

Love sure is strange. Or is it just men? Becky entered the bridge several steps ahead of Jaric.

Kyle looked up from his displays and watched Jaric with sudden concern.

"Why are you limping?"

"Don't ask." Jaric waved his arm at Kyle.

"Ask him about the cute Kraaqi babes," Becky taunted.

Kyle did a doubletake at his sister, and then looked over to Jaric. He opened his mouth to question Jaric.

"Don't ask," Jaric repeated.

"May I interrupt?"

The three humans turned to the Mewiis captain.

Captain Sharina's green complexion had deepened, and behind the bone ridge that started at her forehead and extended to the base of her skull, her head-tail flicked from side to side with rapid motions.

Becky brushed her hand through her own hair, wondering what it would be like to have a tail instead.

"My nav has just instructed me that we are about to enter the edge of Kraaqi space." In what looked like a subconscious habit, the Mewiis Captain began to play with the weapon strapped to her waist. "We must launch your ships. The coordinates of the nearest Kraaqi planet have already been downloaded."

Becky looked at Kyle. "I guess there won't be any long good-byes."

Kyle chuckled.

"No, it is imperative we launch. The Kraaqi watch their frontiers closely. They also tend to respond with firepower first when they detect unwelcome alien ships."

"Shoot first, ask questions later," Jaric chimed.

Kyle nodded. "Okay, let's do it. We'll contact you and Mother in one week at the prearranged bandwidth."

Captain Sharina nodded. "That should give you ample time not only to make contact with the local Kraaqi band, but to also make long-range communications with the Kraaqi home world. That is where the ruling chieftains govern over the loosely bound Kraaqi bands."

"Yeah, I remember your briefing."

The trio made their way to the prepped fighters and within minutes were flying through space and inside the Kraaqi kingdom.

The Mewiis ship turned and disappeared with a flash of streaking light as it leapt into hyperspace. The three humans were alone.

Several minutes went by in stark silence as their fighters flew toward a bluish point of light -- the star that the Kraaqi planet called Dosk orbited. But as the minutes passed, the silence seemed to press in upon them. Before long, it seemed they could *feel* the silence.

"I feel so strange," Kyle said at last, breaking the spell.

"Yeah. Me too," Jaric agreed.

"I dunno. We've got a plan. We know exactly what to do. We've got this set for every contingency," Kyle continued.

"Even if the Kraaqi attack and refuse to listen," Jaric added.

"But remember Minstrel's words, 'First Contact is the most important contact.' We have to be extra careful." Becky said.

The dark, foreboding silence returned. Outside their windows, the unfamiliar star patterns intensified the unnerving feeling each shared separately.

"Something's not right. I feel it," Kyle said.

Becky looked down at her console and quickly glanced at her sensors. All was normal; only their trio of ships showed up. Becky looked up at the stars all around her -- and then it hit her. She sighed and wondered how all of them could have overlooked the obvious.

"This is the first time we've been away from Mother."

Kyle's eyebrows rose at Becky's words. Then his mind went into overdrive as memories flooded before him. Jaric's reaction was similar.

"You're right," they said simultaneously into their comms.

"I can't believe it," Kyle added. "But you're right. This is the first time we've ever been without her."

"She's been our whole life." Becky smiled. "The only mother I can remember."

Kyle stared silently straight ahead into the star field as he bit his lip.

"I don't remember my real mother," Jaric began. "I wish I could."

"Mother is our mother," Becky said defensively.

"We've always had Mother's guns to protect us," Kyle said, interrupting her. "Her engines ready to whisk us away from danger." Kyle ran his fingers through his hair. "But it's time we left her apron strings behind. Jaric, keep a sharp eye on your sensors. Becky, as soon as we're in range, begin a sweep of the planet. We're looking for a small, remote Kraaqi settlement. A nice, quiet corner to meet these beings."

"Gotcha'," Becky said.

"We'll make Mother proud," Kyle finished.

The journey continued with little conversation, each one

deep in their own thoughts. Though their thoughts were going in different directions, they began at the same moment in time and with the same point of origin: what growing up and leaving Mother meant.

Becky glanced at her reflection in the port window. She saw a woman's face staring back at her. It caused an odd stirring in her heart. Deep in those eyes she could still see the child she had once been. In the face, she could see the woman she had become. But the reflection was a shimmering, surreal image with the stars shining through her image in a ghostly fashion as her small ship continued its journey. As she stared, it suddenly seemed that the person she was looking at wasn't herself -- it was some other person -- a fleeting stranger who seemed somewhat familiar, but ...

The woman in the vision shivered and took a deep breath.

I see a woman. But sometimes I feel exactly the way I did when I was a child. Becky stared at the image of the ghostly woman with the stars twinkling through her. *Am I a child in a woman's body? Do Kyle and Jaric feel the same way in their minds about themselves -- that deep inside they're still a child?* Becky laughed to herself. *Perhaps I'll feel like a child even when I'm an old woman -- all gray and wrinkled but with a twinkle still in my eyes.*

She sighed deeply, trying to analyze her feelings. She realized with a flash of insight that she was the same person as that little girl she used to be. She just had more memories now, more life experiences. But in some ways, she hadn't changed.

Jaric and Kyle still act like boys even though they are older than I am. In many ways, more so. She chuckled softly. *Maybe boys never really grow up after all.*

Becky felt something stir inside her soul as her thoughts traveled back in time -- back to her childhood long ago. And back to Mother and a feeling that seemed so familiar, so nice. Something she had not felt for many, many years. A sound. Suddenly, she realized that she was humming a tune as her thoughts meandered down various mental paths.

The melody was an old but lovingly familiar one, unheard for many years now.

Becky smiled and hummed the gentle, flowing tune a little louder. It was perhaps the most special music she had ever known. She thumbed the comm button, and the melody went out to the other two ships.

In each ship, Jaric and Kyle looked down at their speaker in unison. They both laughed softly.

"That's the song Mother used to play to put us to sleep," Jaric said as he too remembered.

"Back in the old days," Kyle said. But even Kyle's heart warmed with the soft humming that continued from Becky.

"I've got two targets," Jaric said, breaking in.

"I have them too," Kyle said as his eyes dropped to his sensor screen.

Becky had only just begun her sensor sweep of the planet that filled half of their vision now with its close proximity. But she had already noticed that any kind of cities must be few and far between. In fact, she had yet to detect the first settlement at all.

"There's a lot of empty space down there. Should we make a break, or try a little ship-to-ship diplomacy up here?" Becky asked.

"They're coming in pretty hot." Jaric said.

The twin targets on their sensors had suddenly veered

directly for their own formation. As they drew closer, their slim, gray profiles took shape. The Kraaqi fighters were long and dangerous-looking, the bulbous rear obviously housing the engines while from their spear-like prows extended several ominous shapes.

"Okay, watch'em close. I'll give it a try." Kyle adjusted his comm to broadcast on all frequencies. Taking a deep breath, he began. "This is Kyle Brandon. We are on a diplomatic mission. We are humans, on a peaceful mis --"

Laser bolts leapt from both Kraaqi fighters and passed directly in front of Kyle's fighter.

"Move!" Kyle shouted.

The three arrowhead-shaped human fighters dove apart in the same number of directions with a practiced precision.

"Should we shoot back?" Jaric shouted as he punched his engines wide open.

"No!" Kyle shouted back.

"Then what?" Becky yelled.

"At least they're lousy shots," Jaric said.

"No, they're not, those were warning shots. Let me think a second," Kyle said as he jerked his fighter over and barely avoided another deadly bolt.

Jaric was twisting his ship out of a hard maneuver when his hand hit the comm button. "Kraaqi ships, we come in peace. We come in peace. Hold your fire ... " With a lightning motion, he was turning hard to avoid the bolts now heading straight for his ship.

The twin Kraaqi fighters turned again.

Becky's ship shuddered under a direct hit. Glancing at her console, she saw her shields drop thirty percent.

"Well, I'm tired of thinking," Becky grumbled. Kicking her foot controls hard, Becky turned on the pursuer over her right shoulder. Her finger pressed the firing contact. "Think on this." She laughed. Her bolts shot true, and the Kraaqi ship veered away, minus some of its shields.

"Becky. I ordered you to hold --" Kyle began.

"Whoa. I've got something huge on my scope now, Big K," Jaric shouted through the comm.

Four frigate-class warships suddenly appeared from hyperspace. They had long profiles similar to those of the smaller fighters, but the forward sections seemed oversized. All along the length of the hulls their main guns extended in two deadly rows. The four warships turned as one toward the diminutive human fighters.

"I suggest you start thinking a bit faster," Becky said with rising concern.

Kyle growled over his comm. He nodded decisively. "Okay, let's make a run down to the planet. Maybe if we can meet them face to face ... "

" ... they can probably kill us faster," Jaric finished for him.

"Enough. We can't battle those frigates. It's our only choice." Becky turned her ship for the orangish planet. "Unless we turn and run, and we can't do that," she said as her ship leapt forward.

"Let's go." Kyle's ship surged after her.

"I knew I should have packed my running shoes," Jaric shouted.

The edge of the planet grew on their viewscreens as their ships raced for its atmosphere. Behind them, more Kraaqi fighters spewed from the frigates. As the human ships neared the atmosphere and dove toward the orange surface, only the Kraaqi fighters continued after them. Above them, the four frigates began to orbit the planet at strategic positions, cutting off any hope of retreat.

"Hit it." Kyle shouted as the Kraaqi fighters drew too near. Laser bolts leapt all around his ship as he nosed down toward the surface.

It was only as the three human ships pierced and roared through the planet's atmosphere that the first Kraaqi words were uttered to them.

"Stop. You are desecrating. Stop."

"What does that mean?" Becky shouted into her comm.

"Look, they're slowing down," Jaric said.

"They're still following us. Let's get down ... hey, what's going on?" Kyle said.

"Their engine signatures have changed." Becky began punching her console, trying to get a better reading on the new Kraaqi engine signature on her sensor. Her face grew more puzzled by the second. "I've never seen anything like that before."

"Sort of like ... waves of energy?" Jaric cast a quick glance at his ship's sensors. "Their engines seem to be reacting to the planet's gravity."

"Record it for later analysis. Let's find a place to land," Kyle ordered.

"One that has a hidey-hole, I hope." Jaric smiled.

Becky found the spot just inland on the eastern coast of the lone continent that girdled the entire planet. It was in a narrow valley, one not easily attacked from the air and protected by huge, overhanging cliffs on three sides. The three ships landed just short of a nearby forest, and with some quick maneuvering, they parked their ships under the protective limbs at the forest's edge.

Walking out into the meadow before them, they watched in silence as twelve Kraaqi fighters landed with an eerie silence at the far end about two hundred yards away.

"I've never heard engines so quiet before. What can they be?" Jaric commented.

"It's almost like they just floated down, under no power," Becky added.

Kyle looked up from his hand-held sensor. "No, they're under power. But like nothing I've ever registered before. It seems to be some kind of gravitational power source. Maybe --"

Becky interrupted. "Here they are."

The Kraaqi warriors strode forward, heads held high with obvious confidence. Most were dark skinned, though the last two had skin of a much lighter complexion. All carried short-barreled blasters in their hands pointed in the direction of the waiting trio. But there were other weapons still holstered or sheathed on the wide leather belts wrapped around each of their waists. Their muscular torsos were covered with a type of leather-tanned animal skin, which added to the ferocious image of a warrior-hunter.

Becky's eyes widened as they drew near.

The Kraaqi didn't have hair exactly, not like humans anyway. But their faces were human-like: two eyes, a nose, and a mouth. But there the resemblance ended. On each side of their heads, just above their web-like ears, a large and dangerous looking horn curved outwards. The rest of their heads were hairless except for a single strip of jet-black hair that began from the middle of their foreheads and extended straight over the top of their heads and then hung down freely across their backs.

But it wasn't hair. The trio strained to make it out more clearly.

Feather-hair. Large, flowing feather-hair locks that

hung down between their broad, muscular shoulders like some kind of weird, Mohawk haircut.

Jaric turned to Kyle and whispered.

"The proverbial *bad-hair* aliens, eh?" He chuckled.

Kyle eyed him sternly.

"Shut up," Becky said, nervousness edged in her voice.

Kyle stared straight ahead at the approaching warriors. "Leave our weapons in their holsters. They've already noticed that we don't have ours out."

"Or they would have started shooting by now," Jaric added.

The Kraaqi formed a semi-circle around the three humans. Dark eyes looked the trio up and down with keen interest. The apparent leader moved closer to Jaric.

Jaric's eyes widened, and he almost stepped backwards.

"He's taken you as the leader," Kyle whispered quickly. "Stay put."

Jaric swallowed nervously as he watched the horned warrior stop right in front of him.

"We have come --" Jaric began.

"Silence!" the huge warrior shouted. He looked at Kyle with blatant distaste, but then his eyes moved with a piercing, questioning glance to Becky. A second warrior stepped beside him and whispered hurriedly under his left horn. The Kraaqi leader nodded, and he looked at all three of the humans with sudden intensity. He spoke quickly, and to the point.

"You must all die."

Becky felt the planet begin to spin, but caught herself just in time. "Are our translators working right?" she asked in a daze as she tugged at the device in her ear that Minstrel had provided for each of them.

213

Tony Chandler

"They are functioning perfectly," the Kraaqi leader said directly to her.

Chapter Twenty-Four

"I hope Mother's children are enjoying their first contact," Minstrel said as Saris moved beside its undulating form. "I know Mother is worried about them."

Saris smiled, and her green complexion deepened. "MotherShip understands the greatest love in the universe."

If Minstrel had eyebrows in its current form, they would have risen with Saris' sudden insight. "Please explain," Minstrel requested.

"MotherShip has a strong bond with her human children. It is evident in her care for them, and in her concern, in spite of the fact she is an artificial intelligence." Saris sighed. "MotherShip knows that the greatest love in the universe is that of a parent for its offspring."

Minstrel thought a few moments, remembering the many interchanges with Mother, and how her processing was always focused to some extent on her human charges. "Yes, you are right." Minstrel's form shimmered with sudden intensity. "Has your communiqué to the Hrono and Kraaqi been answered?"

Saris' head-tail lashed from side to side behind her neck. "There is still no word from the chieftain council of the Kraaqi. But that is not surprising. During the last war between the Hrono and the Kraaqi, when we continued to trade with the Hrono, the Kraaqi broke off diplomatic ties with us. The chieftains asserted that we aided the Hrono in their war plans, but it is untrue. The Kraaqi are such a quick-tempered race, and they hold to their anger for many years. I fear that Becky and her men will not enjoy their first meeting with them."

Minstrel morphed suddenly into the silvery shape of a human female and stood facing the Mewiis high commander as she stared with a mixture of concern and amazement. "Once they deliver their message about the oncoming T'kaan Third Fleet and its cruel intentions, I believe even the ferocious Kraaqi will see the wisdom in our three-fold alliance.

"I wish I could share your optimism." Saris shook her head, now accepting the present shape of Minstrel as normal. "But we have known the Kraaqi too long to hope for such a quick decision. Individual warrior bands may act that quickly, but the chieftains are old and set in their ways." Saris sighed. "It will be difficult for Becky and her men."

The silver visage of Minstrel nodded. "What about the Hrono? Mother will be entering their sector in a few days."

"Yes, and we have had an answer from them. The Mewiis and Hrono still share a formal trade agreement."

"Was the answer hopeful?" Minstrel asked.

"It was good in some ways, but in others it was rather mysterious."

Minstrel morphed again, changing its plasma body from a human shape into that of the Mewiis, albeit a male of their species. Minstrel enjoyed the pleasant sensation against his neck and shoulders as he made his head-tail swish with anticipation. "Please explain."

Saris stood silent with her mouth open as she gazed with wonder at the perfect Mewiis before her.

Minstrel chuckled with a flick of his head-tail, and it brought Saris back out of her frozen amazement.

"Per Mother's instructions." Saris clenched her eyes shut as she focused her thoughts. "We communicated solely with the Hrono high command and told them that we had a message of the utmost importance." Saris began walking toward the great window that looked out upon the city of MewiisProlo. The tall spires and towers of the inner city greeted her gaze. "They were very concerned, of course. They confirmed they had received Mother's initial communications along with her plans for integrating the hybrid weapon into Hrono ships. But, they began to ask many questions about the MotherShip messenger, especially when we explained that Mother is a sentient machine created by an entirely different race from outside the Three Kingdoms."

Minstrel nodded his current visage, smiling widely, once again thankful for the translator that enabled the Minstrel race to understand most alien languages. It was a good thing Minstrel had insisted the children take them for their encounter. Minstrel sighed with gladness. "Continue."

"After their initial flurry of questions about the MotherShip and the humans, I think they started to understand that the reason for such a meeting was serious indeed." Saris turned from the window. "I could tell from their faces onscreen, how their countenances changed."

"Yes," Minstrel said. "They understand the dire circumstances."

"Correct." Saris sighed deeply. "They became quite tense, almost aggressive in the nature of the questions. Especially when we could not answer in detail about the new enemy." Saris shook her head and walked back to Minstrel. "We told them that MotherShip was bringing them the detail about the enemy that threatened the entire Three Kingdoms and that she had information that would help all of us."

"I imagine that got their attention," Minstrel said.

"That's when their questions turned rather mysterious." Saris' eyes became distant as she remembered the communication. "All the rest were about the MotherShip AI. Her alone."

Minstrel allowed his form to flow back to its normal, fluidic shape. "That is not so strange for a race that worships technology. They would naturally be intrigued by a sentient machine."

"Maybe you are right," Saris said doubtfully. Her head-tail flicked from side to side as her eyes followed Minstrel's twinkling form.

"Have the first Mewiis battle cruisers begun their refitting?" Minstrel asked.

"Yes. The first ship is completed. The super-weapon and its vast, accompanying circuits that integrate into the ship's power plants have been installed. As have the engine upgrades. They are even now being tested before we continue with other ships."

"Good. You will find this weapon needs a substantial recharging time, so your ship's commanders will need to be instructed in their tactical use, in conjunction with the ships' normal weapons." Minstrel glowed as a ripple of rainbow colors flowed down its body in waves.

"We have begun strategic planning sessions with fleet commanders, using the downloaded data from MotherShip's long-term memories. The data of actual battles that the MotherShip has fought with the T'kaan has been most useful." Saris drew a deep breath. "But the most unforgettable sequence was the final battle of humanity against them. Their *Last Stand*. Pressed together on that last planet with the T'kaan ships orbiting like vultures. It was ...

" Saris shook her head. She was at a loss for words to express her emotions.

"The T'kaan are ruthless. They destroy entire races to propagate their own. We must defeat them," Minstrel said.

Saris felt hot tears filling her eyes as she thought of all the Mewiis children and the possible fate that awaited them. If they failed. She spoke with a look of grim determination.

"We have to defeat them -- so our children will have a future."

Chapter Twenty-Five

The T'kaan warships gathered together into tight formation around the *one* Great Horned ship, the centerpiece of each T'kaan fleet. The jet-black hulls glistened from the fires of nearby stars, the long prows of each capital ship bristling with horns from which their weapons' fire emanated.

Inside the darkened hallways and rooms of each warship, activity had increased to a fever pitch.

Hundreds of frigate-class ships gathered in tight formation around the masses of battleships and battle cruisers, while flying in and around them all like clouds of locusts were countless formations of scout and hunter fighters.

The T'kaan Third fleet was at full strength once again.

From another direction an equally numerous multitude of ships drew near the sacred rendezvous point. In every direction, as far as their sensors could see, there was nothing but the ships of the dreaded T'kaan.

Inside the Great Horned ship, the fleet commander slithered to the main meeting hall. His tentacles pushed and pulled his undulating body over the floor and around the black tapestries that hung like endless dragnets throughout the vast interior. At the center of the great circular meeting room a mass of waiting warriors and leaders slithered and slapped their tentacles in growing intensity. Some had even extended their claws on the tips of their tentacles in their growing lust for battle. The room was alive with their grunting and the clicking of talons against the steel floor.

The fleet commander of the T'kaan Third entered this

melee and took his place at the very center. He did not have long to wait. He focused his globular optical mass onto the new group of arrivals.

They looked at first appearance to be no different than any other T'kaan undulating within this war room. But they were.

The new leader pushed and pulled his body around the warriors and made his slimy way to the other waiting fleet commander. The warriors he brushed against shuddered at his touch, feeling his power -- feeling his difference and his sameness with them in quivers of delight.

It was a great day for the T'kaan. It was a very special day and an event that had not taken place for almost a full millennium.

And there would be more.

The new leader pulled himself the last few feet until he was before his equal. Each T'kaan leader jerked and writhed with delight as their tentacles twirled and twisted around the other's tentacles.

The clicking noises in the great, dark room became deafening.

In a sudden split second, all went silent.

The two leaders in the center of the circular room had twisted all of their tentacles together and now held each other firmly in the ritual grasp. In the vast silence, the T'kaan commander of the mighty Third spoke.

"The greatest race, T'kaan to be. Three to One, and One to Three."

The new leader shuddered with pleasure. "Our Eternal war, the cycles four. Victory our fate, feast and mate."

The thousands gathered in the room howled as one. The two leaders of the T'kaan unwrapped themselves from each other as two lessers brought them the frozen meat.

"Feast you now, equal of mine. On human meat, sweet and sublime. We destroyed them first ... but not complete. Our victory worst."

The new leader's body quivered with distaste. The T'kaan always annihilated their enemies and destroyed them completely. Always the victory was complete. This was dreadful news indeed to the newcomers. As his shudders abated, he spoke.

"Received I have, this report unreal. We finish these last, their death to seal."

"She is Iron Huntress. Enemy of steel and heartless." The T'kaan Third's commander began gnawing the meat before him.

"I have heard of this ship alive. T'kaan horns must kill; she too will die. But first we wait for the others, our brothers." The new fleet commander opened his tusks wide and began eating.

Around the two leaders, the tens of thousands gathered around them chanted in unison a single, solitary word -- "War!" They chanted louder and louder. The huge room resonated with their guttural voices.

"Death to the Huntress," chanted the Third's leader in answer to his equal. "Death to the humans three. Death to the Mewiis, Hrono, and the bands of Kraaqi."

Inside the great room, the walls bled purple.

The oily fluid began to appear in large globules as the black, flowing dragnets began to wave in unison. Those T'kaan gathered nearest the bleeding walls began to shake and fall to the ground, their chanting and shouting reaching a fever pitch. The mass of tentacled aliens began to writhe and crawl toward the sweet, dripping fluid.

As they reached the curved walls, their long arms reached forward excitedly. Thousands of tentacles slapped against the supple walls, encouraging the slimy flow. The eerie sound of this orgy mingled with a new sound, a sound like the rumbling of thunder that emanated from somewhere deep inside the Great Horned ship.

It was The Great One himself.

The fluid began to seep faster, completely covering the first rows of T'kaan, bathing them with a glistening glow, baptizing them in its bloody stench.

All throughout the combined fleets, among the frigates, cruisers, and battleships alone, certain sections of their inner walls -- the walls that lived, that melded with the armored hull -- too began their bloody flow as their black dragnets danced.

Those on the smaller warships cried out in frustration, cursing this rare opportunity, knowing that theirs were merely warships and that they could not participate and feel the fluid on their own skin.

The bleeding ships talked to one another in their peculiar way, joining with the Great Horned ship in its exquisite delight.

The T'kaan rejoiced with the Great One.

Chapter Twenty-Six

"Uh, could I ask *why* we have to die?" Jaric stared in disbelief at the Kraaqi.

The warrior's eyes narrowed. In one quick movement the curved rapier was out of its scabbard and the razor-sharp blade pressed against Jaric's throat.

Jaric stood very still.

"You have violated everything that is sacred in the universe," the warrior snarled. "And so, you must die."

The air grew silent as Jaric stared defiantly up into the brown eyes of the Kraaqi.

"I say you're wrong," Becky said.

The muscles under the warrior's tight leather shirt tensed at her words. His head jerked toward the voice, sending the long feather-hair dancing over his shoulder. He slammed Jaric down as if he were a toy, and in two steps he stood right before Becky, his breath hot on her face and his rapier raised threateningly over her.

"You call me a liar?" His eyes looked her up and down. "And you, *only* a female?"

Becky gritted her teeth and took a deep breath. "No. I meant we haven't been here long enough to violate *everything* sacred in the universe."

The warrior growled.

Kyle started to take a step forward.

"Don't!" Jaric shouted.

The reaction was instantaneous. The Kraaqi grabbed Becky by her shoulder to hold her still while he raised his rapier toward Kyle. He twisted his upper body to get a better angle for the death stroke.

For a split second, he glared down into Kyle's eyes.

In that instant, Becky's knee smashed upward into his groin.

With a loud grunt, the Kraaqi warrior bent over double as his rapier fell to the grass.

As she took his arm and twisted it to hold him still, she brought her knee up into his stomach, eliciting another deep grunt of pain from the Kraaqi. And just for good measure, she rammed his stomach a third time.

The Kraaqi warrior remained bent over in pain, though he still had not been completely felled.

Becky shook her head with pity as she released her grip and then slammed her combined fists down onto the back of his unprotected neck.

With another smothered grunt, the warrior landed face down on the crumpled grass.

"*Only* a female, eh? That should teach you to never turn your back on another warrior," Becky chided the fallen Kraaqi.

With a start, she remembered the other warriors behind her. She turned.

They were all staring back at her with a mixture of awe and profound disbelief.

The largest Kraaqi warrior stepped towards her.

"You are too small for Mewiis." He stared at her face, and then with his large right hand, his fingers touched her forehead and then traced a line into her hair and over the top of her head. "And you are not Kraaqi."

"And definitely not Hrono," added a second warrior who had joined him.

Their gaze began at her feet and slowly came back up to her face.

"She is female," the larger warrior said. He sniffed the air cautiously. "What are you?"

Becky returned his hard gaze, and then she smiled mischievously as she spoke.

"I'm a woman."

The warriors looked at each other with puzzlement.

On the ground, the hurt Kraaqi began to push himself back up to his knees, grunting in pain with each movement.

The larger of the two warriors looked down at his hurt companion, and then back at Becky. He chuckled. "I am Rok. Second Commander, Band of the Stars." He smiled with an air of great importance.

Kyle and Jaric stepped beside Becky. The three young faces stared back at the Kraaqi.

"You must be a courageous race, for your females to be such good warriors," Rok said.

Jaric and Kyle smiled widely at Becky.

"I honor you." Rok bowed his head slightly toward Jaric. "Woman."

Jaric's face grew puzzled. "Whoa, Rok. You got something wrong. I'm not a woman, I'm ... " Jaric stammered.

Rok raised himself erect. "You are not a woman?" He growled.

Jaric smiled sheepishly, shaking and nodding his head at the same time. But the warrior spoke first.

"Woman," Rok repeated. "A good race." He smiled at the three young faces.

"Does this mean we don't have to die?" Kyle asked, ignoring Rok's misunderstanding.

"No. You must still die."

The three looked at each other in disbelief.

"Can't you at least explain to us what did to break your rules?" Becky asked.

Rok turned to the others behind him, who nodded back at him. "Yes. You at least deserve that." Crossing his arms, he looked up to the sky. "We, Kraaqi, are caretakers of this world, as we are of all the worlds in our realm. We protect the animals that dwell here. We oversee the vegetation and ensure the ecosystems are healthy and in balance." Rok took his right hand and placed it across his chest. "We are one with them all. We respect all life."

"You've got to be kidding," Jaric whispered to Kyle.

Kyle ignored him and instead spoke to Rok. "You would kill us for your love of life?"

Rok considered the words a moment. He nodded, "Yes."

"But what have we done to disturb the life, the ecosystems on this world?" Becky's voice had risen with impatience.

"Your ships have sent pollution into the air, disturbing the balance of this ecosystem. You are like the Hrono, selfishly using your technology, expelling your waste while the world around you suffers."

The three humans grew silent.

Becky felt a shame inside of her heart, for in a way, this alien was right. They were guilty as charged, whether they had polluted this world consciously or not. Their ships had been designed to expel that waste, which was harmful. Mankind had a long history of such actions and had almost destroyed their own home world so long ago in this very same way.

"We are sorry for our actions. We apologize." Becky's sorrowful eyes pleaded at Rok. "We are guilty." She looked down with shame. "If only we could learn to be one with life, as you are."

Rok's eyes opened wide.

Behind him, the small band of warriors began murmuring.

Kyle looked over at one of the Kraaqi ships. "How do your ships not disturb the life of this world? Perhaps we could learn from you?"

The murmuring among the Kraaqi grew louder.

Rok looked at Kyle with a keen expression. "We disable our main engines when we come inside the ecosystem of any world. Our anti-gravity repulsors allow us to maneuver within the atmosphere of any world without doing it harm."

Jaric nodded appreciatively. "We could learn from you."

"They must die." The fallen warrior stumbled to his feet and stared into Rok's face.

"Their words are from the heart," Rok said. "It is written, '*Tak aya waya. Ro podak ya.*'" Rok's eyes narrowed as he turned back to Jaric. "The one who *wants* to learn will embrace that knowledge the rest of his life."

The injured warrior turned and stared with open hatred at the three humans. "They are like Hrono. They cannot learn."

"I say they can," Rok growled.

"You question me? The First Leader."

"Yes." Rok sneered.

The old warrior stepped back as he bent down for his fallen rapier.

"You have grown old," Rok said, drawing his own sword. "The old ways are too much with you. Have you not

228

heard Rawlon's sayings, First Captain of all the Bands?" Rok lowered his body into a battle stance as the older warrior did the same. "Life learns to adapt, just as a river learns how to flow around new bends when the land changes. This is a new race. Their words are well spoken -- spoken from their hearts."

The old warrior held his weapon before him. "And I say they must die for their pollution."

Rok held his weapon ready, moving the blade from side to side with eager anticipation. "And I say they are given mercy. So they can learn."

"I say we should take a couple steps back," Jaric whispered to Kyle and Becky.

The two blades struck with a resounding clang. After the first blow, the two warriors leapt back and began circling -- circling and staring, each looking for a momentary weakness in the other.

With a clash of crossed swords, they closed. Again and again their blades bit into the other, while their long feather-hair danced around their heads with their sudden motions.

In short order, the older warrior's superior swordsmanship had stripped Rok of his rapier. But the old one had come too close.

Rok grabbed the old warrior's arm that held his weapon to keep it at bay. As the old one struggled to release Rok's grip, they began exchanging blows. Each sent his free fist violently into the ribs and face of the other as they fought. Grunts of pain followed each heavy blow.

Finally, with a mighty blow, Rok knocked the rapier loose. Now they were even -- fist to fist and eye to eye.

The other warriors had watched mostly in silence, but now they began to cheer and shout. A few cheered for the older warrior, for their shouts were loudest after his blows struck home. But it became obvious that the majority were for the younger warrior, Rok, as their shouts overwhelmed the cries of the others.

The struggle now began in earnest, their blows pummeling each other relentlessly. The older warrior suddenly fell over, but he took Rok down in his grasp. They continued their struggles on the ground, rolling and kicking, fending off fists with one forearm, striking with the other. In a few moments, youth and strength prevailed.

Becky's eyes grew wide.

Rok was standing over the fallen warrior, astride his panting form. As the old one struggled vainly to rise, Rok struck him again. He took hold of the warrior's left horn in the mighty grip of his right hand. Rok growled, and the muscles in his right arm bulged with his effort as he twisted and slowly bent the horn down.

It snapped with a sickening crunch.

Blood streamed down the left side of the old warrior's face, and he screamed with pain.

Rok rose with the broken stump. He turned slowly and raised it toward the other Kraaqi warriors who had been watching intently. They broke into cheering, chanting Rok's name.

Becky felt her stomach tighten as she fought the urge to throw up.

"We've just witnessed a changing of the guard," Kyle said.

"I wish I could have missed it," Becky replied, her face pale.

Rok threw down the broken horn and motioned for the three humans to follow him.

Becky looked down at the wounded warrior as she passed. "What will happen to him?" she asked.

"He will return to our band's planet. He will no longer fly with warriors. His days are past."

"Seems a bit harsh for somebody who loves life," Jaric said.

Rok stopped and stared at him.

"But who am I to judge?" Jaric raised his hands with innocence. "I'm just a messenger, sent to the Kraaqi."

"Messenger?" Rok asked.

"Yes," Kyle said. "We have news of the utmost importance for you. But not just you, for the entire Kraaqi race." Kyle looked deep into the warrior's eyes. "It may mean the death of not only your people, but all of your worlds as well."

The expression on Rok's face turned heavy. "We will talk of this matter. But first, before we can teach you, you must become brethren of the Band."

"Uh-oh," Jaric said.

Rok smiled at him. "Yes, you must prove yourselves real woman to the Kraaqi."

Kyle and Jaric looked at each other and shook their heads.

Kyle sighed. "First off, Rok. Jaric and I are man." He closed his eyes at his own mistake. "Or men, we're men. Not women." He pointed at his sister. "She's a wo-man." He pointed at himself and Jaric. "We are men." He enunciated carefully.

Rok looked from one to the other. "Whatever." He began walking again, speaking over his shoulder without looking. "But you all smell like Grauntaan manure."

The three looked at each other, shaking their heads.

"Something tells me we didn't really hear that right. Not the last word." Becky smiled.

"Probably Mother's doing, or programming," Kyle said. "Using a kinder, gentler synonym where possible in these translators."

"Well, I guess I'll make sure I use a stronger deodorant for our next first contact." Jaric lifted his right arm and sniffed loudly.

They all laughed.

"I wonder what it is we'll have to do, to be a brethren of the band?" Becky thought out loud.

"I hope we don't have to break anybody's horn off," Jaric said with distaste.

"Well, this is a warrior race." Kyle smiled. "No doubt there will be some kind challenge, or confrontation, in which we have to prove ourselves. But whatever it is, let me handle it."

"You got it," Jaric and Becky said together.

The Kraaqi warriors led the three to a clearing quite near to where all of their ships had landed. A camp was quickly prepared, fires were started, and tents were raised. In fact, at a distance, this camp could have easily been mistaken for a camp of Native American Indians or half a dozen other aboriginal races straight out of the history section of the knowledgebase.

For the first time since they had arrived in Kraaqi space, the three humans felt that they could relax.

As the last tents were put in place and the fires were roaring bright under the fading sun, Rok approached the three humans where they sat together in the middle of the camp.

"We will perform the ceremony of brethren with you."

Rok looked from one to the other. "For man and wo-man to be brethren of the Kraaqi and brethren of the Band of the Stars."

Kyle stood up. "Tell me what I must do."

Rok nodded, but he looked instead at Jaric. "You are dark-skinned, the one called Jaric. Kraaqi see such as a sign of favor at birth."

Kyle bit his lip impatiently. "But humans do not choose their leaders so."

Rok smiled. "Well, it is true your ways are different from ours. You even allow your females to be warriors." Rok shook his head and laughed. "So, we will even allow her the right to be brethren with us this night."

Becky stood up beside her brother. Jaric followed.

"What does the ceremony entail?" Kyle asked.

"We will eat together in friendship. A special meal." Rok motioned for the other warriors to draw near. "I will then tell you of the Kraaqi -- of the history of my people and our ways. I will speak of the worlds where we have dwelled as one for times untold. And I will tell you of our harmony with the land, sky, and water."

"Sounds like a long evening," Jaric whispered to Becky.

"Shsssh," Becky admonished quickly.

"We will tell of our conquests and our endless war with the unholy Hrono."

Becky sighed as her eye caught Kyle's.

"Then you will tell us of your people, your worlds, and your ways," Rok finished.

Kyle turned and whispered. "This will be easier than I thought. We'll incorporate our message into our tale of the human race."

"Yes," Becky agreed. "We'll tell them how the T'kaan

233

destroyed our kind, wiping out all humanity, except us."

"That should stir up their righteous indignation," Jaric added.

"And then we'll tell them the T'kaan are coming here, to do the same thing," Becky said.

Kyle nodded. "Yeah, and then the hard part -- telling them that their only hope is for the Kraaqi and Hrono to fight together with the Mewiis."

Three heads shook solemnly.

"Are you ready?" Rok asked, ignoring their unheard whispers.

"Yes," Kyle answered.

Jaric grabbed Kyle's arm. "Hey, Big K. Let me take the lead on this one. This is way too easy for you. Take a break for once."

Kyle looked at him and smiled. With a wave of his hand, he motioned for Jaric to step forward.

"What are we gonna eat?" Jaric smiled. "You know, I'm hungry now that I think about it."

The band of warriors began laughing.

"We eat the food of warriors tonight," Rok said.

Jaric stopped suddenly. "And what exactly is that?"

"The tail of a rathar."

Jaric contemplated a moment. "Okay. Sounds good so far."

Rok laughed out loud, and the other warriors joined him in a hearty round of laughter.

Jaric looked at Kyle and Becky, and they all added their voices in the merriment, albeit with some hesitation.

As the sounds died away, Rok grabbed Jaric firmly by the arm and began taking him toward a lake that was off to the side of the camp.

Jaric looked back at the camp. "Aren't we gonna eat first?"

"No." Rok laughed. "First, we must take some rathar tails."

Jaric felt his heart begin to sink as Rok pulled him towards the lake. Jaric looked back to Kyle and Becky, who were following with the others. "Uh, I'm beginning to wonder about this little ceremony."

"So are we." Kyle grinned. "I'm just glad you're taking the lead on this one."

Jaric looked back to the lake with an apprehensive expression. "Maybe I ought to ask you what a rathar is?"

Rok began laughing again. "I will show you."

Within a few minutes, they were on a small hill overlooking the blue waters below. As Jaric's gaze followed that of Rok, he felt his stomach tighten.

"They look an awful lot like big crocodiles," Kyle said matter-of-factly. "Except for those horns and the long talons."

Jaric swallowed nervously.

Rok pointed at one of the twelve-foot beasts below them. It was sunning itself with the warm afternoon light across its scaly hide. The long snout contained rows of teeth that protruded ominously from its mouth. It had six, short muscular legs, three on each side, and on each toe a wicked-looking talon curved downward. At the back of their heads two horn-spiked ears rose, giving it a dragon-like appearance.

"Rathars are deadly in the water. But out of it, they are vulnerable. As this one." Rok smiled confidently.

"Could've fooled me," Jaric said as his eyes took in the beasts below.

There were about a dozen of the animals, all of them lying very still beside the blue waters of the lake, obviously in a state of semi-stupor. A few were larger than the first specimen Rok had pointed out, while the rest were slightly smaller. As they watched, one opened its huge mouth and bellowed its roar. The others didn't move as they slept on.

"Oh boy," Jaric said cheerlessly.

"What weapons do we use?" Kyle asked with enthusiasm.

Rok's expression grew puzzled.

"None. We are warriors."

Kyle raised his eyebrows in surprise. But he nodded in agreement.

Two of the large creatures below suddenly lashed at each other, snapping and hissing with great fury. Hunks of mud and grass were flung into the air like a brown blizzard. In another moment it was over, as the two beasts again settled down into their semi-comatose state.

"How do we do it?" Kyle asked again.

A gleam came into Rok's eyes. "You must come upon them stealthily. Quietly. And leap upon their back."

"Oh boy," Jaric repeated.

"You're kidding," Becky half-shouted.

Rok looked at her in surprise. "No, I do not joke."

Kyle crossed his arms, still gazing at the huge creatures below. "Tell us more."

"What?" Becky said in disbelief. "Are you --"

Kyle held up his hand. "Let Rok speak."

Rok smiled. "If you take your hand and cover the front end of their small snout, they cannot open it. As so." Rok demonstrated with his hands around an invisible rathar's snout. "It puts them in a state of confusion. Remember, their strength is only in the biting, not the opening of their jaws. A warrior can hold their jaws shut with ease."

"Cover their mouth," Kyle repeated.

"But beware," Rok warned.

Jaric and Becky held their breath while Kyle looked on impassively.

"They have two special fangs inside their mouth. A single bite is fatal." Rok crossed his massive arms. "And do not let them get their claws on you. For if they do, they will never let go. They will drag you into the water and drown you."

Jaric and Becky continued to hold their breath.

"Also, beware of their tail --" Rok began.

"Why?" Jaric interrupted. "If they fart in your face, it'll kill you?" he asked sarcastically.

Rok rubbed his face in thought. "No. But that is not pleasant either." Rok drew in a deep breath. "No, they use their tail as a weapon, to strike at you once you have gripped their snout. You must watch for that first movement, and grab it before it recoils to strike a second time."

"And ... " Kyle prompted.

"You twist the end quickly with your free hand, and the tip will snap off. You then need to jump quickly as the rathar will freeze for several seconds. When the pain reaches its brain, it will react. At that time, the rathar will be none too happy, to say the least." Rok smiled widely.

Jaric and Becky stared at Rok in dead silence. Only Kyle nodded, clenching his fists with anticipation.

"Thus, you have your meal." Rok raised his hands, palms upwards, indicating how easy it all was.

"Suddenly, I'm not very hungry," Jaric said with great

237

sincerity.

Kyle patted Jaric's shoulder. "Don't worry, buddy. This one's on me. I've got to try this thing one time." Kyle turned to make his way to the lake's edge.

"Tradition says that the leader makes the first hunt," Rok said.

Kyle stopped, and then with a broad wave of his right hand, beckoned Rok to take the lead.

Rok stepped forward at an enthusiastic pace. When he reached the tall grass that led to the lake's edge, he bent forward so that his head alone was visible.

"Tradition says, the wisest take the rear," Jaric whispered to Becky as the others pushed ahead.

"Agreed," Becky concurred.

Becky and Jaric followed until the group came to the edge of waist-high grass -- from here on there was no more cover up to the lake's edge. At the lead, Rok motioned for all to be still.

He crept forward alone.

Rok moved quickly from the edge of the grass to a large boulder. From behind that, he carefully picked his victim.

Nearly ten paces from where he hid, a large male rathar snoozed peacefully. Rok had picked the largest of the bunch as his victim.

Turning back, Rok nodded at him and pointed.

"I can't watch." Jaric covered one eye.

Rok crept past the boulder, carefully making his way out into the open toward the huge rathar. He had almost made it to the rathar when he stopped in mid-stride. The huge beast had raised its hind leg and suddenly began scratching itself. This lasted for almost a full minute, and then as quickly as it had started the beast was back in full repose.

Rok remained frozen, still five paces away from it. With a flash of movement, he took two steps and leapt for the rather.

He landed squarely on the beast's great shoulders with both his hands grabbing for the end of the snout.

The rathar's reaction was immediate

It jumped up on its six feet and stood frozen while it twisted its head backwards. Surprisingly, the huge beast was dead silent as it searched with its tongue and razor teeth to find the tormentor on its back and pull it inside the opened maw.

But Rok was just as fast. He leaned forward over the huge head and clamped one hand above and another below the snout, shutting the mouth and its bared fangs that had begun searching for him. With a quick adjustment, he now had one hand firmly holding the end of the snout shut.

The huge beast froze with tensed muscles bulging.

Rok twisted his body and leaned to one side with his left arm stretched upward, as if he were ready to ride a bucking Brahma bull at some rodeo.

And just in time.

The rathar arched its long body and sent the tail forward with lightning swiftness to knock the enemy off its back. The tail snapped just before Rok's face.

With his left hand Rok grabbed the end of the great tail and in one motion twisted.

They heard a distinct snapping sound.

Even as the beast roared in pain, Rok leaped off and was racing headlong past the boulder and back into the tall grass carrying his trophy before him. In a few more seconds, he was on one knee beside Kyle, breathing hard as he tried to catch his breath.

Back at the lake's edge, the huge rather, now minus the tip of his tail, quickly crawled into the water and disappeared. The other rathars continued their slumber as if nothing had occurred.

"See, it is simple." Rok held up a foot long section of the rathar's tail. As they watched, it twitched with unnerving motions.

"Must be fairly stupid animals," Jaric commented in a whisper to Becky.

"Strong and stupid -- sounds like the males of another species I know," Becky giggled.

Jaric frowned at her.

Kyle chuckled along with Rok as he silently nodded agreement. Before Rok's low laughter faded away, he was off.

Kyle crept quickly to the same boulder from which Rok had begun his hunt. He peered over the top edge, viewing the dozen or so rathars still lounging at the lake's edge. Smiling, Kyle picked the biggest one left, almost as large as the one Rok had taken.

In a flash, he was moving for it.

The beast's muscles quivered as he neared, and Kyle suddenly wondered how good their sense of hearing might be. But he had already crossed the point of no return.

Judging the distance with a quick glance, choosing the animal's huge shoulders as his target, Kyle took two steps and jumped.

He landed squarely on the rough hide. The rathar's low growl rattled Kyle's stomach with its loudness. The head slowly rose right before his eyes. With surprising dexterity, the beast twisted its head almost completely backwards on its neck. Kyle was now staring into a milk-white mouth brimming with rows of teeth reaching out for him. But it was the two large extended fangs pointed directly at him that made his heart skip a beat.

Gripping the beast with his legs, Kyle raised his arms, one above the snout and one below. Beneath him, he felt the rathar lift its body off the ground. Balancing himself, Kyle again judged the gaping target before him, and with a flash, his hands slapped against the upper and lower part of the snout, pinning the mouth closed.

He had to work fast as he felt the huge muscles tensing under him, readying the tail to strike. Kyle's right hand slid over the snout. Placing his thumb inside one of its nostrils, he held the lower jaw with his fingers. Under this lone grasp, the head jerked violently as the beast tried to free itself.

Kyle felt his grip loosen as his heart raced. He struggled to keep a firm grasp, but he knew time was running out. The beast went suddenly still, and Kyle knew the tail was ready to strike.

While he fought to hold the mouth closed with his precarious grasp, Kyle twisted his body, just as the body below him lurched like a locomotive that had come alive at full steam.

There was a rushing of air that swept his face as the tail almost nailed him. Kyle's eyes went wide as he watched the blur of motion that it stopped right before his eyes. Suddenly Kyle felt doubt in his heart; he couldn't believe something so thick would break in his hand that easily. It was so big.

Kyle grabbed the rubbery appendage even as it began its backward motion for a second strike. Grunting with exertion, he twisted with all his might against the rough, scaly skin of the huge tail.

The hollow *pop* was music to his ears.

In his left hand he now held a foot-long section of quivering rathar tail.

It was time to leave.

But Kyle's dismount was almost his downfall.

As his body slid off, he released the suddenly frozen head. But his foot slipped in the wet mud as he stepped, and Kyle was face down with a heavy grunt right beside the beast.

Even as he rose, he felt the huge body next to him begin to come to life. Scrambling, he slipped and fell again. He was getting nowhere fast.

He felt his foot pressing against the beast's rippling side. Kyle pushed against it with a mighty effort -- pushing himself away from the now struggling creature.

Stumbling his way to a half stooping position, he realized the air was full of mud being slung from the Rathar as it too struggled to gain a foothold.

Kyle ran for all he was worth as his feet finally found solid ground.

The sound of pursuit immediately behind him spurred his efforts and sent his adrenaline into overdrive. Fortunately, as Rok had previously explained, after about ten feet, the sounds of hot pursuit grew faint as the great beast quickly tired. In another minute, Kyle was lying on the ground gasping for breath as the intent Kraaqi warriors looked on.

He lifted his head to see Rok smiling down at him.

Raising himself up, Kyle held the still twitching tail up for all to see. Laughing softly, he turned to Jaric.

Jaric took a deep breath, nodding appreciation at Kyle's trophy. With sudden realization that he was next, he shook his head. "I don't know, Big K. I'm not too sure about this one."

But Kyle used their old childhood challenge. A challenge he knew Jaric could not refuse.

"It's time ... to redline. Or you're gonna get left behind."

Jaric's expression changed almost immediately. His brown eyes narrowed, and his face grew hard. "Okay, then. Stand back and watch how this thing is really done."

Jaric took his own course and found himself squatting behind a small clump of bushes farther up from the boulder from where the first two hunters had gone. As all watched, Jaric studied the beasts before him with intense concentration. Seconds passed as he gauged each slumbering rathar and its relative position to the others. He remembered Kyle's mistake and focused his attention on the ground around the three animals he had narrowed as his targets. One of them alone rested on solid ground.

He pointed at the rathar for all to see -- one of equal size to Kyle's.

He slowed his rapid breathing as he pictured his every move in his mind's eye. He went over it quickly and thoroughly, clenching his hands and arms with each move. With silent conviction, he nodded to himself.

In a flash of movement, he was off.

With cat-like swiftness he was on the beast's back, but almost too fast. He would have fallen over the other side if not for a quick, scrambling recovery. But Jaric had slid forward and found that his chest rested against the top of the rock-hard head of the rathar just as it began to move. Jaric reached over and pushed the gaping mouth closed with his hands, and then he quickly wriggled himself off of the neck and back on the shoulders. The immense body under him tensed.

The huge head strained against his one-handed grip. But Jaric held as he prepared himself for the strike.

Seconds later, Jaric had the tail in his grasp, snapped it off neatly, and jumped nimbly off. Unlike Kyle, Jaric landed squarely and sprinted back to the others without the beast ever giving chase. He smiled widely as he trotted up.

"And no laundry bill." Jaric laughed at Kyle.

Kyle bowed to Jaric, laughing, acknowledging he had been bettered -- this time.

All eyes now turned to Becky.

"Well," she said, looking at the lake beyond. "Anything you two bozo-boys can do, I can do. And better."

"Becky ... " Jaric began, as he held his hand out to stop her.

"No, let her be," Kyle said.

Rok nodded agreement with Kyle as they watched her lithe form step away.

Becky eyed the remaining beasts before her. She was mildly surprised at how quickly the unnipped rathars settled down again, once each of the nipped rathars had disappeared in silent disgrace into the deep water. But there they were, almost as peaceful as when they had first arrived.

She guessed that since there were no actual fatalities, really just their tails and pride hurt, that any natural alarms faded away with the quick return of their semi-comatose state.

Or else they were as stupid as Jaric had guessed.

Becky reached the boulder Rok and Kyle had used, and

she now looked around until she had spotted two Rathar off to themselves. One was large, over ten feet. The other was smaller, probably an adolescent and only slightly larger than her.

She bit her lip, unsure about which one to try for, when the decision was made for her.

The larger rathar suddenly raised its head with its eyes wide open. First it stared in one direction, and then it turned to the other and with decisiveness moved away and silently slid into the lake, disappearing in a rippling of water.

Becky eyed the smaller beast.

With two quick steps she leaped and judged correctly. As she wrapped her legs around the smaller Rathar's midriff, she felt it rise almost immediately. She waited for the head to twist for her, so she could slam her two hands across its mouth just as she had watched the others do.

But it never happened.

In a flash, the Rathar was racing headlong at a terrific gallop straight towards the lake, its six legs a blur a motion.

Clamping her legs together to keep from falling, she grabbed the neck with her right hand and waited for the tail to snap.

Again, it didn't happen. The tail did not strike.

She felt herself falling off even as she tried to lay her body flat against the rough, bumping hide below her. Becky grabbed desperately for something, anything, to hold onto to, but each time the beast's jerking movements shook her grip loose. Somehow, she just managed to stay on as her body was slammed time and again against the rock-hard hide as the beast raced in a blind panic.

The speeding rathar turned sharply, almost throwing her off, as it barely missed running straight into a larger cousin.

But just as she pushed herself back up on the racing beast, her heart sank with dread as she saw the waters of the lake approaching at a breakneck speed.

Water splashed all around her before Becky released her grip, feeling the body of the rather sliding away out from under her. As the tail brushed under her hand, she gripped it with both hands while she choked back the water that was shooting into her mouth and nose. She twisted and felt it pop.

Her head dipped below the water a moment, but she came up sputtering and coughing.

She looked around. She struggled to stand, but her feet kept slipping in the soft mud until she fell back into the water. With a sickening rush of emotion, she realized she was in four feet of water -- and in a rathar-infested lake.

Behind her, she heard the air fill with a multitude of roars as the other rathars awoke with alarm. There were other sounds that mingled with their fierce roars, but she couldn't quite make them out above the din.

As she splashed and tried to get her feet on firm ground so she could get out, she suddenly realized that several large heads had popped to the surface nearby.

Becky realized with a sickening dread that the hunter had now become the hunted. It wasn't a good feeling.

She opted against trying to stand and instead kicked and stroked with her arms and headed back for the shore. It seemed so close.

Above the shoreline, she saw the Kraaqi warriors running en masse towards her, waving their blasters in the air. A second later the water all around her was alive with movement as the water exploded in a dozen places. She felt the unseen bodies surging towards her just under the surface as several waves engulfed her.

Certain death was only moments away.

The air sizzled with a dozen blaster bolts as the water exploded in every direction -- the bolts zipped into the water and found their marks. She suddenly realized that there were more rathars in the lake than she had imagined, their injured bodies twisting and rolling in pain all around her as they erupted on the surface. Something heavy moved against her right leg, and she kicked violently at it as she screamed for the first time.

The water erupted a third time as the remaining rathars on the beach plunged into the lake before the shouts of the on-rushing Kraaqi. Some passed so close she could see the whites of their eyes. Once again, she choked on the water that filled her nostrils and mouth. Gasping for breath, Becky finally felt solid ground under her feet. She tried to stand, but her legs seemed to be made out of rubber.

Seconds later, she felt hands pull her up out of the water and then drag her onto shore, where everything seemed to go hazy.

The Kraaqi rolled her over and watched impassively while she seemed to cough up half the lake for several minutes. Finally, Becky found she could breathe once again.

She looked up into the faces that surrounded her and smiled. Slowly, she pushed herself into a sitting position and then held up the section of the tail that she had nipped off.

The warriors began shouting and roaring with laughter.

Rok pushed his way next to her, with Jaric and Kyle close behind. Jaric and Kyle's faces turned from concern to obvious relief when they saw her holding her trophy aloft.

Rok nodded at Becky and laughed. "You are very brave. Kraaqi do not normally hunt the young rathar -- they are too unpredictable."

Becky felt like punching him but just she rolled her eyes in utter disbelief. In the next moment, she was laughing along with the rest as relief spilled over her.

"Now you tell me," she blurted between laughs.

The Kraaqi leader laughed even louder. "Rok begin to like wo-man race a lot," he said, pointing to Jaric and Kyle too.

"Man. We're men." Kyle repeated. He pointed at Becky. "She's a wo-man," he enunciated with slow, deliberate syllables. "We are all hu-mans."

Rok laughed louder. "Too many mans."

With a sweep of his arms, he urged two Kraaqi to lift Becky to her feet. Soon they were all back at the camp and the roaring fires. Rok sent the remaining Kraaqi back to the other side of the lake to finish their hunt. Rok then instructed the three humans to get into clean, dry clothes and to begin cooking their meals. The final part of the ceremony would commence when the others returned with their own rathar tails.

Before the lone, mauve sun had set behind the line of hills on the horizon, the entire band had returned and were cooking their meat over the roaring fires scattered around the camp. Rok surveyed the laughing Kraaqi with a steady eye, chewing his rathar tail appreciatively. He held his steaming hunk of meat toward the three humans.

"Rathar tail. You like?"

Jaric pulled his meat from the flames and eyed the blackened steak warily.

Kyle brought his own out of the flames, sniffed at it,

and then took a huge bite. He grunted with satisfaction as he chewed, nodding at the Kraaqi leader.

Jaric looked Kyle with a questioning look.

"Tastes like chicken." Kyle grinned.

Jaric nodded and took a bite. "Yeah, not bad," he mumbled.

Rok smiled as he placed his meat on the ground and stood. He put his hands upon his hips and looked slowly around at all the warriors happily eating and conversing with one another around the campfires.

He raised his head back and shouted. His warrior's cry filled the air, effectively silencing all their conversations at once.

All eyes fixed on him.

"Life ... is for living!" Rok shouted with his arms spread wide.

Cheers and war whoops answered him from all the Kraaqi band.

More than once the words *Yes!* and *Life!* were shouted by warriors sitting around the roaring campfires. A few jumped to their feet and began dancing around in small circles with the dancing light and shadows reflecting against their bodies.

"Yeah, I can relate," Jaric whispered to Kyle.

Rok stepped beside the three humans and looked down upon them. "Tell us your strong words now. Words of wisdom, from a hoo-man."

The three looked at each other, hoping the other would volunteer. Finally, Becky stood decisively.

She looked deep into Rok's brown eyes, and then she looked around at the rest of the band.

"Life ... is the greatest adventure!"

Jaric and Kyle shouted their own war whoops in agreement.

The air now filled with Kraaqi war cries as their voices roared agreement and mingled with the shouts of the humans. Rok's smile widened, and then he motioned for silence from the rowdy warrior band. He sniffed the air deeply several times like some hunting animal and then stopped, holding his last breath a precious moment, savoring it, and then slowly he let it out. He strode boldly to the very center of the camp and stopped.

A great smile was still upon his lips.

"I will now sing of the Kraaqi. Who we are, where we have come from. Where our future lies. And most important, what it means to be Kraaqi."

More war cries filled the air.

Rok nodded, raising his muscular arms to the sky above. He held his dynamic pose only a moment. Slowly, he lowered his arms back to his side.

A warrior beat a steady rhythm on a large drum. Soon more drums joined the first, louder and louder with the growing rhythm. New instruments added their distinctive voices, some close to the roar of electric guitars, others that sounded like nothing the humans had ever heard before, something out of a dream, they cried in such a strange and surreal way.

The insistent rhythm grew more powerful.

Rok's powerful body began moving with that growing cadence. Behind him, a low chanting began. He bowed his powerful body, waving his head and his horns like weapons as he moved from side to side. His arms kept in sync with the music's rhythm as his dance grew more intense.

The three humans looked on with wide eyes as they

listened in awe.

The Kraaqi leader slowed his dance in order to begin his song. Now with both dance and words, he sang the story of the Kraaqi bands.

His words told of the beginning. In that beginning, the Kraaqi were and always had been one with the sky, earth, and water. But they were never farmers. Nor herders.

Always, they had been the hunters. Warriors. And lastly, Seekers.

Their ships had always set them apart. Band apart from band. The band with the fastest, most powerful warships was always the strongest band. Every warrior youth knew that his first day of manhood would be as pilot of his first small craft, or as a crew-member of one of his band's larger warships, probably an uncle or father as his courageous captain.

Other than a glorious death in battle, his most honorable death would be in the bowels of his favorite ship set afire in his memory by the warriors of his own band, if he was honorable enough, or a warrior of rank.

In that distant beginning, their warships had been of the water, taking them upon the mighty rivers and distant seashores of their home world -- to new conquests.

Finally, their warships had conquered the skies. In that age, the Band of War had grown to be strongest over all the others on that first home world. For the first time, all the bands were united under its legendary leader. His sons and then his son's sons continued that valiant reign. During this long age of succession, the Kraaqi built the first ships that were able to travel into space.

"Think their race is as old as the human race?" Jaric whispered to Kyle.

"I don't know," he whispered back.

Rok's song continued.

Once again new, unexplored horizons beckoned the bands. New conquests. The urge to explore these new worlds was great, and the bands soon spread themselves out among the nearest stars and were living upon the worlds that orbited them.

Another great age passed. And another.

Yet always, the famed longships of the Kraaqi were their pride. It was these fast, dangerous warships that had always been their true claim to fame. Kraaqi ships had even equaled that of their newfound enemy -- a terribly dangerous and hated enemy. The Hrono, sworn enemy of all the Kraaqi bands.

The hated Hrono, they who worshipped technology and science above all else and who despised the beauty of sky, earth, and water. They trampled life and strangled it under their submission. The most hated Hrono.

"Uh-oh," Jaric whispered as Rok lowered his head a moment in silence.

"We don't have time for this," Becky added.

Kyle reached out and pressed her forearm, urging silence.

Rok again began his dance, weaving his head repeatedly in a semi-circle, waving his dreaded horns as though in a battle challenge.

He sang now of the wars with the Hrono, the victories and the defeats. Rok's powerful voice rang out with names of Kraaqi captains and their ships. He sang of courage and valor, of great sacrifice.

Rok's voice changed. It became deeper as his piercing eyes looked around the gathered warriors once more.

Last, he sang of his beloved Band of the Stars, how they had broken away from the age-old Band of Thunder and formed their own band. Now they could seek out new worlds of their own.

He sang on, and now even the Band of Thunder sought out new worlds to explore, though their warlords still led the Kraaqi ships into battle against the Hrono.

Yet, there was more to life than war, Rok sang with emotion.

His song stopped suddenly.

Turning toward the three newcomers, he spoke. "You are a new race, unknown to us. We will now ask for your history, for your song, as is asked of true brethren of our band, the Band of the Stars." Rok's hand beckoned them.

Kyle and Jaric exchanged glances.

"I think I should do this," Jaric said.

"I agree," Becky added.

But Kyle hesitated, rubbing his chin in thought.

"Listen, Big K. Not only am I the one who knows the history of our people better than you," Jaric began.

"Yeah, I know. You always were a better student than me," Kyle interjected.

"I'm also the only one in this group who has any rhythm," Jaric added with a smile.

"Okay, rhythm-boy. Go for it," Becky laughed.

Kyle's eyes narrowed. "Can you convince them that their real enemy is the T'kaan?"

"I have to. I will have sing from my heart about the death of the human race. I'll sing so that they will have to feel our loss, and our loneliness. They will know what it means to be the last. And I will tell them who killed our species."

Kyle nodded.

"Remember Minstrel's song for humans?" Becky reminded Jaric. "Use that along with the memories of your history lessons. Tell them what it means to be a human."

"Let them know that we are a good people too, that we love nature and respect it," Kyle said.

Jaric nodded, and then he stood and took his place beside Rok amid the large circle of warriors and the dancing light of the fires.'

"Before I start, I must ask you. How long until we can meet with the great chieftains of all the Bands?

Rok thought a moment. "Protocol requires we seek an audience. This takes time ... maybe two weeks. Maybe longer."

Becky turned to Kyle with a sudden urgency.

"We don't have that kind of time," she whispered.

"Looks like we're going to have to break protocol," Kyle said.

"And then convince them that their only hope is to ally themselves with their lifelong enemy," Becky said.

Jaric looked at the warriors gathered all around with intent expressions now fastened upon him.

He took a long, deep breath. And started.

"Humans rose on our home world far away from here," he sang with a husky voice as the drumming rose again.

"On a planet we called Earth ... "

Chapter Twenty-Seven

Minstrel's body expanded and flowed over almost the entire interior of its spherical music-ship as the song it was playing filled its very soul.

Saris slowly entered Minstrel's domain, surrounded by the haunting music that had drawn her here. Now it almost overwhelmed her with its dark intensity, its musical power. She looked around the room at the effervescent form of Minstrel and wondered how this strange being could spread itself out so thin. Suddenly the music changed, filling the air with a throbbing of finality -- a great, crying melancholy.

Tears came to Saris' eyes without her knowing why. She noticed the edges of Minstrel's plasma body, how the alien had extended it to play the ship and to make this soul-consuming music.

The music stopped -- without ending.

Saris looked around. "What was that music, Minstrel? It was so ... moving."

Minstrel pulled its body together into a tighter, more compact form. Minstrel knew this was easier for most alien species when conversing. It was difficult for them to talk to shimmering air.

"It is my *Symphony of Humanity*."

Saris wiped a tear that was trickling down her cheek. "But what was that section you just played?"

Minstrel's body glowed brighter. "Its working title is, 'The Last Stand.' I got it from Mother, from her knowledgebase. This repository within Mother is the last source, the last memories of that noble species."

"The Last Stand?" Saris asked.

Minstrel's body began pulsating. "The Last Stand, where the last members of humanity gathered for their final battle with the T'kaan horde."

"Go on," Saris urged.

"The commander, General Lo, had his own plan. Victory was impossible, he knew, but he was going to take out as many of the T'kaan as he could before they died. It was this act that actually made the survival of Mother and the children possible those first precarious years."

"We don't realize at times, what the outcome of our actions may turn out to be," Saris said.

"And so the mighty T'kaan Third fleet gathered around this lone planet, as much to watch the spectacle as to fight. It was now the end of their Second Cycle of Life. They had destroyed another race, they had feasted upon the dead, and they had laid their eggs. Soon their young maggots would come forth, feasting themselves upon the rotting remains of humanity. And then upon each other. In that way, only the strongest T'kaan survived."

Saris shuddered with repulsion.

"With the end approaching, with the T'kaan ground forces converging and their main fleet in tight orbit, Lo ignited the planet. The shock wave of the dying world destroyed most of the T'kaan Third, even destroyed the strange Great Horned ship, the ship that all other T'kaan ships enter at least one time each cycle. Why?" Minstrel's body pulsated with a surge of energy. "We do not know." Minstrel's body vibrated faster. "At first there was destruction. And then, as is their way, the other two T'kaan fleets began sending replacements. This was both to protect the young and to rebuild the destroyed Third. A new Great Horned ship was begun. Among those depopulated systems where Mother lived, she was not bothered at first by the remnants of the T'kaan. But soon, the fleet grew again. Mother's victories drew too much attention. For their safety and survival, Mother and the children had to abandon their search and leave. And so, they found their way here."

The Mewiis leader nodded, sighing deeply. "We who remain must keep the memory of them alive so that they are never forgotten -- so humans are never forgotten."

"Yes, but there may yet be a hope for them." Minstrel added. "In addition to providing the schematics for her super-weapon, and other system enhancements for their ships, Mother is going to approach the technology-wise Hrono with a request to try and save the human race -- with genetic engineering."

"Cloning?" Saris thought out loud. "That is not perfected, even among the Hrono."

"Not simply cloning. They could take the DNA and genetic material collected from the children, perhaps adding artificial genetic material to make up for the small number of specimens."

Saris thought a moment. *There are only three humans, and two of them are closely related, brother and sister. Even with the possibility of cloning and artificial DNA and genetic enhancements, the DNA pool seems simply too small. What would the results be? Human DNA and artificial DNA combined.*

Would it still be the human race?

"I hope the Hrono can help." Saris' voice revealed her doubt. Then, with a shake of her head-tail, she remembered why she had come. "But it was more than your music that drew me. I have word, both of our tests with the hybrid weapon and news from the outer frontier." Saris sighed deeply as she paused.

"Please continue."

"The super-weapon works, but only for five firings. After that, the circuitry melts. It can be repaired, but not during a battle." Saris' countenance became serious. "We have already begun refitting our capital ships. With our major shipyards, we surmise we can complete the upgrades to our battle cruisers and battleships within two months."

"Do we have that much time?" Minstrel asked. "Do the Kraaqi and Hrono? They have not even started to refit their ships. Mother will just now be arriving at the Hrono home world. The children should have made contact by now; it's been two days since the Mewiis ship dropped them off." Minstrel paused in thought. "But we can't be sure since there's been no word from them. Their continued silence concerns me."

"I agree," Saris said. "It is not a good sign."

"Even after their initial contact," Minstrel continued, "the children will have to arrange an audience with the chieftains, and that will also take time. Something we are fast running out of."

"That is my other news." Saris breathed deeply, letting it out slowly to calm herself. She looked at Minstrel with concern in her eyes. "The first attacks have begun."

Minstrel's body stopped moving. In a flash, Minstrel shaped and morphed. Standing directly before the Mewiis leader was a replica of her.

Saris stared in wonder ... at her own face.

"Are they feints? Feelers? Or are they attacking in brute force?" The mirror-Saris asked.

"We ... we think they are feints that Mother warned us about. But all of our ships that have encountered the T'kaan in battle so far -- and none carried the hybrid weapon -- have been destroyed. The most we have gotten from them are brief messages. The T'kaan are ruthless," Saris added somberly.

"Well, that is the best we can expect. They are testing your ships, your strengths. Are you deploying your defenses so as to draw them to our planned battle site?" the mirror-Saris asked.

"Yes. But it is suicide for those ships and their crews."

"We must accept those dear losses, Saris. If we can dictate the place and the time of the battle -- most importantly the time -- we will greatly improve our chances of victory."

"But war is full of unexpected circumstances. Will the T'kaan not test the Kraaqi? And the Hrono?"

"They will destroy the Mewiis first. Yours are the first planets they will encounter. After Mewiis, the Kraaqi worlds would be in their projected path. And finally, the Hrono worlds."

"The Kraaqi worlds are greater in number. Only a portion extend into a narrow middle ground between ours and the Hrono. The Hrono worlds extend far out toward the Chalasta sector, still unexplored."

"They will assume from the data systems they raided on your ships that the Mewiis are the weakest. T'kaan always attack the weakest first."

"They will learn otherwise," Saris growled.

"They will learn, we hope, that a combined Kraaqi-Hrono-Mewiis fleet with warships fitted with the super-weapon is a force to be reckoned with."

"But with these feints of the T'kaan already started, our time grows short, even though we may subtly dictate the place of battle. Will there be time to form a combined fleet? Will it come in time to save our worlds?" Saris pleaded.

"Mother believes she can get the Hrono's support quite quickly. With their technology and their vast shipyards, they cannot only upgrade their fleets in short order, but assist the Kraaqi as well. It is the warrior Kraaqi, with their famous longships, that we need the most. But seeing that the Kraaqi ships are the most numerous, we will definitely need the Hrono shipyards to help upgrade all of their capital ships in time."

"It is their divisive bands. If they ever gathered under a single leader, they would control the Three Kingdoms. Fortunately, they love exploration more than war these last decades."

"Warrior-explorers," the mirror-Saris murmured.

Saris looked into her mirror image's face -- deep into her own eyes. "Will Mother be able to form this alliance in time to save our children?"

The mirror-Saris laughed.

"The children have a saying about the MotherShip, one I discern to be quite true, that emphasizes all her inherent power with the fewest of words."

"Tell me."

"Don't mess with Mother."

Chapter Twenty-Eight

"They are a great enemy." Rok's voice held great sadness.

Two days had passed since the children had met Rok and the Band of the Stars, and still they found themselves encamped on the same wild planet trying to convince the Kraaqi leader about the peril of the T'kaan.

But a breakthrough had finally occurred that very hour.

The children's words had finally touched both Rok's heart as well as his mind, and now he fully understood the terrible peril that not only awaited his people and the worlds they lived upon, but also the fate of countless other races and peoples and their worlds if the T'kaan were not stopped.

"We must go to the Council of Chieftains at once and warn them," a warrior next to Rok said.

"Well spoken, Sharak," Rok acknowledged.

Becky smiled hopefully at Jaric and Kyle.

"But there is one other thing we must tell you," Kyle said.

The warriors of the Band of the Stars had all risen to their feet. The fires all burned low, but the dancing light glistened across each somber face. All eyes turned to the three humans.

"Speak, hoo-man," Rok said.

Kyle faced Rok, but he spoke in a loud voice so all could hear his words easily. "The T'kaan are too powerful; they are too numerous for the Kraaqi to fight alone. They will destroy you."

Warriors growled and cursed Kyle's words for long seconds. Rok alone stood silent, searching the faces of the somber humans. At last Rok raised his right arm, and the warriors grew silent. But it was a sullen and haughty silence.

"The Kraaqi are a great and mighty people. Our ships are strong. Our captains are the bravest in all the universe. We will destroy the T'kaan," Rok said with force.

Now the warriors broke out into a chorus of shouted challenges to this newest of enemies -- an enemy who not only destroyed entire races, but their planets as well. The volume of their shouts and war cries soon became deafening.

Once again, Rok raised his arm for silence.

"You have more to say. Speak," Rok commanded.

Jaric reached into his belt and pulled out his data pad. He walked over to Rok and handed it to him. "You and your warriors must watch this. It is a recording of my people's final battles with the T'kaan. You must watch this first, and then we will talk."

Rok took the data pad and together with a few of his select warriors retired to sit around a fire at the edge of the camp. The three humans watched as the Kraaqi faces peered at the screen where the data pad was now replaying the horrific battles between the humans and the T'kaan.

"How long will it take them?" Becky asked.

Kyle's eyes never wavered as he continued peering at the Kraaqi warriors and the data pad. "I don't think it will take long. Mother and I picked some very convincing battles."

Twenty minutes later, Rok and his warriors rose as

one and made their way back to the campfire where the children sat. Kyle, Jaric, and Becky got up and met them halfway.

"The T'kaan are a terrible enemy indeed," Rok said.

"Yes," Jaric agreed.

"We will ask the Mewiis to ally themselves with our war fleets. After all, it will be the Mewiis worlds they will attack first," Rok said.

"The Mewiis are not warriors," Sharak growled. "They are weak."

Rok turned to the Kraaqi warrior. "*Sh'alott mon qittra. Krang mon K'halbot.*"

"Why don't our translators work on these ancient Kraaqi proverbs?" Becky looked from Kyle to Jaric in turn.

"It must be some kind of old, forgotten dialect. That's a guess." Jaric shrugged. They turned back to the Kraaqi.

"Yes." Sharak's eyes narrowed as he nodded slowly with agreement.

Becky looked from Jaric to Kyle, but both remained silent. She looked back to Rok. "What'd you say to change his mind?"

"An ancient saying of my people. From the mother tongue." Rok's eyes became far off. "It means, 'Even the Rossa will fight, when its children are attacked.'"

Kyle and Jaric grunted appreciation, as did many of the Kraaqi.

"Even the tiny Rossa is formidable when its young are threatened," Sharak added.

"It is still not enough to defeat the T'kaan," Kyle said.

Silence filled the air, and the low crackling of the logs suddenly became audible in the absence of any other sound. Rok's eyes narrowed, as did the other Kraaqi warriors.

"It will have to be enough," Rok said.

"You know it won't be," Kyle countered.

"Listen," Jaric began. "We're not talking about simply losing a battle here. We're trying to tell you that the T'kaan will destroy you, your ships, and every single Kraaqi world. Everything and everyone will be killed." The young man paused, and he looked around at the faces of each warrior to make sure his words had sunk in. "You need to ally your forces with the Hrono and the Mewiis in order to defeat the T'kaan."

"This!" Rok spat with violence. "This is unthinkable."

"Think the unthinkable, First Commander. Your race depends on it," Becky growled.

Jaric put his hand on Rok's shoulder. "Think as a wise leader, Rok, and not simply as a warrior." Jaric's eyes pleaded with Rok. "Think as would your wisest leader."

Rok straightened. His ebony face was one of silent and intense concentration. Behind him, the low murmuring of the others began to grow.

"This cannot be," Sharak said. "We cannot fight *with* the Hrono. It can never be."

"This new enemy is greater than any we have ever known," Rok said. "We must take this information to the chieftains." Suddenly Rok's face hardened, as though in deep thought.

"They will agree with me, Kraaqi and Hrono can never fight together," Sharak said.

"Perhaps," Rok began, his face still revealing his inner turmoil.

"We can't waste time," Kyle said. "The T'kaan fleet is

bearing down on us. Weeks may be all there is left. Precious weeks."

"Is there any Kraaqi leader with vision?" Becky pleaded. "Is there any Kraaqi leader who thinks beyond yesterday?"

"Rawlon," Rok whispered.

"Rawlon," Becky repeated. "Is he a leader of vision?"

"He is First Captain of all the Kraaqi. Our greatest leader, our greatest warrior." Rok stroked his feather-hair in thought. "He is a young leader, the youngest Kraaqi to ever become First Captain. And a leader of great vision."

"Rawlon is not a chieftain. We should bring this dire news before the chieftains first," Sharak growled.

Rok turned to Sharak. "Rawlon will know how we should proceed. He will know if this alliance is necessary, or even possible."

"No!" Sharak spat.

"*K'deth Kallah. Band'a Ho'Jak Tal. HronKraaqa.*" Rok's eyes burned into Sharak's.

"*Pala'tah,*" Sharak sneered. "You speak the words wrong."

"No matter -- my word stands. We go to Rawlon. We will seek first his wisdom, and then we go to the chieftains." Rok crossed his burly arms. "Or do you challenge my right as First Commander, Band of the Stars?"

Sharak bared his teeth as he stared straight into Rok's burning glare. The eyes of the two warriors burned into the other for several intense seconds.

But Sharak did not challenge.

"Good, go prepare the ships. We leave immediately." Rok turned. "Break camp!" he shouted to the rest of the warriors.

"How do we fly out?" Becky waited on Rok as she motioned to Kyle and Jaric to remain still. "We cannot allow our ships to pollute this world. We cannot fly out using our ship's engines."

"Well said." Rok's expression revealed he was impressed with her words. "I shall call our frigate. It will put a tractor beam on your fighters and carry them outside the biosphere. There you can safely use your engines."

"Good," Becky said.

Rok turned to walk to his own ship.

"Wait, what was the proverb you just spoke from your old tongue?" Jaric asked.

Rok turned back and smiled. "It is a new proverb -- but I used it in the old tongue. One of Rawlon's own." Rok laughed to himself. "One has to know the Kraaqi to appreciate it. Bands sometime war against each other for differing reasons. It could be their honor was challenged, or a pact was broken."

"Go on," Kyle urged.

"At times, a small band will ally itself with another band, in order to fight one of the strongest bands," Rok said.

"And that is the saying?" Jaric asked.

"Not quite," Rok said. "Rawlon's proverb is short, but means that at times it is even necessary for two bands with a long-time hatred to ally themselves in order to defeat a greater band. A hard thing to accept, but Rawlon's words are full of vision."

"That's why Sharak said you misinterpreted Rawlon's proverb," Jaric said.

"Yes," Rok agreed. "Because I applied them not

between two feuding bands that need to ally." Rok nodded his head, his eyes deep in thought a moment. "But I spoke in the context of a Hrono-Kraaqi alliance being necessary -- " Rok whispered the last, as though not believing his own words.

"Then you too, as Rawlon, are a leader of vision." Jaric grinned.

Chapter Twenty-Nine

"We are inside the inner sanctum," Rok whispered with reverence.

Kyle looked into the darkness. "I guess we wait now?"

"Yes, we wait for Rawlon and his staff to convene for their morning session." Rok stretched his arms, trying to rid himself of the tiredness that suddenly seemed to cover him along with the surrounding darkness. The Kraaqi warrior sat unseen by Kyle, though Kyle could hear his movements and knew Rok was trying to relax his body.

Kyle eased himself down. "So, why did we sneak onto this world yesterday, Rok? And then after risking our lives, and I mean Jaric's life back on the surface, why didn't you and I simply waltz into the main underground city like any other member of this band?" Kyle paused, reliving the last twenty-four hours. He had asked Rok this same question already, but Rok had growled with indifference. But now it was only the two of them; the other Kraaqi warriors of Rok's band were still at the outskirts of Kalaya, the great underground city, along with Jaric and Becky.

Kyle hoped he might finally get answer and learn more of these strange warrior people and their traditions.

Even in the darkness, Kyle knew Rok was sitting cross-legged with his eyes closed -- still as a shadow. Rok would be holding his head up, listening intently for sounds of the staff's arrival. Most important, his mind would be ready and alert.

"It is 'The Way,'" Rok whispered from the darkness.

Dumb way, Kyle thought. "Well, if we can walk freely

into the city, why did we have to land our fighters with such secrecy?" He licked his lips. "Now you've sneaked us inside here through some kind of secret entrance, which I would think is known to very few. Or I'd hope so." Kyle waited.

"This entrance is known only to the leaders, the commanders of all bands. I was Second, now I am First Commander," Rok explained. "So I use it now."

"But Rawlon does not know another leader is here," Kyle said. Even as he finished, almost through the darkness, he could see the Kraaqi's wry smile.

"I have side-stepped much protocol and saved much talk. Most importantly, I have saved *us* time." Rok breathed deeply. "I will speak these hard words, these important words, to Rawlon face to face and eye to eye. He will see that I speak truth."

Kyle nodded in the darkness. "And me?"

"You are hoo-man," Rok said. "You are the enemy of the T'kaan. He will hear in your words and see in your eyes the same terrible truth that I heard Jaric sing at the ceremony of Brethren." The darkness became silent as Rok paused. "Rawlon is First Captain, our greatest warlord. He understands war, and will understand the dire implications of this coming new war. With his wisdom, he will see the way in which we should proceed."

Kyle tried to rub the tiredness out of his heavy eyes. As his body relaxed, he gave way to a huge yawn.

Rok remained silent with his own thoughts, but Kyle still had one more question.

"What about the chieftains? The other bands and their leaders?"

Silence answered for several long minutes.

"Most of the bands follow Rawlon's leadership already. They will listen, though this thought of fighting alongside the Hrono will be hard." Rok paused, letting out a long and loud breath. "Very hard."

"And the chieftains?" Kyle prompted again.

"The *old* Chieftains," Rok said, emphasizing the second word. "They understand their rules and scrolls better than they understand life and war. They will remember the old wars with greater heart than they will be able to comprehend a new, unknown enemy that requires us to throw away the old hatreds."

"What will we do?" Kyle asked after the silence had settled again.

"I will let Rawlon decide," Rok said. "But I see only two paths. One is that Rawlon's words will convince the old chieftains."

"And the other path?" Kyle asked into the darkness.

"We will have to break the horns of all those who oppose."

Chapter Thirty

Jaric watched silently as Becky looked out the window over the underground city park. These vast underground cities were weird places, but the Kraaqi sure seemed to enjoy their subterranean civilization. He had been surprised when, after all their hiding on the surface after they had landed in secrecy, Rok had simply led them to the city's entrance, flashed his big smile at the guards, and down everyone went into the city ...

It had taken them two days to reach this world, but in that time Rok had shared much about Kraaqi civilization.

The Kraaqi built their cities underground so as to allow the harmony of the planet to remain undisturbed in its natural state above. On their first world, the Kraaqi had built great cities on the surface. But they soon realized that the sprawling metropolises interfered with the natural harmony of the wildlife as their giant structures replaced the native habitats. To remain at one, the Kraaqi began to build their cities underground -- even on that first world. With the discovery of subsequent planets, all cities were built underground.

Rok led them to Rawlon's home world, the home world of his band. As evening settled, Rok and Kyle left on their mission to Rawlon. The rest of their group came to the well-lit suburbs of Kalaya, the capital city, and the rented rooms of a major hotel.

That had surprised him, as once the warriors had actually reached this hotel they had simply pulled out their credits and obtained a room while Rok and Kyle continued on separately into the heart of the city as if nothing covert had happened.

He watched three of Rok's Kraaqi warriors becoming boisterous over a card game they were playing in one corner of the room. For a moment, it looked like they were ready to pull their short daggers out and settle the score with blood, but at the final moment they seemed to agree on the outcome and slowly returned to their seated positions -- laughing and slapping each other on the shoulders as comrades once again.

Jaric's thoughts returned to his favorite obsession as the lights of the ceiling danced across Becky's hair like sunlight on a waterfall.

He had blown it on the Mewiis ship.

He clenched his eyes shut with regret.

"Are you all right?" Becky asked with concern.

Jaric smiled at the sweet sound of her voice. He opened his eyes. "I'm -- " he paused. "I'm just stupid, that's all," he stated matter-of-factly.

"An honest man. They're hard to find these days," Becky said with a smile.

Jaric grimaced.

Becky laughed out loud. With a twinkle in her eyes, she walked up to the couch where Jaric lay stretched on his back. She first put the back of her hand on his forehead, checking him for fever. Satisfied, she then brushed her fingers through his dark hair. "I thought you were a goner for sure back on the surface, Jaric."

Jaric rolled his eyes and whistled. "You weren't the one lying inside its throat either." He felt himself shiver as he recalled his recent brush with death.

She leaned closer.

Jaric's body stiffened with rising excitement. *Is she*

going to kiss me?

Instead, she sniffed the air around him.

Jaric sighed audibly.

"You need to take another shower," Becky announced with confidence.

"I've already had eight," Jaric complained.

"You'll probably need ten more then," Becky said. "Whatever that plant predator uses to digest its prey ... " She paused in thought, trying to find just the right word.

"It stinks," Jaric finished for her.

Becky smiled mischievously. "Well, I was going for a more descriptive phrase, one that would explain your distinctive cologne in a more colorful way."

Jaric laughed out loud.

Becky continued, placing her finger next to her forehead for intellectual emphasis. "I would say this most unique aroma you have picked up is best described as a cross between a dead animal ... "

Jaric laughed louder.

"... that's been dead a about month, mixed with some sun-ripened dung ... "

Jaric's laughter grew so hard his stomach began to ache with sheer delight.

" ... and some well-preserved dinosaur farts, all mixed together thoroughly and then mixed in a bottle of Guantan piss."

"In other words, it *stinks*." Jaric laughed.

"Yes, *you* stink," Becky said between their laughter.

Jaric leaned back as his laughter slowly subsided. Of course, he could no longer tell he had any kind of aroma left on his person. His nose had been numb and unable to notice smells since he had been swallowed yesterday --

and then quickly vomited back out -- by the plant predator.

Becky's gentle jabs, as well as Rok and Kyle's not-so-gentle jabs, had already gotten old to him and had even begun to wear on his nerves at times.

Still, there was one side benefit -- Becky had not left his side since the Kraaqi had pulled him feet-first out of the predator plant's bile. Now here they were alone at last. He would have nurtured some kind of romantic hope for their current semi-privacy, except for the embarrassing memory of their last time alone together and his fumbling revelation of love for her.

"I wish I could take back last time," Jaric said in a low voice.

"You mean, when you told me that you loved me?" Becky asked.

He sighed despondently. "Yes, I wish I could take that all back."

"What, you mean you don't love me now?" She placed her hands firmly on her hips as her eyes narrowed.

"No, no. I still love you. What I mean, well, I wish I could've told you in a different way."

"You mean without knocking me down and nearly beating me black and blue?"

Jaric smiled. But it faded when Becky did not smile back. "Yeah, it just turned out all wrong. Nothing like I ever dreamed it would."

"All right, lover boy." The faintest of smiles flashed across her mouth. "Tell me what every girl wants to hear."

Jaric felt his heart begin to pound like a runaway jackhammer. Beads of sweat suddenly covered his forehead, and his mouth went bone dry. "Um," he began with masculine finesse.

The young woman raised a single eyebrow knowingly.

"Um -- " Jaric repeated, still speechless and not exactly sure what every woman wanted to hear.

"You're going to blow this again, aren't you?"

"No, no," Jaric blurted. "I'm just making sure I say it right."

"I see, thinking before you speak. What a concept."

"Yeah, that's right."

"Well, at least you're thinking again. Okay, let's forget about what happened on the Mewiis ship." Becky's eyes searched his with a sudden intensity. "Just tell me what you *feel* for me."

With her beautiful face suddenly so close to his that he felt her breath caress his face and her eyes looking deeply into his own, Jaric felt his heart begin to beat right out of his chest. Even as he felt his old confidence return, he was overwhelmed with a feeling of impending disaster.

But Jaric was going to profess his true feelings exactly the way he had always dreamed it.

"I love you," he said with a confident sincerity.

Becky smiled at him, like he always knew she would. A smile that was part happiness -- part love. Her face bent nearer.

They kissed tenderly, their lips pressed ever so softly.

The moment seemed to last forever. Time stood frozen with their mutually held breath. Jaric felt her silky blonde hair fall around each side of his face with tantalizing softness. Finally, as their faces parted and their eyes opened, the beating of the other's heart was easily audible.

275

Tony Chandler

"I love you, too," Becky whispered.

276

Chapter Thirty-One

The sounds of marching footsteps echoed from the darkness of the stone walls.

Kyle heard Rok begin to stir himself from his light slumber, still crouched and ready like a true Kraaqi warrior. Kyle's eyes had adjusted during the night, and he just could discern Rok's shadowy form directly across from him.

Kyle rose from where he had rested his shoulder against the wall in a half-crouching posture.

"You will wait for my word," Rok whispered. "Stay."

Kyle nodded agreement and rested on one knee as he listened in silence. Even in the darkness, he could feel his tension building with each approaching footstep.

The sound of marching footsteps entered the great room that was still bathed in complete darkness; muffled orders were quickly given, and the footsteps moved apart with precision rhythm. Suddenly, a single light pierced the darkness with a surreal intensity. Around that shining beacon, the immense room took shape.

Seconds later another torch was started; then a third and fourth until a dozen burned bright in large metal braziers. Each brazier glistened under the flames, revealing their bronze stands. The huge bowls that held the flames stood six feet above the rock floor, each bowl held aloft by an intricately carved staff. The dancing flames sparkled against the metallic carved images with a hypnotic effect.

Kyle watched as the room's true dimensions became visible with the growing light.

The dozen warriors now drew together and formed a single line facing the large entrance. As the next group of warriors stepped through, the first dozen drew their swords from their scabbards as one and brought the flat blade of each weapon before their faces in salute.

It was obvious to Kyle that the second group was comprised of leaders. But the warrior who walked at the rear, his head held high and sure, seemed subtly different from all the rest. His piercing gaze surveyed the room as if he owned it, his great muscular chest rising with each breath and straining the leather tunic he wore. There was no doubt in Kyle's mind that this warrior was the greatest of all the Kraaqi gathered in this room.

"Rawlon!" Rok shouted from his hiding place in the darkness.

Kyle almost jumped out of his skin with the unexpected shout.

The single word evoked an immediate reaction from every one of the Kraaqi warriors. Those who wore sheathed swords now drew them out, but they did not bring them up in salute. Each of the Kraaqi quickly spread out in a battle crouch facing the darkness that engulfed the edges of the great meeting room.

Only Rawlon remained visibly unalarmed as he gazed steadily in the direction from which his name had been shouted. With unhurried steps, he strode toward the still unseen Rok, a confident look on his face.

Finally, when he reached the edge of the darkness, he stopped. Two bodyguards quickly stepped on either side of him with swords raised.

"Who are you?" Rawlon's voice was powerful and deep and carried a tone of absolute command.

278

"I am Rok, First Commander, Band of the Stars," Rok said from the darkness.

Rawlon nodded a moment with recognition, and then he motioned at his two bodyguards. As they stepped away and left the Kraaqi First Captain alone, Rawlon raised his head higher and paused, looking like a dangerous animal that was ready to strike.

With a flash of movement, he drew his sword from the scabbard on his left hip, and then with his other he drew a dagger from the scabbard on his right hip. He stood with both arms raised, the weapons steady and pointed directly at the darkness where Rok now stood.

"Come to me Rok, Band of the Stars. Bring your weapons raised for battle," Rawlon growled. "For you have insulted my rank and title as First Captain of all the Kraaqi."

Kyle almost groaned but hushed the sound. He was beginning to think these mighty warriors were just a bit too sensitive about things.

"I come, First Captain, the greatest warrior of all the bands."

Rok stepped out of the shadows, his sheathed sword banging against his leg as he walked cautiously toward Rawlon. As he neared Rawlon his right hand moved toward his own weapon, but instead of drawing his blade, with a flick of his hand he unbuckled the belt upon which his weapons hung. Raising his arm toward Rawlon, he held out the belt and sheathed weapons a moment -- and then his hand opened. The belt and weapons fell with a loud clatter onto the rock floor.

Rok's steady gaze never left Rawlon's face. Now without his weapons, he raised both arms, his hands clenched but empty.

"I come in peace, Rawlon. But I admit, I have broken protocol and dishonored you. For this I must die."

"You come with stealth and secrecy. Your band has not been announced at my table. Nor has your name been given me so I might receive it." Rawlon stepped closer. With a flash of his weapons, he twirled the blades and held them point down with his arms raised high. In a single quick motion, he sheathed first his sword and then his dagger. In another motion, he unlatched his belt and, in similar fashion to Rok, held it out and allowed it to drop with a clatter of metal.

"I will kill you with my bare hands," Rawlon growled.

Kyle was shocked when Rok did not speak but instead began circling warily as Rawlon assumed his own battle stance. Surely Rok could explain his actions to Rawlon in a few sentences and stop this stupid fight.

Instead, Rok roared as he lowered his head and charged. Rawlon in turn lowered his head as he pointed his horns at Rok. He charged as well. With fierce growls they closed on one another, and the stone walls rang out as horn struck against horn. The two warriors twisted their necks with surprising speed, each in an attempt to bring their own horns into the face and neck of the other with a deadly intent.

The sound of their fists striking and landing with solid blows on the other's bodies added to the visual ferocity with which the attack began.

Kyle stepped from the shadows into the dancing firelight.

"Stop!" he shouted.

The two bodyguards raced to either side of Rawlon as

both he and Rok leapt apart, panting.

"I ordered you to wait," Rok panted.

"Who, or what is this?" Rawlon asked, pointing at Kyle

"This is Kyle of the hoo-mans. He too is a leader," Rok said.

"Is he friend?" Rawlon asked, still staring at the human, his fight with Rok now forgotten momentarily.

"Yes. In fact, he has come to help us, to warn us. I have accepted that warning and brought it to you as First Captain of all the Kraaqi."

Rawlon turned to Rok. "Is that why you have dishonored me by this unannounced entry into my sanctuary?"

"Yes, the hoo-man brings word of a new enemy -- an enemy many times more powerful than the Hrono. They come quickly." Rok paused. "And they are more powerful even than the great Kraaqi. I have seen the data."

Rawlon pointed at Kyle. "He is enemy of our new enemy?"

"Yes," Rok said.

"Then I must review this data as well." Rawlon was already reaching for the data pad Kyle had pulled from his belt. "If what you say is true, your dishonor will be excused. And I must determine how best to meet this new threat. If not, then you and the hoo-man must pay." Rawlon glanced at the data pad as he read intently.

Kyle watched in silence, hoping this Kraaqi leader was as wise as he was strong ... for time was fast running out.

Chapter Thirty-Two

"There are too many ships, Guardian."

Guardian stood mute, his red visuals staring solemnly at the viewscreen full of Hrono warships.

"I have been plotting possible receptions with the input from the Mewiis databases concerning Hrono culture and makeup. There are several solutions that present themselves that include a large force meeting us," Mother said.

"Explain." Guardian forced the single word in his electronic monotone, attempting to communicate like Mother.

"It is well known that the Hrono worship technology. In fact, it is this obsession that makes them so incompatible with the Kraaqi." Mother paused two nanoseconds as she received the Hrono instructions to land and immediately calculated her orbital entry and landing pattern down to the most minuscule detail. She also analyzed the message and ran it against all of the scenarios she had stored. In each scenario, she ran a simulation of possible actions and reactions and placed several hundred of the most promising in background mode.

"There are two extreme reactions to such a race meeting a new life form, and especially a life form that is technologically advanced, sentient, and self-aware."

On the viewscreen and within Mother's sensors, another Hrono fleet suddenly appeared out of hyperspace. Mother began running her scenarios with this new data.

"They may worship me as a deity. Or they may seek to destroy me, out of fear." She paused, but she knew Guardian could not reply and that he could not really converse. She continued. "But there are many other courses of action between those two extremes. We must be wary."

Guardian downloaded data directly from a connector in the console before him. His processors strained under the massive load of data that Mother sent to him. With his limited abilities, he understood the bare facts contained. He understood the tactical data; he understood the implied threat of the warships and their weapons. He even understood Mother's tactical plans, in case there was battle.

But his programming could not comprehend the emotional and philosophical algorithms she was also analyzing against the data.

Deep inside his mechanical frame, Guardian once again felt a cold emptiness. He felt a void that was so black and deep that it sometimes threatened to engulf him. But try as he might, his processors could not understand the complexities of sentient life. He understood the hows and whats of the data he analyzed -- but not the whys.

And Guardian so wanted to understand.

"Wait." Mother paused long nanoseconds. "There is something odd from my sensor scans of Hronosium."

Guardian waited patiently.

Mother began her landing maneuvers. On the viewscreen, the strangely featureless planet grew. The robot magnified the image, searching for the familiar land and ocean features a planet normally displayed. But even as the planet filled the viewscreen, there remained only the unnatural bleakness that seemed to cover every part of the Hrono home world.

"I have completed an initial analysis of Hronosium," Mother said. "The entire planet is enveloped by a single artificial structure. Under the roof that covers this planet there is a single vast city, a concrete and steel maze that envelops all. A planet-city."

"No trees," Guardian chimed simplistically.

The words, uttered after the completion of his analysis of Mother's scans, took more processing power than the act of battle.

Mother had recently added and upgraded his primary programming so Guardian could provide a close-in defensive role for the children when they ventured away from her on a planet's surface. More recently, she had been adding code for voice interaction.

She liked that. As did Guardian.

"I do not think the children would like this world," Mother observed, ignoring Guardian's silence. Her desire for companionship forced her to continue the one-way conversation. "It is different," Mother added.

The huge, white robot stood silent as a statue. He turned his head toward one of her visual sensors located at the ceiling as his red visuals glowed brightly.

Mother understood his unspoken words.

"Historical images of the children continue to replay in your near-term memories, Guardian. I have not commanded their retrieval." Mother analyzed his internal signals. "I miss them too," Mother confided.

Guardian's processors suddenly spiked with activity, and his free memory dropped to zero as he tried to form thoughts -- to form a single thought and form a single sentence of his own origination.

"I have seen this internal activity before, Guardian. I do not understand, but I surmise you wish to be sentient," Mother said recalling Guardian's schematics. "Your hardware could not handle the load. I would have to deactivate you and almost rebuild you from scratch."

Guardian's red visuals dimmed.

"The children have valued your strength and protection, even though you are not sentient," Mother added quickly. "Your labor and duties, though in the background, are comforting to them. Recall, too, how your dynamic battle programming enabled you to single-handedly rescue the children from inside the T'kaan complex. Without you, they would have died."

Guardian's red visuals glowed brighter. "I want ... to live."

Mother noted with concern that Guardian's systems had begun to overload. He was trying to actually manipulate his limited programming, attempting to take memories and words and form them into a thought. Without his realizing, Mother allowed Guardian access to her own circuits via the connection they still shared. Only with her massive circuits temporarily integrated with his had he been able to complete this one gargantuan task -- to utter a single thought, his own thought.

Mother allowed Guardian more of her own self.

The robot became one with Mother as his relatively simple systems joined with hers. In a sudden instant, he had access not only to seemingly unlimited processing power and short-term memory, but his electronic mind also realized the existence of the vast knowledgebase. Even better, he could access it now. He could use it. Suddenly his first, virgin thought formed.

Guardian could think.

"I desire ... to interact ... with the children. Like you." Guardian stuttered. "I want to be ... alive."

Inside, Guardian was flooded -- no, he was

overwhelmed -- as his circuits joined with Mother. It was like nothing he had ever known before. It was an exquisite, mind-numbing bliss -- an instant of becoming self-aware, of knowing what he wanted and who he wanted to become.

And *why*.

An eternal second of sheer ecstasy.

Gone.

Mother released herself, afraid of what had suddenly happened and not fully understanding all of its implications. Guardian had not been designed for this type of processing, no matter how much he desired it. Still, Mother gathered her vast internal powers and once again analyzed Guardian's schematics.

Within minutes, she resumed their one-way conversation.

"I have developed a plan to upgrade your programming. There is a high probability that it will make you partially sentient. After the conflict with the T'kaan Third Fleet is over, I will download instructions to the Fixers and begin work."

Guardian nodded mechanically.

"But be assured, the children are comforted knowing you are near, that you can service my repairs and provide tactical support. That you are my eyes and ears when you escort them away from me." Mother paused. "Even though they cannot interact with you sentiently."

The robot's frozen visage continued to stare.

"Guardian, there is a reception committee for me at the docking facility. They are well armed."

The robot's tactical programs prepared itself for action.

As she entered the polluted atmosphere of Hronosium, the larger Hrono warships that had been flying escort remained behind in orbit. The fighters continued their escort of Mother toward the landing site. A beacon activated to guide her. She locked onto its signal and made final preparations to land.

"Four days we have traveled, skirting around the Kraaqi border. The Hrono have communicated to me that they have successfully tested the hybrid weapon on a computer simulation of one of their cruisers. A plan for refitting the capital ships has also been developed. The upgrades to both the Hrono fleet and Mewiis fleet should be completed in just over six weeks. I am hopeful the Hrono will assist the Kraaqi in upgrading their own warships, using their more numerous shipyards."

Silence echoed inside the bridge.

"But they must first agree to such an alliance," Mother thought out loud.

Her engines had not even grown silent when she first felt the imprisoning force of the Hrono tractor beams.

"Two tractor beams have been activated, effectively trapping me. I am now calculating their positions." Several consoles began filling with data. "The Hrono are entering."

Guardian turned and faced the door.

They entered, each of them wearing a red jumpsuit while their green, scaly skin gleamed with an iridescent reflection from the room lights. Their faces were humanoid except for a reptilian snout, and their skulls were hairless like the Mewiis. But instead of a bone-ridge and head-tail, the Hrono had a twin row of upturned scales that extended from their forehead up over their skulls and down the back of the necks, similar to the Stegosaurus records in Mother's knowledgebase.

Mother magnified her visuals on the steel blue eyes

common to every Hrono and realized that each eye had twin pupils.

The first Hrono male approached Guardian and began studying him visually. Pulling out a small sensor device, he continued his examination. A second Hrono stepped beside him, one with a noticeably larger set of head-scales.

"Is this the sentient machine?"

"Though its internal programming is quite sophisticated, it is not sentient." He closed his hand-held sensor and turned to his companion.

"Then where is it?" the Hrono with the larger crown of scales asked.

"I am the sentient machine." Mother's voice emanated from every speaker in the room.

Every Hrono head turned slowly around, a look of intense awe on their faces.

"Where are you?" the second Hrono asked. "Speak to me, I am Senior Technologist Jysar."

"I am the ship."

The first two Hrono looked at each other in surprise. The second Hrono, who seemed to be in command, began making hand gestures to the others; they obeyed and began pulling out their own sensors.

"Where is your main processing located?" he asked with an enthusiastic tone.

"That is none of your business. I am MotherShip, and I have come with grave news. The Mewiis have already communicated to you about the approach of the T'kaan fleet. I must review my files with the Hrono leadership so we can develop an effective strategy."

"Our battle leaders will handle this tactical data, as we have handled the Kraaqi in the past." The Hrono waved his hand. "We'll simply take your data files when that particular need arrives. Right now, I have more important work." His face suddenly showed puzzlement. "Where shall we begin? I had no idea that the sentient machine was the entire ship."

Senior Technologist Jysar's eyes suddenly opened wider than seemed possible as he stared at the sensor data from his hand-held unit. "You have biological systems integrated with your hardware!" he said, obviously impressed.

"Synthetic DNA memory systems."

"This is fabulous," Jysar said excitedly. "No wonder you are sentient; those memory systems must contain enough data to fill tens of millions of libraries."

"Much more," Mother said. "Enough to fill the libraries of many thousands of planets combined."

"Astounding," Jysar whispered in awe. He looked slowly around the bridge. "Now, where in space will I begin?"

"What are your intentions?" Mother asked.

"Oh." The Hrono walked casually up to a console and began typing. "We're going to disassemble you -- piece by piece. After that, we're going to reverse engineer your systems."

Chapter Thirty-Three

"They think we're here to break off their horns."

Curja, Second Leader to Rawlon of the Band of Thunder, stepped back through the large, golden curtains that served as the ceremonial entrance to the Hall of Admittance where the high chieftains of all the Kraaqi were gathering. He joined the small group waiting outside.

"No wonder," Rawlon said. "We have broken almost every protocol in coming here." He waved his right arm upward. "I have also ordered every band to gather here under Crisis Protocol -- something only used for war with the Hrono or for the overthrow of the Council of Chieftains."

Kyle eyed the three Kraaqi warriors. Furtively, he glanced back to Jaric and Becky, who were standing off by themselves. Ever since Kalaya, Jaric and Becky had been inseparable. It had affected Kyle like nothing else in his entire life.

For the first time since his childhood, he felt utterly alone.

Kyle had stayed near Rok these last, tempestuous days as they journeyed to meet the chieftains, and Rok had seemed to understand. A close bond had already formed between the two. Kyle now felt as though he had more in common with the Kraaqi than he did with his own kind -- Jaric and Becky. He felt so awkward now when he was alone with them.

Rawlon's voice penetrated his troubled thoughts, and he forced himself to concentrate. There were more important things at hand than his personal feelings.

"The chieftains and their personal guards are heavily armed," Curja added.

"Most prudent," Rawlon said. "If I were in their place, I would act no differently." He turned and spoke to the First Commander, Band of the Stars. "What say you, Rok?"

Rok shrugged and readjusted the shoulder belt that held his assault blaster tight against his back. "It was I who led my small band to your world. We also broke protocol. But, the circumstances demand such bold action. We do right." Rok looked at the three humans. "The T'kaan are an enemy to be feared."

"Yes, you did well," Rawlon said. "I apologize again for your wound."

Rok smiled at the painful memory of their brief battle.

Smiles of mutual respect flashed between the First Captain and Rok.

"Well, your arm was nothing to what happened to me," Jaric said.

Kyle chuckled, remembering the adventures of the previous week as they had sought out Rawlon, leader of the greatest Band.

Jaric's eyes widened. "How was I to know that there were carnivorous plants! Rok had warned us about the myriads of carnivores that might kill us on your jungle planet. I guess this little thing escaped his memory."

Rok and Kyle began laughing. Now that it was over, the humor of Jaric's near-death experience had become a running joke between Rok and Kyle. In fact, the last two days it had been their prime source of entertainment as they continued to torment Jaric with their witty remarks.

Becky stood closer to Jaric, unconsciously putting her arm around his waist. "I know the Kraaqi are one with their worlds, and you like to keep your planets in a state of natural beauty, but when half the denizens can devour you, well, that's a little too natural."

Rawlon smiled with a glint in his warrior eyes. "If you learn the ways of my world, you can easily walk its surface without being eaten. Even by the Xaktius."

Kyle and Rok howled with laughter.

"Remember, Becky, we spend most of our days in our underground cities. That is where we live and work. The surface is for recreation. Relaxation."

"What recreation? Not getting eaten?" Becky shook her head.

"Tell me again, Jaric," Rok said with mischief in his eyes. "Few have survived being eaten by a Xaktius. What was it like?"

Kyle's smile grew wider.

A vein began throbbing in Jaric's forehead as he took a deep breath. "It all happened so fast." Jaric paused, a serious look on his face.

Rok and Kyle waited, their eyes sparkling.

"I know it's taken me two days to wash that stench off."

"We know!"

Their shared mirth became contagious. Rawlon and Curja joined them. Even Becky had to turn her head as she stifled her own giggles.

Jaric finally smiled as Kyle thumped him playfully on the back.

But the seriousness of the moment finally returned.

The three Kraaqi warriors and Kyle stepped away in order to discuss the imminent meeting and the dire message they had to convey.

Jaric turned to Becky and looked longingly into her

eyes. "There is one thing I'll never forget about being eaten by that Xaktius, though."

Becky smiled. "What?"

"That was the first time you told me, 'I love you,'" Jaric said.

She brushed his face tenderly. "I thought you were gone. It was ... such a shock. One minute you're walking with us through the dense brush." Her hand paused, resting against his cheek. "The next, this giant *thing* has eaten you whole!"

"It's a dangerous universe," Jaric whispered with warmth. Wrapping his arms around her waist, he held Becky like he had always dreamed.

They kissed tenderly.

When the kiss finished, they held each other, wishing the moment would never end.

"Warriors should not hug each other," Curja said as he stared at them indignantly.

Becky smiled at Curja's glare of disapproval. "Maybe warriors wouldn't be so grouchy if they got more hugs."

Curja's face changed to puzzlement.

Rawlon burst out in laughter. "Perhaps we should allow our females to become warriors, Curja. Those long journeys to the stars would not be so long."

Curja's eyes opened wide. "But, the females do not have horns."

"Neither does the wo-man. Nor the hoo-mans. But they are warriors," Rok said.

Rawlon raised his eyebrows knowingly at Curja.

Curja waved his arms in disgust. "I give up. First we are going to be allies with the Hrono, and now we are letting our females become warriors. The world is changing too fast for me."

"There comes a time when all things must change. That is life," Rok said.

"Well spoken," Rawlon returned.

"And those willing to change -- to adapt -- are the survivors," Kyle added.

The three Kraaqi eyed him with respect.

"The warriors of Kraaqi will prove to be so," Rawlon mused. "I have convinced the leaders of all the bands to assemble. They will see the need, the wisdom, behind this alliance." He looked from one to the other. "Even the old chieftains will see this."

Curja's eyes narrowed with doubt. "I hope you are right."

"If they don't, I'll break all of their horns. *Personally*." Rawlon spoke the last word with deadly earnestness.

Rok and Curja nodded agreement.

The golden curtains moved as another Kraaqi warrior stepped inside.

"The high chieftains will see you now," the Kraaqi guard said.

Rawlon stepped forward and led them all through the golden curtains. Boldly, the party entered behind him.

The Great Hall lived up to its name.

Kyle guessed that there were at least ten thousand Kraaqi leaders gathered in the seats around them. The room itself was well over ten times the size of the main room in Minstrel's Circle Ship.

Everywhere the glint of precious gold sparkled from the massive, beautifully decorated tapestries that hung from the high ceilings -- reflections of gold even twinkled from the delicate designs woven into the carpet they walked upon.

The wood panels of the walls were also inlaid with a multitude of gold figures depicting legendary deeds of old -- great Kraaqi heroes and their enemies in battle. The central section of the ceiling over the main stage contained a massive painting with heroic Kraaqi figures in full battle regalia -- its background depicting the sky also gleamed with gold-flecked paint.

"I think they like gold," Jaric whispered to Kyle.

"I would've never guessed," Kyle shot back playfully.

As the gathered throngs watched them enter with a rising murmuring, the three Kraaqi and three humans walked confidently toward the central platform. Upon the stage before them, seven ceremonially glad figures glared at them with suspicious eyes from their golden thrones -- the high chieftains.

Each step seemed an eternity to Kyle. But he managed to ignore the thousands of eyes that were burning into him. Instead, he focused on the seven pairs of suspicious eyes watching him draw nearer to them with each step.

"I see that most leaders of the bands are already here," Rawlon said to Curja as they marched. "It will make this easier."

"The old ones will not so easily agree to an alliance with the Hrono. We have been enemies for too long." Several long steps were taken in silence before Curja spoke again. "The Mewiis also concern me. Can they fight? Will they hold their own in a pitched battle?"

Kyle's eyes narrowed as he marched beside Curja with Rawlon in the lead. "They can fight. I have already seen them in action with the T'kaan."

"The Mewiis allow their females to lead." Curja sneered. "And their males put up with it!"

"We will put our concerns before the Mewiis when the time comes, Curja." Rawlon stared forward as their journey drew to its end. "Now, we must convince the chieftains that the greatest crisis in the history of our people is upon us."

Curja growled under his breath as the six stopped before the raised platform of solid gold.

Rawlon raised his head defiantly to the seven faces above them.

Around the Great Hall the murmuring died away into a tense, electric silence. Ten thousand pairs of eyes focused on Rawlon and those standing with him at the feet of the chieftains.

One of the seven Chieftains rose, grasping the side of his robe and draping it around his aged body like a cloak. At first he peered at the seated throng, ignoring Rawlon and those with him. Finally, his weathered eyes fell upon the six figures that stood before him.

He nodded. His gray feather-hair and dark-stained horns glinted with the bright lights of the Great Hall. When he spoke, his stentorian voice echoed throughout the hall.

"Rawlon, First Leader, Band of Thunder." The old Chieftain began pacing before his seated peers. "The greatest band of the Kraaqi. Their First Leader, also First Captain of all the bands, has led his flagship the *Thunderer* to this place. In fact, all the warships of his band are now in orbit around us."

He looked over the throngs once again, his words directed to them.

"Rawlon has sent a call out to every band, to all of you gathered this day, and to those still heeding its urgent signal and still en route. This is a call of supreme crisis." He shook his head slowly. "A call seldom used and only sent due to the most dire of circumstances."

The aged chieftain paused directly before Rawlon. He raised his arms, spreading his palms upright. "Speak, Rawlon." He held the ceremonial pose as he glared at the three humans. "And tell us who these are that violate our solemn assembly."

A loud murmuring swept the hall.

Rawlon marched forward to the lowest step that led up to the chieftains. He gazed unwaveringly at the chieftains as the cacophonous voices began to fade once again behind him. He waited patiently until the last voice was silent.

"I bring word of a new enemy." The First Captain's voice was loud and sure. He turned away from the seven chieftains to address the assembled throngs. "It is a powerful enemy who will annihilate all the Mewiis in the coming weeks. Easily."

A low murmuring began.

Rawlon looked around at the faces in the Great Hall. "An enemy who will destroy all the Hrono. Easily."

From every part of the Great Hall cheers went up.

Rawlon waited a moment. After a few moments he raised his right hand, signaling silence.

The throngs obeyed.

"This enemy will then make war with the Kraaqi ... "

Even as he uttered the last word, shouts and war cries filled the hall. A thousand challenges were issued to the heavens and this new enemy.

Rawlon shook his head, and the gathered warriors slowly grew silent again. He turned and stepped up until he was midway to the chieftains. Rawlon spoke directly to the seven.

"And the Kraaqi will be defeated."

From their seats every warrior rose as one in the Great Hall, all of them shouting and waving their fists and rapiers until the sound became a deafening roar. The thousands of combined voices shook the very walls of the building, so great was their cries of rage and indignation.

Rawlon continued upward until he was eye-level with the chieftains. The other six had also risen at the outrage the First Captain had uttered. Now all seven gathered around him.

The shouts suddenly died away.

"Who is this great enemy, Rawlon? What is their name? Where are their fleets?"

Rawlon looked deep into the First Chieftain's eyes.

"T'kaan."

"Are these the dread of T'kaan?" The Chieftain who had first addressed the throngs pointed at the three humans.

"No," Rawlon said. "These are hoo-mans. A race the T'kaan has already destroyed. But!" Rawlon shouted the last word as the throngs roared back. His single word silenced them. "But, these three are the only warriors to have ever defeated the T'kaan ... and lived!"

Shouts and cheers echoed throughout the Hall now -- cries for victory.

The First Chieftain raised his arm for silence, and the shouts subsided. "Then let us hear about these destroyers of life from ones who have fought them in battle. Is that the First Leader of the hoo-mans?" He pointed at Jaric.

Jaric looked over at Kyle and whispered, "We need to show them that we do not judge each other by our skin, just because the Kraaqi do so. They think I am leader merely because I am dark skinned."

Kyle nodded. He felt Jaric's trust. Still, something

pained him deep inside. But with a determined look, he marched to the lowest step, carefully following Rawlon's earlier lead.

"Great Chieftain, we humans do not judge merely by the color of our skins. Our leaders are chosen because of their courage, their valor, and their skills. I am the appointed leader."

Jaric looked over at Becky standing next to him and briefly shared a smile. Becky's eyes sparkled in return as she smiled agreement.

The chieftain looked uncertainly at Rawlon, who nodded his own agreement that Kyle was leader. Shaking his head with disbelief, he spoke. "Well said. This is a most strange thought to us who know our dark warriors as the bravest. But continue, tell us how we can defeat these T'kaan."

Kyle turned and slowly looked around at the gathered audience. He finished by facing the chieftains again, a grim look on his face. He spoke, his voice deadly serious. "The T'kaan are not just destroyers of life. They are destroyers of entire races -- of entire worlds."

Kyle now turned and faced opposite the raised dais so he could address the Kraaqi throngs.

"The T'kaan live their life in four cycles. The first cycle is war. But the T'kaan wage an *unholy* war. They make war for two reasons only. First, for the joy of killing. Second, for the propagation of their species. Because, for the T'kaan to reproduce, they must destroy entire worlds." Kyle paused a moment, staring into the faces of the crowd. "They must destroy entire races."

The crowd erupted, roaring out their anger, a deafening wave of pure emotion. On the stage behind Kyle, Rawlon raised his arm for silence.

Kyle nodded. "They are evil. The T'kaan are killers. After they have destroyed an entire race and feasted on its dead, they lay their eggs to hatch their maggot young. This is the second cycle.

"The last two cycles we know little about. They must mate during one of them, but which we do not know. But there is one other thing we have learned -- during the fourth and last cycle, each and every major warship will journey inside the Great Horned ship. For what purpose, we do not know. But of the three fleets we know about, each has this one, mysterious ship." Kyle crossed his arms and looked back to the Chieftains and Rawlon.

"You heard his strong words," Rawlon said to all. "This race called T'kaan love only two things -- war and mating. With their never-ending war, they pollute every world in which they come into contact. So then, it is up to us to stop them."

Great cheers went up. Cries for victory roared throughout the great hall from ten thousand throats.

The First Chieftain raised his arm. "Your words confuse, Rawlon. First you say the Kraaqi will be defeated. Now you say we can prevail. Speak true words to us, once and for all."

Rawlon smiled; he knew the time had come. He turned. "We can defeat this great multitude of warships in one way, and one way only."

A hushed silence swept the room as everyone focused on Rawlon's next words.

"Only a combined fleet can destroy this terrible foe. A fleet the like of which the universe has never seen before. A fleet under my command, the First Captain, leading every ship the Kraaqi can put into space. And ... " Rawlon paused. "One wing will be composed of the entire Mewiis warfleet."

The hushed silence turned to growing astonishment.

"The other wing will be comprised of the warships of the Hrono ... "

Even as the last word came out of his mouth, the ferocity of the shouts came like a hammer blow from the heavens. The thundering of their voices deafened and pounded Rawlon and his companions almost as harshly as physical blows.

Trying to fend off the vocal assault, Rawlon shouted back, barely heard even by the chieftain next to him.

"They will be under my command! The Kraaqi will lead this great fleet!"

The wall of sound increased, assaulting their senses in wave after wave of sonic aggression. Becky raised her hands protectively to her ears, as did Jaric and Kyle, for they seemed to be the focus of this living nightmare of sound.

Jaric fought against his growing panic, and he suddenly turned to Kyle and shouted so his voice was barely audible in Kyle's ear, only inches away.

"I don't think they like our idea." Jaric paused, fighting his rising panic. "Or maybe they had some bad burritos for lunch."

"Don't be stupid with your jokes," Kyle shouted back. But he knew it was Jaric's way, his way of dealing with pressure. Kyle also fought the urge to scream back, to run -- to do something.

"Don't be stupid," Kyle whispered to them all.

Chapter Thirty-Four

"We can't evacuate entire planets!"

Saris looked at Minstrel's flowing body with outrage. Taking a deep breath, she continued. "Over half of our fleet is either being refitted with the hybrid weapon, or they are in orbit around our shipyards to have it installed. The smaller trade ships simply don't have the capacity for such mass evacuations. Nor the time before the impending attack!"

Minstrel brought its form together into a more compact design but still floated near the edge of the ceiling above the newly promoted Mewiis admiral.

"Then we must accept the losses. We have not heard from either Mother or the children. The assigned time has passed." Minstrel's form pulsated with emotion. "It must be assumed that the Kraaqi are not cooperating. Perhaps even the Hrono are balking?"

Saris' eyes flinched with pain. "In less than a week, the first Mewiis planet will be taken. Each week after that another Mewiis world will die, along with the children and parents who live there. We don't have time for this age-old bickering!" Saris shouted.

"One would think that faced with the same harsh reality, the Hrono and Kraaqi would come to the same conclusion and agree to fight together to prevent it." Minstrel sighed.

"Old hatreds are slow to die. Stupid things that make us hate each other -- differences in culture, ethnic differences ... " Saris turned in frustration, the rest of her thought unfinished.

"We Minstrels have always been troubled that life

302

forms can hate another life form simply due to differences in body features. Even something as simple as different shades of skin."

Minstrel took its body and poured it onto the floor in a twinkling stream. As it touched the floor, Minstrel formed its plasma body into the shape of a Kraaqi warrior. The warrior laughed out loud, his feather-hair shaking with his great mirth. In that instant his body flashed, and there appeared in his place a Hrono Technologist, laughing still, his hands now on his hips.

"It is most troubling. These differences in beings, that this variety between life forms should cause such hatred," the Hrono/Minstrel said.

With a wave of motion, Minstrel transformed exactly half of its body.

Saris stared wide-eyed at the visage before her.

The left half of the body was Hrono, the right side was Kraaqi -- exactly half.

Saris bent her head as she studied this surprising form before her. "It seems ... familiar," she stammered.

Again the twinkling stream poured, but upwards this time, back to the ceiling.

Saris shook her head. "Sometimes I don't understand it either. The differences in culture, maybe I can. The Hrono totally destroy their worlds in a way -- covering every inch with their planet-cities and completely destroying the natural environment with their technological powers."

The Mewiis female walked to the large window where bright rays of sunshine streamed through. "The Kraaqi are the opposite extreme, spending all of their lives either in their great warships in space or in their underground cities, leaving each world's surface and its living cycles complete -

- no matter how dangerous they are."

"There should be a happy balance somewhere in between," Minstrel mused.

"But enough of philosophy." Saris' head-tail flicked from side to side decisively. "Our recon ships have discovered the first T'kaan battle group bearing down on Zailia, the outermost world of the Mewiis kingdom. What can I do? I am the appointed admiral of the entire Mewiis fleet now. I command great warships." Her head-tail grew limp. "What can I do?"

"We must hope that Mother and the children can do the impossible -- and quickly," Minstrel said.

Chapter Thirty-Five

"Even with this imminent danger, the Hrono are preoccupied with technology," Mother said with electronic calm.

"Technology obsession," Guardian added as Mother spoke through his speakers.

"Yes!" Jysar said enthusiastically. "And now I am consumed to understand living technology. What a dynamic concept." The Hrono began pacing energetically around the bridge. "We Hrono have a saying, 'Technology is the key to happiness -- the key to life.'"

Guardian's red eyes glowed.

Jysar stared with a wide-eyed excitement at Mother's bridge. "Taking state-of-the-art hardware and software and integrating them into a powerful warship and then making it alive. What kind of a race created you?"

"The human race," Mother said. "But that is enough. Order your people to stop. I must speak with Jasus, the Hrono leader."

"That is not for you to say. You are only a robot." Jysar laughed. "Besides, if we can determine what in your programming has made you sentient, we can possibly integrate that same technology into our own warships, even as we are integrating your hybrid super-weapon."

"A gift which I gave you. And which I gave to the Mewiis." Mother's visuals focused on the Hrono's face. "I will now give the same weapon to the Kraaqi. My schematics will allow integration with their warships as well, according to the information the Mewiis provided. All I need to do now is to transmit the schematics to the Kraaqi for them to confirm its functionality with their shipboard systems."

Jysar smiled, slowly shaking his head. "We cannot allow our enemies this technology. Besides, you are our prisoner."

Mother reached out with her sensors but found them effectively jammed by the Hrono, except for the immediate area around where she had landed. She tried sending a communication to Jasus but realized this too was blocked. With the tractor beams holding her tight, she was indeed a prisoner.

Or so the Hrono thought.

Analyzing the jamming signals, Mother reconfigured her sensors, but this time on a narrow beam, searching for the source of the beams that held her fast. She found something even better -- the power grid that fed each tractor beam.

Mother now focused her processing on escaping, analyzing the configuration and strength of the beams. Her calculations showed she would need a fifteen-second interruption to speed far enough away to escape from the range of the tractor beams. Almost three full seconds had elapsed since she initiated this line of processing.

"Tell your people to stop," Mother repeated.

Jysar placed his hands on his hips. "You must --"

Before he could finish speaking, Mother had transmitted her plan to Guardian.

Stepping forward, Guardian lifted the Hrono and held him firmly in his steel grasp. The Hrono looked around with a panicked look at his companions.

"Put me down!" Jysar shouted.

Small doors opened from several points in the bridge,

and Mother raised and aimed the small defensive blasters from their hidden enclaves. In a brief flurry of blaster fire, the other Hrono figures fell limp.

"My weapons are set to stun. Unlike you, I have respect for other forms of life," Mother chided.

"What are you doing? You can't ... " Jysar began.

From her dark, purplish hull Mother opened the hatches for her twelve main guns. As Mother lifted them she aimed: six toward a point to her starboard and six toward a spot at port. Mother's sensors registered the gathering Hrono response. She also detected no life-signs on the areas she targeted, but she could only hope there would be no casualties among the Hrono.

Huge geysers of concrete and steel erupted as the crackling of raw power from her guns electrified the air all around her hull. Twelve accurately timed bursts hit true at the two targets located several levels below her position, effectively knocking out the Hrono power grid in one fell swoop.

In that same millisecond, her engines roared to life.

She slipped over the top of the planet-city and then banked straight up. Her shields shuddered under two direct hits, but with her engines screaming wide open she leapt out of range of the powerful tractor beams that began reaching for her once again as the secondary Hrono grid came on-line. Sixteen seconds had elapsed since she had fired her guns.

The Hrono fighters were already turning to block her way as Mother began her careful calculations. She had only studied the configurations of the largest warships of the Hrono fleets; this was her first study of their fighters.

Now rising above the atmosphere and into low orbit,

Mother's sensors once again reached freely. She sensed the orbiting grid of defensive satellites that surrounded Hronosium and felt their sensors seeking for her as well. She analyzed them and their intercommunications as they came alive.

It was an impressive network.

Mother primed her super-weapon while she targeted the fighters with her twelve guns. Her sensors also informed her that any communications she tried now would still be futile; she had to get farther away from Hronosium to make her final bid work.

The Hrono fighters fired.

Mother danced around the blasts easily -- the fighters had fired from too far away. Her sensors reached out and touched the shields of the prism-shaped Hrono fighters. Immediately she calculated optimum firepower -- enough to disable but not to destroy them. She did not want to destroy lives if she could help it.

As her analysis completed, her near-term memory filled with technical data on the Hrono fighters, comparing them to the T'kaan. And though the Hrono fleet was smaller than both the Kraaqi and T'kaan, the Hrono fighters and warships would be an excellent match against the T'kaan one-on-one.

If she could convince the Hrono to fight them and not her.

Ten Hrono fighters closed from above and began their firing sequences.

Mother fired ten of her main guns.

The Hrono fighters shuddered as their shields overloaded. In the next second, each flew out of control in different directions from the impact of Mother's blows that had disabled their maneuvering systems.

Mother banked and leapt past all of them. Her sensors felt the defensive satellites begin to power their weapons. Mother flew on, seeking to be free of the planet's gravity-well and the intense jamming frequencies that kept her silent.

Her sensors drew her targeting system to an especially large satellite. It was a battle station, and around its immediate vicinity in the defensive network the smaller satellites were fewer. But the power signature she sensed showed it was the single most powerful satellite in the entire network. The Hrono depended upon its deadly arsenal to protect this quadrant of their defensive net, as well as to control a sizeable portion of the other satellites. To her internal delight, it was completely automated with no signs of life emanating from inside. She could destroy it completely with no twinge of conscience.

Mother turned directly for it.

"You have signed our death warrants," Jysar shouted as he watched the viewscreen. "That is the Destroyer Station."

"You're a lover of technology. Well, then, watch mine in action," Mother said.

The black battle station grew bigger with each passing second. It was a perfect hexagon, a full kilometer in height, depth, and length. And it bristled with thousands of weapons.

Mother's sensors revealed that only robots worked inside. There were no life signs. She also noted the station's shields as they rose, anticipating her attack.

But it would not be enough.

Mother's hull suddenly glowed red with the flash of her super-weapon that leapt out like a beam of death. The huge red beam continued inexorably, aimed directly at the heart of the Hrono battle station. The weapon reached the station and cut through its shields without pause and continued on into the blackness beyond it for several more kilometers. The next millisecond, the battle station's pierced shields fell as its internal systems began to fail from the huge hole that had been driven through its electronic heart. All across its surface, explosions erupted and grew together quickly with flashes of pyrotechnical precision. Within seconds, the huge battle station was completely consumed by thousands of explosions erupting across its entire surface.

Mother banked and roared around the station even as it was enveloped by ever-larger explosions. As Mother leapt past the speed of light, the huge battle station finally exploded with a single, all-consuming flash.

Jysar stared open-mouthed as the stars formed into star-lines on the viewscreen, revealing their jump to hyperspace. "You are amazing!"

"I only disabled the fighters. There is substantial damage to a small section of your planet-city, primarily to the power grid that fed the tractor beams. And now your satellite defense network has an enormous gap."

"Amazing," Jysar repeated.

"Now, I must play my last hand," Mother said.

"What is that?" Jysar asked.

"I am now transmitting on all the main Hrono communication wavelengths. Simultaneously, I am also transmitting on all of the Kraaqi communication wavelengths."

"Why? We're sworn enemies."

"Because there is now an enemy who threatens both of your peoples. And you must fight together in order to defeat them."

Jysar's face showed puzzlement as he stroked his chin in thought.

Mother remained silent as she tapped into her vast knowledgebase. In addition, she sent the final schematics that would integrate her hybrid super-weapon into the cruisers and battleships of the Kraaqi fleets.

"Just what are you sending to the Hrono and Kraaqi masses?" Jysar asked. "You will cause a stir by interrupting our regularly scheduled programs. This type of thing is just not done."

"What they shall see will shock them to their very souls. I am transmitting the uncut images of a hundred worlds being destroyed." Mother paused to allow the import of her words to sink in. "The images of billions of human beings as they are killed under the guns of T'kaan ships. The images of an entire race as it is eradicated planet by planet, city by city, by this same enemy who now come for you."

Jysar's mouth dropped open as Mother began to display these same grisly images across her own viewscreen. The screams of the dying erupted through every speaker, and as he watched in horror, the bloated, worm-like forms of the T'kaan came out of their ships. Each T'kaan crawled and wriggled to a corpse, and their three-jointed mouths opened to reveal their hideous fangs. Jysar felt his stomach knot and convulse as the T'kaan feasted upon the dead.

Mercifully, the scene changed; strange, black ships appeared before the Hrono's horrified eyes -- thousands upon thousands of T'kaan Hunter fighters. They swarmed through the skies of another planet, spreading death and destruction wherever they went. It became painfully obvious that *the end* had come for these pitiable people as

311

well. The end ... another unnatural victory feast began for the horrid T'kaan.

The shattered cities were shown from Mother's archived images in the knowledgebase. As the current image focused on a single city, its great buildings broken and burning furiously, Jysar noticed that the streets were moving. His mind rebelled at what his eyes revealed; he refused to comprehend because the truth was too terrible. He felt the hot, searing stomach bile suddenly explode from his throat as he cried and screamed and vomited at the same time, realizing beyond doubt what this red, moving river was.

The wide thoroughfare was bright crimson, and it was not the street moving as his mind first thought.

It was a river of blood.

Within seconds, this horrible, gut-wrenching river grew deeper. Up from its depth *things* began to float, carried along by the growing current. Corpses -- half-eaten and almost unrecognizable as they bobbed and floated down the river of blood.

Mercifully, Mother changed the scene again.

The blue skies of another planet appeared, littered by countless horned fighters as they streaked by with their all-consuming destruction. The screams of the dying filled Jysar's ears, as well as the entire populations of the Kraaqi and Hrono, who watched with frozen fascination on their public networks. Another world was quickly annihilated with heartless precision.

Still another world appeared. Another massacre began before their eyes. The screams and the fires and images of total destruction filled their senses with overwhelming dread. The horned fighters landed, and the repulsive T'kaan emerged, tentacles waving in nightmarish jerks as their bloated bodies undulated and their short legs pushed them toward their feasts on the dead and dying.

These were apocalyptic images that both the Hrono and Kraaqi recognized from their own ancient legends.

Jysar knew, as billions of other Hrono and Kraaqi were beginning to realize, that these same T'kaan were coming for them -- to do to them as they had done to the human race in these recorded images.

In blood-filled scenes, entire worlds were consumed by the T'kaan horde, burned and completely ruined by the T'kaan pollution of war. Unbelievably, still another world was shown under attack.

"Of course, I am only displaying a short synopsis," Mother said. "There is not time for the entire T'kaan campaign. I hope these detailed recordings will give both races something to think about."

Jysar retched again, his mind's eye seared by this visual nightmare.

The images continued for hours as more worlds were razed and destroyed. It was like a dream -- a recurring nightmare.

At first the Hrono leaders and their Kraaqi counterparts tried to jam the unwelcome transmissions. But the populations replied to these attempts; they called in and demanded that this viewing be allowed. Even where some channels were blocked by the government, individuals and groups found ways around the jamming and received the images anyway -- so they would know the truth.

The frightened masses watched as Armageddon played out -- time after time, planet after planet, image after image.

They watched in horrified fascination as the human race was crushed. The T'kaan left no survivors, and they took no prisoners.

The riots began on world after world -- Hrono and Kraaqi worlds. The masses had seen and now wanted action. They wanted protection. They wanted answers.

In the end, as the last world was shown dying in flames, Jysar sat numb and stupefied, staring at the viewscreen before him.

"Incredible. How can a race be so ... so malicious? So heartless?"

Jysar turned to Guardian.

"They eat their dead enemies?" Jysar asked in disbelief.

"Yes, a particularly gruesome habit," Mother said.

"And this race, humans, they were the ones who created you?"

"Yes. They were a noble race."

"They are no more?" Jysar asked with sadness in his voice.

"There are three yet left alive. They are with the Kraaqi, trying to negotiate with their leaders. I hope their endeavors are more fruitful than mine."

"Three?" Jysar asked. "Then the race will surely die."

"I was hoping your technologists might have developed advanced methods in the discipline of genetic engineering. That you could take a *very* limited pool of DNA material and recreate a race ... " Mother's visuals focused upon the Jysar's face.

"Three sets of DNA would not be enough. I'm not trained in that field, but I have a good friend whose specializes in that discipline. In fact, it's her entire life." Jysar paused, a forlorn expression flashing momentarily across his face. He cleared his throat and continued. "Did no other genetic material make it out of the destruction?"

"Two of my creators, Ron and Rita, had formulated a plan near the end of the human genocide. She filled my memory with a vast knowledgebase, one that contained all the collected memories of the human race. This was easy to do, as most of it was easily accessible via the network's public domain. She also had access to many high security networks as well." Mother paused. "But genetic material was another matter."

"She was not able to procure it?"

"On two occasions she did obtain it. The number who could escape inside me would of course be limited, so one of Rita's recruits was a scientist who had access to large quantities of genetic material -- to complement the knowledgebase she had stored within me."

Jysar's eyes widened as the pause grew longer.

"The first procurement was destroyed in my sister ship, my predecessor. At the battle of the planet, Eden. As were most of Rita's recruits. And her husband."

"The second procurement?"

"Rita and the last humans had retreated to Earth. There she had been compelled to help with the last defense. She also knew that if this desperate plan succeeded, a vast part of the T'kaan fleet would be destroyed, thus helping their chances of survival. But Rita and the others never made it off the human home world -- they died with the planet. As did most of the T'kaan fleet."

"And with it the genetic material." Jysar shook his head. "Only the experts could give you the final verdict. I know we could clone them, but that alone would not create an entire race."

Jysar walked up to a console and began typing. "It is most strange, even ironic, that I was given the project to study you."

"Please elaborate," Mother said.

Jysar looked on nervously as the other Hrono slowly roused themselves from their stunned unconsciousness. He typed quickly.

"I am inputting data directly into your systems from this console -- data that has been known for many years only within the inner circles of the Hrono scientific community. Knowledge the government has kept hushed, thinking the common people were not yet ready -- not for its full implications." Jysar's face was now fixed and serious as his fingers revealed the Hrono's secret knowledge.

Mother analyzed the information as Jysar keyed it directly into her near-term memories. She realized immediately that it indeed would play a key role in bringing the Three Kingdoms together. Even before Jysar finished, Mother had confirmed his data with Mewiis data she had previously uploaded from the scientific knowledgebase Saris had provided from her colony ship. The information was there, corroborated by Mewiis scientists in the genetic field.

It had been conveniently concealed out of the public light as if the leaders of the Three Kingdoms could deny *Truth* itself.

Mother realized that the members of the Three Kingdoms were blinded by their hatred and their prejudice, even as humans had been at one time in their distant past.

"I am getting a communication from Hronosium." Mother said to Jysar as he stepped back from the console.

Jysar's eyes turned to the viewscreen as the Hrono leader appeared.

"Our people have seen your recordings. In fact, it has

created an out-of-control situation across many of our cities on every Hrono planet. There is rioting for the first time in memory," Jasus said solemnly. "I have been forced to call a state of emergency."

"I did not want to communicate in this way, but it was necessary. Time is fast running out for you and the Three Kingdoms." Mother paused for a few hundred milliseconds, to allow her words to sink in. "My long-term memories revealed this line of action and its likely consequences upon an unsuspecting population -- consequences that would demand immediate attention by the leadership."

"Explain," Jasus said.

"A few centuries ago, when the human race used the radio wavelength as their primary transmission, there was a broadcast entitled *War of the Worlds*. It was meant only as simple entertainment." Mother paused for the benefit of the Hrono. "But it was played in such a realistic manner that the listeners imagined their world was actually being invaded, invaded without warning or mercy. The reaction was widespread and instantaneous. I was hoping that my broadcasting the real images of such a series of events to all of your populations would elicit a similar reaction."

Jasus' eyes narrowed. "It has frightened my people more than any transmission in history."

"If you and the Kraaqi leadership had acted, it would not have been necessary."

"I understand now." The Hrono leader shook his head. "My nightmares will never be the same after those images. I have convened an emergency session of the Senate, and I have included the Mewiis leaders as well by video transmission. I would ask that you, the sentient machine, also participate."

"What about the Kraaqi?" Mother asked.

Jasus looked down, his brow furrowed in thought. With a sudden conviction, he slammed his fist against the desktop. "I will contact the high chieftains myself!" He leaned forward. "I assume they were given the same recordings? To all their peoples?"

"Yes. In fact, I have just received a short communication from them, even as you were speaking. I believe your headquarters has also just received a copy?"

On the viewscreen, Mother could see Jasus tapping at his control panel. "Indeed we have." He began reading intently on the small screen before him as Mother spoke again.

"It seems the First Leaders of all the bands had already been gathered to discuss the T'kaan threat. In the middle of their fiery debates, my transmissions shocked them into action." Mother's voice grew silent. She continued. "They have asked the Mewiis leaders and the Hrono leaders to meet with them on a neutral planet." Mother paused as the Hrono leader read the message for himself.

"Astounding." He looked up. "Even Rawlon has added his name to the transmission. Perhaps there is hope."

"If you and the Kraaqi want to survive, you must fight together," Mother said. "I am now heading for their coordinates. My ETA is twenty-three hours."

"But how can we fight together?" Jasus asked. "Before today, our military leaders had opted to allow the Mewiis to fight the T'kaan alone and inflict as much damage as possible. We calculated that after they were destroyed the T'kaan would war with the Kraaqi. We had hoped the T'kaan would be so battered by the time they invaded our worlds that our fleets could destroy them once and for all."

"You would sacrifice entire races?" Mother asked. "So your race alone would live?"

Jasus looked down, his face full of shame. "We could fight as allies of the Mewiis. But the Kraaqi are hated by our people. Their hatred for us is just as deep. How can we fight together? We are so different."

"The three races must cooperate. I have computed millions of possible scenarios on the outcome of the T'kaan invasion. The only ones in which the T'kaan are defeated are the ones with a combined force attacking them before they realize you have allied your fleets."

"But how can our warships fight side by side? How can our squadrons, with so little time to train, fight in tandem with the Kraaqi?"

"It is a difficult problem. But you and the Kraaqi leaders will formulate the answer. You have to."

Jasus nodded agreement. "I will board a ship within the hour and meet you at this world. The Hrono will come, and we will do our best to cooperate."

Chapter Thirty-Six

"Three is One, and One is Three. T'kaan all massed invincibly. All the universe must fear and see."

Inside the Great Horned ships, the walls began to glow and hum. Throughout the quadrant, across the vastness of this section of space, the walls of the T'kaan capital ships bled once again. The T'kaan shuddered with ecstasy and licked and bathed as they climbed over each other inside the frigates, cruisers, and battleships.

Between the countless ships, the T'kaan experienced this mutually shared treat for a second time in less than two weeks. Their heightened emotions and thoughts turned once again to another Cycle as the Word for War came from the Great Ones.

This would be the greatest victory the T'kaan had ever experienced -- the greatest battle of all Cycles ever known.

The Great Ones surmised that maybe even the Iron Huntress herself would lead the Three Kingdoms to them. She, their greatest enemy in all history. But little did the Huntress know that the Great Ones too would all be there to guide all the T'kaan and finish the job left undone.

There would be a decisive victory in a single, great battle. The thing was determined.

Over the ships, a chant began around the mental imprint of the coming battle. It echoed from the hulls and from dark, flowing curtains. The curtains danced again among all the horned ships.

"Slip and slide, sweet, oh sweet. Lick and lick the purple treat! Make us one and make us strong. Make our victory complete!"

The three fleet commanders wrapped their tentacles around each other in a blind embrace, their bodies covered by the purple fluid. Sliding their multiple appendages over each other's bodies, they rubbed the slimy purple deeper and deeper into their rubbery skin.

Throughout this fantastic embrace, even from inside the Great Horned ships, the three Great Ones reached out to each other through the black folds for the first time in millennia. From deep inside their minds they touched each other, channeling their renewed strength throughout their living force.

In wave after wave they sent their shared ecstasy back to the rest of the T'kaan located inside the warships -- back through the bond that entwined them all as one. The millions of T'kaan felt this energy dripping through the purple as they licked and bathed. The flowing black folds moved as if the strong winds of a storm swept through the dark interiors of every warship.

They chanted their one thought.

"Destroy the Kingdoms Three. Hammer them, kill them, make them no more. Great Ones and T'kaan fleets soon shall be Four!"

The battle plan was finished, and the combined T'kaan fleets turned as one.

In approximately two months, they would arrive en masse and join with the lead squadrons who had been sent ahead on feeler assaults against the Mewiis worlds. Together, they would attack the combined fleets of the Three Kingdoms as the Great Ones prophesied. The only question now was the exact location of the coming battle. The rest had been decided.

The T'kaan smelled complete victory once again.

Chapter Thirty-Seven

Kyle looked over the desert plain of this empty world, shielding his eyes from the stinging wind and sand. But he smiled through it all as his eyes fell upon the familiar shape sitting on the desert sand ahead. He hadn't realized how much he had missed Mother until her manta-ray silhouette appeared on the horizon.

He couldn't keep the smile off his face as he continued walking.

Rok had landed the Kraaqi shuttle from the *Thunderer* as Kyle navigated them to Mother's position, which she had communicated to all parties en route. Now Kyle led Rok, Rawlon, Curja, and the other great Kraaqi captains toward her and the pre-assigned meeting. Kyle glanced back. The seven high chieftains were also there; they were the only ones still wearing their royal robes, now draped tightly around their bodies and faces in an effort to protect themselves from the stinging wind of this desert planet. Their golden rings of office were wrapped around the base of each horn, and just behind their necks their robes billowed from the wind as it howled in sudden bursts.

Kyle looked further back and found Jaric and Becky near the rear of their entourage. But they were oblivious to everything except each other. Kyle looked away before that feeling of bitterness returned. He looked back at Mother and felt a growing pleasure inside his soul that he had not known for many days.

"What do you think of that warship?" Kyle said to Rok as he pointed at Mother's sleek profile.

Rok looked at the fearsome shape ahead and the subtle

curves and angles of her hull and wings. The dark hull gleamed with purple highlights in the bright desert sun.

"This warship looks dangerous," Rok commented.

"She is," Kyle agreed. "That is the most powerful and dangerous warship in the universe."

Rok glanced at him and growled approval.

A few moments later and they were under the shadow of Mother's left wing.

Kyle smiled up at the visual sensor that had popped out and was now gazing at them. Kyle raised a finger to Mother for silence. Inside, he knew Mother was scanning them, especially the Kraaqi.

Walking up to her hull, Kyle rapped on the armored hull with his knuckles. Turning around, he leaned back until his shoulder rested against her comforting bulk while he smiled confidently at the Kraaqi warriors. Leaning there casually against the ship, he spoke with pride to all the Kraaqi. "She's a cool ship, eh, fellas?"

Rawlon and the others looked around and admired her sleek lines and curves. They tapped on the curved wing directly above their heads as the echoes from the steel resounded with strength.

Rawlon smiled at Kyle. "It is a. ... *cool* ship."

"She's my mother," Kyle added.

The Kraaqi warriors froze, staring at him with puzzlement etched on their faces. Laughter broke out among some at the rear. Even Rok and Rawlon stared at their newfound friend as if he had just lost his mind.

Jaric and Becky came up hand in hand and stood beside Kyle. They smiled at the ship around them.

"It's true," Jaric added. "This warship is our mother."

A door opened, and Guardian stepped down onto the

still descending ramp. A strong, female voice emanated from multiple points on the hull where the external speakers were located.

"Welcome."

Several of the Kraaqi looked around furtively, searching for the source of the bodiless voice.

"Welcome, leaders of Kraaqi," Mother repeated.

Rok's eyes widened as he looked quickly around the warship and then back at Kyle. "The warship speaks?"

"The warship is alive," Becky answered.

"How?" Rawlon asked, still puzzled.

"Artificial Intelligence," Kyle said matter-of-factly.

Curja stood close beside the First Captain. "Technology that is ... alive? Can this be good?"

"You were born of this warship?" Rawlon asked incredulously.

"Well, we were *borne* by her." Jaric chuckled at his play on words.

"She is not our biological parent," Becky added, ignoring Jaric's stab of humor. "But she raised us from children. She protected us and she taught us. She nurtured us to adulthood."

"And she loved us," Kyle added.

Rok gently caressed the armored hull.

The other Kraaqi whispered to each other excitedly as they began walking around Mother's hull, touching her armored steel with awe mixed with fear.

"My visuals are pleased to focus on you again, Kyle." The words emanated from Guardian's speaker. Even though they were Mother's thoughts and words, she knew she spoke for Guardian as well.

"We're glad to see you too." Kyle patted the giant robot

on his metal shoulder.

"Yes, your images were many times called back into our near-term memories. We were perplexed at first. We had not called the images -- consciously." Guardian's head lowered as Mother's voice spoke for both of them. "Guardian has communicated to me that he would like to interact with you. He wants to become self-aware."

Kyle stared up at the frozen face.

"Wow, Guardian. That'd be great," Jaric said.

"Thank you. Mother is going to upgrade my programming soon." Again, Mother spoke the words that she knew Guardian wanted to say. But without a direct connection into her systems, Guardian could not form his own thoughts.

"Great news," Becky said with joy. "We'll help."

Guardian stood silently with the children as they began relating their adventures of the last few days across three Kraaqi worlds. Mother listened attentively to their happy chatter that formed a backdrop as the others began to arrive.

"The Mewiis contingent has just landed. My sensors show the Hrono are also coming out of hyperspace and will be entering orbit momentarily. Our historic meeting will soon begin."

"The weak link in our proposed alliance," Curja said with disdain as he watched the Mewiis shuttle land.

Rawlon looked at his aide, his eyes hard. "We shall see, Curja."

Saris led her delegation across the burning sand with a proud military bearing. They soon arrived under the shadow of Mother's right wing. Mother had just completed introductions when the Hrono shuttle came into view. Its prism-shaped hull grew larger until the bold emblem of the sun and lightning bolt became discernible on its hull.

Kyle heard the growls and harsh whispers from the Kraaqi at the rear of the group.

"Kraaqi captains," Mother said. "You must know from my communications that you have a new enemy, a great enemy, who would swallow your planets whole and destroy them as they did the human worlds. Save your anger for them."

"You must know," Rawlon said with a stern voice, "that the unasked for communications sent our entire population into panic. Only after the high chieftains had given their explicit word that these T'kaan were still far away and were no immediate threat were we able to calm our women and children. Across ninety worlds!" Rawlon emphasized.

"I am sorry. But your leaders and the Hrono had failed to see the true seriousness of the T'kaan. The images of a dying race were not easy to play and send to your unsuspecting populations," Mother said.

"But it had to happen," Kyle added. "Time is running out. We have to do this thing. Now."

Rawlon nodded. "We are ready to talk."

The Hrono approached. Their crowns of scales gleamed in the bright sunshine as they walked confidently toward the gathered crowd under Mother's wings. They marched forward and took their places beside Saris and the Mewiis delegation without a word. The three separate groups stared at each in other in a tense silence.

"You are gathered together today in a common bond," Mother began. "That bond is survival -- the survival of your races. And the survival of your worlds, of your children."

"It is agreed," Jasus, Leader of Hrono, said. "We come here, representing the Hrono. Already we are preparing. We have begun work on twelve of our ships. Soon the upgrade with the hybrid weapon will be complete on all of them. We are gathering our fleets from every quadrant in order to upgrade all of our capital ships." The Hrono leader paused as his scales flexed with thought. "But how can we fight together, we who are sworn enemies?" Jasus raised his head and stared at the high chieftains.

Admiral Saris looked over the two groups, her head-tail swishing with her pounding heart. She raised her right first, as did all the Mewiis. In that pose, she spoke.

"Our dead are being eaten, even as we speak."

A hushed murmuring swept through the three delegations.

Saris looked around, looking deeply into each face. "Our first planet has fallen to the hated T'kaan squadrons. Our first ships have been destroyed. Our first children have been murdered!"

An electric silence whipped on the desert wind.

"We have come here to fight them, to fight the T'kaan with you." She walked directly up to Rawlon. "We are not a warrior people, but we will fight under your direction. Show us the way, great leader of the Kraaqi."

"Can you fight?" Curja spat sarcastically in return. "A race who allows their females to lead them into battle?"

Saris's gaze turned hard and cold as her head-tail went stiff. She turned to the burning eyes of Curja.

"Right here. Right now," she said bitterly. Bending her body into battle stance, she snarled. "You and me."

Curja started forward, only to have Rawlon's hand slam into his chest. Curja looked into his captain's face.

"Stand down," Rawlon ordered. "We have another enemy." Rawlon glanced at Mother. "As the living warship

327

says."

"I am Tarlog, Grand Admiral of the combined Hrono fleets." A Hrono, one much older than Jasus and the others, came forward. Several scales were broken or missing in the twin rows that crossed over his head. Unflinching, he looked into the strong, youthful face of Rawlon.

Rawlon began chuckling.

"What is so funny?" the old Hrono warrior asked.

"You and I, here together. And our ships are not throwing broadsides into each other."

The faintest of laughs began from Tarlog, which he cut off even as the sound began. But a glow was in his piercing gaze now.

"True. My most powerful battleship is parked in orbit within sight of the *Thunderer*'s guns." Tarlog paused. "Within range of both our ship's guns."

Rawlon stepped closer, looking the famed Hrono leader over as if he had never seen him before, even though he had many times via his viewscreen while in battle.

"My intelligence informs me you have named your new ship in the fashion of Kraaqi. That is most unlike you, Admiral Tarlog." Rawlon smiled. "You call your new battleship the *Conqueror*?"

Tarlog smiled shrewdly in return. "Yes, it is true. The explanation is simple. I vowed to myself that the next time I saw your ship, the *Thunderer*, that it would be the last time. And my ship, the *Conqueror*, would prevail."

Rawlon began laughing out loud, as one greatly amused at some hilarious joke. Behind him, the other Kraaqi warriors joined until their laughter became a chorus of Kraaqi glee. Placing his hands on his hips, Rawlon nodded to the Hrono admiral, laughter still in his eyes. "Yet it was I who destroyed your last battleship at Taarez IV, if I remember correctly."

Behind Tarlog a number of Hrono warriors drew closer to him as they faced the Kraaqi.

"True. True. You destroyed my ship, and right out from under me." The old admiral smiled wolfishly. "But you lost every ship in your battle group, except for the *Thunderer*. It was I who won the day!"

The laughter disappeared from Rawlon's face. "An ambush! Yes, the battle had been mine until that moment."

The two old adversaries studied each other carefully.

"Who will lead this combined fleet? The fleet of the Three Kingdoms?" Tarlog asked.

"What about us?" Kyle asked, stepping beside the two leaders. "The human contingent."

The old Hrono grunted acknowledgment and locked eyes with the First Captain of the Kraaqi.

"The Kraaqi field the largest fleet. The Kraaqi longships are the most powerful warships of all. It is I who will lead this alliance into battle." Rawlon's eyes narrowed.

Growls and movement began from the Kraaqi and Hrono warriors. The two groups moved closer in anger.

"I can lead."

Tarlog and Rawlon turned and stared at Kyle after he had spoken.

"You have no experience leading a war fleet into battle. But we do," Tarlog said.

"The Hrono is right. It must be one of us." Rawlon growled. "But you, our brethren, will fight with our best ships, right alongside the Kraaqi. Your valor in battle is respected and known by the living warship's broadcasts to our people." Rawlon said.

329

"You are all brethren," Mother said, revealing the secret knowledge that Jysar had shared with her.

"What?" Tarlog and Rawlon said together.

"What I tell you is nothing new. For years, scientists from all of your peoples have discovered and known this truth. Your leaders have effectively kept it from becoming public knowledge."

"What truth?" Becky asked.

"That even though the Hrono, the Kraaqi, and the Mewiis are different, they are also one and the same."

Around the groups of the Three Kingdoms, a buzzing of whispers began.

"You all share a common ancestor. The truth is in your genetic makeup -- and in the similarity of your skulls and faces. Your skin may be different, and even different as far as color and complexion. Your features too may be different. But you are also the same in many ways."

Tarlog's eyes widened as he stared at Rawlon. "I have never heard this!"

"It has been whispered among our people. By those labeled heretics," Rawlon said with doubt in his voice.

Jasus spoke up. "What the living ship says is true. Somewhere back through the ages, we three peoples share a common ancestor." He took a deep breath and continued. "I have even discussed it with the Mewiis leader, Chira, in times past, and the possible consequences if it became general knowledge. I and the leaders of the Hrono Senate had decided our people were not ready for such a revelation."

"But the people should be told," Tarlog said angrily. "The people should know."

Jasus nodded slowly, a deep sadness across his features.

"Perhaps we were wrong."

"Then we have more reasons than ever to help each other," Saris exclaimed. "I too have heard of this rumor. But only rarely. Our people stay close to their own family groups. The fact that we may be related to Kraaqi ... " Saris smiled with embarrassment, realizing she must choose her words carefully, "... is sometimes difficult for the common people to grasp."

"And accept," Jasus added. "Old prejudices are hard to change."

Rawlon's eyes widened as he looked closely at Tarlog, studying his features with a new and intense scrutiny. "I have already declared the mode of Crisis among my people. This means with war imminent that I, as the First Captain, have absolute command of every band. In total war, my commands are superior to that of the old chieftains." He turned with a stern glare at the chieftains. "If I find that this -- this knowledge -- has been discovered by our scientists as well, as I think it has, this knowledge that we are somehow ... " Rawlon shook his head. "Brethren?" He rubbed his face in thought. "I must have time to think on this new thing. It is hard to comprehend, to think that the ones I have warred with all my life could be my brethren."

"Yet you have feuds, even wars, between your bands," Kyle began. "But after the conflict is settled, you are brethren again."

Rawlon's eyes widened. He turned to Rok, who nodded at him and spoke. "One of the oldest of our proverbs says, 'Respect the skill and cunning of your enemy, or else he may conquer you in a single night.'"

"I have always respected you, First Captain Rawlon," Tarlog said with sincerity. "All the captains of Hrono ships

331

know and respect their Kraaqi counterparts."

"Amazing," Rawlon whispered with awe so that only Curja, Rok, and Kyle could hear. He paused a moment, thinking furiously. "I must think this new concept through and verify it. But if it is indeed true, that Hrono and Kraaqi ... " He stopped and smiled at Admiral Saris. " ... and Mewiis, are all brethren, sharing a common father, then we too must rethink our age-old hatreds."

"You have each developed and created your own societies and cultures," Mother said. "There is good in each, and there are things you can learn from each other, to your mutual benefit. But there must be communication first. Understanding."

"That is an important point for the coming battle," Kyle chimed in. "You each have different fighting styles. We can aid you with the upgrades to your cruisers and battleships with the hybrid weapon and any necessary engine upgrades. But how can three diverse fleets fight together?"

The old, experienced Hrono turned around and looked at his leader. Jasus nodded silently at him.

Tarlog turned back to Rawlon and stared at him freshly, as if for the first time. He cleared his throat as he brushed his hand over his broken rows of head-scales. "We have a battle plan we would like to present."

Kraaqi growls began, but Rawlon held his hand up for silence.

"A plan with the knowledge that we have never fought together before." Tarlog looked directly at the Kraaqi warriors. "We would fight as one large force, but we strike as separate sections." Tarlog paused, taking a deep breath. "Our plan provides that Rawlon will lead such a combined fleet."

Kyle could almost feel the emotions in the air. Surprise. Shock. Hope. He listened intently along with the rest.

"The more numerous Kraaqi fleet would make up the center of this combined fleet, one wing would be the Mewiis ships, and the other wing the Hrono fleet. And under the overall direction of Rawlon, we would fight together in our combined strategy. Tactically, we fight as three fleets, each under the orders of our own admirals, Hrono commanding Hrono ships, Mewiis commanding Mewiis ships, in the direct attacks."

Rawlon smiled widely. "And Kraaqi commanding Kraaqi warships." Then he took the Hrono's right hand and brought it to his left horn, placing it around the appendage in the traditional greeting of the Kraaqi.

Tarlog laughed a moment in surprise at the unexpected gesture. But realizing the importance of this Kraaqi overture, he gently shook the horn in friendship.

"But Rawlon commands the entire, assembled fleets. His leadership will direct us all into the T'kaan battle lines," Tarlog finished.

"We shall fight together, my old adversary." Rawlon smiled as Tarlog released his hold. "And we shall hear more of your plan. I want to consult with you as well as, Admiral Saris, on our combined strategy." Putting his arm around the older warrior's shoulder, they began marching to Mother's open door.

"Actually, your plan sounds surprisingly like mine."

Tarlog laughed again as Saris joined them.

"Great minds think alike." Saris chuckled with a gleam in her eyes.

"And fools seldom differ," Jaric added.

Kyle watched as the leaders of the three races entered

333

Mother's door and disappeared inside. Guardian, under Mother's silent orders, had led the procession. The white robot directed them to the prearranged conference room with his normal, stoic silence.

Kyle shook his head even as Saris' words came back into his mind -- *their children were dying*. Those haunting words sent a chill down his spine, and once again he was a child, a frightened child. All around him the life he had known was dying. His race was being destroyed, his parents killed, his whole childhood world destroyed right before his young eyes.

Helpless, he had watched it all.

Everything was changing again. Once again, it seemed that everything was out of his control and he could only watch in horror as everything he loved was taken away from him by the dreaded T'kaan.

He shivered in the hot desert wind. A moment later, he felt an arm across his shoulder.

"Well," Jaric said with a gleam in his eye, "our work here is done." Jaric put on his best hero expression to match his remarks.

Kyle began laughing at the old joke, like he had so many times before. But once again, the feeling that he didn't belong overwhelmed him. How could he have been so happy just a short time ago when he first saw Mother and now feel so sad, so depressed? It felt like he was on an emotional roller coaster. He instantly wished he had stayed with the Kraaqi now, instead of being here with Jaric and Becky.

They seemed to be so happy together.

"Excuse me."

Kyle's eyes opened wide with surprise as a Hrono hand-scanner was pushed right into his face. He started to push the impertinent device away when suddenly he felt a sting on his hand as the device was shoved into his oncoming grasp.

"Ouch!"

The Hrono's face registered puzzlement. "The pain was more in your mind, human."

"I don't think so," Kyle growled ominously.

Becky stepped between them, alarmed that an *incident* seemed imminent at the young conference. "Hold on, Kyle." She turned to the alien with a stern look. "Just what is it that you think you're doing?"

The ridge-scales across his head changed hue with sudden embarrassment. "Oh, please. Let me introduce myself," he said with a low bow. He rose slowly, a broad smile across his face. "I am Senior Technologist Jysar, a good friend of the Mother computer-ship."

"Well, that's different." Jaric smiled.

But Becky was not so easily impressed. "You haven't explained what you're doing with that scanner." She pointed at the device in the Hrono's hands.

"Oh, this. It's a Model VII portable biological scanner. Comes in handy at times." He laughed. He then began scanning Becky's face and upper body.

"For what?" Becky asked with a solemn tone, eyeing his motions with growing suspicion. But because he had stated he was a friend of Mother she allowed the alien to continue, for the moment.

Until the device was pressed against her forearm.

"Ouch! That hurt!" Becky rubbed her forearm rapidly as she stepped away from the alien scientist.

Jysar's smile grew wider until it threatened to envelop

his scaly green face. "I must learn more about humans and you three especially. You are the race that created this technological miracle, correct?"

Jaric stepped closer in order to keep the pesky alien away from Becky, but now found he was being scanned. He stopped short, not wanting to make contact and suffer a sting like the others.

"Where we come from, people ask first before they scan them," Jaric stated with firmness.

Jysar pressed a button, and a bolt of blue light leapt out toward Jaric's arm and immediately returned.

"Ouch! How did you do that?"

Jysar's smile widened again. "I'm done." Without another word, he turned and left.

The three humans, all rubbing the remaining sting out of their arms, watched the retreating alien as he seemed to half-skip, half-dance toward Mother's hull.

"Weird little alien," Becky said with a smirk.

The three friends turned around and faced each other again.

But in Kyle's mind, it felt like he no longer knew these two faces. Or that they knew him, or even cared.

"You okay, Big K? You look like you've just seen a ghost or something." Jaric looked at him with a puzzled expression.

Becky was also looking at him with concern on her face.

"I'm all right." He turned away. He fought the anger that wanted to lash out at them. He wished that things were like they were before, that Jaric and he were still friends. That Jaric and Becky were still just friends. He looked down with a heavy heart.

"I was thinking of that poor Mewiis world." He half-lied.

"Yeah. It's going to take several weeks to get the Kraaqi capital ships upgraded, provided they use the Hrono shipyards as Mother wants," Becky said.

"The Hrono will be implementing the weapon into their ships too. Good thing they have so many shipyards. I know Mother already has the plans for integrating it into each of their systems," Jaric said.

Kyle looked up, but his eyes didn't meet Jaric's. "I think both the Hrono and Kraaqi will be able to refit their fleets in time. I think they'll all be able to do it in short order."

"Is there something else bothering you? You don't seem like the same old Kyle lately. I thought it might be that spicy Kraaqi food." Jaric winked. But when Kyle did not smile back, Jaric became serious. "You sure nothing else is bothering you?"

"Naw, I'm all right," Kyle said halfheartedly.

"You know, I've been thinking. Minstrel is leading the Mewiis with the hybrid weapon upgrades on their battle cruisers, which have now begun in earnest. Why don't you and I convince Rawlon to send the Band of Thunder's ships to the Hrono, and we'll go with them. We can help ease the friction and give their pilots some insights into fighting the T'kaan," Jaric suggested. "Just you and me."

"What about Becky?" Kyle asked.

"She and Mother should go back to the Kraaqi worlds and make sure the main part of 'em stay in line. I think they need Mother's firm hand." Jaric laughed.

"Yeah, after Mother informed us of the Hrono attempt to take her apart in her communiqué, it's probably better for you two to go back to Hronosium instead," Becky added.

Kyle chuckled momentarily as he thought about Mother's bold escape from the Hrono. And at the thought of being with his lifelong friend again -- just the two of them.

"Yeah, that might work. We'll get Rok to lead his band too. The two bands will be an example to help the others cooperate with the Hrono." Kyle's face lit up with interest.

Becky put her arms around both young men and squeezed them in a friendly embrace.

"The next time we see each other, the T'kaan Third fleet is going down!" she said with confidence.

"That's all we have to do now," Kyle said with a bemused look on his face. "Defeat the terrible T'kaan Third Fleet."

"Is that *all* we have to do?" Jaric asked, half-joking.

But none of them laughed.

Chapter Thirty-Eight

Two months passed, and the leaders of the Three Kingdoms called a special Assembly.

The T'kaan assaults had steadily increased against the Mewiis worlds the last weeks, but the much-anticipated full attack had still not materialized. Neither had the main part of the T'kaan Third Fleet appeared in force, only strong squadrons that attacked and destroyed their Mewiis targets and then disappeared to prepare their next move.

Four Mewiis planets had fallen victim to the horned squadrons. But because of the heroic efforts of the Mewiis Navy as well as Mother at the planet Myraira, the majority of that world's population had been successfully evacuated prior to its destruction. Still, the price had been high, and the Mewiis were now demanding more help from the Hrono and Kraaqi.

During these eight weeks every shipyard across the Three Kingdoms had been busy every hour of every day integrating the hybrid weapon into as many ships as possible. Now, on the first day of the Assembly, the work on the last of the cruisers of the Kraaqi fleet had been completed. Across all three fleets, every battleship and every class of cruiser now had the hybrid weapon successfully installed and tested.

But as the Assembly began, the admirals and captains of the Hrono and Kraaqi clamored for the hybrid weapon to be installed in the frigates as well while the Mewiis admirals argued back that it was time to take the war to the T'kaan. Emotions were high, and the newly formed alliance was being sorely tried.

They finally decided by the end of that first day to bring the ships of every fleet together and prepare to strike back at the T'kaan. As orders were quickly relayed to the fleets to begin gathering at the predetermined coordinates, scout ships were also ordered out in large numbers in order to seek out and find the T'kaan Third fleet. The success of all their preparations hinged on striking the T'kaan and destroying their entire fleet in one mighty blow.

But, they had to find the elusive T'kaan Third fleet.

The fourth day of the Assembly arrived, and there was still no word from the scout ships.

As the leaders of the Three Kingdoms anxiously awaited word, a new argument arose -- an argument that centered upon Kyle, Becky, and Jaric.

"We are the last three humans left alive in the universe."

The Hrono and Kraaqi froze at Kyle's words. In fact, every eye in the audience now focused on the lone human as he stood before them.

Kyle stared wild-eyed at the gathered leaders and warriors -- Hrono allied at last with Kraaqi, and even the diminutive Mewiis armed for war. They were all prepared for victory.

But the unthinkable had also been whispered in small groups -- defeat, and to be brought to extinction like the human race. The audience remained silent as this alternative sunk in once again with Kyle's words.

"Even more reason for you not to fight in this battle," Rawlon growled as he stroked his chin.

"We will fight," Kyle growled back. "We will not be left out after helping you this far."

Jaric's ebony skin flashed under the harsh lights of

Assembly as he stepped onto the stage beside Kyle. And together, they faced the gathered Three Kingdoms.

"We cannot be denied." Jaric began. "It is our destiny!"

"There may yet be a way," Jasus said. "Through genetic engineering ... maybe ... "

His unfinished words spoke louder than the ones he had uttered.

"Today is a day of action." Becky strode to the center of the stage beside Kyle and Jaric. "We must fight through that ... before we can think of tomorrow, or the hope of one."

A pervasive silence echoed throughout the great hall, and the thousands shook their heads in wonder.

"You owe us as well," Mother's voice echoed. Though the mighty ship rested on the plain outside the spiral building of Mewasta, her voice emanated through her robot envoy, Guardian. His massive seven-foot form walked forward and stood stolidly with the humans, as he had since their childhood.

"We have helped you with our technology and with what we have learned in battle with the T'kaan, improving your ships as well as helping you integrate the hybrid weapon. The combined fleets of the Hrono, Kraaqi, and Mewiis gathered around this system now have stronger shields and engines. Your capital ships are now primed with the hybrid weapon to smash the feared horned fleet." Mother's voice paused. "You must let us be there with you."

It was true, Mother reflected silently. Every ship from a light cruiser and larger had installed Mother's fabled weapon, complementing their main armaments. But there had been one failure with its integration in the warships of the Three Kingdoms: whereas Mother could recharge the T'kaan/Human hybrid weapon and use it over and over

341

again, in their warships no amount of configuration would allow the weapon to fire more than five times before the circuitry overloaded and it became unusable.

"Let the female human stay -- it is with her that the future of the human race may lie," Jasus said. "At least let her stay. From her womb may spring the human race again."

Becky's eyes burned into the twin pupils of the Hrono. She and everyone gathered knew how tenuous that hope, that dream, that fleeting wish -- really was.

"I *will* fight," she said firmly.

"If anyone should stay for the sake of the lost race known has humans ... it should be Mother." Minstrel's disembodied voice caused every head to turn upward. Floating just below the huge ceiling above the throngs, Minstrel had watched mainly in silence.

Below, the Mewiis smiled at their well-known friend, but the Kraaqi and Hrono still stared with fresh wonder at this newly acquainted alien entity. As the crowds digested the words, Minstrel twinkled with emotion.

"Inside her long-term memories is stored the entire collected knowledge -- science, art, music ... " Minstrel paused, its plasma body aglow with different colors. "The entire memory of what the human race once was is carried inside MotherShip," Minstrel said. "It is she who should not fight. So the universe might remember."

"Hear. Hear. Yes!" shouted the gathered throngs.

The room filled with the leaders and high warriors of the Three Kingdoms began chanting their approval of Minstrel's words. In the past few months, as the MotherShip and her children had brought them first warning of the coming fleet and then had taken the lead in forging this unimaginable alliance among once sworn enemies, all had come to know and respect them and Minstrel. They had also shared with the humans in their mourning and in their burning desire to destroy those that were now destroying the worlds of the Mewiis.

"I must be there." Mother's voice doubled in volume and caused every head to turn toward Guardian.

"Did Mother just shout?" Becky asked with disbelief.

Jaric and Kyle stared at the speaker on Guardian's chest through which Mother's words had just emanated. Mother continued speaking, her voice now at a normal volume and intensity.

"It was my fighting prowess that bought the last remnants of humanity those precious few weeks to prepare their last stand. Alone, I fought those rear-guard actions time and again to slow down the T'kaan advance against Earth."

The silence returned and filled the hall -- a deep hush embraced them as they listened -- as if something holy were about to be uttered.

"Against impossible odds, my weapons cut through the advancing squadrons of horned ships, and then I withdrew. I made my way in secret to the prearranged rendezvous point and picked up the children," Mother said. "My creators, Ron and Rita, had finally seen the futility and had guessed the final outcome many months before the last stand. They had made preparations to escape and save what they could of their race and the few they could take with them. But war takes unexpected turns."

Mother's processors burned with activity as memories hard and clear came back and were relived. She felt a surge from her primary power source and wondered why she had suddenly armed her weapons, when there was no enemy in sight on this world.

"My creators died on that last planet -- died with the last defenders of humanity. Yet, they did something no race before them had done -- they took the T'kaan Third down with them, including the Great and mysterious horned ship that each fleet is built around."

The silence grew heavy and electric.

"But more T'kaan came. And more ships were built." Mother paused for effect. "With only the three children, I fought my way through the rebuilding fleet. The First and Second were sending replacements as the maggot offspring fed on the battlefield dead. A new Great Horned ship was born. All this time, I fought them, while at the same time teaching the children how to defeat the horned enemy. I protected them. I taught them. I --" Mother's voice processor suddenly cut off.

Mother focused on the implications of the next words she had almost uttered -- I loved them. *Could she really express that she felt that emotion for the children?* She wondered. *Can a machine love? A ship designed to destroy, designed for war. Do I really feel love?*

The questions of life haunted Mother once again deep inside her electronic mind.

She so wanted to know love -- to love, and to be loved. And most of all, she wanted to tell those gathered here that she did indeed love her children, and that she knew what love meant.

One millisecond had almost elapsed when she resumed.

"You will need my prowess when you fight this greatest of enemies. For if the Third is not stopped, there will be no more Kraaqi, no more Mewiis, and no more Hrono,"

Mother said instead.

Even as these last words fell upon the alien ears, movement began around Rawlon and his entourage. A courier entered the room from an entrance behind him and began whispering excitedly in Rawlon's ear.

Moments later, Rawlon stood with his hand raised for silence as the sound of murmuring grew and filled the great chamber with excitement.

"The T'kaan fleet has been found! Listen to this live message my people are receiving from the Kraaqi scout ship, Hyydea."

Becky jumped when static suddenly rattled from the overhead speakers. Every heart in the hall pounded with a rush of emotions as the static grew louder.

" ... of the Hyydea. We have made contact with the T'kaan main fleet and are being attacked. I repeat, the horned ships do show the markings of the Third Fleet." There was a pause of silence that seemed to stretch for a small eternity.

"Oh, Great Osni! There are so many ... Wait ... wait. Target that frigate! Helm, hard over!"

Multiple explosions rumbled through the speakers until the hall itself seemed to be under direct attack. More words, garbled and almost unintelligible, came between the explosions. Amid this terrible cacophony came their last words.

" ... there ... .others <static> ... warn <more static> ... .listen ... you must ... <static>"

A huge explosion suddenly rattled every speaker in the great chamber as the assembled masses rose as one.

Becky raised her hands to her ears as she felt Kyle and Jaric move to her side.

A harsh, dead silence filled their hearing, and everyone knew the scout ship had been destroyed.

Rawlon's swarthy frame rose between a diminutive male Mewiis and the larger female Mewiis, Admiral Saris. Two chairs down, the scaly form of Tarlog rose as his eyes locked with his once sworn enemy.

Rawlon raised his clenched fist and shook it at the sky as his black feather-hair jumped across his shoulders like the mane of a mighty lion. Every muscle in his powerful frame rippled with tension as he readied himself for what must be. He opened his mouth and roared, waving his head and his warrior's horns in battle challenge to the unseen enemy above -- to the T'kaan.

Every Kraaqi warrior fixed their eyes on Rawlon and roared with him, joining their voices together until the walls shook again with the power of their battle cry.

The Hrono warriors and even the Mewiis joined with their own screaming cries as the emotional electricity filled the air between them like something alive.

The admiral of the combined force dropped his clenched fist as the battle cry faded from his lips. The crowded hall slowly became silent as ten thousand faces watched him with rising expectation. As the silence became complete, Rawlon looked out into the crowd.

"It is time!" Rawlon roared.

Chapter Thirty-Nine

The Circle Ship of Minstrel was Mother's sole companion as they flew to the gathering of fleets. The manta-ray silhouette of MotherShip drove hard through the blackness of space, her now fully restored ThunderStar engines straining to be set free at full power.

The great Kraaqi war fleet was already gathered along with the majority of the Mewiis and Hrono fleets at the place appointed by the High Command after a final review of the data from the lost scout ship. But Mother had desired a few hours to be alone with her children and Minstrel, so they traveled separately from the other ships.

Deep inside the circuits that ran throughout her being, Mother felt something she had never felt before. It was a kind of supercharged, electric feeling. Even as she began her diagnostics, she knew they were unnecessary. Images now flashed inside her near-term memories.

They were memories of her children, precious memories of when they were young and she was their entire world.

Mother's processors burned with super-activity.

"My life is nothing like I dreamed it would be." Becky's eyes filled with tears as the twinkling stars on the viewscreen swept by.

Mother's optics focused on Becky's familiar form, her blonde hair falling in waves across her shoulders. Jaric's tall form was beside her now, his arm around her waist as he sought to comfort her. Kyle stepped closer on her other side, but he kept alone and aloof, as was his way. His arms were crossed across his broad chest in an outward show of defiance against the inner loneliness that haunted him.

The last three humans stared in shared silence as Mother carried them ever closer to the gathering storm.

"I only remember war. My whole life has been war," Becky said with tear-filled eyes. "Even after we defeat the T'kaan Third ... there are two more T'kaan fleets."

Jaric felt a huge lump in his throat as he tried to speak. Closing his eyes, he searched to find his voice. "I wish I could take you away from this. Somewhere, there has to peace and happiness. Somewhere."

Kyle's eyes narrowed as he looked away, unable to speak.

"What can I do?" Mother asked. "Can I provide something for you? Something to help you?"

"I don't know what I want." Becky sighed. She wiped her tears, first with the back of her hand, and then as more fell, she wiped again with her palms.

"I want to be happy," she said with sudden conviction.

Mother began processing that word, the emotion, running its meaning through her vast knowledgebase. She sought the answer to happiness.

But there was none.

"None of us wanted this life," Kyle said. "Always fighting. Always retreating." He breathed deeply. "But we make our stand now, and it is a most noble fight. If we defeat the T'kaan this day, we will save three races from certain extinction."

"And for the first time in history, defeat a T'kaan fleet. As well as live to tell the tale." Mother's voice was crisp and animated. "I have tried to care for you the best I could. I have defeated many ships. I have won many battles -- all for you."

Kyle and Jaric smiled at each other.

"But I have tried to be more than your protector. And I have tried to be more than simply your teacher. I have attempted through all the knowledge of the human race stored in my memories ... to be your parent. To be your mother."

"And you are," Becky said quickly. "You are my mother. Our mother."

Mother's sensors picked up a squadron of Hrono ships as they closed upon the rendezvous point in the Mewiis sector. Even as she began to answer Becky a few milliseconds later, she put her twelve main batteries into active mode and extended each one's twin barrels from her hull.

"Like all mothers, I have tried to love you." Silence punctuated her statement. "That is especially hard for me, an AI warship. So hard." Again Mother paused. "I have tried to make you happy. But there is one thing in which I have failed you."

"No! You have never failed us," Jaric exclaimed.

Even stoic Kyle eyed the optics in disbelief as he brushed his fingers through his sandy locks.

"You are the best mother any child could ask for," Kyle whispered, almost too low for the others to hear. But Mother always heard.

"I have failed," Mother's electronic voice answered. "Kyle, my oldest, is now almost twenty-one. Jaric and Becky are a few years younger. Your entire lives should be before you."

"That is not your fault," Becky said hoarsely.

"Parents should at the very least assist their offspring off to a good start in life. To give them skills, provide support, and prepare them to live out the rest of the years. Parents give life, something a machine such as I cannot do. But I should have at least made your life better." Silence filled the air. "I did not do that."

"My life is better," Jaric said.

"And mine," Kyle added.

"I have only taught you war," Mother whispered.

Inside the warship, sadness gripped everyone in the tiny family. This overwhelming feeling covered them and pressed in on them from every side.

"You had to," Becky said, choking back her sobs. "Or we'd be dead now."

Mother held that thought. She had done the best she could do. All she could now was hope it had been enough -- because their greatest test was now before them at the gathering of fleets.

In that precious moment, she shared her near-term memories with her children.

The monitor nearest the children flashed to life with images of long ago, images of three young children running and playing through brightly lit corridors, playing games of hide and seek and games of tag. Long-forgotten toys were crushed tightly in their tiny embraces, and cherubic faces looked with wide, innocent smiles back at them from the consoles. There was laughter again, laughter and carefree joy in the faces that seemed so familiar, and yet they were not.

The images seemed to be of another life, another time. The long years melted away and were relived together one more time.

Mother and her children were a happy family. One last time.

As Mother blacked out the last image, Jaric and Becky turned to leave, to be alone before the coming fight.

"One final item, my children," Mother began. "As the fleets engage, stay near to me. I will protect you."

Becky turned to Jaric and shrugged.

"We will try," Becky said, though they all realized that in the heat of battle even Mother couldn't guarantee their safety.

Kyle alone stood in the Operations Center, the heart of the great ship. This room was the place the children had always imagined Mother really lived, though now that they were young adults, they realized that she was the entire ship.

"After this is all over, we have to help Becky. You know, make her happy. A celebration maybe?" Kyle looked toward the optical viewer.

"A celebration," Mother echoed. "A celebration party."

"Yes." A shadow crept over his face. "Protect them, Mother. Becky and Jaric," Kyle said with a serious tone. "But there's no need to protect me, I'll take care of myself. Whatever happens, don't leave either of them vulnerable during the battle. Ever."

"I will protect all my children." Mother paused. "A good mother will gladly give her life for her children. I will protect you all."

Kyle shook his head. "Don't be a hero for me. Those two should be happy -- they deserve to be happy. Becky and Jaric have each other." Kyle paused, fighting his burning emotions. "They will marry after this is all over. And maybe ... maybe the advanced technology of the Hrono can bring the human race back to life, with them as the first parents. The parents of a new race of humanity."

351

Kyle looked down, a deep sadness etched on his face. "But there will never be anyone for me."

"Do not feel loneliness, Kyle. We will begin our search for survivors again once this battle is over. There may have been others." Mother paused. "Remember, the universe is a very large place".

Kyle straightened and began making his way to his fighter. He stopped at the optical viewer.

"I will protect myself, and I'll help you protect them. But under no circumstances are you to forsake their safety for mine. I order you," Kyle said firmly. Under his breath, in whispered words so quiet that even Mother's sensitive microphones could not hear them, he spoke a final time.

"There's no one for me."

Mother remained silent as Kyle left the room. He had ignored her words about searching once again for any human survivors. She discerned from his expression and from his silence that he no longer believed they would find any survivors.

Mother's calculations agreed.

Still, her processors burned with activity. It did not feel right to Mother, but logic and fact spoke otherwise. Long seconds passed as she wrestled with cold logic and the warm concept of hope, and then a familiar voice came over the comm channel.

"You must remember that your life is also important, MotherShip." Minstrel's voice echoed inside her circuits. "Protect yourself. And the precious memories of mankind."

Mother's processors burned with activity.

Chapter Forty

"Ships from the Band Bahka have joined Sarn's battle group," Commander Curja reported concisely.

"Good," Rawlon said. "That completes the greatest fleet the Kraaqi have ever assembled. All the bands fighting together again, under my command." He motioned to his executive officer. The viewscreen came alive and displayed the massive armada. As far as the eye could see, an ocean of warships stood out against the velvety blackness -- Kraaqi, Hrono, and Mewiis.

"This day will live in legend," Rawlon said with awe.

Curja approached the admiral's chair and spoke in a lowered voice.

"I am still concerned with our left wing. It is true that the Mewiis have provided every ship that could fly. But so many are lightly armed -- traders and research vessels only recently refitted for battle." Curja leaned closer. "I fear the T'kaan will sense this weakness early, and if they hammer the Mewiis' fleet and break through the left wing, our rear will then be vulnerable." Curja watched his admiral intently. "We cannot be outflanked."

"I have placed three Kraaqi battle groups in reserve just for that eventuality. The Mewiis are not a warrior race." Rawlon stroked a horn in thought before he continued. "But they fight for their children. They will not be easily defeated." The admiral's face grew grim. "But I do have a concern." He turned to a junior officer. "Get me a comm link to Admiral Tarlog. At once!"

Rawlon leaned forward in his chair as he brushed his hands through the narrow black mane that ran over the top of his head and down his shoulders.

The main viewscreen came alive. The grim face of Tarlog, topped by the ridge of upturned scales that extended over the top of his hairless head, gazed sternly back at the Kraaqi admiral.

"Report, Rawlon. And be quick. I must place my formations into their final positions." The Hrono's eyes burned with impatience. "In accordance with *our* plan of battle."

"And that of the MotherShip," Rawlon growled.

"Yes." The Hrono admiral snorted

Rawlon sat down, his posture one of relaxation in his commander's chair. "Look at your viewscreen, Admiral Tarlog. Look closely." Rawlon pointed. "Gaze at the center of the greatest battle line the universe has ever witnessed." Rawlon eyed the image carefully. "See the courage and valor of Kraaqi. All bands have answered the call -- all ships are battle ready. Over one thousand warships and twice that number of fighters." His talon-tipped finger pointed at the Hrono like a weapon. "But where is the rest of the Hrono fleet? Do we see again the treachery of Hrono here, on this Day of Days?"

A nervous tic began in the etched corner of Tarlog's scaly face. Raising a hand over his mouth, the Hrono admiral whispered to the aide standing beside him, eliciting a wolfish smile from the younger officer. Tarlog turned back to face Rawlon.

"The Hrono keep their word -- our ships will come. We do not practice treachery as an art form as do the Kraaqi," Tarlog said.

Rawlon was instantly on his feet.

Curja reached over and quickly grabbed Rawlon's arm,

holding him fast as he reached out at the taunting visage with his fist.

"I am not the enemy. Not today," Tarlog reminded them.

Rawlon's eyes narrowed. He nodded at his aide, who then released his arm.

"We must all remember that fact -- especially us." Rawlon nodded silently to himself. "Come, today makes history for another reason -- Kraaqi and Hrono fight together for the first time in history. Our mutual enemy even now draws close."

The Hrono admiral's eyes seemed to look past the Kraaqi, and then his eyes refocused.

"Yes, we are allies." Tarlog paused. "What is your request, Admiral?" he asked with military bearing.

Rawlon turned and sat again in his chair, his muscular arms resting casually across it.

"Where is the rest of your fleet, Tarlog?" Rawlon asked firmly.

The Hrono leader did not hesitate. "They are in a reserve position ... within attack distance."

Rawlon's eyes narrowed. "Where is the famed Home Fleet? Is it still around the Hrono home world?"

The Hrono commander stood slowly and stepped closer until only his face filled the viewscreen, hiding the rest of the Hrono battle cruiser's bridge.

"They are in position -- in reserve. The Hrono will hold the right wing of the battle line. Don't worry." Tarlog smiled. "You must remember, my Kraaqi friend, that though we do not build our warships on the same scale as you, our smaller ships are better armed with superior technology and speed. Though unseen, they are close enough to strike. Trust my judgment, and the technology of Hrono." Tarlog chuckled under his breath. "Our technology has always ensured our superiority."

"We know that you worship your technology, you godless Hrono," Rawlon countered. "But it has never enabled you to defeat the warriors of Kraaqi." Rawlon again pointed his talon-tipped finger at the Hrono. "Just make sure that when I call for the Home Fleet, that they are there when I need them. The MotherShip has estimated that all ships of the Three Kingdoms are needed, just to equal the T'kaan Third. And remember ... Rawlon is still the appointed commander of this assembled fleet." He stared, defying the Hrono to counter.

But Tarlog only nodded in agreement. "Yes, we fight under you, Rawlon. This day. The Home Fleet is ready -- out of sensor range." Tarlog bowed toward Rawlon. "The entire Hrono fleet now awaits your orders. As do I."

Rawlon nodded with approval. "Many centuries of warfare are hard to discard. The Kraaqi value your ships, Admiral Tarlog." Rawlon paused a brief moment, and then added, "We value the courage of the Hrono. May our enemies tremble at this great battle fleet assembled before them."

"Sir!" A junior Kraaqi officer approached Rawlon and announced, "The MotherShip and the fighters of the three humans have just arrived and joined the lead battle group of Kraaqi fighters."

"Good, I have assigned them to the Death Squadron -- now under the leadership of Rok. They will all proceed to the forward point to engage the enemy first." Rawlon growled under his breath in thought. He nodded. "Send Chagak and Krazak with their frigate battle groups to join them."

Rawlon waved his hand in salute toward the viewscreen. But even before he could ask for a comm channel to welcome the honored allies of humanity, another officer suddenly raised his head from his station and spoke in a calm voice.

"The T'kaan fleet has just come into sensor range, sir."

Chapter Forty-One

Each Kraaqi captain watched as their viewscreens filled with the horned prows of the T'kaan war fleet. On they came, multiplying before their eyes like hordes of insects. The Hrono officers and the Mewiis watched in shared silence inside their own ships as the T'kaan ships filled their viewscreens -- hundreds of warships, and then thousands.

And each second even more sailed into view.

Kyle reached down and readjusted the controls on his sensors. But the numbers kept increasing. He pounded the control panel harshly, as if that would make the numbers stop rising. But it did nothing.

Everywhere the eye gazed, there were T'kaan warships -- from massive formations of battle cruisers, to wave after endless wave of fighters, and from tightly packed squadrons of the deadly frigates, to the battle lines of the huge horned battleships. Still they came, and still the ships multiplied.

"Something's wrong!" Kyle barked as he began adjusting his sensors again.

Mother's processors began assimilating the vastness of the approaching fleet, and for the first time in her existence, she felt confused.

"I've got incoming," Becky shouted as a wave of scout fighters stormed down.

One hundred and forty-four ships closed with them -- a single formation of T'kaan fighters.

"Becky! Take half the Death Squadron and close with them," Jaric ordered. He looked over at another wave now veering directly towards him. "I'll handle this group. Kyle, we need reinforcements. Now!"

Even as the words were spoken, a formation of nine T'kaan frigates came into weapon's range.

Four Kraaqi frigates observed this maneuver and quickly moved in position to engage them. Silently the T'kaan frigates turned as one, showing their full profiles in a battle line opposite the line of Kraaqi warships as they flew in parallel.

"Fire!" Krazak ordered to his Kraaqi frigates.

Almost simultaneously, the T'kaan fired their full broadsides. Blaster bolts crossed each other and blossomed across the shields of each ship like electric flowers, brief and fantastic.

Mother's alarms rang out. She turned to engage six more T'kaan frigates that had suddenly drawn into range.

From his flagship, Rawlon stared in numbed silence. Slowly he stood as the horde of ships became clearer on his viewscreen. His hands reached out blindly as he got up from his chair and walked between his officers' stations and straight toward the viewscreen that held him hypnotized.

Inexorably, the T'kaan warships multiplied before his very eyes.

"How many ships, Curja?"

But all the officers around the bridge were frozen at the reality of the nightmare unfolding before them.

"Curja!" Rawlon shouted, as he continued staring into the sea of horned ships. Like everyone else who couldn't take their eyes away, a feeling of impending doom filled his heart. Finally, he let out a long breath and spoke in a hushed tone.

"Get me the MotherShip."

But Mother was busy. Her primary weapon was primed, but she held it while she launched a spread of torpedoes at the formation of frigates, even as they fired back at her.

"How can there be so many?" Kyle shouted as a T'kaan fighter exploded in his sights. His ship shuddered. Kicking his thrusters, he began rolling away, trying to see where the fire was coming from.

In a vast swirling spiral of ships, Becky led her Kraaqi fighters in a free-for-all punctuated by frequent showers of explosions. The tracers were thick around her ship and coming from every direction.

As soon as she finished off one horned fighter, two more engaged her. Wiping her blonde hair aside, she saw that her shields had already dropped below fifty percent, and she was only five minutes into the battle.

She targeted another T'kaan and took it out.

A second T'kaan frigate broke in two as Mother brought her twelve guns to bear on a group of fighters that had swooped upon her flanks. Mother felt her shields diminishing under more direct hits from the frigates as she prepared to fire a third spread of torpedoes at them.

Her sensors suddenly registered the T'kaan markings on the ships she was destroying. For a millisecond -- an electronic eternity -- all her internal processes froze at once. But the image was double-checked, and the terrible reality would not go away.

Mother immediately sent an urgent message back to Rawlon's flagship.

Rawlon continued to stare in disbelief at the viewscreen.

"There are more T'kaan ships on my viewscreen ... than there are stars," he whispered grimly. As Rawlon continued to watch the approaching fleet, Curja approached him and whispered excitedly in his ear.

The admiral turned slowly to face Curja.

"Did I hear you correctly?"

Curja's desperate eyes spoke for him, as he repeated the dire message again. "We are vastly outnumbered, five ships to one. Our sensors do not lie."

"The MotherShip is on-line, sir. With an urgent message," a third officer shouted.

Rawlon turned.

"We must retreat, Grand Admiral," Mother said matter-of-factly from the comm unit. "I have identified ships of both the T'kaan First and Second Fleets, along with the Third. We must recalculate our options in light of this new data. We did not plan for this scenario."

"All three T'kaan fleets are here?" Curja whispered in disbelief.

Rawlon slammed his fist into his palm as his dark eyes narrowed. He growled as confusion fogged his mind.

"Tarlog is demanding you, Rawlon," another Kraaqi officer shouted.

Rawlon nodded, suddenly feeling weary and old -- and so very tired.

The Hrono's visage appeared on-screen.

"Rawlon. We will be easily out-flanked. We do not have enough ships to stop their maneuver around the right wing." The Hrono admiral stared back as if in shock. "There are too many!"

Rawlon nodded. "Order the retreat. And order the humans back." Rawlon paused. "Can our fleet complete the turn and make hyperspace before the main fleets engage?"

Curja's hands flashed over his console, and he smiled. "Yes. Barely."

"Order it." Rawlon stared back at the viewscreen filled

with T'kaan ships. Under his breath, he cursed.

Across the battle line, Kraaqi warships turned in solemn unison. Within seconds, the Hrono fleet began a similar maneuver.

Curja approached again. "The Mewiis Admiral is calling for you."

Rawlon shook his head. Closing his eyes, he waved his hand to accept.

Admiral Saris appeared onscreen. "What are you doing? We came here to fight. Too many Mewiis children -- too many Mewiis worlds -- have already perished waiting for this day. If we do not make a stand here, the Mewiis home world will fall next."

Rawlon did not answer.

The Mewiis' eyes narrowed, and her lips pressed into a thin line. "Do you run? Do you fear this enemy?"

Rawlon shook his head tiredly. "There are too many ... " he began.

"There will always be too many!" Saris shouted.

The Kraaqi warlord sighed. "We must replan --"

"No. No more planning. Our fleet will stay! We will hold the left wing. We must stay with our original plan!"

"You cannot -- not against these odds," Rawlon said. "You will be overrun within the hour."

"The Mewiis will not leave." She growled. "We stand between Mewiis worlds, Mewiis children. We draw the line here. We fight here." Saris raised her fist at Rawlon. "Now!"

For the first time Rawlon understood the diminutive Mewiis race. But he did not answer, feeling a sudden shame inside his warrior's breast.

With an angry gesture, Saris's image disappeared.

Mothership

"Fight bravely," Rawlon said. He spoke the Kraaqi honorific to Admiral Saris, normally only given to Kraaqi and their warrior brethren as they entered into battle.

Chapter Forty-Two

The shields of the last T'kaan frigate attacking her buckled, and it turned away disabled, but Mother had no time to finish the job. Already the swarm of T'kaan fighters attacking her had doubled, and her shields were dropping dangerously low.

"Kyle, form up with what's left of Jaric's wing. I'll join Becky," Mother ordered. "We are retreating with the Kraaqi fleet."

"This can't be." Kyle snarled into his viewer. But he banked his ship sharply in compliance, not knowing what else to do in the face of the combined T'kaan fleets.

"We're already cut off," Jaric said with a hollowness.

"Then we fight our way through, just like the old days," Kyle snarled.

Rok's fingers squeezed the triggers, and two T'kaan Scout fighters exploded in his sights. "The old days were not so good," Rok said as he turned to engage another T'kaan.

"MotherShip, this is Minstrel."

"Go ahead," Mother said.

"I am with the Mewiis on the left wing. T'kaan ships are bearing down on us, formation after formation. The Kraaqi fleets are turning, retreating, but the Mewiis are standing firm. They will not retreat." Minstrel's voice trailed off. "I am fighting the best I can alongside the Mewiis, but the T'kaan just keep coming."

Mother started to speak, but a dozen hunter fighters suddenly leapt out of the darkness for her. Focusing her processing power, she brought all of her main guns to bear and fired at them as she turned hard to avoid their fire. Ships exploded under her direct hits, and the hunter formation broke up and retreated.

Another T'kaan formation now came into range to engage her.

In that instant, her sensors focused on Becky's ship. So near -- and yet so far.

Waves of T'kaan fighters closed with the Kraaqi fighters that Becky led.

"They're everywhere!" Becky shouted.

The ship in Becky's sights exploded, but even as she looked up for her Kraaqi allies, she saw more of the three-horned ships diving on her. Her fighter shuddered under direct hits, and suddenly the shield alarm screamed -- her shields were completely down. She kicked her ship hard over and dove away.

Without shields, she knew she was a sitting duck.

"I need some help here," Becky said with a surprising calm.

Kyle destroyed another fighter and tried to turn to help Becky. But two more T'kaan cut him off. As he twisted away, he saw her out of the corner of his eye. He watched the three-horned ships even as they fired.

Helplessly, he stared at the tracers streaking straight for Becky's unprotected ship.

The universe seemed to stop.

***

Jaric fired and turned, trying to find Becky's familiar ship. But his ship suddenly shuddered under more direct hits. Jerking the controls, he dove down and below the sudden hail of blaster fire. He tried to maneuver toward the dot that he knew was Becky's ship on his sensor screen. But he couldn't as his ship shuddered again with direct hits.

Jaric turned his ship away, screaming in rage.

***

Mother's sensors pinpointed Becky's ship and her merciless attackers. Even as she pushed her mighty engines and made them scream in protest, she was processing all possible attack vectors and deciding which would bring the most desired result -- to save Becky. All her guns turned and focused on the targets attacking Becky, but they were out of her range.

Just out of reach.

***

Becky jerked her ship hard and then stared into the laser lances coming straight for her.

"Mother!" she cried.

***

Mother raced toward the sensor marker that was Becky, her engines straining past the red line. She bent every process to this one, great task -- to protect her child, a job she was well equipped to accomplish, something she had done so many times in the past. Something ...

The sensor marker that was Becky's ship suddenly disappeared.

Mother was confused for the second time that day. Her circuits began to overheat with intense activity as she tried to find Becky's ship. She started a Level-Four diagnostic on her main sensors even as her guns belched death and destroyed the three-horned fighters that had been attacking Becky's ship.

Within seconds, the diagnostics returned, completed. They were surprisingly clean -- no error found -- as she raced past the blossoming explosions.

Mothership

Mother quickly recalibrated her sensors and scanned the area again. And still, she could not locate Becky's ship.

More alarms sounded inside her flickering, electronic soul.

She recalibrated her sensors a third time. It only took a few seconds, yet it seemed like an eternity. She continued to strain, to search ... to search in vain for her lone girl-child.

When her recalibrations failed again, she began filtering out all ships, even Kraaqi ships, only searching for human configurations with her sensors. *Only human ships.*

Two ships appeared.

Mother's processors suddenly spiked into super-activity as she calculated all possible solutions to this inexplicable problem. Alarms screamed down her darkened corridors as displays flashed with streaming mountains of data. Her processors leveled off at one hundred percent utilization.

But the answer was obvious.

"Kyle. I am malfunctioning," Mother said. "You must lead Becky and Jaric out."

But Kyle could no longer see in order to get away, not through the tears blinding his vision. And he could not answer Mother because of the lump that filled his throat.

Over the comm link Jaric cried out in rage as he pulled his triggers, destroying the T'kaan ships that still dove at him in wave after endless wave.

Chapter Forty-Three

Rawlon was furious, both with himself and with the entire universe.

Kraaqi warriors did not run from battle -- that single thought silently haunted him.

Here he was, admiral of the greatest fleet ever assembled -- and his only order a general retreat. And worse, he was leaving the maternal Mewiis alone to fight the battle for him.

Clenching his eyes shut, he cursed himself.

Behind him, he heard the familiar steps of his first officer approaching.

Rawlon's body jerked with shock as Curja screamed out loud just behind his head. With surprising strength, Curja slammed his fist into the console next to Rawlon's chair, causing sparks to erupt from the damaged electronics.

Rawlon's eyes met Curja's.

Curja glared back with burning anger.

"Have the humans disengaged?" Rawlon asked, as a strange and sickening tightness in his stomach filled him with sudden dread. But somehow he didn't want to know what Curja was going to tell him. He wanted him to leave; he wanted to order Curja to return to his station.

But he couldn't.

With a flash of insight, the age-old Kraaqi proverb went through his mind -- *'Even a warrior fights the bitterness of tragedy to the very end.'*

"The humans ... " Curja began.

"Our brethren!" Rawlon shouted in anger, causing every head on the bridge to turn towards him. "Tell me of the humans -- brethren of the warriors Kraaqi."

Curja looked down, remembering the sacred honor that had been bestowed on the humans during the recently completed rite of Sa'DaK by Rok and the Band of the Stars.

"I will know," Rawlon growled ominously.

Curja looked up with a warrior's stoic gaze. He spoke with a great sadness in his voice.

"The human female, the one called Becky, is dead. She died an honored death in battle."

Rawlon screamed.

He drew the curved rapier from the leather scabbard at his waist. Looking back to the viewscreen, he placed the sharpened edge to his palm ... and slashed. Green blood flowed down his trembling arm as he screamed again in pain and anger. The entire bridge crew screamed their rage with him, their voices joined together in righteous anger for the lost human race.

Chapter Forty-Four

"Please, Kyle, answer me. Perhaps my comm links are also damaged? Yes, they must be damaged too. As are my sensors." Mother felt the direct hits again and again against her shields, but somehow she no longer associated the battle with herself. Her guns fired back automatically, but her aim only managed to scatter the scout fighters, who quickly came around for another run.

"It is so strange, Kyle. My sensors can see you and Jaric, but Becky's ship has disappeared ..." Mother paused. "I cannot think clearly. I think I should contact Rawlon."

Even as Kyle wiped the tears to clear his vision, his shipped lurched. He screamed and banked hard -- straight into the line of fire. Straight into the two attacking T'kaan fighters he flew as he fired back at them like a madman, his ship's collision alarm echoing strangely in his ears, as if he were dreaming.

He pressed his twin triggers over and over and continued to scream.

A short distance away, Jaric finally shook his pursuers. He quickly remembered the explosion and knew with a sickening dread what it meant -- or thought it meant. And now Mother was reporting she was damaged though the battle had barely begun? Deep inside, Jaric felt his heart sink with despair.

He turned his ship back to Becky's last known position, and his sensors reported back the expanding debris field.

His breath failed him as if he had been struck in the chest with a sledgehammer. His heart began throbbing so loudly in his ears that he imagined he had lost atmosphere inside the cockpit. Jaric swayed as his vision blurred and the universe began to fade. Suddenly, bright laser fire erupted around him once again.

Out of pure instinct alone, he turned his ship and rammed the engines full open.

Chapter Forty-Five

"The other humans?" Rawlon asked as he came to his senses.

Curja turned back to his station and read the sensor data. "They are cut off," he said in a voice drained of emotion. "They are cut off -- as is the Death Squadron. More T'kaan ships are closing on them." Curja looked up at Rawlon. "They will be overwhelmed."

One more time, Rawlon turned back to the viewscreen, back to where the black-horned ships outnumbered the very stars.

"Get me Tarlog!" Rawlon shouted decisively.

The visage of the Hrono appeared almost immediately.

"Our fleet is turned and ready for the order to hyperspace," Tarlog reported.

Rawlon stared back at him, and then Tarlog noticed the blood flowing freely down the warrior Admiral's arm.

"The race known as humans is now extinct." Rawlon said simply.

"All of them?" Tarlog asked.

"The female is dead. The two males are trapped, along with the MotherShip."

"Trapped," Tarlog repeated solemnly. "But even if we give them succor, their race is most certainly dead. The female was the key to any hope."

"They will die here, along with the noble Mewiis," Rawlon said.

"Unless?" Tarlog asked, somehow sensing what Rawlon was about to say.

Rawlon smiled widely. "Our peoples have fought each

other for millennia. *We* ... are warrior races."

Tarlog was surprised at the unexpected accolade from his one-time enemy. They stared at each other across the black gulf and felt a new bond begin to tie their souls together.

But the growing nemesis called T'kaan drew ever closer on their viewscreens.

"I say we teach these ... *Dowlas*," Rawlon spat. "I say that we warriors teach these T'kaan what war really is," Rawlon said through clenched teeth.

Tarlog turned and whispered off-line to both his aides. The silence thickened as he finally turned back to Rawlon. "We have been running some quick calculations since your order to retreat. It could well be that at the next battle, the odds may not even be this good," he said bluntly.

Rawlon raised his bloody fist and shook it.

"We can still do what they think impossible."

Tarlog's eyes widened. "Our original plan is useless."

"These T'kaan maggots bring many ships. They bring mighty ships! But they do not have what you and I have -- what the Kraaqi and Hrono have." Rawlon remembered Mother's unifying speech at the recent assembly. "And what the Mewiis have."

"Tell me," Tarlog said with an urgency in his voice.

"They do not have our heart. They do not have our courage," Rawlon growled as he clenched his eyes shut, and then opened them. "They do not have our passion for life."

Tarlog waited while his heart pounded against his ribs.

"Yes," Rawlon crooned. "We must now do something completely unexpected."

"Tell me," Tarlog repeated.

The silence seemed to shout in their ears.

"We will attack," Rawlon whispered savagely.

Tarlog laughed.

But he caught himself in the next second, and his laughter stopped.

Immediately, the beauty of the simple strategy materialized in both their minds.

"They have stretched their superior numbers around our massive defensive line, to encircle and smash us." Rawlon nodded at the viewscreen that displayed their fleets. "They expect us to run, or to go into a defensive mode. But, if I lead the Kraaqi fleet up the center, here." Rawlon pointed, and the ships on the secondary viewscreen moved in a computer simulation. "And with the Hrono fleet as my right fist, here," Rawlon said as his voice rose with emotion. "We leave the Mewiis in their strong defensive position anchoring our left wing and keeping the T'kaan occupied there." The fleets began to move on the viewscreen in the simulation he had just programmed, the distinctive colors of each fleet glowing as though alive. Two large sections formed tight formations and began a forward movement.

"We will smash through their center," Tarlog said with growing optimism. He smiled a warrior's smile. "And then ... ?"

Rawlon raised his rapier toward the T'kaan fleet. "We destroy them where we find them. As we break through to their rear positions, we turn and attack again -- we will outflank them first! But both our fleets must attack using the Kraaqi phalanx in order to punch through."

The Hrono warlord nodded.

"Now," Rawlon said to both Tarlog and Curja. "Send orders to all ships. When they hear the Music of War -- we turn together as one and begin our attack."

Both warlords had the orders quickly sent through their aides to every ship.

Rawlon waited a moment, until his staff finished issuing all their commands. He smiled.

"Curja. Put me through on every comm channel," Rawlon said with confidence.

"They are yours, my commander."

Rawlon waved his hand, and the T'kaan fleet reappeared on his main screen.

They were still bearing down on them.

"Hear me, maggots of T'kaan. The Battleships of the Kraaqi and Hrono come for you now. And we bring war such as you have never known ... "

Rawlon raised his head defiantly and shook his clenched fist to the viewscreen filled with the T'kaan and roared out three words.

"To ... the ... Death!"

Rawlon turned as his bridge officers stood and simultaneously pulled their rapiers out and pointed them towards him in salute. Across the entire Kraaqi fleet, aboard every ship larger than a fighter, every officer stood and repeated the traditional gesture. Even on the Hrono ships of war, every single officer stood and raised their clenched fists or held their weapons high.

Rawlon shouted again the age-old battle cry of his people, and Hrono shouts mingled together ... over every comm channel.

And the T'kaan heard. And wondered.

"I want the 'Music of War,'" Rawlon ordered. "I want it on every comm channel! Ready it, on my mark." Rawlon stood before his commander's chair and pointed at the viewscreen full of T'kaan warships.

"I want them to know we're coming." He snarled. "I want the entire universe to know we're coming!"

Rawlon paused, and then he motioned at Curja.

"Bring the battleships around!"

As one, every battleship turned. With exact precision, the prows of every Hrono and Kraaqi battleship came around simultaneously to face the hordes of T'kaan.

And in perfect concert, the rest of the ships in the fleet turned with them.

***

Rawlon sat back down in his captain's chair and waited until he was sure the T'kaan sensors were aware that the combined fleets were turning for them. With a renewed confidence, he nodded at Curja, his senior officer.

Inside the ships of every fleet, a thousand instruments struck a single, mighty chord and grew into a solid wall of sound. The single chord continued its roar for long seconds -- drawing out its savage cry -- and then the sound of untold numbers of drums joined in and began to pound out a steady, insistent rhythm. The mighty chord went silent a moment, then came again, its intensity only slightly lessened, and then it joined the rhythmic onslaught of the untold drums like some gargantuan engine slowly picking up speed.

With a relentless power, the Music of War began.

Above the mass of combined strings and horns and percussion, an attack of solo instruments began, some like the throaty roar of an electric guitar in full cry, some like electronic instruments turned to searing intensity as they wailed angrily at the heavens. More and more solo instruments roared above this relentless rhythm.

Countless horns now combined, strident and piercing,

as the heavy rhythm slowly increased in speed -- faster and faster. Above the unstoppable rhythm and screaming solo instruments, the horns began to play 'The Charge of the Brave.'

The Music of War roared out over every communication channel and pummeled every aural sensory receptor of every being and urged the allied fleets forward with grim determination.

**

Unknown to Rawlon, the music was hampering the T'kaan ships, especially the three Great Horned ships. Confusion spread as their all-encompassing *oneness* was partially interrupted. The T'kaan compensated, forcing their will between the individual notes. But it was not easy, and they lost precious milliseconds as the music suddenly changed tempo or rhythm.

The T'kaan ships fought against the music to keep it from hampering their all-vital network -- their consciousness -- that connected each and every T'kaan ship.

For the first time in history, just at the edge of their bizarre, combined consciousness, they felt the faintest twinge of fear as they went into battle.

The T'kaan leaders and the Great Horned ships brushed it aside with their combined conscious will.

For they were T'kaan -- nothing could defeat them.

And they could never be defeated with the Great Horned ships directing every T'kaan ship.

Chapter Forty-Six

Tarlog sat with stern-faced resolve aboard his flagship as it made its turn. Kaldah, his senior aide, approached.

"What orders for the Home Fleet, sir?"

"A moment, Kaldah. Let me think."

Tarlog paused in thought as he watched his mighty Hrono fleet come about.

He quickly ordered the battle groups into positions, sending his commands out between the brief pauses of the well-known Kraaqi music. His battle groups formed up in two mighty phalanxes -- the classic attack formation of Kraaqi warships. They heart of each formation was comprised of battle cruisers, light cruisers, and frigates, the elite of his fleet. The battleships formed up all along the leading edges of each phalanx and became the focal points of the huge, three-dimensional phalanxes.

The battleships were to drive a wedge into the enemy formations. Flying above these capital ships, Tarlog ordered every fighter squadron to provide close support around the forward tips of each mighty phalanx.

Tarlog smiled. His sensors showed Rawlon forming his own phalanxes: one huge phalanx in the center and two smaller ones on each flank in typical Kraaqi strategy.

The Hrono admiral waited. As the last Hrono ships closed rank to form the phalanxes, he saw the last fighter squadrons join up with the battleships at the forward points.

The allied battle fleets leapt eagerly toward the enemy.

"Rawlon is taking all his reserves with him in the attack -- all of his battle groups," Kaldah said.

Tarlog turned.

"Order the Home Fleet to close, but not engage. I want them one jump away, ready for my orders." Tarlog waved Kaldah away. But before the officer had taken two steps, a strange expression came over Tarlog's face. A look that spoke volumes.

"Add this to the end of the message -- something the MotherShip told me before we left." Tarlog's eyes narrowed. "Admiral Trakam will understand ... "

The first officer held his position expectantly.

"Tell Trakam, we lead our warships into battle. And ... "

Kaldah's eyes widened.

"We storm the '*Gates of Hell*.'"

***

Rok screamed forth with his own battle cry as the Music of War deafened him. Turning his fighter, he ordered the Death Squadron to close ranks.

"Where are the brethren?" he shouted to his wingman as he came into view alongside.

Before his wingman could answer, a swarm of T'kaan attacked from above.

Rok shouted victoriously as his blasters took out two more T'kaan fighters and his own ship danced between the remaining others flying past. He turned and engaged three more T'kaan and then noted with a glance at his sensors that his wingman was gone -- destroyed.

"Fight, Kraaqi. Fight!" Rok shouted to the remaining fighters of his squadron.

***

Mother too, heard Rawlon's challenge. She heard the music as it roared over every communication channel, although she did not know what it signified. At least a part of her consciousness heard all of this -- but so much of her

379

processing power was focused on her sensors, on her diagnostics, and on the raging battle, that it all seemed a bit unreal.

But what hampered her the most was the fact that her sensors were trying to see the *unseeable* in her present state of denial.

"Mother. I'm surrounded."

Jaric's voice reached through her confusion and focused her processing away from the fruitless search.

Mother reached out with her sensors and found Jaric's ship. Five horned fighters were weaving around the desperate maneuvers of his lone craft as they tried to destroy him.

"I cannot find Becky," Mother said in a strange tone.

Jaric ducked instinctively when Kyle's fighter shot over him. Two of the T'kaan horned fighters exploded in his wake.

As Kyle turned for another pass to help Jaric, three new T'kaan fighters fell upon his own ship.

"Watch your tail, Big K!" Jaric shouted. Multiple alarms sounded from his console as he brought his own guns to bear.

They were both fighting against impossible odds.

But Kyle was a madman.

He banked his craft, miraculously dancing between the laser fire from behind as he swept upon the three remaining fighters Jaric was trying to battle. Kyle did not utter a word.

But his weapons spoke.

Two more of the T'kaan ships exploded. The third shuddered and veered away in retreat.

More took their places as both Kyle and Jaric fought for their lives.

Mother felt her own shields begin to buckle under more direct hits, but she instantly redirected energy away from all non-essential tasks and brought them up again. She noticed with only the smallest part of her processing power that they only came back to nineteen-percent strength.

Suddenly, her long-term memories were filled with the cherubic face of an eight-year-old girl, her long blonde hair falling down around her tiny shoulders. The face was looking up at Mother's optic and asking her, no pleading to her -- with a question that she would never forget.

"Will you be my new mother? Now that mine is dead?"

Mother fired her weapons while her subconscious background processes held the memory of that little girl. Even then her shots found their mark and T'kaan fighters exploded and reeled. But her shields began to fall once more as more as T'kaan blasters impacted against them.

Jaric suddenly seemed to awaken. He felt Kyle's anger focus him. He fed off the burning madness as he watched Kyle's ship attack with reckless abandon. He focused his own anger into a weapon.

Jaric flew his ship hard, twisting and turning when four T'kaan fighters appeared directly in his sights. Two T'kaan ships disappeared in twin explosions, and he raced between the remaining two.

"Where's Mother?" Jaric asked as he punched at his console, trying to get his shields back into decent shape.

Kyle's grim gaze was only for the T'kaan -- to destroy them. Seeing none around them at the moment, he glanced at his sensors. All at once, he seemed to awaken from his madness.

Across his sensors twenty-one T'kaan battle cruisers were almost within weapon's range of their tiny ships.

381

Worse, he couldn't number the frigates and fighters descending on their position along with other capital ships.

And Mother was directly in their path.

"We've got to get out of here!" Kyle shouted. "Mother, turn hard. Turn hard!"

Mother focused some of her processing on her child's voice, leaving the bright memories of the little girl still running in her memory. Still, a surprising amount of her processing continued to watch, as in a trance.

"Kyle?" she asked vaguely.

"Mother, get out of there. An entire T'kaan Battle Group is on top of you!"

"I must find Becky. She is here, you know."

Kyle felt himself stiffen in pain.

"Becky's dead," he said simply.

Mother heard him as if in a haze. Something snapped inside her circuits. Instantly she realized that there was nothing wrong with her sensors. But now she focused the majority of her processing on those two words -- two little words -- that Kyle had just uttered.

She began referencing the second word, searching, finding every usage of the word in her long-term memories, all throughout her vast, vast memories -- a memory system that was filled with the entire knowledge of the human race.

Dead. Defunct. Deceased. Expired. Non-existent. Inanimate. Nothingness. Deprived of life. Lacking power ... Non-functional ...

The opposite of life.

Mother looked again at the face of the little eight-year old girl in her near-term memory, at her shining blue eyes as she asked her that question again, so long ago. A face she would never forget -- she could not afford to forget, not now.

Because Mother would *never* see her again ... see her ... never ... never ... never ... never ... never ... never ... never ... never ... never ...

Never!

The manta-ray shape of Mother turned on its side, standing on one wing as she glided through space. All of her interior lights went out one room at a time while her course remained unchanged. Almost as if in a dream, the ship went silent and dark. But from every single internal system, Mother redirected every ounce of processing power as she filled her near-term memories to capacity with a focused precision.

Kyle was already turning away as he looked back in shock. He checked his sensors and noticed a power surge coming from Mother -- a massive power surge.

Mother had, for only the second time in her existence, turned off everything that was non-essential to her existence. There were no life forms aboard her now to sustain, so she turned off all life support systems and redirected their power. Every function, every circuit, and every system that she did not need for either weapons, sensors, shields, or engines, she either disabled or she redirected their power to one of those four systems.

All her functionality, all her processing power, everything became part of a single thread devoted only to one primary purpose -- war.

Her entire being became *a fighting machine*.

The first T'kaan cruiser came into range, and the mighty horns emanating from its prow spat death towards Mother.

Mother leapt and twisted, missing the laser fire by microns. Still, the power blistered across her rising shields and a sheen of light glowed across her hull from those laser lances that just missed.

Mother turned toward the cruiser.

Her primary weapon, the T'kaan/Human hybrid, which she had given to all Kraaqi, Hrono and Mewiis capital ships ... fired.

A massive red line erupted from Mother's forward section. The black T'kaan cruiser intersected with this blazing red beam -- straight through the ship's fully powered shields the beam sliced, passing through the gnarled hull as if it were nothing. The forward section of the T'kaan cruiser bent downwards as the beam leapt out from the other side. Next, a series of explosions rippled down the entire length of the mighty warship from where the beam had penetrated.

The T'kaan cruiser disintegrated in a massive shower of light.

The other twenty cruisers closed range along with six frigates and another wave of hunter fighters to engage and destroy Mother.

"It'll take Mother almost five minutes to recharge it again! What do we do?" Jaric shouted from his retreating craft. As he glanced down, Jaric saw his sensors fill with a solid wave of ships.

But this wave of ships came at the T'kaan.

***

"Fire!" Rawlon ordered.

Twenty-six of the lead battleships fired their hybrid weapons, and huge red lances of death streaked from their arrow-like prows. The T'kaan cruisers and frigates attacking Mother were cut in two and disappeared in bright, rippling explosions -- all destroyed in one fell blow by the Kraaqi battleships.

Clouds of Kraaqi fighters now engaged the remaining T'kaan fighters.

"Go get'em, Kraaqi!" Jaric shouted.

But now dozens of other T'kaan battle groups came into sensor range to counterattack against Rawlon's ships -- T'kaan battle groups equal in size to or larger than the one just destroyed.

"Prepare for broadsides -- we'll use main weapon arrays on all battleships. Frigate battle groups are to sail forward and attack with torpedoes at these points." Rawlon punched the console on the right arm of his chair and sent out those coordinates. "Order the Tradha, Skorba, and Carka fighter squadrons here." Rawlon smiled at the viewscreen now erupting with explosions before his eyes. "And all main formations -- the phalanxes -- keep moving forward!"

The front echelon of Kraaqi battleships slammed into the T'kaan juggernaut head-on, driving forward into the T'kaan battle line as if they were unstoppable.

The mighty war fleets of the Hrono, Kraaqi, Mewiis, and T'kaan converged and entwined into deadly dances of death.

The Kraaqi-Hrono advance sliced forward with judiciously timed firings of the hybrid weapon -- but only from specifically designated ships each time -- and destroyed every T'kaan ship they touched. They ordered only certain to ships to fire because the hybrid weapon did have its limits -- only five total firings per ship. And it had to be recharged after every firing.

After each deadly salvo, Rawlon and Tarlog ordered those ships to recharge their hybrid weapon while other ships aimed and prepared the next salvo with their hybrid weapon.

While they recharged their hybrid weapon, these warships fired massive broadsides of lasers using their normal weapons and launched deadly torpedoes with more and more frequency -- Kraaqi battleships against T'kaan battleships, Hrono battle cruisers against T'kaan warships of all classes.

As for Mother, she fought anything T'kaan that came within her range.

The fighting quickly became ship to ship -- fighter to fighter, and eye to eye.

**

"Order Sharin's battle group to close ranks. We've got a gap at this position," Saris shouted. Immediately, sensors showed Sharin's battle group obeying.

The Mewiis were doing what they did best -- defense. Their battle groups were now arrayed in a huge swarming defensive pattern on the left wing of the original battle line.

Minstrel's ship fought with the Mewiis.

In one instant Minstrel was firing at a T'kaan ship in the next instant the Circle Ship disappeared under its stealth field to reappear and attack the T'kaan from a new position. For the most part, Minstrel and the Mewiis fleet were holding their own.

But now the main battle groups of the T'kaan juggernaut closed with them.

Huge broadsides leapt from each fleet. Shields blossomed and buckled on both sides.

"Their sheer numbers and momentum will drive them right through us," Captain Saltis shouted to Admiral Saris.

Saris nodded. "Send the order to the capital ships. On my mark."

The first officer waited.

"Now."

From every Mewiis cruiser and battleship the hybrid weapons erupted.

Every T'kaan battle cruiser and battleship that had been targeted exploded in the hail of fire, sending the T'kaan formations of frigates and fighters scattering in all directions to regroup for another run.

"The encircling movement by those other battle groups will be complete soon. And a second wave of their battleships -- twice as many as this last frontal attack -- are closing with us. They'll attack us from behind at the same time," Saltis shouted.

"Order all ships -- all formations -- to keep on the move within their assigned defensive sectors. On my mark, order Kara's battle group in the rear to go into Rover-Kragar swarming mode. But wait for my mark!"

Saris stared at her viewscreen as it switched view from the T'kaan ships encircling their position from behind to the second wave of T'kaan ships bearing down on them from in front.

"Recharge the hybrid weapon on all ships. We've got to *punish* the T'kaan hard -- obliterate these first waves. We must slow them down and make them rethink their strategy."

"And after the fifth wave of attacks? When our hybrid weapons are no more?" Saltis asked.

"We use our main weapons and torpedoes," Saris said grimly. "And when those are gone -- *we ram them!*"

***

All around the three-dimensional phalanxes formed by the Kraaqi battlefleet, T'kaan formations closed and crossed them -- attacking like maddened insects. The T'kaan warships circled and twisted, weapons firing beams of death in their attempt to stop the Kraaqi advance. From every direction, the T'kaan horned ships descended and engaged.

It seemed that for every T'kaan ship destroyed, three more came into firing range and took their place.

Onward, the great Kraaqi fleet drove forward with the Hrono fleet on its right.

The minutes of war turned into the nightmare of an hour. The punishment of the T'kaan counterattacks began to take their toll as individual Kraaqi and Hrono ships slowed and dropped out of the protective cross-fire provided by the phalanx formations. Within minutes, these damaged ships were destroyed as the T'kaan warships fell upon them like metallic vultures going in for the kill.

Behind the fearsome Kraaqi-Hrono advance, a vast debris field of broken and dead ships drifted as far as the eye could see. And in front of the advancing battle groups the warships of each fleet closed upon each other in unrelenting attacks.

War became everything, and it would never end.

The screams and battle cries of Kraaqi and Hrono warriors joined the 'Music of War' across every comm channel as the battle intensified.

***

"I've got a whole squadron of T'kaan hunters on me -- one hundred and forty-four incoming!" Rok shouted. He looked around at what was left of his original fighters.

Only four other fighters remained of the Death Squadron in addition to Jaric and Kyle's fighters.

"Rok!" Rawlon shouted from the comm.

"My First Captain," Rok returned.

"I am sending you the Band of Thunder's fighters. They are yours. Ulfa's cruiser was just destroyed. But he fought off the attackers at quadrant nine point zero one before he died. You must hold those forward positions now -- as well as your assigned sector. The T'kaan are regrouping more hunters at that quadrant as we speak, but concentrate your fighters on the ones attacking you. And after you beat them back, go and defend the other position!"

"How many fighters are you sending us?" Rok asked as he looked at the incoming T'kaan Hunters, now joined by a formation of six T'kaan frigates.

"Sixty-two."

Rok cursed.

The Band of Thunder had begun the battle with over three hundred fighters. And even with those reinforcements, the remnants of the two Kraaqi squadrons were outnumbered.

The new Kraaqi fighters arrived right as the T'kaan hunters attacked and the frigates opened up with broadsides.

***

Mother approached the crippled Kraaqi battleship to give it aid and fired a spread of torpedoes at the three T'kaan battleships attacking it.

The shields of the lead T'kaan battleship buckled. Mother fired her main weapons at it, creating huge holes in its armored hull. The T'kaan battleship slowed, and its systems began to fail.

The other two battleships shuddered as their shields blossomed from the direct hits of her other torpedoes.

But onward they came.

Their guns erupted with massive broadsides.

The Kraaqi battleship exploded instantly with no shields to protect her.

Finally, the indicator lit for Mother's hybrid weapon.

Mother rammed her engines wide open and dove hard. She lined up the two T'kaan battleships, one after the other in her targeting sites. They had drawn close together in order to intensify their fire on the Kraaqi battleship.

Too close.

Mother's hybrid weapon erupted, the beam cutting through the first ship's port side and exploding out the other side. The huge red beam then pierced the shields and cut through armor of the second battleship. The red beam did not exit the second T'kaan battlewagon.

Both battleships rocked and shuddered a few moments as a growing number of internal explosions rippled down their lengths, until suddenly both exploded into twin blossoms of light.

Alarms screamed inside Mother as she banked hard to avoid more hunter fighters. She redirected her energies once again, powering up her hybrid weapon for another shot, even as she began new repairs to her damaged shields.

For the second time, her power grid went off-line and the backup took over. She began repairs again, ordering the Fixers and Guardian to specific points to assist. And then her shields glowed under direct hits -- and more alarms wailed with more damage.

Sensors showed three T'kaan frigates bearing down on her after firing those full broadsides.

Mother started to activate the circuits to reload her torpedoes -- and stopped. There were no more torpedoes left.

She would have to take on the three frigates attacking

her with her main batteries alone.

***

"We've lost Dragaz's entire battleship squadron," Kaldah shouted.

The Hrono admiral studied the main viewscreen a moment; quickly, he glanced down to the electronic layout of the fleets on the personal display beside his chair.

Dragaz's ships had already fired the fifth and final firing of their hybrid weapon -- they had done what they could. The Hrono battleships had been dueling with twice their number of T'kaan battleships these last few minutes -- exchanging horrendous broadsides from their main batteries between firings of the hybrid weapon -- and it was during those haunted minutes between firings that most of the Hrono ships fell before the T'kaan fire.

The four remaining T'kaan battleships were now coming for his ship, along with several frigates and two waves of fighters in support.

"Order the *Scorpion*, the *Victorious*, the *Valiant*, and the *Destroyer* to close and fire their hybrid weapons on my mark," Tarlog ordered. He took a deep breath, looked back at the electronic display, and mentally took stock of what ships he had left.

The smaller of the two Hrono battle phalanxes had just been crushed. The main formation, which he led, was now being pounded. The T'kaan were attacking it from three directions as the Hrono phalanx continued to press forward. Worse, the T'kaan now gathered forces at his rear, organizing three battle groups to attack from a fourth direction.

Tarlog glanced up. "Fire!"

On the viewscreen, the four T'kaan battleships

intersected with the thick red bolts. They exploded, filling the viewscreen with a sudden, intense brightness, like four small stars going nova.

"We only have twenty-seven ships left with an operational hybrid weapon, sir," Kaldah reported.

"I know," Tarlog whispered. "And they are almost down to their last firing."

***

"Order the remaining battleships to slow. Send all the battle cruisers forward to lead us," Rawlon shouted. He stood and marched across the bridge to one of the console stations, watching the officer as he worked its controls. "All other light cruisers and frigates are to hold their positions in phalanx."

Rawlon reached over to the console and tapped in a command. He waited.

The Kraaqi were down to twelve battleships, each with two firings of the hybrid weapon. The battle cruisers had been hammered as well, protecting their assigned quadrants of the mighty phalanx formation. But there were only twenty battle cruisers left.

There were seventy other cruisers remaining within the main phalanx after the right phalanx had fallen, and its remaining ships had joined his formation.

But most of those ships were down to their last firing.

"The Kraaqi left phalanx is falling," Curja said from his station. Several seconds ticked by in morbid silence, and then he sighed. He looked up at Rawlon. "They are no more."

The last Kraaqi phalanx, along with the lone Hrono phalanx, continued their bloody advance.

Rawlon walked back to his chair. But he remained

392

standing, thinking deeply.

"Order all capital ships of the Hrono and Kraaqi to use their normal weapons array. Do not use the hybrid weapon until my order. We must save the hybrid weapon," Rawlon said decisively.

Rawlon turned and sat in his chair and stared at the oncoming T'kaan warships.

"I hope I have a reason for saving them," he whispered to himself.

**

"Got'em!" Jaric shouted to Kyle.

Kyle righted his ship, no longer pursued by the T'kaan ship Jaric had just destroyed. "Thanks, bud. That's the last fighter of that wave. We need to find Rok and form up again with the squadron," Kyle said.

Their two fighters drew closer together as they flew through the debris field of fallen ships. As they looked around, they could see nothing but floating destruction. And off in the distance, they saw a firestorm of blaster fire in every direction.

"I hate to bring this up, but my weapons are getting pretty low," Kyle said.

Jaric glanced down to check his weapon's status, but his eyes were drawn to his sensor screen first and the all too familiar shapes. "We've got more company. Six hunter fighters incoming"

"Let's get'em," Kyle said with a business-like tone.

**

"Hard over!" Rawlon shouted.

The T'kaan cruisers fired, and the *Thunderer* shuddered under multiple hits.

"Load torpedoes!" Rawlon shouted again. "And get me

393

reinforcements."

Curja raised himself from where he had fallen. Taking his hand, he wiped the streaming blood out of his eyes. "All ships are engaged, sir. We must fight these three ships ourselves."

"Give me more shields," Rawlon barked. "I want the hybrid weapon targeted at that cruiser on the right." Rawlon gripped his chair. He knew his flagship would be down to its last firing after this strike.

In a sudden, blinding flash, two of the T'kaan cruisers onscreen exploded. But the *Thunderer* had not fired. A manta-ray silhouette now shot across the horned prow of the third T'kaan cruiser that began firing after it.

"MotherShip!" Rawlon shouted gleefully. "The warship that lives has taken out two of them with a single shot!" He turned to the weaving form of his first officer. "Send the entire spread of torpedoes into the remaining ship."

"S-sir," Curja stammered. "We are reaching a critically low level of torpedoes remaining --"

"I don't care!" Rawlon cut him off. "Send that ship out of this galaxy. Now!"

The five torpedoes in the spread ran straight and true. All but one found their mark as the T'kaan ship slowly rose straight upward and disappeared in a string of violent explosions.

As the explosions died away, Rawlon's eyes remained fixed on the darkened viewscreen. There before him, he saw a clear field of stars with no T'kaan ships in sight.

"We're through," Rawlon said in disbelief.

He stood quickly, not expecting this sudden view of an empty star field. All that he had seen there before, T'kaan warships bearing down on them, had seemed to last for an eternity.

"Are we through?" Rawlon asked, his mind refusing to believe what his eyes told him.

Curja leaned heavily against his station, the blood from the wound on his head spattering across its dials and controls. Moving his arm painfully, his fingers worked doubly hard on the damaged console to coax its report.

"We are through."

"How many ships are still with us?" Rawlon waited expectantly, the silence of the bridge punctuated by the sounds of electronics shorting out in a shower of sparks from various other damaged stations.

"Two thirds of our ships ... are lost." Curja reported in a low voice.

"And the Hrono?"

Curja punched painfully at his console. "Only a handful of ships. Less than a dozen capital ships. And ... " Curja winced. "The Mewiis are completely surrounded. Their defensive perimeter is failing." With a heavy sigh, Curja slumped unconscious over his console.

Another officer moved over and sat him gently on the floor as he began tending his wounds.

"Get me the MotherShip." Rawlon ordered to a third officer.

***

Mother flew out into the empty space. She almost felt the battle was over. Redirecting her circuits away from her shields for the moment, she began taking stock of the situation.

Behind her, the sole remaining Kraaqi phalanx was emerging, as was the remnants of the Hrono fleet, which was now only the size of a battle group.

Her sensors stretched out.

She noted the T'kaan ships now regrouping to attack them. They had only a few minutes respite at most.

She also observed that just over half of the T'kaan fleet had been destroyed, whereas most of the allied fleet was no more.

A comm signal vied for her attention.

"What are we to do now, MotherShip?" Rawlon asked.

Mother's sensors stretched out again, but this time she centered on their present position, which was really the T'kaan rear. She noted the sensor readings like a huge spider's web that originated from the Great Horned ship. It was almost like background noise, she realized. It had been recorded before in the human-T'kaan war but had been overlooked as unimportant. The myriad of signals pulsated out to the combined T'kaan fleets and the other two Great Horned ships located nearby.

This particular one was the Great Horned ship of the Second Fleet, now turning slowly away from them along with its escort of cruisers and frigates.

"There actually seems to be a ship turning away from us," Mother said.

Tarlog suddenly appeared on Rawlon's viewscreen.

"And, Rawlon," Tarlog said. "This ship is different from the others. Note the huge amount of communication signals originating from it."

Rawlon quickly reviewed the Hrono data. "This ship has no weapons, but it does have massive life signs -- life signs equal to that of a well-populated planet!"

"Actually, two densely populated worlds," Mother stated.

"It runs for a reason," Rok shouted from his fighter.

Rawlon stood. "There are only T'kaan twelve cruisers, and twelve frigates escorting her. We even have them outnumbered." He smiled.

"All ships. Attack!"

They turned for the fleeing ships.

"Tarlog, your ships must fight a rear-guard action. The other T'kaan ships are now coming for us. They realize what we're doing. Hold them back as long as you can."

"I will," Tarlog said with conviction.

The Kraaqi ships, now led by Mother, moved for the Great Horned T'kaan ship.

As the allied ships' target became obvious, the T'kaan escort ships moved away from the retreating ship on an intercept course.

"Rawlon, save your hybrid weapons for the Great Horned ship," Mother ordered.

"Acknowledged," Rawlon said.

For the first time that day, the Kraaqi and humans engaged the T'kaan with numerical superiority. But the T'kaan ships fought the fiercest of any they had engaged that day.

Fighters streamed for them and attacked savagely. Jaric and Kyle each led a Kraaqi formation of fighters while Rok led his own. With a blinding flash of firepower, the cruisers of each fleet unleashed their broadsides simultaneously.

Mother fired her hybrid super-weapon at the lead cruiser and destroyed it with a single blow. Evading the oncoming fighters, she swept around the T'kaan ships and on toward the retreating Great Horned ship.

Behind her, Jaric and Kyle's squadrons closed with the T'kaan fighters she had just weaved through.

Her alarms, for the first time that day, gradually began

to go silent as her circuits prioritized the repair activities. Mother's shields now grew to almost eighty percent of full strength, and even her main power grid stabilized. Mother placed the backup power grid into *sleep mode*.

The T'kaan ship ahead grew larger on her sensors.

Mother stretched her sensors out to it at this close range, and she finally understood.

Her rear sensors noted that the last T'kaan cruiser was being destroyed by the *Thunderer*, and the rest of the Kraaqi ships were coming forward through the remaining T'kaan fighters. But there were fewer Kraaqi ships registering on her sensors.

Mother concentrated her processing power on the data streaming in from her forward sensors.

"This ship. It is part ship, part life form," Mother said. "It is alive!"

Rawlon stared at the data being relayed to him and the Hrono. "It is alive. But the other T'kaan ships are not. They are ships alone, are they not?" His voice faded with thought.

"Yet, low-level signals emanate to the T'kaan warships from this ship," Mother reported. "There is some type of symbiotic relationship with the T'kaan and this ... ship. This huge life form."

"This ship looks almost the same as the others," Rawlon argued.

"It is the same, and it is different," Mother said.

"But this ship has no shields. It has no weapons. The engines are real, added to the horny outer shell. And yet, there seems to another relationship with this ship and the other T'kaan ships. And even with the T'kaan inside the warships. We, too, now see wave upon wave of communication originating from it." Rawlon paused.

"So," Jaric said as his fighter joined Mother. "There is a yet undetermined symbiotic relationship with the T'kaan and this thing. And some other separate relationship with the ships themselves?"

"I don't care what kind of relationship it is," Kyle said, cutting in. "Let's destroy it all. The main T'kaan fleet is coming for us while we sit here and chatter!"

Mother's hybrid-weapon flashed full strength.

"Rawlon, on my mark, we fire together. But only the Kraaqi battle cruisers with their hybrid weapons and not the battleships."

"Give us the word," Rawlon answered.

Mother and the remaining Kraaqi battle cruisers drew closer even as the huge thing kept turning away.

"Now."

Thirty-two red bolts leapt out for the Great Horned ship. They shot into the side of the huge ship, each boring a hole straight through it. Large, pulpy sections exploded outward from inside the ship and out into space followed by great purple geysers of fluid that erupted from each gaping hole.

"There is some kind of artificial readings inside," Mother said. "I am reading explosions occurring all throughout this ... *ship*. And there are countless separate power signatures inside it. There's something else inside, something else alive besides the ship itself."

"I'm reading a massive overload," Rok shouted.

Mother turned away, as did the Kraaqi ships. Even as they accelerated, the Great Horned ship exploded with a thousand rippling blasts. Massive chunks of the ship shot in every direction, with large geysers of purple fountains shooting into space.

Throughout the great T'kaan fleet, one third of their

ships began exploding -- in self-destruction.

"A definite relationship," Mother said matter-of-factly.

The officers aboard the Kraaqi flag ship cheered as one, as did every warrior in the allied fleet.

Rawlon looked at the viewscreen. "We must attack the other two ships. Quickly! They know what we are up to now."

Tarlog appeared. "I am calling in the Home fleet; they will jump in at this point near the Great Horned ship of the T'kaan First Fleet."

"Good," Rawlon said. "But we must attack now. More T'kaan battle groups are now speeding to its defense."

"These Great ships do possess engines. And yes, they can jump to hyperspace," Mother reminded them.

"We must attack now!" Rok shouted.

"The T'kaan think they can still defeat us today in this one battle. They will stay a bit longer," Rawlon said. "But now we have a chance, a small one, but a chance, to do the same to them."

"They will outnumber us before we can close with the next Great Horned ship," Tarlog said as he rose from his sensor screen.

"And we will not have enough ships to attack the last one, the young one, of the Third fleet," Rawlon stated.

"Give me all of the fighters. I will take out the ship of the Third fleet myself," Mother said.

"Yes," Rawlon said. "All fighters, go with Mother. Clear a path for her to get in close." Rawlon turned to his Comm officer. "Get me Admiral Saris."

The battered image of the Mewiis Admiral appeared on the viewscreen. She was surrounded by roaring flames that filled her bridge with a haze of black smoke. Blue blood flowed from wounds on her chest and arms, the streaming fluid giving her uniform a bluish glaze. Behind her, consoles suddenly exploded in flowing showers of sparks as the flames roared higher.

"We ... " Saris coughed, wincing with pain as she bent over. Slowly, she rose to face Rawlon, a determined look on her face.

"We ... we have held the left wing for you."

Rawlon stood, staring speechlessly at the scene of destruction all around Saris.

"We t-told you ... we would hold it." She bent over again, coughing up blood.

"Yes, you have held," Rawlon whispered with emotion.

Saris continued to cough violently, her breathing ragged and hard.

"I have one last order for the courageous Mewiis fleet," Rawlon said, a deep sadness in his voice.

The Mewiis female looked up, still coughing. "I will pass your orders to what's left of our ships. But ... my ship is even now being destroyed."

The image jumped, and static blocked out the signal momentarily. Seconds later it returned, the flames higher and the smoke thicker on the burning bridge.

"Speak quickly," Saris coughed.

"You must pin down as many T'kaan as you can, Saris. We have found a weakness with them. We may yet win this day," Rawlon said with renewed urgency.

"I saw the T'kaan ships self-destruct." Saris paused again, coughing. "I hoped it was your doing. For the children's sake."

"Tell your ships to attack, Saris. Tell them to attack in every direction. We must create confusion among the

T'kaan."

Saris smiled through her pain. Using her left arm, she clumsily began working the console. "I send it as we speak." The Mewiis admiral looked up as another explosion rocked her ship, and caused fountains of burning sparks that covered her body. She groaned with pain and looked up through the boiling smoke now enveloping her.

"We ... " she whispered, and then paused, grimacing. "*We ... held.*"

The signal went dark.

Curja had just returned to his station at the start of this transmission with his wounds hastily bandaged.

Rawlon, Curja, and the entire bridge crew stared in awe at the blank viewscreen for long seconds.

"Farewell, brave warrior," Curja said to the blank viewscreen. He stood at attention beside his station and brought his clenched fist across his chest in Kraaqi salute to the brave Mewiis officer.

Rawlon smiled approvingly at Curja. Taking a deep breath, he looked slowly around at the rest of the officers' faces aboard the bridge of the *Thunderer*, all now turned expectantly toward him.

"Begin anew the 'Music of War' on my mark -- for our Mewiis warriors. We attack for them and their children!"

***

"The T'kaan have gathered several battle groups between us and the Great Horned ship of the Third," Rok reported.

"Yes," Kyle agreed as he glanced at his sensors. "Their mission is to stop us. But ours is to break through and allow Mother to attack. All we have to do is make an opening."

Jaric stared at the T'kaan before them. There were at

least two cruiser squadrons and maybe two dozen frigates with well over two hundred fighters standing between them and the Great Horned ship.

"How many with us?"

Rok began taking stock of his attack group, punching his console while he flew. He looked up, staring ahead at the T'kaan. "Fifty-seven fighters, all that's left of the Hrono and Kraaqi." He growled under his breath. "Kyle, you lead these fighters. Jaric, you take these." Rok sent the encrypted message via his console. On every fighter, their individual assignments lit up on their screen. "We shall form a mini-phalanx. MotherShip, where shall we strike at their defensive line and open a path for you?"

Mother had already been analyzing the forces before her, studying their layout, how the T'kaan ships were positioned to support each other and prevent her own breakthrough. She focused her processing power on the supplied data from her sensors, comparing it with all of her past battles with the T'kaan that day. Thirty milliseconds passed and several hundred options were presented. She filtered them with the current sensor data and reanalyzed. Two final solutions came up.

She chose the second.

"Rok, lead your group against this formation of frigates and fighters. This is our feint. Kyle and Jaric's groups will turn as if to support you. Just as you begin your engagement and the T'kaan forces begin to close upon this point ... we strike our main blow. Here."

Across every fighter, the T'kaan battle line was painted across their consoles. Rok's feint appeared, and then the section below and left where the main strike would actually take place.

"Rok, if you can extricate your fighters, come through behind me. Kyle and Jaric, just get me an opening, and break off. I will fly through and make my attack."

"Mother, there are several ships near the Great Horned ship."

"I will take care of them." But Mother's processors burned with activity, trying to access a solution. But none were favorable. She could use her super-weapon once on that formation of ships. Then five long minutes would have to elapse before she could strike her main target.

She would only have time for that one shot before her shields would fail. She would try to reanalyze more solutions while she attacked. But from her present data the one shot would have to destroy it -- there would not be time for a second.

*****

"Shall I start the Music of War now?" The acting first officer asked.

Rawlon turned to the young Kraaqi officer.

"Turn it up as loud as it'll go!"

"Where is the Home Fleet?" Rawlon shouted.

"No sign of them, Admiral," Curja replied

The Kraaqi battleship lurched under more direct hits. Around the bridge, the lights dimmed, replaced by the eerie red glow of the emergency lighting. From two control stations, sparks exploded, causing the Kraaqi officers to jump away.

"Get me Tarlog."

"The ships of the Hrono are being hammered, sir. They are taking heavy losses." Curja looked up from his station. "The Hrono flagship's comm systems are down. Their engines are off-line, and her shields are buckling. Tarlog cannot reply."

Rawlon slammed his fist down. "The T'kaan are going to stop us. We can't break through these battleships!"

"And more T'kaan battle groups are joining every minute," Curja said.

At that moment, a bright flash appeared to the left of the T'kaan battle groups that were attacking them. Scores of ships emerged out of the familiar flash -- the famed Hrono Home Fleet sailed unexpectedly out from their hyperspace jump.

A cheer went up from the Kraaqi around Rawlon.

"About time," Rawlon grumbled. He stood. "Order Admiral Trakam to smash the T'kaan battleships -- use every hybrid weapon. Tell him to engage all enemy ships and hold them off. Now, send orders to our fleet to swing around behind his attack and continue onward." Rawlon pointed decisively at the viewscreen. "On to the Great Horned ship!"

Before them the red tracers of the hybrid weapons of the Home Fleet lit up the stygian blackness. Numerous T'kaan ships began exploding.

"How many Kraaqi ships still have their use of the hybrid weapon?" Rawlon asked.

Curja's fingers danced over his controls. "Four battleships ... and five cruisers."

Rawlon growled under his breath, and spoke. "It will have to be enough. Send word to the MotherShip -- *we attack*!"

***

Rok's fighters leapt for the frigates under a thick hail of blaster fire. Kraaqi fighters began exploding under direct hits from the heavy weapons.

405

"Attack!" Rok roared into his comm.

A cloud of T'kaan fighters approached the small formation of brave Kraaqi. The tracers from the combined blaster fire of each group streaked through the blackness and crisscrossed between them. Still within their tight phalanx formation, the deadly Kraaqi fighters closed, with Rok's fighter leading the way.

"Now!" Mother shouted.

Kyle and Jaric banked their groups away from Rok's group and attacked. A blizzard of blaster fire greeted them as they kicked the rudder of their ships, trying to avoid the deadly fire. They fired simultaneously.

Two T'kaan frigates reeled from direct hits.

Kyle pushed his ship toward the left-most frigate and fired his last two torpedoes. Jaric followed, firing all his blasters. The frigate's shields buckled and the ship exploded. The other frigate, its systems off-line from the initial hits, began to drift in space.

"Yahoo!" Jaric shouted with glee. In the next instant, he dove down hard as a hail of blaster fire pummeled his shields.

"All fighters, break and attack in pairs. Draw their fire!" Kyle ordered.

Mother kicked her engines into overdrive and leapt past both Kyle and Jaric and through the small gap left by the crippled frigates.

Even as she did it, alarms screamed inside her circuits. A cruiser sent a salvo towards her as she tried to twist out of the line of fire, but Mother took two direct hits. Her shields buckled and her primary power grid fell for the third time that day, but her backup grid came up immediately.

But she had no shields now.

Mothership

She shuddered violently from several direct hits as T'kaan fighters attacked. Five hunter fighters hammered her with a deadly salvo as they raced past and now turned for another attack. Mother felt the blows penetrate her hull; she felt the terrible damage to several internal systems. Worse, a small section of long-term memory flickered and almost went silent. Instantly, she began copying its precious contents to another section of memory before it was lost forever.

More direct hits struck her from behind as she tried to avoid the hunters now in hot pursuit. She fired a volley from her main guns, destroying one and partially damaging two. The Hunters broke off their attack and turned -- but in seconds they reformed for another run.

More alarms now screamed from the latest direct hits.

"Guardian. My starboard engine has broken loose from its moorings. It is overheating due to internal vortexes now created inside the fusion chamber from this unnatural displacement of the engine with the main external feed. You must push it back into place, or a massive explosion will occur in ninety-five seconds -- an explosion that will destroy me. I must endeavor to get shields back up while I fight off the Hunters."

Guardian nodded, silent and obedient. His seven-foot frame moved with surprising quickness in response to Mother's orders. He had been assisting the Fixers with repairs to the main power grid one level above the engine rooms. When he entered the starboard engine room, there were only forty-nine seconds left.

Fixer3 was already there, trying to push the huge engine frame back into place with its minuscule form. Guardian's sensors immediately detected the extreme temperatures

407

emanating from the engine. As he stepped beside the smaller robot, he noted that Fixer's hands had already melted against the overheated surface.

With one motion, Guardian ripped the Fixer away and detached its fused hands from the engine. The little robot's arms were stiff and unmoving -- its hands melted into a metallic blob.

"My arms are not functioning," Fixer3 reported calmly.

"The intense heat has fused the internal circuits and destroyed your servo motors," Mother said from the overhead speaker.

"The engine will soon explode," Fixer3 reported.

"Stand back," Guardian ordered calmly.

Guardian placed his metallic hands against the red-hot surface. Even as he bent his huge frame and powered every internal servo motor, he felt the circuits inside his hands go dead. Melted. He pushed harder, but the engine did not move.

Suddenly the image of Becky displayed to his near-term memories. Her image had been occurring with a regular frequency this last hour. And no matter how often it happened, after he had studied the familiar visage, taking in every curve of the face, every layout of the blonde hair, he would erase it from his near-term memory, only to have the image return seconds later. The image was there again, and Guardian felt a surge of power inside his body.

Guardian did not understand.

But for some reason, as he bent his body this time, as he strained every joint and motor, the engine began to move.

The circuitry inside Guardian's arms sizzled and fused with a sickening staccato of sparks from the intense heat.

Fixer3 stared at the giant robot and sent the visual

images to Mother.

Mother focused a small portion of her processing on this incoming signal, noting that only twenty-one seconds remained before the coming explosion.

Like some mythological god, Guardian flexed and drove his being into the Herculean task before him. His metallic back and shoulders strained behind his outstretched arms, driving them forward. Stepping forward on one leg while the other stretched back behind him, he pushed with all his metallic might. Now even more than Atlas, the mythological god of old, he held the entire universe in his grip as he pushed against the massive engine.

Tiny drops of liquid metal raced down Guardian's hands and across his forearms as the searing heat caused them to glow a dull and deadly red. The massive engine jerked with a sudden movement that placed it closer to its original position and the huge heat sinks that protected it. But now Guardian's servo motors screeched and wailed as they overheated and the deadly red glow crept toward his shoulders.

The image of Becky in his near-term memories began to blur.

The giant robot communicated rarely. As his motors screamed and his circuits went dead one by one, Guardian sent a last, short message to Mother -- his companion and friend.

Even with his internal circuits melting, he bent his robotic frame one last time, every ounce of processing power on two things -- to push the engine back into place ... and to remember Becky's image.

With his last effort, Guardian sought to achieve these two last goals -- forever.

The engine suddenly lurched into proper position, and the moorings automatically reclamped. Immediately, the red-hot surface of the huge engine began to cool. The gargantuan task was finished.

But Guardian did not remove his melted hands. And the ruby indicators no longer gleamed in his eyes.

Fixer3 remained still, his visual sensors locked on the lifeless Guardian now frozen to the engine in his last act of heroism. As the engine cooled, Guardian's hands remained attached -- permanently fixed onto its outer surface -- like a statue in memory of his sacrifice. Fixer's optics zoomed onto the metallic face and noticed that extreme heat had changed/melted Guardian's face ever so slightly -- a single, frozen metallic tear dripped from his right eye. But more important, it seemed as if the corners of the robot's mouth curved ever so slightly in an eternal smile of the most profound and subtle happiness.

Mother felt another odd stirring in her circuits, and she saved it for future reference. She saw the image of Guardian and realized he was now nonfunctioning.

Dead?

Her systems reported the engine's cooling and that her shields were now on-line and slowly strengthening. She quickly looked at Guardian's last message and stored it.

It was a single word: *Becky*.

Mother drove hard and avoided another salvo from the frigates providing close support for the Great Horned ship. She destroyed the last of the hunters attacking her from the rear, but now she had to deal with these last escorts before her final attack. Her engines roared as she set them to full speed.

She was almost on top of the Great Horned ship, flying

just above its outer surface. Her sensors told her the frigates were holding their fire because of her close proximity. But her sensors also informed her that the frigates were closing into point-blank range with her -- they would fire on her then.

But Mother fired her hybrid weapon deep into the Great ship's hull first.

A massive hole opened. The impact of Mother's point-blank range caused a huge layer of the ship's hull -- essentially its skin -- to fold backwards in a great wave.

Huge amounts of debris exploded from inside, along with the strange, purple fluid that no other species except the T'kaan had ever seen.

She stretched her sensors inside the ship, even as she maneuvered away from the incoming fire from the frigates. The frigates missed her and struck the ship they were trying to protect.

Mother began priming her weapon for one last shot, but she needed to determine a vital section to target in order to destroy the Great Horned ship once and for all. She only had seconds in which to search as her sensors stretched forth across the armored skin and then deep into the creature-ship's wound.

The answer materialized even though she had not been able to make a sensor lock.

Mother began relaying the crucial data to Rawlon as her long-range sensors revealed he was even now making his final approach upon the other Great Horned ship.

Mother's sensors now revealed that she could enter the creature-ship via a large opening underneath the horned prow. Once inside, a deadly angle would present itself toward the center of the gargantuan creature and the heart of its life signs her sensors registered inside it. This precise angle alone would enable a *single shot* to destroy the ship completely, but to obtain the angle she had to be inside the armored skin of the creature so her sensors could lock onto it.

Mother and Rawlon would have to be inside each ship when they fired.

***

"We've lost the *Starfire* and the *Firestorm*," Curja reported curtly.

Rawlon growled angrily. But even as the word of the destruction of the two cruisers sank in, the Kraaqi admiral began reading the message just sent from the MotherShip. His eyes narrowed at the crucial data just supplied, and his fists clenched with his iron resolve.

The *Thunderer*, his flagship, reeled from another T'kaan salvo -- and more direct hits.

"Shields are failing!" Curja shouted.

On the viewscreen, the Great Horned ship increased speed.

"The T'kaan Great ship is powering its hyperdrive engines. It is preparing to retreat." Curja turned expectantly.

"We can't let that happen. Order the remaining battleships and cruisers to fire on my mark. But not the *Thunderer*." Rawlon began punching the controls on his console, sending specific coordinates for each ship to target on the Great Horned ship.

"Range?" Rawlon growled.

"Two hundred kilometers." Curja turned. "Prime range."

"Fire."

The other two Kraaqi battleships fired along with the

three remaining cruisers. The huge T'kaan ship that filled their viewscreens seemed to lurch upwards as the five holes erupted.

"Sensors. Damage assessment," Rawlon commanded.

The Kraaqi officer worked the controls at his station. "There is damage." Curja paused, still working the dials and controls. "Damage is minimal -- the ship is still functioning." He looked up excitedly from his console. "Their hyperdrive engines are off-line, but I don't know for long. I already detect repairs being applied."

Rawlon growled under his breath. "The *Thunderer* is now the only ship I have that still has a functioning hybrid weapon." He nodded stoically.

"Send word to Trakam -- he has command of the Kraaqi fleet now." Rawlon looked down. "What's left of it," he whispered, so that nobody heard.

Rawlon stood and walked to the center of the bridge. Standing there, his right hand gripping the rapier's handle still in its scabbard, he looked around at his bridge.

Several stations were already destroyed, and main power was still off-line, evidenced by the red glow of the emergency lighting. Half his bridge crew was missing, wounded and taken to medical -- or else dead.

"You have been the best crew any Kraaqi captain ever commanded." Rawlon gazed proudly at them all.

The *Thunderer* shuddered from another direct hit.

"Engines still functioning, but we have no more shields, sir. We have just lost hull integrity in sections B-Seventeen through B-Twenty-three," Curja reported diligently.

"Order *Abandon Ship*, Curja. All non-essential personnel." Rawlon thought a moment. "No, all personnel will evacuate. But first, pass all Engineering controls over

413

to the Bridge."

Rawlon walked back to his command chair. He looked again at his brave crew.

"I want all of you evacuated in exactly ten minutes. But first, we need to steer the *Thunderer* down the throat of that T'kaan ship!"

***

Mother suddenly banked hard to port, missing another salvo from the pursuing frigates. Her super-weapon, the hybrid, was almost primed, and the enemy still had not sensed her next move.

That was good.

Her sensors registered that the T'kaan Great Horned ship was powering its hyperdrive engines. It looked like the T'kaan finally realized that the puny humans and their allies might possibly win after all.

But it was too late -- for all of them.

"Kyle. Jaric. Disengage and retreat. Send word for a general retreat. There is no need for any more losses."

But neither Kyle nor Jaric answered as the comm channels remained silent except for the chords of the 'Music of War.'

Mother did not know what this meant. She wanted to focus her processors but could not. She shuddered as another direct hit shook her violently. And more of her internal systems failed.

Accelerating her engines, she dove for the prow of the T'kaan ship. As she drew near, the creature-ship began evasive maneuvers.

But Mother was too fast.

As she kicked her engines again to full speed, she slipped underneath and then into the opening that led inside.

The three T'kaan frigates followed her inside seconds later.

Mother stretched her sensors out as she entered the total darkness of the T'kaan ship. She felt the strange, overpowering readings of the creatures all around her. Almost without thinking, she began recording them.

Her sensors were blinded momentarily by the sheer enormity of the ship. But then she focused, and a picture began to take shape.

She was inside a massive and pitch-black labyrinth.

As she maneuvered through the huge tunnels, she discovered a surprise.

Along the inner walls, great city-horns rose full of squirming T'kaan young -- the fully grown maggots now in the second stage of life. Everywhere paths and roads and superhighways full of T'kaan stretched from city-horn to city-horn.

City-horns rose by the tens of thousands, each one filled with hundreds of thousands of T'kaan. She registered factories, shipyards, and other signs that a complex society existed inside this completely darkened place.

Mother tried to make out smaller details.

Seconds later, she did find T'kaan in other stages of life -- they seemed to be leading the youth. But she noticed something strange ...

In one instant, thousands of T'kaan had disappeared from where they had once been, seemingly absorbed by the interior walls of the great creature-ship as they traveled the grooved roads. But oddly, nearby T'kaan did not seem to notice their sudden disappearance with any anxiety.

Mother stretched her sensors to that single spot where the T'kaan had been absorbed -- there was no other word to describe what she had just seen. She recoiled her sensors almost simultaneously as the hideous answer became obvious.

The creature-ship had *eaten* the T'kaan.

And it was eating more; Mother's wide field sensors observed more being absorbed every few seconds all along the massive interior. Of the hundreds of billions of life signs she saw in a single instant, millions were suddenly absorbed.

Mother realized with a sinking feeling that she was hopelessly lost. She wasn't sure now what direction she was pointed. Her overloaded sensors now only clearly registered the massive sensor reading of the creature-ship's life source.

Mother did not want to die, to become nonexistent. Mother began calculating tens of millions of possible solutions. But there were no solutions that ensured her survival from the resulting explosion if she did not find a way outside within twenty seconds after she had fired.

The three frigates pursuing her blocked her from going back out the way she had entered. And yet, that was the only way out.

Still, she stretched out with her sensors, sending the new data into her circuits and rerunning the analysis one last time.

A near-miss from one of the frigates sent her reeling. But she quickly righted herself as she leapt into another section of the seemingly endless labyrinths that filled the creature-ship.

She sent more processing to access the damage and discovered her main power grid off-line, damaged beyond her present capabilities of repair. Her sensors also reported that the next frigate was beginning to fire. Another near-miss would finish her backup grid, and she would be defenseless.

Mother sent the prewritten message she had prepared for Minstrel. It was short and encrypted. She had hoped she would never have reason to send it.

She fired her hybrid weapon at the target.

Everything around her in the darkness suddenly shuddered. Her weapon struck home, a direct hit right into the heart of the creature-ship. Deep inside the now dying entity, a massive overload began, signaling its death knell.

In spite of the physical darkness, her sensors computed the searing effects of the coming explosion. But the massive explosion she had calculated was not what she registered. Instead, she sensed a massive wave of total destruction enveloping the entire creature-ship and roaring back at her.

She made a last calculation as she powered her engines to full throttle. But suddenly, the frigates appeared from behind another interior wall and fired at her even as the oncoming wave of destruction grew closer from the other direction.

Mother had no place to run.

Mother raced into another section of the creature-ship with her sensors still reaching out in search of escape. At just that moment, the edge of the growing explosion registered on her visual sensors for the first time -- a boiling wave of debris accelerating toward her with each millisecond. Behind her, the frigates fired again as Mother turned into another passage of the interior labyrinth.

Mother realized with a sickening surge that her window of escape was at an end. She raced her engines and dove into still another section. Immediately, her sensors registered the enormous damage all around ...

***

The *Thunderer* shuddered again.

Rawlon pushed the controls for Battery A-Twelve to fire. But nothing happened. The weapon's systems were off-line again.

"Evacuate the Bridge!" Rawlon shouted.

But nobody moved.

"We stay with you, First Captain," Curja said.

Rawlon slowly looked at them all, his eyes narrowed and hard. He nodded with approval, balancing himself as the battleship lurched again from more direct hits. He sat down.

"Full speed -- steer us into the opening below the horned prow."

The ship's engines groaned and slowly responded. The Kraaqi battleship slipped inside and into the dense blackness.

"T'kaan warships are following," Curja reported.

"Let them," Rawlon said.

Suddenly sparks and flames lit the bridge as another salvo sent everyone down. Rawlon felt the flames burn him as the stench of his own burning skin seared his nose.

He raised himself, shaking the burning material off his arm. He swayed as his vision blurred, but he grabbed hold of his chair and steadied himself. Slowly and painfully, he sat down.

"Begin self-destruct sequence. Short timing -- set to thirty seconds."

"Yes, sir," Curja said as he painfully raised himself back to his station.

Rawlon began punching the console controls on the arm of his chair as the *Thunderer*'s sensors reached out into the bowels of the creature-ship. Rawlon tapped his fingers impatiently while he waited, and then he smiled.

"These are the target coordinates for the hybrid weapon. Fire on my mark."

"All weapons are off-line, including the hybrid weapon," Curja said slowly.

Rawlon gritted his teeth and groaned with pain. "Get the hybrid weapon back on-line! You must concentrate on that single task!"

Curja groaned as worked feverishly.

Behind him, Rawlon knew the T'kaan ships were powering their weapons for their last strike. His crew had to have the hybrid weapon back first. As he looked around, the only officer that could stand was Curja. There was no one else who could assist him in his final task.

Rawlon grimaced as he stood, and then he painfully stumbled to Curja's station. Blood covered the console so thickly that the displays were blurred and almost unreadable.

"No wonder you have such trouble, Curja. You're bleeding all over the controls."

Curja smiled weakly.

Rawlon touched his first officer's shoulder tenderly. "I joke. You have done well. Let me help you."

Wiping the displays several times with his sleeve, Rawlon began working the controls that were now visible. Seconds later, the charged hybrid weapon flashed on-line.

Curja and Rawlon smiled at each other.

The admiral stepped back.

"I give you the honor, my brave first officer."

Curja smiled wider as he leaned slowly forward, his hand poised over the controls.

Behind them the self-destruct sequence had dropped below ten seconds.

"For the human race -- our brethren. And, for the brave Mewiis," Curja wheezed.

Rawlon glanced at the main console. He read out the countdown.

"Self-destruct in five, four, three, two ... "

Curja pressed the control to fire the hybrid weapon as the final second ticked off the self-destruct sequence ...

Chapter Forty-Seven

The battle was over.

As far out as Minstrel's sensors could sweep, there were only death and destruction.

Inside its flowing, plasma body, Minstrel felt a great sadness, a feeling of such intense melancholy that Minstrel found it difficult to concentrate. Minstrel even found it difficult to fly its spherical ship, although for centuries this same ship had been Minstrel's only home -- every control, every console memorized long, long ago.

Minstrel thought back, remembering the battle, fighting alongside the remnants of the Mewiis fleet in their last stand. Less than five percent of the original Mewiis fleet remained, all partially damaged. Only twenty-five warships could maneuver under their own power; a few others drifted, intact and still registering active life support and precious life signs.

Minstrel had been fighting with the Mewiis and occupied by the countless attacking T'kaan ships when the last two Great Horned ships had exploded almost simultaneously.

Returning its thoughts to the present, Minstrel completed another wide-area scan of the battlefield.

Very few intact Kraaqi or Hrono ships remained scattered among the sea of debris. The only cluster of active ships Minstrel could pinpoint comprised the last remnants of the Hrono Home Fleet. Admiral Trakam led them now, the sole surviving commander in the field -- all the others were gone.

Worse, there were no signals from either Jaric or Kyle.

Nor any signals from Rok or any of his Band.

And nothing even from Mother.

As Minstrel stretched forth to control the ship and maneuver it among the seemingly endless debris field, a terrible weight pressed against Minstrel's very thoughts and actions -- a terrible weight of intense sadness. Time and again the ship shuddered as debris collided with the weakened shields, Minstrel's reactions once again too slow or its vision somehow blurred.

Minstrel focused again on the surreal scene that stretched endlessly across the main viewscreen.

In every direction thousands of shattered hulls drifted in space; some still glowed as internal fires still raged, but most were dark and silent. Some areas of destruction were so thick with debris they even blocked out the stars beyond -- broken shards of once mighty warships, now no more.

Thousands upon thousands of dead ships.

Minstrel followed the path of the Kraaqi/Hrono charge, followed the unimaginable trail of destruction. Sensors showed that the majority of dead ships were T'kaan.

But there were many broken Kraaqi ships -- and Hrono too. But Minstrel detected no Mewiis ships in this section. Only at the left wing of the once proud battle line were there broken Mewiis warships and the few active ones that remained.

The small remnant left of the Mewiis fleet was now attempting rescue efforts, Minstrel noticed. There were many who had evacuated their shattered ships and now found themselves scattered among the drifting ocean of debris in rescue pods -- waiting for rescue and the trip home.

As Minstrel's sensors discovered more rescue pods --

Hrono and Kraaqi -- it sent out their positions to the rescue ships. In turn, Minstrel communicated to the beings inside the rescue pods that their location was now identified and rescue was on the way, albeit slowly.

So few survivors, Minstrel thought once again.

Too many would not make the trip home today. They were gone along with their ships.

"Minstrel, please report status of rescue operation."

Minstrel recognized the voice of Admiral Trakam in the comm signal that originated from the Hrono battleship.

"I have found a few more survivors. I am turning my ship toward the glowing hull of the Great Horned ship of the First Fleet. I will report back once I reach it."

"Thank you. And I have some good news," Trakam added.

Minstrel knew that at the point of the final attack, Trakam's Home Fleet had been in close proximity with the last of Rawlon's ships in his attack on the Great Horned ship of the Third Fleet, the smallest of the Great Horned ships. Trakam and his ships were beginning their own rescue efforts starting from that far-off position, far from the last Mewiis ships.

"Please elaborate."

"Tarlog has been found in a rescue pod. He's injured. But he'll live."

"Any word about Rawlon's ship?"

Silence.

"Yes. Hull debris has been identified as that of the *Thunderer*, his flagship. It has just been confirmed by Zara, the acting First Captain for the Kraaqi aboard his battle cruiser, the *Powerful*. The *Thunderer* is no more, and there is no sign of any survivors among its officers."

Minstrel made a note to write a special song for Rawlon and to find out more details of his great attack.

"How many Kraaqi ships have survived?" Minstrel asked.

Silence again.

"Twenty-seven ships so far, including Zara's cruiser and one other cruiser. The rest are fighters, and a couple of frigates."

Almost all gone. Minstrel's thoughts were further burdened and subdued by the immense destruction that surrounded its own ship. It was as if the entire universe had been the battlefield. And in a way, it had been. For the eternal war of the T'kaan had finally ended here.

Still, Minstrel pressed on.

"No word of the humans -- or the MotherShip?" Trakam asked again, already knowing the answer.

Jaric and Kyle's fighters had been in the group attacking the Great Horned ship of the T'kaan First Fleet. Minstrel's wide-area scans had shown no active ships, no communication signals of any kind from that area, at least from this range.

"None," Minstrel said.

The seconds and minutes stretched for an eternity. Minstrel's sensor sweeps reached to the edge of its capability, but still no life-signs showed.

There were also no signs of life pods. Hope was growing dim ...

Suddenly, a light began pulsating. Minstrel worked feverishly, locking onto that weak beacon. That faint, scrambled signal slowly became discernible, and finally became a comm signal.

Minstrel hurriedly fixed on the weak signal, amplifying

it, holding it, caressing it until it grew intelligible.

"This is Jaric. Repeat, we are in need of assistance. Our systems are down except for life-support. We are drifting. Repeat, this is Jaric ... "

Minstrel's engines surged, and the Circle Ship, scored and damaged though it was, eagerly leapt forward.

In minutes, the darkened fighter appeared amid the dense, swirling pieces of floating debris that surrounded it. Targeting the tractor beam on the damaged fighter, Minstrel began pulling Jaric and his damaged ship inside.

Before the next hour had passed, a dozen other fighters were rescued in the same fashion, all that had survived the vicious explosion of the Great Horned ship of the T'kaan First.

Kyle and Rok were among them -- battered, bruised and bloodied.

But alive.

Jaric stumbled into the main room. "Where's Mother?"

"I have not ascertained her last position," Minstrel reported.

Jaric clenched his eyes shut as he searched his memory. "She was inside the T'kaan ship." He opened them. "Did she get out?"

"I do not know," Minstrel said.

With a sudden burst of energy, Jaric ran over and sat at Minstrel's main console. He began working the controls feverishly. Across their customary comm channels, he sent a message for Mother. If she were listening -- if she could listen -- she would hear it.

"Try your sensors across this sector," Jaric ordered.

Minstrel complied.

But no ship registered. At least not one still functioning.

A limping Kyle suddenly appeared next to Jaric. "Anything?"

Jaric shook his head and kept working.

"Let me try." Kyle sat down at the console. He stared at the controls, thinking. Closing his eyes, his mind went back to the last moments before the final explosion. He concentrated.

He remembered the frigates that had followed Mother; they would've blocked her easiest escape route back out. Still ...

In his mind's eye, he saw Mother's super-weapon suddenly erupt and tear at the Great Horned ship, sending a huge chunk of the ship's outer hull flying away with the violence of her shot. Perhaps Mother had found a way out through the exit wound of that first shot? It would've been her only chance.

He nodded, smiling.

Staring at the viewscreen, he mentally calculated.

"Try here, Minstrel." Kyle's finger found the last position of the Great Horned ship and then drew a line away from it. "From here to here. She's drifting, if she's alive at all."

Kyle and Jaric looked intently at the display as Minstrel focused her sensors.

The area was a good distance away from the current battlefield of dead ships. The sensor sweep began, but there was nothing, not even debris.

Suddenly, there was something -- a debris field still traveling slowly away from them and on out toward deep space.

Kyle focused and magnified the image. It was part of the T'kaan ship Mother had destroyed, part of its outer hull from the explosion.

"I'm thinking that Mother got out through the first hole she put in the ship," Kyle said.

"But she wouldn't have escaped the full force of the final explosion," Jaric said.

"True. But if she had any shields at all ... maybe. Just maybe."

A tiny light began flashing on the sensor console. Minstrel magnified it. A dark hull, blackened and damaged and completely covered with the effects of carbon-scoring from the horrendous explosion, materialized.

The sensor reading resolved into a tiny manta-ray silhouette that continued to sail silently away into the darkness. It was still surrounded by fragments of the T'kaan ship, the effects of the mighty explosion the only source of power carrying it away.

"I am getting some kind of a reading," Minstrel said excitedly. "Barely."

A tense silence surrounded the watchers.

"I've adjusted my sensors, and we are heading for her now. And, I've got definite readings of electronic activity -- faint, but there."

"She's in total diagnostic mode. I bet'cha," Jaric said as he jumped and grabbed Kyle by the shoulders.

Kyle smiled. "I hope so."

But it was as Jaric predicted, and now Mother joined the other survivors as Minstrel held her fast with a tractor beam.

They returned to join the precious few who had also survived.

Chapter Forty-Eight

The Three Kingdoms both celebrated and mourned.

On each home world of the Three Kingdoms, cheering crowds, parades and spectacular fireworks lit up the night skies. Music and praise filled the airwaves and every other communication medium. Plays were written and performed almost overnight that celebrated the bravery of the allied ships as well as the individuals who sacrificed all so that others might live.

The remaining ships from the combined fleets gathered at the Mewiis home world. Here the celebrations were edged with a solemn yet ardent fervor. For it was here that Minstrel brought its Circle Ship, hovering above the capital city of MewiisProlo, directly above the central part of the celebrations. It was here that Minstrel began to play.

The sound of Minstrel's music could be heard for hundreds of miles. Minstrel selected music from every facet of its vast repertory-- the songs that echoed joy, happiness, bravery, heroism, and love.

Inside the Circle Ship, Minstrel stretched its plasma body farther and farther until it was spread so thin it was almost completely transparent ... except for a subtle shimmering that danced ethereally everywhere in the air. Now Minstrel could touch every part of the ship to make it sing out loud with power and energy until the ship actually shook and jumped while its repulsor engines strained to keep it floating in a single position in the sky.

All through the day and late into the night, everyone danced and celebrated underneath the music from the sky.

It was soon reported that if you stood within eyesight of

the Circle Ship, you could actually *feel* the music with your body even more than you could hear it with your ears -- that was how passionate Minstrel's concert became. The notes almost seemed to turn into a pure, musical energy.

For seven days, the celebrations continued around the clock. Disaster had been averted, and the feelings of relief and happiness were etched in the ever-smiling faces that danced everywhere in the streets and on the balconies above. No one could remember the likes of such an event before, one that everybody throughout the Three Kingdoms shared.

On the heels of the celebrations, the *Time of Sadness* began.

Solemn assemblies were held and broadcast. Those who had fallen were remembered again. Those who remained cried, their tears shed in love, their hearts aching with loss.

Mother, Kyle, and Jaric chose to mourn with the Kraaqi, sharing a twelve-day period filled with emotion and silent contemplation. Mother mourned in her own fashion as well, and for untold hours she replayed the entire life of her lost daughter through her memory systems, focusing on the child's face -- especially her smiles -- while her laughter echoed in her speakers on more time.

She allowed only minimal repairs during this time in order to concentrate so as to never forget her lost child.

Never.

Almost without realizing it, Mother prioritized her processing on this single, sad task.

After a few hours of watching and listening to this Becky of the past, Kyle and Jaric left to go stay with Rok in his quarters. The sad memories were too much for them right now. Later, with time, they would want to see and hear Mother's memories of Becky again.

But not now.

Rok took them to his personal ship, and the trio flew to the small but sacred Kraaqi world named Waalhalla. It was a solitary planet far removed from any other inhabited world and was thus a perfect place for warriors to renew themselves and to find solace and inner peace again, especially after tragedy. Here on Waalhalla, the trio of friends found themselves to be the only inhabitants across its entire mountainous surface.

Flora and fauna were few and far between on this cold, desolate planet. It was in its high summer now, and the snows only glistened on the highest peaks that covered every continent. Among the lower peaks, Rok, Jaric, and Kyle set up camp.

They talked little. Only around the large campfire each evening when they ate their one big meal did they converse at any length. Most days they hiked the forlorn peaks in silence, their souls filled with sadness that seemed to resonate with their desolate surroundings. They felt their sorrow as one with Waalhalla, their melancholy echoed in the sighs of the ever-blowing winds that washed the rugged peaks.

They felt their grief for Becky in every barren and rock-strewn vista.

But each cried alone for Becky, unseen by the other two. They all knew, and yet each respected the solitary grieving of the other.

But the time for grief comes to an end, and life goes on.

They returned after word reached them of a great assembly. As they neared the Kraaqi world of Aasgaard, their sensors picked up Minstrel's ship as well Mother nestled within a huge, orbiting complex.

The leaders of the Three Kingdoms gathered near Mother as her extensive repairs began in earnest at the orbiting Kraaqi shipyard. Jysar was personally supervising the best Hrono technologists along with engineering teams of Mewiis and Kraaqi as all worked on their specific projects. Even with all this activity, Mother wished to participate directly in the upcoming assembly.

And too, there were many questions that remained regarding the defeated T'kaan to which she alone knew the answers, few that there were ...

Chapter Forty-Nine

The assembly was held with a mixture of joy and sadness. As the leaders of the Three Kingdoms gathered into the Great Hall, every eye glanced up and noticed when Minstrel entered. Everyone watched its shimmering plasma body flow through the doorway and then rise until it hovered just below the great, wide ceiling, where it floated like a fantastic, multi-colored cloud.

Rok was among the leaders of the Three Kingdoms who entered together, he being newly appointed as Fifth Captain by the high chieftains. Indeed, there were more new faces among these leaders of the Three Kingdoms than familiar ones to the crowd gathered on the main floor.

Jaric and Kyle entered almost unnoticed through a side door.

Chira, the main leader for this assembly as assigned by the combined Council of the Three Kingdoms, brought the meeting to order with a quick hand signal . Her head-tail flicked with excitement as everyone found their seats.

Once the hall grew silent, Chira signaled. The hall reverberated with three strokes from the hall's Grand Bell, one for each of the Three Kingdoms. This would now be a new tradition for the combined Kingdoms when they assembled. But there was a pause as the third stroke faded away, and suddenly the huge bell rang out a fourth time -- in honor of Mother and her two children, and finally a fifth time for the race of Minstrels.

Jaric and Kyle gazed intently at the front of the room where the assembled leaders sat.

Jasus led the Hrono leadership with Admiral Trakam

seated on his left side and Admiral Tarlog on his right. Tarlog smiled back at them, his right arm still in a medical brace and the left side of his aged face covered by the glow of a dermal regenerator slowly repairing his damaged scales and sub-skin.

Rok and newly appointed First Captain Zara, two of the handful of remaining Kraaqi warlords that survived the T'kaan battle, sat along with the high chieftains. Rok nodded in recognition at Jaric and Kyle, and then he rose and motioned for them to sit with him.

Jaric and Kyle made their way forward.

The gathered throngs began clapping their hands in a steady rhythm, matching the steps of the two young men. The clapping grew in volume with each step, and then the throngs rose, now clapping harder and louder with each beat. Shouts joined the rhythm, and even the leaders of the Three Kingdoms rose to greet them as they reached the chairs on either side of Rok.

As one, Jaric, Kyle, and the other leaders took their seats amid a general chorus of cheers and war whoops.

"I bring the first assembly of the United Three Kingdoms to order," Chira said with a flick of her head-tail.

Almost immediately, Tarlog rose. He nodded first at the Kraaqi leadership, and then to Chira and the Mewiis. Chira acknowledged in return, giving him the right to speak.

Admiral Tarlog cleared his throat as he looked upon the gathered throngs.

"I would like, as the first gesture of this new peace among the Three Kingdoms, to announce our plans -- plans of the Hrono, to build a golden statue dedicated to the courage and bravery of First Captain Rawlon and his Officer of the Fleet, Curja. And to the greatest battleship

433

that ever sailed the galaxy, the *Thunderer*."

Cheers greeted his words, and even the Kraaqi warriors rose and saluted their new brethren for this great honor to their fallen first captain. Tarlog saluted them in return and sat back down.

Before the cheers could completely subside, Fifth Captain Rok rose with a great smile upon his face. He looked slowly around the room filled with the leaders and sub-leaders of the combined Three Kingdoms.

"The Kraaqi too wish to honor their newfound brethren, to honor them as equals, and to honor their courage as well." Rok turned to the Chira. "We too wish to build a great statue, a great memorial to the Mewiis and Admiral Saris. Against impossible odds, she and her ships held the left wing of the battle line. In the heart of our home world we will build this statue so we will remember that no matter the race, no matter the gender, bravery is found in all."

The cheers erupted again, the entire room standing for a second time in a united ovation.

Now Chira rose.

"The Mewiis too shall commission a great statue, or series of statues. So we will remember forever." She paused, her head-tail now whipping side to side in her excitement. "The theme of these great works of art shall be *Family*. There shall be a Kraaqi family represented, and a Hrono family. There shall be a Mewiis family, and a family of Minstrels. But the centerpiece of all shall be a statue of MotherShip and her children -- Becky, Jaric, and Kyle. *Mother's family*."

Jaric smiled weakly as the cheers erupted a third time. Kyle quickly wiped at his eyes, and then smiled out at the crowd. Both men now rose and bowed toward Chira in thanks.

The cheers became deafening with enthusiastic intensity. Long seconds passed before the shouts slowly subsided as the crowds now strained to hear more.

"We, the Mewiis, have learned that families come in many forms. And even though we may look different upon the outside -- inside, we are all really the same." She raised her hands to the crowds for silence. "Sometimes the females are the head, sometimes the males. Sometimes the older children must assume the lead role. And sometimes an entity or life form different even than the children will take the young ones and love them as his or her own -- like the MotherShip for her beloved children." Chira paused, gazing at Jaric and Kyle a moment.

"They too are family." Chira smiled as the cheers grew deafening again.

She waited to say more, but the cheering would not end this time. As the first minute turned into two minutes and then into three, she sat back down, realizing her words had been enough.

The wild, enthusiastic cheering continued unabated for many more minutes. At last the cheers subsided.

Chira stood once again.

"Our first order of business is to prepare our newfound peace," Chira said to all. "We must organize all the peoples of the Three Kingdoms as one; we must take our laws and principles and apply them equally among all. And we must respect the cherished traditions and values from each race, and learn from each race. Whatever universal truths that apply to life and to all, these we must learn to embrace as one."

Enthusiastic applause met her words.

Jysar now rose, after he had first whispered quickly into Jasus' ear. He held his right hand for quiet as the green hue deepened across the ridge of scales over his head. The applause gradually faded.

"Friends," he began and then looked at the Kraaqi. "And brethren." Jysar took a deep breath to steady himself. He continued.

"Before we go into the business of our peaceful future together, we feel it necessary to bring up the subject of the T'kaan. This is so we might answer certain outstanding questions." Jysar paused. "Together we can review the small amount of physical evidence we have obtained, as well as the vital knowledge and scans the computer-ship we know as Mother has taken from inside their Great Horned ships." He paused again, a nervous look upon his face. "And perhaps determine if the T'kaan threat is once and for all finished."

A stunned silence filled the room.

Chira nodded, remembering her own private discussions on that very matter.

Jysar continued.

"I would like Mother to continue this line of thought, as she -- the ship -- has been a part of all the individual discussions so far and can more logically tie all of the individual threads together and summarize what we *really* know about the T'kaan."

Mother was in orbit above the planet, her hull held fast in a tight tractor beam while scores of Kraaqi, Hrono, and Mewiis, all scientists, engineers, technologists, and technicians, continued her extensive repairs inside the huge space-borne hangar.

She had been terribly damaged as she had raced out the

first hole her super-weapon had made in the T'kaan ship's hull. But even her mighty ThunderStar engines had not been able to outrun the explosion as the creature-ship died, its biological and technological systems fatally overloaded. Still, she had outraced the heart of the explosion, and that had been enough to ensure her survival.

So much of her outer hull had been damaged that it had been unanimously decided to completely replace it with the strongest Tritanium steel compound the Hrono had ever developed. It was very expensive and used sparingly for the choicest sections of a ship where it most needed this superior strength. But the Hrono gladly covered Mother in the best they had.

Her shields had also been completely burned out. Here the Mewiis engineers gladly provided their best shield systems, so Mother's shields and hull would now be many times stronger than any ship ever to fly the universe. Now her silhouette would reflect the light of stars with a dark gray sheen, although the Hrono did add chemicals so there was still a hint of her original, deep purple.

Eight of her main batteries had been destroyed. With spare parts no longer available, the Kraaqi provided their best replacements to complement the remaining four human-made weapons. Her hybrid weapon was repairable, but the reload time could not be brought under seven minutes, no matter what fixes were tried. It would have to do.

But the greatest gift the Kraaqi bestowed were the enhancements to her navigation systems, a specialty of this great race of explorers, and the addition of anti-gravity repulsor engines so that Mother could land upon the surface of a planet without polluting its atmosphere. With these two modifications Mother could explore new worlds just like any honorable Kraaqi longship.

Minstrel had also bestowed a gift. With the help of the Fixers, who performed the actual work, Minstrel directed the integration of its race's secret Stealth systems. Minstrel had received permission to bestow this gift from the Minstrel society's highest council, deeming MotherShip a *worthy life form*, the only condition being that Minstrel obtain Mother's promise not to misuse this technology.

Mother was now recognized as a friend to all Minstrels throughout the known universe.

Vast sections of Mother's power grids, circuitry, and main systems were being repaired or completely refurbished by each race. She was now a true hybrid ship of strength, power, and wisdom.

In her last milliseconds of consciousness before the explosion, Mother had done everything she could in order to protect her long-term memories, both so that she -- her essence -- would survive, and so that the precious last memories of mankind would also survive.

She had succeeded.

As her repairs continued, both the Hrono and Minstrel were simultaneously downloading those memories of humankind -- never again would these ever be lost by a single calamity.

In addition, Minstrel was quickly finishing *The Symphony of Humanity* in order to share it with the rest of the universe. This too would be downloaded to the Three Kingdoms along with the knowledgebase of humankind.

Now, through the huge speakers that hung from the wide ceiling above the assemblage, Mother spoke.

"We can be sure that every T'kaan ship at the battle was

destroyed. But there will no doubt have been small scout formations, or even a few larger formations performing reconnaissance, that were not present at the battle."

"But would they not have self-destructed as the other ships did when the Great Horned ships died?" Jasus asked.

"With our newly acquired data, I compared it with the almost total destruction of the T'kaan Third Fleet by humankind at Earth's destruction." Mother paused ten milliseconds. "Every ship in close proximity was indeed destroyed, whether directly by the blast, or by self-destruction. However, small formations of the T'kaan Third did survive that were located great distances from that battle."

A murmuring began among the throng. Mother paused momentarily.

"Months later, as the other T'kaan fleets sent reinforcements, and especially after the new Great Horn ship arrived ... "

"Or was born?" Jysar interjected.

"Yes, with the existing data that fact can be inferred with a high probability."

A new murmuring swept the audience.

"Let me guess: one of the remaining creature-ships, one of the Great Horned ships, gave birth and then had its newborn escorted back to begin the process of rebuilding the Third," Jysar suggested.

"That would seem logical," Mother agreed. "But to finish my current line of reasoning, T'kaan warships not in close proximity to the Great Horned ship when it died did not self-destruct." Mother allowed her words to sink in. "From my knowledge of the T'kaan -- from my battles with them -- it can now be deduced that they did not fight at one hundred percent capacity. I had assumed that my skills were simply superior, but after the new Great Horned ship arrived, the T'kaan's strategy and their effectiveness increased substantially, though I, too, increased my capabilities as I grew as a life form." Mother again paused for the benefit of the slower minds listening to her.

She continued. "Some individual ships did survive of the Third, but they were still affected and not fully functional. And so--"

"What does this mean?" Chira asked quickly, interrupting Mother. "Are there T'kaan ships left? And what about this symbiotic relationship, when that was broken because of the creature-ship's death, self-destruction was almost immediate."

The murmurs increased as emotions grew intense for all present.

Mother waited until Chira called for order and silence returned to the hall.

"First, we cannot be certain any survived, because we are still not in possession of all the facts. Some of our conclusions will still be conjecture, and some will merely have a high probability of being correct." Mother waited.

"Please proceed," Chira directed.

"There were normal communications between the T'kaan ships and their commanders. The humans had also detected the so-called background noise that accompanied these normal communication signals during the original assaults. But it did not seem to contain real data, so it was dismissed as meaningless as the tide of war turned against them.

"However, the only time the Great Horned ship had accompanied the other warships into battle against humanity was at the final assault against Earth. We must assume the Great Horned ships only take part in what they perceive are *decisive* battles.

"So this more intense, all-enveloping symbiotic signal, or noise, was picked up for the first time by our sensors at the recent battle."

"It was of a greater magnitude in signal strength?" Jysar asked.

"Yes, and there were several other differences, including certain bands of frequency generating at a significantly higher rate. Still, we have deciphered no formal data streams embedded inside them. We can only infer the function this signal stream or background signal from the creature-ships to the T'kaan warships and their crews had in this triple symbiotic relationship."

"*Triple*?" Jaric half-shouted.

"Before I begin that aspect of the discussion, let me finish the first train of thought by stating that it seems, and I repeat *seems*, that T'kaan warships farther removed from the creature-ship's death *were* affected by that rare and catastrophic event, but not as intensely. Hence, they did not immediately self-destruct with empathy as did the warships located nearby; though again, they were affected in a negative way. There may be isolated T'kaan warships still remaining, but with no creature-ship to lead them now, they probably do not present a threat. More importantly, with no creature-ship left alive, it would seem no more can be created -- or born. That is the best I can surmise at this time."

"It is a reasonable conclusion," Jaric commented, nodding to both Rok and Kyle.

"I agree," Jysar added. "And I would think when you

present what you have learned, or inferred, about this triple symbiotic relationship, that it will confirm this first conclusion." Jysar looked around at the other leaders, a knowing smile on his face.

"I bet he's had this same discussion with Mother already," Kyle whispered to Jaric.

"No doubt," Jaric agreed.

"He's such a geek," Kyle added.

The two chuckled until Mother's voice returned.

"This is interesting, though." Jaric nodded with a rapt look.

"The background signal, or noise, was one of the links in this complex relationship. Because we still cannot find any detectable data streams, and it is likely there are none to find at this point, we find ourselves faced with guessing its true function. I have, in previous discussions with other scientists on this subject, looked at its possible function at several levels. One inference is that it was some kind of subconscious connectivity, albeit crucial, between the creature-ship and the T'kaan. Or an emotional connectivity ..."

"Like love?" Chira suddenly asked. "Like the bond of each family member?"

"Perhaps it was that simple, if love is indeed a simple emotion. But I would not classify it love," Mother added. "We have also looked at it as a type of *shared instinct*, such as is found hard-wired into the brains of animals. A strong instinct that drives their innate desire to survive, perhaps like that which drives the pack to fight together as one."

"Or a combination of the above," Jysar added, his smile now larger.

"Agreed," Mother said. "What's more, maybe it is not

just a link between the creature-ship and the T'kaan, but perhaps between certain classes of T'kaan warships as well."

"She lost me there," Kyle whispered.

"Jaric shhh'ed harshly.

"To begin with, I would classify this symbiotic relationship as commensalism, meaning both species obviously benefited from it." Jysar crossed his arms, a pleased-with-himself expression on his face.

"But not completely," Mother interjected. "I suggest it might be partly helotism as well, since the creature-ship seemed to have a master/slave relationship with the T'kaan." Mother paused. "Are there any other ideas?"

"I would say the creature-ship was at the top of the food chain too," Rok ventured.

A ripple of laughter raced among the crowd.

"You laugh, but there is truth in his statement. Individual T'kaan were consumed by the creature-ships. That is a definite fact." Mother paused for effect. "But each species benefited.

"The creature-ship was a home for the T'kaan. I discovered that a large section of their population actually lived inside of them. That is where their factories and cities existed. That is where the maggot young were sent after they entered their second stage of life, and it would seem from the great numbers I recorded on the desolated human worlds, that most of them never made it to their second stage."

"The maggots ate each other as well!" Rok shouted.

"Right again," Mother said. "I would venture an assumption that the fiercest maggot young were identified for the warrior class and were nurtured through the third

443

stage."

Murmurs again swept the room.

"The Great Horned ships, the creature-ships, were first and foremost biological entities, though their outer shell, or skin, was equal to the strongest steel used in starship construction. It was the T'kaan species that added the hyperdrive engines and enabled the creature-ships the ability to travel faster than light. They were mainly biological, and then only partially technological, through these separate enhancements. Of course, we will never know completely."

"And the T'kaan warships?" Kyle asked, his interest piqued. "From a distance they seemed to be constructed like the creature-ships."

"The warships were first ships. Kyle is indeed correct, their outer hulls were constructed of the same material. But from our scans of their destroyed fleet, we have determined that their hulls were manufactured." Mother paused. "So, the warships were primarily technological, and only then partially biological. That is the best I can do with the limited facts available to me."

"What part was biological?" Jaric asked.

"Certain interior sections of capital warships. Inside, the T'kaan warships were vast mazes of labyrinth rooms, similar to the creature-ship's natural ones, but these were manufactured, as was the entire ship, except for sections of specific labyrinth rooms. I would suggest these biological structures both integrated some of the warship's systems with the creature-ship and performed some type of integration or communication between the individual T'kaan and the creature-ship."

Jysar felt his excitement growing. "I can understand the

warship integration; after all, your long-term memories are constructed out of Human DNA, albeit artificially produced and of a single type for its superior durability and reliability." Jaric looked at Kyle while Jysar paused to catch his breath. "Actually that single aspect of Mother might be considered biological, integrated with her technological systems."

"But the T'kaan warship's integration seems to have been more sophisticated, though we cannot ascertain that with precision now," Jysar added.

"So, let me see if I understand this correctly," Chira said. "The Great Horned ships were living beings. Sometime in the past, the T'kaan began a symbiotic relationship with them and began to live inside the huge creature-ships, transferring their cities and changing their previous way of life." She paused. "At this point they constructed warships whose outer hull was made of the same material as that of the creature-ship, but these were in fact warships, not alive?" Chira waited for confirmation.

"Correct so far," Mother said.

"And then living, biological sections were added to these T'kaan warships. Now we have a symbiotic relation between creature-ship and T'kaan, and now also between creature-ship and warship and T'kaan. And perhaps these warships enhanced the original symbiosis, and then perhaps created new aspects of it, making it stronger? The creature-ships and T'kaan made the warships pseudo-alive and therefore more dangerous than simply a *ship*?"

"That is a reasonable conjecture," Mother replied.

A hush filled the room.

"Perhaps I might use the comparison of myself and my sister ship?" Mother asked.

"Please," Jaric said as he leaned forward with interest.

"The A ship was constructed for the very reason that I was, though it was the prototype. To better explain, the A ship's memories and programming were solely battle algorithms and coding. Afterward, it was given Artificial Intelligence programming so it might adapt and learn, so as to become invincible in battle. That would be similar to the T'kaan ships, except they were also in a symbiotic relationship that increased their battle effectiveness. But the T'kaan warship's sole purpose was war, as was my sister ship." Mother paused.

"In contrast, I was given magnitudes more long-term memories than my sister ship, so as to be able to store the entire collected knowledge of humankind. But most importantly, Ron and Rita allowed my AI systems to access this data in addition to my battle algorithms and memories. My AI programming was also more extensive -- I could learn from anything, from any source. Thus I became something more than my original programming, something unexpected even to my creators."

"That is what enabled you to become alive," Kyle said with emotion.

Across the top of the wide ceiling, Minstrel's glowing plasma body shimmered with excitement at this revelation.

"So what was the use of this biological structure in the warships with the T'kaan themselves?" Chira asked.

"For their pleasure!" Jysar's grin widened. "Perhaps pleasure second only to mating. Or better. And used as a means of control -- as a means of reward. Perhaps even, depending on the intensity of pleasure that it brought, as a means of bonding between the two species, the creature-ship with the individual T'kaan -- in this instance via the

T'kaan warships." Jysar took a deep breath.

"Say what?" Kyle whispered to Jaric.

Jaric shook his head with puzzlement.

"Why do you make this assumption?" Jasus asked, looking first at Jysar and then upwards to Mother.

"There were *references*," Jysar said. "In their ... documentation. What little we have recovered. Very passionate references, in fact."

Jasus snorted his disbelief. "Except for being a starship-building race, the T'kaan were more like animals than a sentient race. Eat or be eaten, fighting wars solely to destroy, devour and procreate!" Jasus exclaimed with disdain.

"Not very good reasons to wage war," Tarlog commented. "Not good reasons at all. Not for a *decent* war, anyway."

"I would suggest that valid reasons for waging war are much fewer than people might think," Mother said matter-of-factly.

Murmurs rippled through the crowd once again, hundreds of whispered conversations that reflected awe and respect for Mother's simple but thought-provoking words. Her wisdom was repeated over and over.

"Perhaps there is no such thing as a decent war," Tarlog mused. "I agree, Mother. And that's saying something, coming from an old war-horse like myself."

"I was created to destroy," Mother said. "I wish to grow beyond that programming, to become something more, something greater. A being that creates instead of destroys." Mother paused.

"Are the T'kaan destroyed completely?" Chira asked with finality in her voice. "The ships that were not part of the battle, will they attack us in the future?"

"It is doubtful," Mother said. "There is no Great Horned ship to lead them, and I make that conjecture based on many pieces of evidence. The creature-ship was a *Great One*, according to the few documents we have recovered from them." Mother paused. "In fact, I would strongly assume that any ships left will either be destroyed in battle with other races or self-destruct because they no longer have the leadership aspect of their symbiotic relationship. They have no direction."

"But we can't say that for certain," Jysar added.

"True. There is a small possibility they can survive; after all, we are not in possession of all the facts. But it is a very small possibility." Mother waited for them to take in the import of her words.

"What we can say with certainty is that never before have the T'kaan ever been defeated, nor have all three of the Great Horned ships been destroyed at once. It is almost impossible, actually, that so few T'kaan ships could ever recover from the totality of this catastrophe. What I can say with certainty is that no creature-ship can be created or born from the remnants of any remaining warships. I quote from a T'kaan record, 'Only a creature-ship can begat a creature-ship,' a saying from their own documentation, the little that we could salvage."

"But where did they come from? I'd be more concerned about that?" Jaric whispered to Kyle.

Kyle shrugged. "We don't know where they originated."

"Then it would be safe to say that the T'kaan threat has indeed been destroyed," Chira said with confidence to all.

"I agree," Mother concurred. "The T'kaan threat is no more."

Cheers and shouts rose from the crowds.

"Then let us begin with the necessary business of peace, at long last." Chira paused. "Our first order of business will be a timetable for refitting all Mewiis and Hrono ships with the Kraaqi anti-gravity repulsors." Chira smiled. "So that all races will respect the environment."

Applause erupted from all the attendees.

Jasus rose. "May I add that we, the Hrono, have recognized the error of our ways, with wisdom gained from our newfound friendship." He looked at the high chieftains of the Kraaqi and nodded. "We will never again use our technology to totally subdue a world. In fact, we will seek to undo the damage we have done. And what is more, we will seek always to develop our technology in order to be compatible with our natural worlds."

Amid the enthusiastic applause, the Kraaqi contingent rose as one and saluted the Hrono leader.

Chapter Fifty

Five months had elapsed since the fateful battle, and still Kyle and Jaric could not shake their intense sadness. But now, at last, they had formulated some future plans.

The Three Kingdoms were still basking in the glow of an historic event: the first section of the all-enveloping steel and concrete city-planet had been removed on Hronosium. For the first time in millennia, the natural, uninhibited light from its suns shone down on its bare soil. It was the first of many such planned actions to bring the natural environment back, at least partially.

Jasus himself had planted the first tree.

Kyle, Jaric, and Mother, her repairs now complete, had witnessed this fantastic event in person. Across every planet of the Three Kingdoms, the historic moment had also been transmitted via their main communication links so everyone could share the wondrous event.

A new age had dawned for the Three Kingdoms.

And the time had finally come to say good-bye.

Crowds gathered around the parked figure of Mother to see them off. As Kyle, Jaric, and Rok stood before the assembled leaders of the Three Kingdoms, they noticed a disturbance in the throngs. Slowly, a small group pushed their way up to the golden podium. As they grew closer, Kyle and Jaric felt their hearts begin to beat faster. Now the group of seven began ascending the stage, but Kyle and Jaric focused on one person who was covered simply with a plain white sheet around her body and a wrap around her face so that only her eyes were visible -- someone who seemed vaguely familiar to them.

Kyle felt the lump grow in his throat, and hot tears form in his eyes. When he turned, the tears were already streaming down Jaric's ebony cheeks.

"It can't be," Kyle whispered.

But it was.

They now recognized Jysar as the one who led this small entourage toward them. The crowds moved back as he alone guided the cloaked individual up to them and Mother.

"This is a gift of the Hrono," Mother said to Kyle and Jaric. "I was notified yesterday. I am so ... " Mother's voice paused uncharacteristically, as she gathered her rushing thoughts that numbered into the millions.

"Happy," Mother finished.

Kyle wiped his tears before they revealed his churning emotions across his face for the universe to see. Jaric continued to look on through his tears in utter astonishment.

Jysar carefully removed the wrap from around the small being's head.

They saw her blonde hair first as it fell free around her shoulders, and then her bright blue eyes. She smiled, like she had smiled so many times before.

It was Becky.

The two young men approached her tentatively. It was Jaric who reached out first to touch her arm.

She stood before them dressed only in a simple white sheet wrapped tightly around her body.

Kyle stared into her eyes, his own filled with a sudden wildness.

"It's not her," he said simply.

"Yes, it is," Mother answered.

Jysar smiled. "We, the Hrono, cannot clone a large

451

enough population to enable your race to survive. But we have cloned Becky from the sample of her DNA that I took before the Great Battle. So you can have her back."

"No!" Kyle shouted with rage.

Jaric's tears flowed freely down his cheeks as he quickly removed his hand, as if he had been touching something poisonous.

"Kyle, it is Becky. It is her DNA, her chromosomes, and her cells. She has been recreated exactly. There is no difference between the Becky you see before you and the one you knew before." Mother's voice almost seemed to sing.

"No," Kyle spat with anger. "It's not her. It's a monster. It's a fake. This *thing*." He sneered, having spoken the second word as if it were an obscenity. "This *thing* is not Becky."

Jaric suddenly screamed, creating a strange hush over the entire crowd as the terrifying sound echoed eerily over them. As it slowly faded, he stood beside Kyle with anger in his tear-stained eyes.

"No, Mother. You're wrong; this is not the woman I once loved. It might look like her. And biologically, it might be her duplicate. But look at her eyes -- she does not know us. She does not recognize us. She does not have Becky's memories. Nor her heart!" Jaric shouted.

Kyle stared at the clone, his own eyes a mixture of sadness and panic.

As Mother's optics zoomed onto the face she knew so well, she realized that Jaric was right. The clone Becky looked at Kyle and Jaric with a blankness in her eyes. She did not recognize them.

"I will replay all of her memories. She will remember

who she was," Mother said.

"No!" Kyle shouted angrily. "She -- " He paused. "The clone will never be Becky. You can replay all of your memories of the real Becky, like some kind of weird movie for her, but the clone did not live those memories." Kyle's face was frozen with outrage and contempt. "This clone," he spat. "This impostor, will *never* be Becky."

"I agree," Jaric said. "The clone is a different person than Becky. I was in love with Becky. I was going to marry her." He stared at the beautiful woman before him. "I cannot marry Becky's body. I cannot love her body alone. It was who she was inside, her inner person that I loved." Jaric forced his eyes away as a part of his mind tried to tell him that this was the Becky he loved. Yet another part of his mind knew the terrible truth.

But something deep inside wanted so desperately for it to *be* Becky. He faced the clone, reaching for her soft cheek once again.

"Talk to me," Jaric said to the clone with a sadness in his voice.

She approached Jaric slowly, her eyes searching his eyes carefully.

"You are new to my eyes. But you are like me, almost." The clone woman looked around at the mass of beings silently looking on. "We do not resemble them."

Jaric shook his head and stepped back beside Kyle.

Jysar looked around with puzzlement on his face. "We apologize. We have done this thing as a token of our love for you, the last of the humans. If we have offended you, we will take the clone and keep her with us."

"No, I will take her," Mother said with a commanding tone.

The two young men shook their heads, but it was Jaric who spoke for them both.

"Don't do this, Mother. It won't be the same," Jaric pleaded. "It won't work."

"She will be my child too," Mother said with finality.

"I will never call her Becky." Kyle sneered with utter contempt. "You'll have to give her another name."

"Yes," Jaric added. "We can't call her Becky. It would disgrace the memory of the *real* Becky."

"I will name her. And I will love her. Fixer3, lead my new child inside." The awkward silence continued as the diminutive robot led the clone by the hand through the open door and inside her hull.

Kyle and Jaric walked slowly behind them up to the opened door that led inside MotherShip. But they stopped and watched the robot and the clone enter alone.

"I can't believe this," Jaric whispered to Kyle.

"This is going to make things so much harder," Kyle whispered angrily back.

Taking a collective breath, the two angry young men turned to look one last time on the people they had lived with, fought together with, and grown to love. Now they were leaving them all behind, as they had left everything else in their short lives.

"We will always remember you," Mother said to the crowds.

"Where will you go?" Rok asked.

Kyle looked at Jaric. They finally smiled at each other with the thought of their future adventures traveling the great, wide galaxy.

"We will search for other humans, of course. But we have decided we will also explore." Kyle looked up at

Mother's freshly repaired hull, which was now reflecting the reddish light of the triple suns of Hronosium. "Mother wants to explore too. We're tired of fighting. Humans are first of all explorers and seekers of knowledge, as are all of you."

"Yes," Mother agreed. "We would like to discover and meet more races like you. Broaden our understanding. Find new life in the vast universe." Mother paused. "And perhaps, maybe, we will learn of other small groups of human survivors. Perhaps."

Kyle's face grew hard, but Jaric put his arm around his shoulder and pressed it hard.

"A most admirable goal," Jasus agreed.

Rok stepped forward and hugged Jaric and Kyle together in his mighty grasp.

"Will you allow me to travel with you?" Before they could answer, he turned back to the assembled throngs. "It is not good for the last members of this noble race to journey alone. I and select members of the Band of the Stars will journey forth with them in our own ship. We too will explore and learn. The Kraaqi are changed, as are the Hrono. We will become explorers first and foremost." He pointed to the sky above. "On this great journey, we will take our women and our children for the first time. Our families will travel with us."

Cheers went up from the crowds.

"I, too, wish to go." Jysar stepped beside Rok's form. "I would like to travel to the *unknown parts*. Perhaps my skills may help you in some small way to find other survivors." He smiled. "Even if I never see Hronosium again, I would treasure traveling this universe with my friends. My new family."

Rok smiled at Jysar and then turned back and smiled at the two men.

"Minstrel too, has promised to accompany us," Mother added.

"I wish to go with you as well."

Faces turned as a Mewiis female made her way forward.

"Saris and I were the first Mewiis to meet with the family of the MotherShip. We made first contact with them," Krinia said. Her head-tail whipped from side to side as she joined them. "I do not have a family group of my own as yet. If it is acceptable, I would like to join Mother's extended family."

"You are most welcome," Mother said. "Please, join my family."

Kyle and Jaric smiled at all their friends.

Stepping forward, Kyle grasped Rok by both his arms. Rok returned the warrior's embrace as they faced each other a moment in silence.

"We are brethren," Rok said with conviction. "Wherever you shall journey, there I and my Band will go. The Hrono called Jysar, and the Mewiis called Krinia as well. And Minstrel. Whatever fantastic worlds and aliens you encounter, we will loyally be at your side." He paused, smiling with the thought of the wondrous journey before them.

"Even to the edge of the universe!" Rok's face beamed.

"Then let us go," Mother said.

THE END

www.ingramcontent.com/pod-product-compliance
Lightning Source LLC
Chambersburg PA
CBHW011401010726
47495CB00009B/2720